PRAISE FOR

CHLOE LIES[...]

"Chloe Liese's writing is soulful, honest, and steamy in that swoon-worthy way that made me fall in love with romance novels in the first place! Her work is breathtaking, and I constantly look forward to more from her!"

—Ali Hazelwood, *New York Times* bestselling author of
Love on the Brain

"Quirky and delicious romance. I could curl up in Liese's writing for days, I love it so."

—Helen Hoang, *New York Times* bestselling author of
The Heart Principle

"There's no warmer hug than a Chloe Liese book."
—Rachel Lynn Solomon, *New York Times* bestselling author of
Weather Girl

"No one pairs sweet and steamy quite like Chloe Liese!"
—Alison Cochrun, author of *The Charm Offensive*

"Chloe Liese consistently writes strong casts brimming with people I want to hang out with in real life, and I'll happily gobble up anything she writes."

—Sarah Hogle, author of *You Deserve Each Other*

"Chloe Liese continues to reign as the master of steamy romance!"
—Sarah Adams, author of *The Cheat Sheet*

TITLES BY CHLOE LIESE

THE WILMOT SISTERS

THE BERGMAN BROTHERS

Only and Forever

A BERGMAN BROTHERS NOVEL

CHLOE LIESE

BERKLEY ROMANCE
NEW YORK

BERKLEY ROMANCE
Published by Berkley
An imprint of Penguin Random House LLC
penguinrandomhouse.com

Copyright © 2024 by Chloe Liese
Excerpt from *Two Wrongs Make a Right* copyright © 2022 by Chloe Liese
Penguin Random House supports copyright. Copyright fuels creativity,
encourages diverse voices, promotes free speech, and creates a vibrant culture.
Thank you for buying an authorized edition of this book and for complying
with copyright laws by not reproducing, scanning, or distributing any part of it
in any form without permission. You are supporting writers and allowing
Penguin Random House to continue to publish books for every reader.

BERKLEY and the BERKLEY & B colophon are registered trademarks of
Penguin Random House LLC.

Library of Congress Cataloging-in-Publication Data

Names: Liese, Chloe, author.
Title: Only and forever / Chloe Liese.
Description: First edition. | New York: Berkley Romance, 2024. | Series:
The Bergman Brothers |
Identifiers: LCCN 2023032409 (print) | LCCN 2023032410 (ebook) |
ISBN 9780593642474 (trade paperback) | ISBN 9780593642481 (ebook)
Subjects: LCGFT: Romance fiction. | Novels.
Classification: LCC PS3612.I3357 O55 2024 (print) | LCC PS3612.I3357(ebook) |
DDC 813/.6—dc23/eng/20230717
LC record available at https://lccn.loc.gov/2023032409
LC ebook record available at https://lccn.loc.gov/2023032410

First Edition: April 2024

Printed in the United States of America
1st Printing

Book design by Kristin del Rosario

For those still waiting and hoping for their happy ending,
and for those who worry they'll never find one:
There's someone out there waiting and hoping,
who'll love all of miraculous, marvelous you.
I promise.

Dear Reader,

This story features characters with human realities who I believe deserve to be seen more prominently in romance through positive, authentic representation. As a neurodivergent person living with chronic conditions, I am passionate about writing feel-good romances avowing my belief that every one of us is worthy and capable of happily ever after, if that's what our heart desires.

Specifically, this story portrays a main character who is neurodivergent (ADHD) and a character living with type 1 diabetes. No two people's experience of any condition or diagnosis will be the same, but through my own experience and the insight of authenticity readers, I have strived to create characters who honor the nuances of those identities. Please be aware that this story also includes the topic of navigating a toxic family relationship.

If any of these are sensitive topics for you, I hope you feel comforted in knowing that loving, healthy, affirming relationships—with oneself and others—are championed in this story.

XO,
Chloe

We are, to be sure, a miracle every way.

—JANE AUSTEN,
Mansfield Park

ONE

Viggo

If there's one thing you should know about me, it's that I love a happy ending. That butterflies-in-your-stomach, rush-of-serotonin, breathless, euphoric, wrapped-up-in-a-bow happy ending. The last page of a romance novel as my eyes dance across *The End*. A shore-front view of the sunset, toes wedged in the sand, watching fading light spill glorious gold across cool blue waves, the grand finale to the perfect beach day. The first bite of homemade pastry, finally perfected after countless recipe tweaks. And, of course, most of all, my family, side by side with their happily ever afters, crammed together at the long, worn wood table in our home away from home nestled in the woods of Washington State, the A-frame.

My gaze drifts around the room, the sound of everyone's rowdy voices and laughter sweetening the bittersweet. I'm surrounded by happy endings—my six siblings, their partners, their children, my still-so-in-love parents—and, given my love of happy endings, *I* should be fully, utterly content, too.

But I'm not.

Because I'm still waiting for *my* happy ending. Irony of ironies, salt in the wound, unlike these lucky ducks, who, in six different ways, serendipitously tripped and fell, kicking and screaming, into meeting their perfect match, I've been *searching* for mine. And I'm the only one who hasn't found them yet.

"Viggo!" Ziggy, my baby sister, the youngest in the Bergman brood, calls my name from across the table, wide smile, freckles, and bright green eyes, flipping her long red braid over her shoulder. "Scrabble doesn't have to be so serious. Play already."

I snap out of my daydreaming and peer at the Scrabble board, tugging down my ball cap to hide my eyes. I don't like being caught in maudlin thoughts.

"'Scrabble doesn't have to be so serious.'" Ziggy's boyfriend, Seb, tips his head her way. "Did you really just say that? The woman who punched my thigh when I built a word off of the letter *u* and compromised her plans for her *q*?"

Ziggy blushes bright red, narrowing her eyes at Seb. "That's different."

His tongue pokes his cheek. "How so, Sigrid?"

I still can't believe she lets someone call her by her full name. Then again, if anyone could get away with it, it's Seb.

"You," she says breezily, plucking a cracker off the plate of snacks, "looked at my tiles. You cheated."

Seb grins. "Now, why would I ever do that?"

"Because you live to fire me up and suffer the consequences."

He sighs dreamily. "And what glorious consequences they are."

"Ew," I say miserably. "Stop with the double entendres— Oh, hell yes." Inspiration having struck, I lean in and spell out *entendre*.

Everyone groans around the table.

"With that double word square," I tell my sister, "I'll take eighteen points."

Ziggy grumbles as she writes down the score. Seb takes the opportunity to whisper something in her ear that puts a smile on her face.

I avert my eyes and try not to slip right back into my mope, but it's hard. Mom leans into the crook of Dad's arm, her hand resting on his as they talk with my oldest siblings and their partners—my sister, the firstborn Bergman, Freya, beside her husband, Aiden; my oldest brother, Axel, born after Freya, holding hands on the table with his wife, Rooney, so at home in how they lean in together and talk and touch. My gaze dances farther down the table to Ren, the next sibling born after Axel, his arm around his wife, Frankie, who sits, hands folded and resting on her very pregnant belly, as she makes some dry quip. Willa, wife to my brother Ryder, born after Ren and preceding me, laughs loudly at what she says. Ryder grins at Willa, his arm stretched across the back of her chair, softly twirling a coil of her hair around his finger.

So affectionate. So effortless. So romantic. My chest feels tight. Pain knots, sharp and sour, beneath my ribs.

A toe nudges me beneath the table. I glance up and find my brother Oliver, just a year younger than me, whom I'm so close to, not just in years, but emotionally, that we've operated like twins for as long as I can remember. Except now he has his someone, too—Gavin, who sits, shoulder wedged against Ollie's, our niece, Linnea, perched on Gavin's lap as they color together, dark-haired heads bent over the page.

Oliver's eyes, ice-blue-gray, just like mine, like Mom's and Freya's and Ren's, lock with mine. *You okay?* he mouths.

I swallow, then force a smile. *I'm fine.*

He frowns, which is rare for my sunshine-bright, often smiling brother. But he knows—he always has—when I'm low. And when he does, Ollie will go to great, often ridiculous lengths to make things better. This is just one thing he can't fix.

Oliver stares at me, brow furrowed. He doesn't buy my *I'm fine* line one bit. Which means it's time to redirect before he stubbornly decides to get to the bottom of it and problem solve. I nudge my chin at the Scrabble board. "Your turn, Ollie."

He sighs, shaking his head, dropping the subject for now, and peers down at the board. A devious grin lights up his face as he brings his first tile to the board and places it beside the *e* at the end of *entendre*.

Tile by tile, they stretch across the Scrabble board, building a word that builds my sense of dread. *E-S-C-O-N-D-I-D-O.*

My brother lays down the last *o* with a jaunty snap. Sitting back, he smiles wickedly, then says, "Escondido."

I glare at him. "Yes, thank you. I can spell."

"You can't use proper nouns!" Seb calls.

"Yes, you can," Oliver and I reply in unison, locked in our mutual stare down.

"Or more than seven tiles," Seb adds. He frowns in confusion. "How did you get so many tiles?"

"You get to sneak one extra tile per turn when you draw," Oliver tells him, still holding my eyes, "unless someone catches you, then you have to return it."

"Bergman rules," Ziggy explains.

To which Gavin adds, grumbling, "It's *mayhem*."

Oliver's smile deepens. "But it's awfully fun mayhem."

I glare at my brother. He's doing it on purpose, taunting me like this. As I once said to him when he was fresh off heartbreak back in college, it's better to be mad than to be sad. Oliver's going for that, poking me about Escondido.

While my trips from Los Angeles down to Escondido aren't a secret, to my family's dismay, their reason is. That reason is the only private part of my life, which is no small feat—I suck at keeping secrets, and my family's so close and communicative, secret keeping is basically unheard of. This is a secret I've kept because it's something I feel deeply vulnerable about—the biggest risk I've ever taken, the greatest dream I've ever let myself cultivate and try to follow through on, which isn't a strength of mine. My ADHD brain loves newness—new ideas to explore, new projects to kick off, new skills to learn. So many things bring me joy. I've never seen why I had to settle on only a few of them.

But this plan, this hope and its possibility, brings me a kind of joy that's eclipsed anything I've ever dabbled in before. So, step by step, I've worked toward making it a reality.

"Escondido?" Linnea, Freya and Aiden's daughter, four and a half, as smart as a whip and highly observant, lifts her head, those dark waves she inherited from her dad frizzy from hours spent running around outside. "Mommy says if she got a dime every time Uncle Viggo drove to Escondido, she'd—"

Freya leaps from the table and scoops up Linnea from Gavin's lap. "Bath time for you!"

Aiden bites back a laugh as he hands over their one-year-old, Theo, to my mom, who takes him with a raspberry to his tummy that makes him laugh. "I warned you she was listening," Aiden tells Freya.

"She," my sister says, tickling Linnea, who giggles, "was supposed to be asleep when we had that conversation."

"But spying on you is so much more fun!" Linnie yells.

Freya sighs and hitches Linnie higher on her hip before starting up the stairs. "You, little miss, are a troublemaker."

Linnie's giggle echoes up the stairwell.

"On the subject of Escondido, and while you have the family's attention," Oliver says, leaning his elbows on the table, "care to tell us why you've been regularly burning two hours' worth of gas each way, driving down there for the past year, Viggo?"

"Up until two months ago," Ziggy chimes in.

I blink at her, stunned.

"What?" she asks.

"How do you know where and when I've been?"

Ollie rolls his eyes. "V, we have mutually agreed phone tracking, remember?"

"To my continued dismay," Gavin grumbles.

I blow Gavin a kiss. He flips me the finger, safe to show his true colors since Linnie's made her exit.

Seb snorts, highly amused by this. I glare at him, then redirect my ire at Oliver. "Ollie, *we* have phone tracking, but since when do you share that highly classified information with the siblings?"

"Since Ziggy wanted to know where you were and what was taking you so damn long to deliver those gluten-free cookies for Seb."

Everyone at the table says, "Awww."

Ziggy turns bright red. Seb wiggles his eyebrows as he throws an arm around the back of her chair.

"So," Ollie continues, "I told her you weren't in Escondido. According to phone tracking, you were poking around Culver City. And, in fact, you hadn't been to Escondido for the past seven weeks."

"You two have a disturbing lack of boundaries," Axel mutters.

Rooney beams a smile our way. "I think it's adorable."

I scowl at Oliver. I used to think it was pretty adorable, too, but I'm not such a big fan now that it means my family knows my migratory patterns have changed. It means they're going to be sniffing around me even more, and if they happen to follow me, catch me at the—

No. I'm getting ahead of myself. My family wouldn't follow me. We're a debatably overengaged bunch, but no one's *that* far in each other's business.

Except maybe me. And I'm me, so I don't have to worry about following myself.

"Well then," Oliver says, setting his chin on his clasped hands, smiling sweetly. "We're all ears. Go on."

I glance around the room, my family's side conversations now brought to a stop. All eyes are on me.

As much as I want to confess and unburden myself, I can't make myself share this risk I'm taking, this hope I have that could fail and fall apart. Not yet, not when I'm already so raw from this family staycation that brought Ziggy's boyfriend here, declaring his feelings, making their relationship official and leaving me surrounded for the first time by *everyone* in my family being happily paired off.

"What can I say?" Scooping up a handful of pistachios and throwing them back, I tell them around my bite, "Escondido's zoo is killer. I can't stop going back."

Everyone groans and grumbles, going back to their conversations.

"You don't believe me?" I ask.

"No!" they all yell.

I snort a laugh, chewing my pistachios, as that bittersweet bubble of being loved yet lonely swells inside me. I adore my family. I'm grateful for them. And I also feel further from them than I ever have before, because of how their lives have shifted while mine has remained fixed.

For now, just a little longer, I'm going to keep my secret.

Ding-dong.

The A-frame's doorbell ring echoes, silencing conversation once again. Ziggy shoots up from her chair and squeals happily. "They're back!"

"They" are Ziggy's childhood best friend, Charlie, and her partner, Gigi. Ziggy met Charlie Clarke when we were young, right after Charlie and her siblings moved to Washington with their mother during their parents' first acrimonious divorce (they have since divorced and remarried each other twice—it's a bit of a mess, according to Ziggy). Knowing my sister and Charlie's history, I wasn't surprised when Charlie showed up with Gigi earlier this week to celebrate Ziggy's birthday, which, in addition to enjoying a spring break of sorts, is why all the family's here. What *did* surprise me was when Charlie pulled me aside this morning over coffee and asked me for a favor that sent me spinning sideways.

Charlie, my baby sister's best friend, looked at me with those big hazel eyes and asked me for a favor I couldn't refuse:

"My sister," Charlie said, "her life has sort of blown up lately, and I'm worried about her, so I'm going to try to bring her here. I have to do *something*, and I feel like if I bring her here, it might help. You Bergmans can make anything better. If she says yes, if she comes, will you help me?"

"How?" I asked.

Charlie smiled, bright and trusting. "Just by being you. Put a smile on her face for me. She needs someone to make her smile. If anyone can do that, it's you."

It was on the tip of my tongue to explain how much harder that was going to be than Charlie thought. But that would have required admitting something I was much too proud to admit:

I'd already tried to make Tallulah Clarke smile, years ago. And I'd failed.

"Did Ziggy mention," I ask Seb, "if Charlie and Gigi were . . . bringing anyone else back with them?"

Seb frowns at his tiles, rearranging them in their tray. "No. Why?"

I don't know how to answer that without giving myself, or the secret favor Charlie asked of me, away.

Seb peers up, clearly curious about my silence, and rakes back his dark wavy hair, frown deepening as his sharp gray eyes lock on me. "Viggo. Why?"

Ziggy grips the front door's handle and wrenches it open. I lean back in my chair, tipping onto its two rear legs, craning for a better view.

In walks Gigi, then Charlie, talking loudly, laughing about something I can't make out, as they shrug off their parkas and ease out of their boots. They step aside, like they're making room for someone else, like they're not alone.

Like someone else is there.

I lean back farther, trying to see past them. That's when I catch it—a full, soft shadow; a quiet throat clear.

Goose bumps bloom across my skin.

And then, behind them, as striking as a sudden silent storm, walks in Charlie's sister, the only other secret I've kept in my life:

Tallulah Clarke.

Tallulah Clarke is obviously not a secret to my family. They know her as Charlie's quiet older sister who kept to herself, who never had the time of day for us Bergmans during the years Ziggy and Charlie were best friends, before we moved to Los Angeles.

The secret is exactly who Tallulah Clarke was *to me*.

And so I'm not surprised that I feel my family's eyes shift my way, curious, as I stare at Tallulah with my mouth hanging open, eyes ridiculously wide. I'm too distracted by the sight of her, the jarring impact of seeing my first bitterly unrequited crush, to worry about my family's observation. Or to pay attention to exactly what my body's doing in its chair.

As I lose all sense of balance, the chair wobbles, creaks, and, like a felled tree, tips back in slow motion. I pinwheel my arms to try to stop myself from falling, but it's too late. I dive off the chair and land clumsily, managing to catch the chair right before it can crash to the floor.

Leaping up, I straighten the chair and shove it in against the table. My fingers curl around the top of it as Tallulah Clarke, seven years older than she was when I last saw her, steps to the side so Ziggy can shut the door behind her.

Jesus Christ. Tallulah is hotter than ever.

I didn't know Tallulah when the Clarkes lived in Washington State. She never came around. Charlie was picked up and dropped off by an au pair with a thick German accent or, on the rare occasion, her mother; her siblings were a mystery.

Until, of all places, Tallulah walked into my very first class at USC.

I didn't know who she was until roll was called, until I did a double take at the name and pieced it together—Charlie's dark hair and wide eyes, her upturned nose. This was *the* Tallulah Clarke.

I watch Tallulah as she stands just inside the door of the A-frame, eyes down, shimmying a highly impractical rain-dappled jean jacket off her shoulders, toeing off even more impractical leopard-print flats. She wrinkles her nose when she sees mud caked on them.

I recognize everything about her that launched my body from awkward adolescent horniness to sexually aching adult *desire*. I'd had wet dreams, fantasies, curiosities, in high school, sure, but seeing Tallulah had obliterated all of that. Simply looking at her in class, being near her, was pure, lusty torture.

There's the beauty mark, right where I remember it—just above and to the left of her pouty mouth. Big brown doe eyes fringed by dense dark lashes. The promise of deep dimples in her round cheeks. Glowing golden skin. And that body. That luscious body. Full, soft arms and thighs; wide, lush hips. The only stark difference is her once dark hair, now dyed icy aqua blue, swept up in a twist on her head.

Her top is white, striped with marigold, the perfect complement to her warm skin. It's half-tucked into cropped wide-leg jeans that hug her hips, ripped in all the right places. She always dressed like the child of Hollywood royalty that she is—stylish, artsy, all LA glam. That hasn't changed. Nor has its impact on me.

As if she feels me staring at her, Tallulah glances my way. Her eyes widen for a fraction of a second before they settle into that cool indifference that I remember all too well.

It bugged me then. And it bugs me now. Because—and I'm sorry, this will sound arrogant, *but*—everyone likes me. At least if I don't stick around *too* long, or if they don't; if we don't spend enough time together for me to wear out my welcome and rub them wrong. When people meet me, I'm playful, charming, gregarious. I make them smile and laugh, I quickly figure out what makes them happy, then try to make them happier. To make them like me. And often, for a while, I'm damn good at it.

Except her. Tallulah was the one person who turned her nose up at me right out of the gate, my first and only semester of college.

It drove me up the damn wall.

Standing there, staring at her as she gives me another chilly glance, I feel the sucker-punch *thud-thud-thud* of my heart whacking my ribs. Just like it did when she walked into my class seven years ago.

I can't stop staring at her, frozen by the memory of Tallulah as she answered quietly to her name beside me, as I turned toward her and pieced together who she was. Our elbows brushed, and electricity flew through my body so violently, I dropped *Mansfield Park* and lost my place. Tallulah glanced at the book, then up my body as far as my wide grin (after having braces for the second time late in high school—losing and forgetting to wear my retainer after braces round one bit me epically in the ass—I'd just gotten them off and was very into flashing my once again straight, bright smile). She gripped her chair and scooched it as far away from me as possible without being in the lap of the person to her other side.

I remember staring at her, crushed, offended, as she opened up her book bag, pulling out a thick novel made anonymous by a stretchy bloodred cover. Dark shoulder-length hair swept around her face, a curtain resolutely shut.

And that was that.

Tallulah and I don't have a history. Or, I suppose you could say, we have a very one-sided history. *I* was fascinated by Tallulah, by her gorgeous looks, her expensive-smelling, sultry floral perfume, her always covered mysterious, thick-spined books. But Tallulah didn't have the time of day for me. My pride was pricked. I could take a hint. I wasn't going to bother someone who didn't want to be bothered.

I can't lie—it stung. It felt serendipitous, that after our families had crossed paths in Washington State, though Tallulah hadn't gone to my school back then, here she was in Los Angeles, at my college, in my classroom. And yet, instead of looking as pleasantly surprised as I was by this turn of events, Tallulah looked thoroughly unimpressed.

I was insecure. I was just turning the corner from a gangly teen with braces, too lanky to fit the deep voice that had taken hold of my body. I'd started to feel like I was finally a little more put together—my body filling in from playing soccer and eating my way through the pantry, my braces finally off, a flattering haircut. College was poised to be even better than high school—I wouldn't be just an entertaining, albeit fairly intelligent, goofball; I'd be respected, admired, appreciated.

Tallulah swiftly took a crap on that.

So I shut up and kept to myself and stewed and pined and stewed some more. Days became weeks, as I wrestled with what the hell was happening to me. I'd never seen someone and felt my chest tighten, my belly do this disconcerting flip-flop, let alone someone who quickly made it clear she thought she was better than me and my countless questions in our shared lit class, the Austen novels I couldn't stop reading and rereading, sensing something in them, searching for something more that I couldn't put my finger on. I didn't know what it meant, the way Tallulah made me feel. Until fall break, when my family made a long-weekend trip up to the A-frame, where I was poking around its bookshelves. I yanked out a small, worn mass-market paperback historical romance, and the back copy caught my eye.

Loathing. Lust. Unrequited, burning desire.

Burning. Desire.

Those were words I'd been struggling to find, feelings I hadn't known how to identify. I picked up the book, turned it over, dropped to the floor, sat with my back to the bookshelves, and started reading.

That was my first romance novel. A historical romance that bore out on page what Austen often told in a few sentences or glossed over entirely. Heartrending confessions of adoration, intimate love-making, dramatic duels, kisses that lasted paragraphs and left my body hot all over. I devoured it, desperate to make sense of the wild power that a silent, chilly girl had over me. And I never looked back. I've been reading romance novels ever since.

"Viggo." Ziggy frowns at me as I rearrange myself, trying for a nonchalant lean against the chair, which wobbles again ominously before I ease off it. "What," she whispers out of the side of her mouth, "is wrong with you?"

I watch Mom hand my nephew Theo to Dad, then approach Tallulah as she smiles warmly, opening her arms for an embrace that Tallulah gingerly steps into.

"Wrong? With me? Nothing. Just tipped in my chair. Gave myself a little scare. Heh, I rhymed. Look at me, the poet."

Ziggy arches an auburn eyebrow. "You're acting so weird. And you keep staring at Tallulah." My sister tips her head, assessing me. "You've never met her before, right?"

My family has no clue I had class in college with Tallulah. I wasn't about to go waltzing to family dinner on Sunday and announce that the woman I was having nightly filthy dreams about wouldn't even acknowledge my existence.

And then I left school after that semester, this antsy feeling that I wasn't where I was supposed to be tugging me toward something else, even though I didn't know what that was. Ziggy doesn't know about my equal parts interest in and resentment of her best friend's big sister because I've kept that embarrassment to myself. No one in my family knows, either. I made sure of that.

Thank God. Because, after my track record of—with the most loving and benevolent intentions, I might add—pushing and nudging my siblings into their romantic happily ever afters, they'd be all too ready to push me right into mine.

Relief buoys me up. My family doesn't know. I'm safe. And I have only one greater consolation than my family's ignorance of my long-ago crush on Tallulah: Tallulah's ignorance.

Because if she knew, this favor I'm about to do for Charlie would take it to a whole new level of humiliation.

Tallulah's eyes meet mine as she peers over my mom's shoulder. She frowns as she catches me staring at her again. I cover my blunder, flash her a playful, winking smile. The frown deepens.

Perfect.

I know how to keep it breezy, make things light. That's my bread and butter—deflect with hijinks and humor, divert with glib goofiness. I've done it for so long, it comes as easy as breathing. Tallulah might have put me down with that arctic front, back in freshman year of college, but not now. I'll make it playful, keep it fun. It's a godsend in a way—with Charlie's favor guiding me, I have a plan, a strategy to cope with being around Tallulah again.

"Viggo." Ziggy elbows me. "Seriously, what's going on with you?"

"Nothing!" I smile Ziggy's way, hiding everything I'm desperate for her not to see. "I'm just being a hospitable Bergman."

My sister's eyes narrow suspiciously.

I'm saved from any further possible inquisition as she turns toward the table where Seb's messing with her tiles and gives him a heated warning look.

Seb grins at Ziggy, but then his gaze slips past her as she starts arguing with Oliver about ending the Scrabble game in favor of making s'mores outside, and I'm not so sure I'm clear of further inquisitions after all.

Slowly, Seb stands and makes a pretense of leaning over the board, cleaning up tiles as Ziggy relents to Scrabble ending. "What's that woman to you?" he asks quietly.

I bend and scoop up tiles, too, shimmying them to the crease in the middle of the board as Seb lifts the bag for me to empty them into. "Nothing."

He snorts. "Bullshit."

"I'm serious," I tell him sharply.

Seb peers up at me, eyes holding mine. "Sure. But when you're ready to walk what you so eloquently talk, you giant hypocrite, I'll be here."

And with that, he turns, tugs my sister his way by the waist, and strolls with her out onto the back deck, in the mass exodus of my family.

Leaving me with the last person I want to be alone with, standing just a few feet away.

TWO

Tallulah

Playlist: "Tempt My Trouble," Bishop Briggs

This is my worst nightmare—I have stepped into a goddamn den of lovey-doveyness. The air is practically saturated with happily ever afters and romance and all that mushy shit that makes me antsy just thinking about it. I stand right inside the door, reeling from the warm welcome, watching the beaming, close-knit Bergman family and their equally beaming, close-knit partners drift out onto their back deck.

Except for Viggo.

He doesn't seem to have anyone around, no one taking him by the hand, walking him outside. But maybe they're here. Somewhere. Maybe they're in the bathroom. Or lying down, taking a nap. They could be anywhere in this massive place, which, Charlie's told me, like the family itself, began small and has since grown big and beautiful, brimming with memories and history, photos crammed on walls, candles flickering on counters and end tables and window ledges, spring's first flowers bursting from mismatched vases.

"Tallulah Clarke."

My head tips up reflexively as I hear Viggo's voice. I process how different he sounds, how different he looks.

Viggo is all grown up.

Gone are those long, lanky limbs. No more boyish bare face. He's even taller than he was freshman year, still lean but more muscular, radiating barely restrained energy like a tightly coiled spring. His face is obscured by a thick, unkempt chocolate-brown beard speckled with auburn, and locks of that same chocolate-brown hair flip out around a beat-up navy blue ball cap. Beneath its brim, bright even in shadow, are those eyes. Those damn lovely Bergman eyes. So deceptively cold for such warm people. They're the pale blue-gray of a winter sky heavy with the promise of snow, yet they throw heat like a fire that could thaw you on the most frigid of days, right to your bones.

Staring at him, I feel a foolish pang of desire. He turned my crank when we were freshmen, and he turns my crank now, somehow even more. But, I remind myself, I'm only standing in front of an attractive guy; this is the hormones talking; it's just biology. I'm ovulating. I'm a horny animal, designed to be horny right now. That's it.

I remind myself that this man in front of me is simply the grown-up version of the guy who read Austen novels and bodice rippers during lecture and talked nonstop during recitation. Whose bouncing legs wiggled our table and who annoyingly smelled like Christmastime—pine trees and the faintest hint of sweet vanilla spiced with cinnamon. The guy I ignored because he scared the hell out of me. He was gregarious and cute and endearingly awkward, and all I could think was, *Once upon a time my mom probably felt these ridiculous butterflies for my dad, too, and look where the hell that got them.*

"Viggo Bergman," I reply.

His eyebrows lift. "So you're acknowledging me now?"

"I'd be rude not to."

"Didn't stop you freshman year of college."

A sigh leaves me. Of course he's going to bring this up. And I probably deserve it, but it's not like I can tell him the truth about why I acted the way I did.

I was taken by you. And terrified of you. Keeping my mouth shut was the only option.

He smiles wider, seemingly pleased, watching me squirm even without earning my explanation. "At any rate," he says, "welcome to the A-frame. Looking forward to some rest and relaxation?"

I shift on my feet, feeling every bit of my soles and toes pressed to the cool wood floors, grounding myself. "I'm just here for Charlie."

Viggo tips his head, curious. "How so?"

I stare at him, silent, thinking through my response. I'm not telling him why I'm actually here, because that's not my truth to tell. I'm not telling him that my baby sister blurted to me in the bathroom of the restaurant over lunch that she's scared shitless to propose to her partner but she can't wait a damn second longer, either, and she needs me as moral support, and I can't say no to her because it's our pattern. For as long as I can remember, it's been this: my parents are a toxic mess whom I put up with more than I should; my younger brother is destructive chaos that I try to manage; and my sister, the youngest, gets scared and needs me, and needs me to be okay so I'm there for her, and I am.

Waiting me out, Viggo drums his fingers on the chair he just nearly fell out of and barely managed to catch, not unlike the first time I walked into our classroom, when his chair teetered dangerously before it slammed back down on the ground, right as my heart thudded against my ribs.

I was nervous, walking into my very first college class. That was the only reason it happened, back then. It wasn't because the first thing I saw was an adorable guy watching me, smiling curiously.

Not unlike how he's watching me, smiling curiously, now.

God, I need an escape. I feel that hum beneath my skin like I did the first day I sat by him. And his scent hasn't changed. Woodsy and warm, a pine tree trimmed trunk to tippy-top and fresh baked Christmas cookies.

I can't take this.

I've got enough on my plate. I've got a horribly long editorial letter that I'm too scared to read, and an accompanying Word doc version of my proposal and the first ten chapters of my new manuscript, which, judging by the brief, terrifying scroll through its comments and Track Changes, is filled with ego-slashing edits. I've got parents who are back at each other's throats, trying to drag me into it. A brother who's sulking even after getting away with a mere slap on the wrist for his latest misdemeanor. And I've got a sister who's about to propose to her partner once she takes her on some "romantic" hike, who's begged me to come along and support her, as if my being here could somehow make this nonsense she's gotten herself into—a long-term romantic partnership—work out.

"Charlie and I haven't seen each other in a while," I finally tell him. "She . . . wanted us to have longer to catch up."

"You met up with her in Seattle today," Viggo says. "I heard. Glad you decided to come back with her."

I arch an eyebrow up at him. "Are you?"

He smiles. "Why wouldn't I be? You think I was going to hold against you that little cold shoulder you threw my way all those years ago?"

My stomach knots. My ego takes another hit. Of course he wasn't. I didn't matter to him. I brushed him off and he moved on. Literally. He left USC after that semester. A few of our classmates who ended up in our next lit class the following semester liked to joke that I'd scared Viggo away.

But I hadn't. I was nobody to him. Just like he was nobody to me. That's what I told myself: *We're no one to each other.* That's what I remind myself now.

"Just so you know," he adds when I don't respond, "my family won't hold it against you, either. They don't even know we were in class together."

I blink at him, surprised. Everything Charlie says about her beloved Bergmans is how close they are, how well they communicate. "They don't?"

"Nah." He shrugs. "Never seemed worth mentioning."

Relief lowers my shoulders. I was worried he'd have told all the Bergmans what a frigid bitch I was. It certainly wouldn't be the first time someone said that about me.

"Our little secret," he whispers, winking. "We can keep it that way."

I nod.

"Can I get you a drink?" he asks. "Show you around the place? The family photos are comedy gold."

I can't take this. His kindness. His easy conversation. He's too cute, and I feel too awkward, oddly ashamed of how cold I was so long ago, given how warm he's being.

I need an escape.

I glance past Viggo to the back deck, where our sisters sit together, laughing. Ziggy lounges beside Charlie, who has her arm around Gigi. Charlie glances past her partner and smiles brightly, waving me her way with her free hand.

"I should probably just join Charlie out on the deck."

He glances over his shoulder and spots my sister. "Good idea." He smiles. "She looks real happy you came." When he glances back my way, our gazes meet. His eyes dance between mine. His smile deepens.

It's charming and friendly and just as aggravatingly attractive as it was back in college. Worse, I think it might be even more attractive now. Growing up suits Viggo. His skin is suntanned and a little weathered; there are already tiny lines at the corners of his eyes, like he smiles too much, laughs too much, spends too much time outside without putting on sunscreen.

Eyes on me still, he says, "You're as quiet as I remember."

"I'm not much of a talker."

I have gotten more comfortable with talking. I've had to. After my debut unexpectedly took off and hit the bestseller list, there were interviews, podcasts, bookseller virtual events, where I could hide behind a turned-off camera but had to embrace my voice.

"My theory back in college," he says, "was that you saved your words for all those overachieving papers."

I arch an eyebrow. "Like you weren't an overachiever in that class, too."

Viggo shrugs. "I didn't give that class my *best* effort."

The hell he didn't. I stare at him, biting back the retort. I won't be baited by him. He can't suck me into talking. I won't let him charm me or flirt with me. It makes me wonder if that's all he wanted in college—a reaction from the cold, quiet girl. Like others before and after him, did he just want what he couldn't have? And like them, would he have dropped me the second I gave him a sliver of myself?

"I frankly didn't pull out all the stops in that class," I tell him offhandedly, picking lint from my shirt, where no lint really is. "It wasn't particularly memorable."

The corner of his left eye twitches. "You tried awfully hard in a literature class you don't find memorable, Tallulah Clarke."

I shrug. "Who says I was trying *that* hard?"

"Did you conveniently forget we swapped papers for peer critique? Your writing was an exercise in perfectionism. Your footnotes had footnotes."

Thank God I don't blush easily. I'd be red, head to toe. I clear my throat. "I don't know what you're talking about."

"Sure you don't," he says, winking.

I want a button to deactivate his winking capacity. It drives me up the wall. "The class wasn't entirely unmemorable, I'll admit that. Some things I do recall quite clearly. Like the unreliable quality of your voice. Don't know many eighteen-year-olds whose voices still crack."

"Ouch." He slaps a hand over his heart. "Harsh blow. Take it easy, Tallulahloo. I was on the cusp of adulthood. That's a delicate time in a man's life."

"*Tallulahloo?* What the hell kind of name is that?"

Viggo shrugs, winking again. That damn wink. "A cute one."

"I'm not cute."

He clucks his tongue. "Sorry, Lula. You are the definition of cute: five foot nothing, bright blue hair, arriving here, all Reese Witherspoon in *Sweet Home Alabama*, like you forgot spring in Washington State requires boots and a waterproof coat, not designer flats and a fancy jean jacket. If that's not cute, I don't know what is."

I scowl. How does he know how deeply I loathe being called cute? This is infuriating. "There's a reason I didn't acknowledge your existence back then," I tell him. "And it holds now. I knew you'd be a giant pain in the ass."

"You are an excellent judge of character, then." He folds his arms across his chest, staring down at me, his expression a bit more serious, settled in. "So, how's the thriller-writing business?"

My stomach drops as I try to orient myself to the abrupt subject change, to figure out why he's asked, what he knows, how to answer him. I use a pen name. I'm deeply private. The only way he must know what I write is because he's all buddy-buddy with my sister.

"Charlie told you."

He nods. "Not your pen name, just your genre. Your anonymity is protected. She did brag that it was a bestseller, and your debut novel, no less. Congratulations."

I balk at the compliment. I don't know what to do with it. I never know what to do with compliments.

My cheeks are hot. "Thank you," I whisper.

Viggo smiles, tipping his head, shifting his weight onto one leg. "So. Why thrillers?"

I frown up at him. "What's with all the questions?"

"Making up for lost time. I've got you talking. Can't quit now."

I stare longingly past him, where I see beers are now being passed around the deck, wine poured, shot glasses set out with a chilled bottle of what I think might be aquavit. Type 1 diabetes and drinking aren't the best of friends, but straight liquor is manageable, and I have practice handling it; if there's any time it's worth the hassle, this is it.

I flick my gaze back to Viggo, who's watching me, those pale eyes locked on my face. "If I'm going to be interrogated, I at least deserve a drink."

Viggo smiles his widest smile yet. "You got yourself a deal, Tallulahloo."

I made three big mistakes last night. I drank way too much aquavit; I looked up my ex-roommate and long-term fuck buddy on Instagram, only to see a photo of him with most of our friends from college—a visceral reminder that just a week ago he kicked me out and imploded every friendship I'd built with him; and I read my editorial letter. Of the three, the last hurt the worst:

> So far, the "romantic" dynamic between your husband and
> wife characters, which is central to this book's proposed
> conflict and resolution, lacks a stitch of soul or sensuality.

Ouch. Ouch, ouch, ouch.

That's my internal refrain as I fumble around the Bergmans' kitchen, desperate for signs of a coffee maker. It's too early to be up, but I couldn't sleep. My head hurts; my stomach aches; my ego is a bruised mess. And I really need coffee.

"Goddamn tree huggers," I mutter at the sight of compostable coffee filters, a kettle on the stovetop emitting soft curls of steam from its open mouth, a glass pour-over carafe with used grounds perched inside. This perfect family in their perfect house in the woods would be hard-core environmentalists. Hipsters and their slow coffee-making methods. I'm going to die. I need a pod to insert, a button to push, and hot, liquid life poured into a mug fifteen seconds later.

That's when I spot a tall thermos just a little farther down the counter, a hodgepodge of mugs gathered around it.

"Thank you, Jesus." I rush toward it, twist off the lid, and nearly cry for joy. The scent of strong fresh-brewed coffee wafts from the thermos. Grabbing a mug, I greedily fill it to the brim, then take a tentative sip.

I burn my mouth, then swear under my breath.

Tears well in my eyes. From the pain of burning my mouth. The head-pounding misery of being hungover. The ache in my chest from Clint and his shitty Instagram post with all my old friends burrowing under my skin. The bitter, terrible panic knotting my stomach that I can't write this book that I barely managed the first ten chapters of, that I'll never get it right, never finish it.

Tears slip down my cheeks, and I clench my teeth, willing myself to stop. I hate crying. I wipe my cheeks and eyes with the heel of my hand.

Taking a deep breath, I steady myself and cross the great room toward the sliding doors that lead to the back deck. I'm still teary-eyed and sniffling, but at least there's no one to see me like this. At least I'm alone.

As I step onto the deck, my gaze fastens on the first moments of dawn, the sun just a faint yellow smudge on the bruised blue-black horizon. I drag the sliding door shut behind me, then start to ease into an Adirondack chair beside me.

"Well, good morning to you, Tallulahloo."

I startle violently, spilling coffee all over my hand. Fuck me. Shaking my hand free of the scalding coffee droplets, I glare in the direction of the only person who's ever used that ridiculous name, who's here, where I was supposed to be alone, left in peace to wallow in my early morning pity party.

Viggo. Of course it's Viggo.

He smiles my way and lifts his coffee mug.

A weird kick knocks against my ribs. There's no ball cap this morning. Just thick, chocolate-brown bed-head waves that almost touch his shoulders, that dense beard obscuring his mouth and jawline. He's wearing an open plaid flannel shirt in shades of deep blue and green over a white graphic tee that features a mug of coffee, a couple embracing on its ceramic surface. Above the mug his shirt says, *I like my romance novels like I like my coffee—hot and steamy.* A pair of hunter-green joggers that are a little short reveal bare ankles and the most grandpa pair of slippers I have ever seen—plaid flannel that matches his shirt, with a little leather bow.

It feels weirdly . . . intimate, seeing him like this.

I'm reminded, as I glance down at myself, that I am in similarly informal clothes, and that feels . . . weirdly intimate, too. My stretchy black palazzo pj pants flutter in the spring breeze. The matching dolman-sleeved pj top is half off one shoulder, cool air kissing my bare skin. I shrug it up. At least, I try to. But it slips right back down.

Viggo's eyes hold mine, not for a second dipping to where my eyes definitely would be, if a lady with as fantastically ample, braless tits as mine walked out onto my deck first thing in the morning.

Well, well, well, we have a gentleman on our hands.

In hindsight, I should have realized that already, given the hot coffee inside. Viggo didn't selfishly make himself a quick single pour-over cup of coffee. He stood at the stove and heated a whole kettle, made a big pot of coffee for anyone who needed it, then set out mugs for them, too.

How despicably thoughtful.

Annoyed, unsettled, I grumble, "Of course you beat me in the wake-up race," before bringing the cup slowly to my lips. I try another sip and stop myself. Still too hot.

"I wasn't aware we were competing for first awake," he says wryly, before bringing his coffee cup to his mouth.

"Ours is a brief history, Viggo, but it is undeniably defined by competition."

He pauses, mug poised an inch from his mouth. His eyes dart to mine. "You saw us as competitors? In class?"

I blink, processing his question. Is this a surprise to him? He seemed so confident in class, so quick to speak and debate, to offer insight. And he was a damn good writer. The man could write a beautiful turn of phrase, though like hell am I admitting that.

"Don't get a big head," I tell him.

His face transforms from serious curiosity to the charming playfulness that greeted me last night. "Too late for that."

I roll my eyes. Viggo watches me as I set my cup on the chair's arm and try to lean back. I nearly fall flat, the chair is so deep. Swearing under my breath, I scooch until I'm nestled against the back of the chair, then scowl at the sunrise.

For a few minutes, nothing but silence hangs between us. At any moment, I'm anticipating some pithy, provoking quip from Viggo, something about me not being a morning person, about how I woke up on the wrong side of the bed, but he's quiet. Perplexed, I glance his way.

Viggo's smiling at me.

I glare at him. "What are you looking at?"

He turns back toward the horizon, then lifts his mug to the sky. "Just a stunning view." After a beat he says, "I get the sense you aren't generally up this early."

"How did you ever guess?" I deadpan, tucking my legs up onto the chair. I'm so damn short, when I'm eased into the back of the chair, my feet don't touch the ground. An Adirondack is usually the one kind of chair I can count on to fit in like an adult rather than a child, legs dangling from a high chair. These Bergman giants and their long legs would have specially made long-legged-friendly Adirondacks.

Viggo sips his coffee, then sets his mug on the arm of his chair, a wry smile lifting his mouth. He's quiet. Which really confuses me. I never got to know him well—I made a point not to—but I did share a classroom with him for a whole semester, and, once he got me my drink last night, I spent my energy avoiding yet nonetheless constantly aware of him. Last night, it was clear he's as much of a nonstop talker as he was in college. Making conversation, telling jokes, laughing, instigating antics and noisy debates.

But not now. Right now, he's surprisingly quiet.

"Now what are *you* looking at?" he asks, eyebrows raised as he turns his head my way.

Dammit. He caught me staring at him. "Just inspecting those trees over yonder."

His mouth cracks with a grin. "Over yonder?"

"Shut up."

He clucks his tongue. "You're a bad liar, Lulaloo."

I sigh heavily. "I was staring at you because I was trying to wrap my head around an unnatural phenomenon."

"Oh?" His smile widens. "And what unnatural phenomenon is that?"

"You being quiet."

A laugh jumps out of him, deep and rich, right from his belly.

It makes a delicious little hum dance beneath my skin. "How would you know that's unnatural for me? One semester of college not talking to me and you know me so well?"

"I didn't talk to you, but it's not like it stopped you from talking to everyone else. You were always participating in class, debating, discussing. You were never quiet."

And I was fascinated. By how quickly he shared ideas, the way he drew others' ideas out, both challenged and respected them. I hated him a little for how good he was at talking to people.

Viggo's mouth kicks up at the corner; another smile. Our gazes hold. Viggo's dips down to my mouth, then darts away, fastened on the horizon again. "I'm not normally quiet, no. But I am in the morning."

"Why?" I find myself asking before I can stop myself.

Viggo shrugs, gaze pinned on the growing dawn. "Just seems unnecessary to talk while I'm watching the world wake up. Feels like something that deserves a little reverence." He sips his coffee. "Even I can shut my mouth for that."

I stare at him because I can't seem not to. Shit, that man has a nice profile. A long, straight nose, sharp cheekbones peeking above his beard. I shut one eye and squint because I hope I'm seeing things, but no, it's true, there they are—a faint dusting of freckles scattered across his suntanned skin.

I'm just horny. Ovulating. Haven't had sex for weeks, since things became silent and tense with Clint, before he said some really nasty things and told me to get the hell out last week. That's all this is.

Taking a slow, deep breath, I stare back at the sun, now grown to a ripe lemon wedge, its zesty rays sprayed into the brightening sky. I bring my mug to my lips and hazard a slow, careful sip.

A satisfied moan rolls up my throat.

Viggo brings a leg up, setting one grandpa-slippered foot on the edge of his Adirondack, and drapes an arm across his knee, coffee cup clasped by the brim between his long fingers. I peer at him over the top of my mug as I take another sip, and his gaze flicks to mine.

"You," he says, "disappeared on me last night. You promised I could ask you questions if I got you a drink, and instead, you took your drink and ghosted me."

"That's rich, coming from the guy who left USC without a single word to anyone."

His eyebrows shoot up. "You noticed?"

Shit. I didn't mean to say that. For it to sound like I noticed ... like I cared. "Every kid in that lit class noticed, once we came back for spring semester; a lot of us had overlapping classes, but you weren't there. You were a big personality that people remembered; then you were just ... gone."

Viggo peers down at his coffee. "I never thought anyone would care."

"Well, they did, but they moved on. As did you, clearly, because here you are, loving life and"—I gesture toward his shirt—"romance novels."

Viggo leans in, smiling. "You want to ask me about them, the romance novels, don't you? It's not every day you meet a spry, strapping specimen of a man who adores the genre devoted to love. You could now be asking *me* questions, if you hadn't been too scared to indulge *my* questions last night."

"I wasn't scared," I snap.

He smiles sweetly. "What were you, then?"

"Too busy meeting your entire family. There's so many of you, it took me all night."

I won't tell him the truth, that when I was overwhelmed by all the people, my gaze kept slipping toward him, hoping he'd break in and save me with that flashy smile and some diversionary tactic.

That I almost caved when the buzz kicked in, almost wandered his way and told him, *Ask your damn questions. And kiss me senseless while you're at it.*

But then I asked myself, what would be the point? Why put the emotionless moves on a hopeless romantic? He believes in destiny and swoons and happy endings. I believe that's all a crock of shit. Not to mention the complications of trying for a one-night stand with my sister's best friend's brother. No, too many entanglements, too many ways it could go wrong.

"Well," Viggo says, before taking a sip of coffee, eyes back on the dawn, "if you aren't scared, you certainly have the time this morning. You *could* answer my questions right now if you aren't too afraid."

"I'm not afraid of your questions."

He glances my way, smiling. "Prove it."

I roll my eyes and slump back in my chair.

"C'mon, Lula. Give me a chance. You might even have fun talking to me."

That's what I'm worried about, I think, sipping my coffee. *And then I'll leave, and you'll leave, and I'll have a happiness hangover when my life shrinks back to being sad and stressful.*

"Fine," I grumble. "Do your worst."

Within five minutes of agreeing to Viggo's questions, I am deeply regretting my decision. He now knows my favorite food (seafood risotto), my first pet (Gertrude Stein, a sheepdog whose death I have still admitted to no one absolutely gutted me), my favorite color (blue), and the last country I visited (Iceland). Each answer I've given is harmless, except it doesn't feel harmless at all. It feels like Viggo is building a stockpile, an arsenal of Tallulah facts stored up to use against me, to draw me in, to know me, like I've never wanted him to. And now he's on to asking the weirdest stuff. The latest question is a bridge too far.

"I'm not telling you the last time I cried," I mumble into my coffee mug before draining it.

Viggo's eyes widen innocently. "Why not? That's a great question."

"It is *not*. Besides, I barely ever cry."

"Why?"

"Because I hate crying."

"Really? I love it," he says. "Crying is so cathartic. I mean, I never love it in the moment, but I always cry when I really need to, and I always feel better afterward. Come on, now, tell me."

"Nope."

Viggo growls quietly in his throat, perturbed. It's extremely satisfying to see his smile slip and watch him get annoyed, too. "Fine, then. I'll guess."

"Viggo—"

"When you finished your next book."

"No." I wish. I'd give anything to have finished this book already.

He narrows his eyes at me, like he's trying to read my mind. "When your sister scored the game winner in their final match of the season."

Charlie, like Ziggy, plays for the LA women's professional soccer team. I felt a fierce surge of pride and happiness when she won the game for them, right before the end of stoppage time. But I didn't cry.

"Nope."

Viggo scratches his beard, peering out at the trees, mouth pursed in thought. "When you hit the bestseller list."

I make a wrong-answer buzzer noise. "Three strikes, you're out. Move on."

He sighs. "Fine. Where do you live these days?" he asks, before draining his coffee, too.

My stomach clenches. I think about the Culver City house that I'd been living in since our friend group graduated college and we got a place that we all agreed to live in. The house that became emptier as people paired off, got jobs, moved on, until it was just me and Clint. I think about the night Clint told me off and left me there, with a warning that I'd better be gone when he got back. "Pass."

Another sigh. "Where's the last place you *stayed*, then?"

"If Charlie hadn't bombed my Seattle staycation plans, an adorable condo right on the bay, but thanks to her, the last place I stayed was a bungalow Airbnb in Escondido."

Viggo chokes on his coffee. Eyes watering, he whacks his chest and sets down his mug, then spins and faces me fully in his chair. "Escondido?"

I frown at him and answer slowly, "Yes. Why? What's the big deal?"

"I . . ." He clears his throat, whacking his chest again. "Nothing."

"It's clearly not nothing. What's Escondido to you?"

Viggo stares at me, his expression growing uncharacteristically serious. He brings a finger to his mouth and bites the nail. He's nervous.

Instinctively, I reach a foot toward him and knock my toe into his grandpa slipper. "Tell me."

His eyes are tight, searching mine. "Why should I? Miss Begrudgingly, Barely Answering My Questions."

I hold his eyes, wrestling with myself. He's right. Why should he confide in me? More importantly, why do I want him to?

Viggo sits back in his chair, still turned toward me, folding his arms across his chest. "My connection to Escondido is a secret. One my family doesn't even know—"

I keep my expression blank, trying hard to hide my interest. I love a good secret. That pent-up anticipation of the truth finally being uncovered. It's one of my favorite parts of thriller writing, building a story's momentum toward that climactic revelation.

"—but I'll tell you," he says, "*if* you tell me a secret, too."

Oh, no way. No bonding secret swaps with Viggo Bergman. "You can keep your secret, then."

He sighs, eyes narrowed analytically, like I'm a code he's trying to crack. "*And* I'll drop the remaining questions I was going to ask. For context, I had twenty-two left."

I lift my eyebrows. Now, that's appealing. After letting him hang for a minute, I stand from my chair and tell him, "Deal. But first, I need more coffee."

"Oh, no, you don't," he says, springing out of his seat. "Last time I made this 'deal' with you, you got a drink out of it and I got a big old goose egg."

Something about the way he says it tickles me, and I duck my head, biting back a laugh. But when I glance up, all amusement drains from me. Viggo is standing very close—not inappropriately, just . . . close. Closer than a person's been to me in too long.

I feel heat pouring off his body, smell that damn delectable evergreen and cinnamon-sugar scent clinging to his skin. I drink in his clothes, soft and worn, draped lovingly over his lean, hard body. I can see two defined pecs beneath his shirt, and one of his flannel sleeves is rolled high, rucked up on his arm, revealing a taut, round bicep.

I swallow thickly. "I'll get the coffees," I say, trying to sound resolute.

"*I'll* get them. You," he says, pointing to my chair, "will sit your butt down, enjoy the sunrise, and be right here when I get back."

"Someone's bossy."

A twinkle settles in his eyes. He grins. "I can be. But generally, I much prefer when it's the other way around."

My mouth falls open as he plucks my mug from the rictus of my clenched hand.

And then Viggo Bergman strolls right by, his arm brushing mine, leaving me to melt into a resentful, lusty puddle on his deck.

THREE

Viggo

Playlist: "Make a Picture," Andrew Bird

I step back onto the deck, a mug of coffee in each hand, dragging the door shut with my elbow. Tallulah glances over her shoulder and lifts an eyebrow at me, her mouth set in a firm, frigid line. My dick twitches in my sweatpants. There's something wrong with me. Tallulah's chilly gaze should not turn me on like that.

But God, is there something about that woman's serious scowliness that my devious self enjoys, that makes me want to tease and play, see if I can get a little rise out of her, or better yet—and as Charlie pleaded—finally turn that frown upside down.

I smile, handing her a cup of coffee. "Your caffeine, madam."

She takes the cup, peering up at me skeptically. "Thanks."

"Very welcome." I plop back into the Adirondack and scooch the chair her way, holding my coffee out and steady with the other hand so I won't spill. "So. Let's swap secrets."

She rolls her eyes as she sips her coffee, but, for just a second, I swear I catch the tiniest sliver of a smile hiding behind her mug.

"You first," I tell her.

She throws me a "get out of here" look. "Hell no."

"Respectfully, Tallulahloo, you already ducked out on me yesterday. I'm going to need you to go first, an act of good faith."

There's that chilly scowl again. I like it way too much. She's quiet for a minute, wide, dark-lashed eyes dancing between mine. I stare at her irises, because I've always wanted to, knowing, in my gut, they weren't as simple as plain old brown.

I was right.

Sunlight bathes her face, and finally I see those irises for what they really are—a dozen slivered shades of amber, topaz, and gold—rich and warm, a dramatic rim of dark chocolate wrapped around them. They're so damn pretty.

Stop, Viggo. Stop romanticizing this moment with a woman who barely tolerates you.

At least she used to barely tolerate me. I can't get a read on her now.

Tallulah says quietly, "I don't think I'm ever going to finish this book."

Her words land with a shocking splash inside me, ripples that echo through my body. I blink at her. I can't believe she actually confided in me, and about this, of all things.

"I'm in way over my head," she adds, staring down at her coffee. "I wanted to write a fresh take on the domestic thriller. Husband and wife both suspicious, marriage on the rocks—the usual deal, except it's not the usual deal at all, the way I imagined it. I had these plans to subvert the predictable arc of the unreliable, jealous female narrator, the duplicitous, scheming husband, and fucking crush this book, but I just can't . . ."

She sighs and massages her forehead with her hand.

"I just can't get it right, and my editor is generally super helpful and insightful, but this time, every email and call with her is just muddying the waters, making it harder to sort out my thoughts and untangle the mess I've made of the plot, and we're on this tight deadline because my first book did so well, and they want to capitalize on momentum, keep a tight publication timeline, but I'm so behind.

I'm fucked." Sighing again, she drops her hand. Her eyes meet mine, a rare flash of soft, raw vulnerability before they slip away, fastened on the horizon. "That's my damn secret. Now spill yours."

I stare at her, warmth spreading through me.

Tallulah trusted me. She talked . . . a lot. Well, a lot for her. That same zip of electricity that jumped down my spine the day she walked into class seven years ago flies through me again.

That's when I know I'm in trouble. If I'm not careful, I'm going to find myself right where I was the day I met Tallulah Clarke.

Thoroughly, unbearably smitten.

FOUR

Tallulah

Playlist: "Direct Address," Lucy Dacus

A thoughtful hum rumbles in Viggo's throat. He stares at me with those keen pale blue eyes—I feel them boring into the side of my head. "Tallulah—"

"Don't." I point a finger at him. "Don't therapize me. Or console me."

He frowns. A frown looks all wrong on Viggo. There's a sharp pinch in my chest. Something dangerously close to regret. I don't think I like making Viggo frown, but dammit, I'm not here to be his buddy; I'm here to get this secret swap over with and move on with my life.

"I told you my secret," I remind him. "Now you tell me yours."

Clearing his throat, he scrubs at the back of his neck, then sets his coffee on the arm of his Adirondack. He tugs the hem of his joggers' right pant leg a little farther down his ankle and clears his throat again. "I'm uh . . . I'm planning to run a bookstore."

I lift my eyebrows. "And what does that have to do with Escondido? I vomited a paragraph of professional crisis on you. I deserve more than that threadbare sentence."

He groans and slumps down in the Adirondack chair, raking his hands through his hair. "I went for a drive last year because . . . I needed to go somewhere. Do something. I was having one of those days when my brain was spinning in eighty directions and my body was antsy, and it was too damn hot for a run, so I got in Ashbury—"

"Ashbury?"

"My car," he says impatiently, as if I should have known this. "I got in Ashbury, started driving south. Took the scenic route, down the PCH to I-5, and by the time I was a few hours in, nature was calling. I took a random exit, dealt with my business, and then when I was done, I just . . . wasn't ready to go back. So I drove around some more and ended up driving into Escondido, right by a quirky little bookstore that just . . . made me stop. I wrenched the car in park, walked in, and"—he shrugs, his expression turning dreamy—"that was that. Love at first sight."

Good grief. "Love at first sight, huh?"

"It was this magical little place, Lula." His voice is soft, nostalgic. "Shelves crammed with every kind of book you can think of. Chipped china cups stacked by the register, a rusty electric kettle, ancient bags of Lipton tea. Movie posters from days gone by, dusty stacks of comic books, grimy windows the light barely snuck through."

"Sounds delightful," I tell him dryly before sipping my coffee.

He smiles, his gaze fastened on the horizon. "It was. It could have been even more so. That's what I saw when I walked in there, its potential."

Silence hangs in the air. I'm on tenterhooks now. Where does this story go? What happens next?

"And?" I prompt.

Viggo's smile deepens. "And I told the owner as much."

"Bet they loved that."

He laughs softly. "Gerry was surprisingly cool about it. Rather than tell me to walk my ass out for implying his place could use some work, he said, 'Well, Mr. Grand Plans, how about you work for me, get a dose of reality about running a store, then see how many of those ideas of yours are actually possible.'" He sips his coffee. "So that's what I did. Worked for him. For the past year, I've been driving down there a couple times a week, opening the place, running it till close."

I blink at him. "You've been driving two hours to work at a bookstore?"

He nods. "Yeah."

"*Two* hours. Each way. To work at a poky little bookstore in Escondido. That cannot have been worth it."

Finally, he glances my way, still smiling. "Hist-rom audiobooks kept me company on the drive. Traffic wasn't too bad because I was always on the road so early in the morning and so late at night. And working at the store itself, training with Gerry, learning everything there was to know about running a bookstore while thinking about how I'd do it differently, do it *my* way? I loved it. That's how you know you really love something, Tallulahloo, when it feels worth the hassle, when even the hardest parts of it feel like a gift."

My heart does something funny in my chest. It bristles and it burns. *Love.* He uses that word so easily, so confidently. I, on the other hand, recoil from it.

Sitting straighter in my chair, I cup my hands around my coffee mug and focus on what I'm invested in: this story's outcome.

"So, the store's revamped now?" I ask. "Gerry let you zhuzh up the place? Make it its best self, right?"

"Nope. Gerry was ready to retire. Sold the building two months ago to some firm that's going to set up their insurance office there, wouldn't even let me buy it from him. Said I had to start on my own, make something from nothing and prove to myself that I could."

My mouth drops open. "What the *hell*? You drove four hours a day, twice a week, to run a musty old bookshop in Escondido that got closed down, and for *what*?"

A flock of birds darts from the trees, startled by my volume.

Viggo blinks at me, surprised. I blink at him, surprised, too. I can't remember the last time I got fired up about anything. When

I was little, I learned getting fired up just made things worse. It gave my parents something else to use against each other; it egged on my younger brother, Harry, to be even more misbehaved, simply to outdo me; it upset and scared little Charlie. So I stopped. I learned to stay quiet and bottle it up and not feel. Feelings made everything worse.

Viggo leans an elbow on the arm of his Adirondack and tells me, "I decided that I'm going to open a place of my own, in LA and here. I've been back and forth on where to start. Here would be cheaper, since I'd keep it out this way, rather than in Seattle. Then again, if I opened up my flagship store here, before I opened my second location in LA, I'd be up here most of the time, far away from the kiddos—"

"Kiddos?"

"My niece and nephew," he explains. "And another one on the way. Frankie, my brother Ren's wife, she's due next month. You saw her last night, I'm sure. Tall, long dark hair. She's the only one in our family right now who looks like they swallowed a prizewinning pumpkin, though never would I ever say that to her face—I value my life."

"So . . . those kids. You don't want to be away from them."

He frowns at me, clearly perplexed. "Of course not. I'm their favorite uncle."

"Like hell you are," a man gruffs beyond the shrubs surrounding the deck, startling us both.

"Jesus," I gasp, slapping a hand to my chest. "Where'd he come from?"

"Oh, he's been up for hours." Viggo sips his coffee, then says, voice lowered, "Ever since he retired, Gavin's been an early riser. I'd guess he's been up since three, probably, if he even slept at all. I'm not sure he isn't a vampire."

"I heard that," says the man I now recognize is Gavin Hayes, former international soccer star and Oliver's partner. He walks slowly up the steps from the backyard to the deck, wearing a gray zip-up jacket and matching black pants with a gray stripe along the side, a black coffee thermos in his hands.

"How's it taste," Viggo asks, beaming up at him, "that hefty dose of delusional thinking mixed in with your morning joe?"

Ignoring Viggo, Gavin lifts his mug in greeting and offers me a polite "Good morning."

"Morning," I tell him.

Then he turns to Viggo. "You think *I'm* delusional about favorite-uncle status? Consider the facts, Bergman. Does Linnie play magical unicorn and sorceress with *you*?"

Viggo blinks, clearly thrown by this. "Not as such, but—"

"I didn't think so," Gavin says, wrenching open the sliding door leading inside. "Enjoy *that* dose of reality with your tepid light-roast hipster coffee."

The door slides shut, unexpectedly quiet.

Viggo smiles after him. "Man, he gets under my skin, but I love that asshole."

I glance between where Gavin was and where Viggo sits. "You are a very strange family."

"No doubt," he agrees. "But we do love each other."

Damn that word, itching like a nettle dragged across my skin. I tug up my sleeve and scratch around my CGM—the continuous glucose monitor secured to my upper arm that keeps track of my blood sugar. The adhesive itches sometimes, and when it does, I can't help but scrape my nails around its border.

Viggo glances at what I'm doing, then tips his head. "Don't remember that from freshman year."

I tug my sleeve back down over it. "Unlike you, I wasn't making best friends with everyone. No one needed to know I have type 1 diabetes."

"So you'd already been diagnosed?" he asks.

"Freshman year of high school."

"That had to have been kinda tough. Especially going through it as a teen. High schoolers can be buttheads about things like that."

"They were," I say offhandedly, staring into my coffee, plucking out a bug that decided to dive-bomb its surface. "But I got over it. I moved on."

"Sure. But just because we've moved on doesn't mean some hurts don't linger."

I throw him a flat, chilly look. "I don't need your empathy. We're here swapping secrets, not becoming friends."

Viggo smiles at me slowly, a mischievous twinkle in his eye. "Uh-oh. You didn't know, did you?"

"Didn't know what?"

His smile widens, and he leans in. "Once you swap a secret with a Bergman, you're bonded to them for life. We're friends now, Lulaloo. Like it or not."

"I do not like. I unlike. Unsubscribe. Unfollow."

Viggo laughs. "Tough cookies. We're friends now, and that's that. Heck, I bet by this time next year, we'll be duetting karaoke at the wedding."

My throat turns desert dry. "Wh-whose wedding?"

"Theirs." He points past the shrubs surrounding the deck, where I see Charlie and Gigi emerge from a thick cluster of trees, clasped hands swinging, sunlight glinting off a pair of sparkly engagement rings. Gigi's got a wildflower tucked behind her ear, and Charlie's short dark hair is covered in petals. Their smiles are incandescent.

Something very close to tears springs into my eyes.

"She did it," I whisper.

"Yeah," Viggo says. "She did."

I tear my gaze away from my sister. There's something about the way he said it that makes it sound like he was in on this, too. "You knew? That Charlie was going to propose?"

"Course I did. I'm the one who suggested proposing here in the first place."

"You and Charlie . . . are that close?"

"She's my baby sister's best friend," he says, as if this should make perfect sense to me. "I'm friends with my baby sister; her friends are my friends. Char Char Binks and I are buds. In fact, *I'm* the one who got her reading romance novels, helped your sister rekindle her belief in happily ever after."

My jaw clenches. Of course he did. There's a small, screaming-angry part of me that wants to launch myself at him and give him a good, hard shake. To tell him he has no business putting absurd romantic ideas into *my* baby sister's brain. But when I glance Charlie's way again, hearing Gigi's throaty laugh and Charlie's sparkly one right behind it, that admonishment, the indignation, just . . . dies away.

I don't believe in happily ever after. But Charlie does, and if she and Gigi are happy, who am I to shit on that? Even if I'm scared she'll get her heart broken. Even if I'm terrified I can't protect her from something she doesn't want to be protected from.

Standing, I set down my coffee and dab the corners of my eyes before I set a hand over my brow, shielding my gaze from the sun. "So my sister believes in happily ever after now, thanks to your romance novels."

"Well." Viggo stands, too, hands on his hips, at least until Charlie and Gigi spot us and wave. He smiles wide and waves back. "Not *just* because of the romance novels. But I sure think they helped."

I sigh bleakly, still watching Gigi and Charlie as they walk closer. "This store of yours, it'll be selling romance books, won't it?"

"Primarily, yes, but I've got lots of plans for the place. Plac*es*."

My eyebrows dart up. "Multiple locations. Grand plans. Awfully confident, aren't you?"

"Better than confidently awful," he says, winking.

I roll my eyes, fighting a smile. "Well, may that confidence take you far, Viggo Bergman."

"Likewise, Tallulah Clarke." Our eyes meet. "You'll figure out that book," he finally says. "I know that you know that you know what you're doing."

I frown. "That was . . . a confusing sentence."

"But no less true. Tell you what," he says, turning fully my way, stepping closer. He raises a pinkie. "Let's make a promise. A pinkie promise."

I barely override the impulse to take a step back. "Why?"

"Because . . ." His eyes search mine. "It helps, when you're doing hard things, knowing someone out there is cheering you on. So, let's promise to put the rocky past behind us, be accountability partners, of a kind. By the time we're celebrating Charlie and Gigi's wedding, let's promise we'll have done what we set out to do: you, kick that book's butt. Take the time you need to make it right, make it something you're proud of. Push back your deadline, tell your publisher, 'Just hold your horses and let me work my magic; great books take great time—'"

Great books take great time. That's actually pretty good.

"—and *I'll* have my bookstore up and running. Now, come on." He lifts his pinkie higher.

I stare at it, then say, "And if we've both done those things—"

"*When* we've both done those things," he says.

"—then what?"

Viggo tips his head, smiling warmly. "Then we'll celebrate, and it'll be nice to know we were cheering each other on along the way. Hopefully, we'll both be happier and less stressed. And maybe, just *maybe*, by then, you'll have come around to actually being my friend."

"Your friend, Viggo? Seriously? We're night and day. Why would we be friends?"

"Why wouldn't we?" he counters. "Consider this. You know your literature—you're a book lover. Think about how many great stories are built on friendships between people who couldn't be more different. Difference is what makes the world beautiful, Lu, it's what makes life interesting." He shrugs, then says casually, "But I get that it might be intimidating—"

"I'm not intimidated by you. Or your pinkie promise."

Viggo grins. "I'm glad to hear it."

Roughly, I lock pinkies with his. A jolt of static electricity jars me as we touch, but Viggo doesn't flinch. He just holds my eyes for a moment, steady and warm; then he pulls his hand away first.

The wind picks up, bringing Charlie and Gigi and a gale of blossoms with them up onto the deck. I scrunch my face against the petals as they whip around me, brushing them away. Viggo reaches toward me and plucks a flower from my hair.

"I could have gotten that," I mutter.

He smiles, makes a fist around the flower, then rolls his wrist before opening his palm, revealing . . . nothing. The flower's gone.

I blink at him. "Got a little magician side hustle going there?"

His smile deepens. "One of many."

As Charlie and Gigi grow closer, Viggo takes a step back and says, just loud enough for me to hear, "Remember, the shop's a secret for now. So don't tell anyone."

"My lips are sealed." I mime zipping my mouth shut.

A laugh jumps out of him. "It's just studs and old windows right now, but the shop is in Culver City. Come by sometime. I'll make you a cup of coffee; you can poke fun at my romance novel inventory and glare at me some more."

Don't ask. Don't ask.

My damn mouth moves before I can stop myself. "What's it called?"

He smiles wide. "Originally, I was going to call it Happily Ever

After, but I settled on Bergman's Romance Books & More—Bergman's Books, for short. Well, it *will* be called that. Right now it's still Joe's Sandwich Shop, according to Google Maps. Anyway, between now and the wedding," he says, "if you ever need a little pep talk from the cheering stands, you'll know where to find me."

Before I can say anything else, not that I'm sure what I'd even say, Charlie throws her arms around me, breaking the moment. And then Gigi throws herself in my arms, too. I hug them both and tell them I'm happy for them.

My sister and her fiancée drag me inside, where every Bergman seems to be up now, the kitchen bustling with cheery chaos. Champagne is popped, toasts given, and the day blurs into an overwhelming stretch of hours of celebration. Viggo's there the whole time, but he keeps his distance. Stays busy. He cooks in the kitchen with his siblings and his mother. He takes his niece and nephew outside, tumbling across the grass, tickling their feet, making them laugh as they sway in tiny swings hanging from a tree deep in the yard.

I try so hard not to watch him. Or dwell on what he said.

I try not to think about him while I quietly pack my bag that night. While I sit in my rental car early the next morning, so early the sun isn't even a hint on the horizon, and text my sister an apology for being gone when she wakes up, along with a promise, the same promise I always make her, that I'm here, whenever she needs me.

I try so hard not to think about that promise *I* was given by that aggravating man with those paradoxically warm-cool eyes—a promise that he'd be there if I needed him, the thought of someone cheering me on, nudging me down the road.

I fail miserably.

FIVE

Viggo

Playlist: "Brass Band," Jukebox The Ghost

One year later

I haven't heard from or seen Tallulah since the day of our early morning coffee conversation. And I've made it a point not to think about her, either.

Well, not too much.

Of course I thought about her when Charlie wrapped her arms around me, one Sunday family dinner the following month, so sure that Tallulah's turn for the better was thanks to me. She'd gotten her own place, Charlie said. Pushed back her book deadline. She'd told Charlie she was going to take some solo trips and try to prioritize some self-care.

That made me happy to hear, but after twelve months of hearing nothing, I've long since given up the idea that Tallulah's one-eighty had anything to do with me. I pushed away thoughts of her and focused on pouring myself into the life right in front of me, making this bookstore happen.

I'm only thinking about Tallulah now because I've got a small section in the bookstore devoted to non-romance, including thrillers—carefully selected titles that vibe with my store's motto: happy endings. Before that trip up to the A-frame and my run-in with Tallulah, I hadn't read a thriller in years, after thoroughly *not* enjoying the few I tried, but since seeing her last year, I made a point to poke around the library, ask the staff for some recs, and give thrillers another chance. More than a little to my surprise, I found a few that I loved and that fit the bill, their bittersweet endings imbued with hope. So, on to my store's non-romance shelf they went.

While a lot of bookstores boast row after row of every kind of genre, romance is often tucked into a little corner, if it's included at all. My bookstore is the opposite. There's a small, curated floor-to-ceiling set of bookshelves containing non-romance, all of which I've read, all of which end on a note of hopeful possibility. I want to take care of my patrons when they come to my store. This place is all about happily ever afters, and I'm not about to mislead them.

I know romance isn't everyone's cup of tea, and I respect that—so long as people don't bad-mouth the genre—but this place is for the people for whom romance reading is their joy. Somewhere they can walk into and scour aisle after aisle of feel-good stories, lost in happy endings to their hearts' content.

That said, I recognize sometimes readers need a genre switch, or maybe their partner or friend or family member isn't big on romance novels, and they want to bring them along, buy them a book, too. So that's what this corner of the store is for.

It makes me smile as I adjust my favorite thriller so far, *Isochron*, and face it out. The cover is beautiful, a watercolor tapestry of orange and red, a dramatic sunrise that fits the story's ending perfectly. I'm sure its design alone has made plenty of people lift it from a shelf, turn it over, then read its intriguing back-cover copy. That's what hooked me.

One chapter in, and I knew—I *knew*—it was Tallulah's. Her elegant, streamlined prose—never too much exposition or description; balanced, well-paced dialogue. Painfully beautiful observations on human weakness and brokenness.

I adjust the remaining copies of *Isochron* on the shelf and let my mind wander Tallulah's way. I wonder how her second book is going, if she finished it, if she took the time she needed to make it something she was proud of. I hope so. I'm standing in my own expression of that—taking the time I needed to finally get it right, at least I hope.

"That better not be adult content you're reading in front of my daughter." Ren steps up beside me and gives me a faux-censorious look.

I grin, leaving Tallulah's book on the shelf proudly facing out. Lucia, Ren and Frankie's eleven-month-old daughter, shrieks with delight as I turn with her safely tucked in the baby-wearing harness strapped to my chest and she spots her dad. Ren's face melts from feigned seriousness to a soft, lovesick smile. He strokes a finger down Lucia's cheek and wipes away the drool that's pooled on her chin.

"Hi, sweetheart," he coos.

"Dada!" she shrieks. Her legs kick out, then back. She nearly nails me in the nuts with her heel.

"Take it easy," I tell Ren, clasping her pudgy feet. "She's got long legs and she knows how to use them."

Ren grins, picking up his daughter's hand and blowing a raspberry in her palm. Lucia giggles. "Course she does. She's a Bergman."

"*And* a Zeferino," Frankie adds, stepping up beside him and arching her eyebrows.

"As if anyone doubted that." Ren ruffles Lucia's dark hair, the same color as Frankie's.

Lucia's legs start kicking wildly again as she clocks Frankie. "Ma! Mama mama!"

"That's it," I tell them, gently lifting Lucia from the baby-wearing contraption. "I'm gonna lose a nut if you two don't stop fawning over her."

Ren takes her from me greedily, like he's been waiting for this moment, and props Lucia up in one arm, pinned to his chest. Her hands go straight to his beard, and she tugs.

"Easy, Luce," he croons, guiding her hands from his face. "Gentle."

"Gentle." Frankie snorts. "That child doesn't know the meaning of the word."

"Wonder where she gets *that*?" I ask.

I narrowly avoid being whacked in the shins by Frankie's cane. I swear, the women in this family rule us with an iron fist.

Leaving Ren and Frankie with Lucia, I set aside the baby wearer, then turn and start a loop around the store. It's my super-soft opening tonight—only my family but *all* my family here, seeing my dream come to life, which I finally found the courage to tell them about last fall—and I'm a bundle of nerves. That's why I was wearing Lucia. Something about holding a baby makes me feel better about everything. The sweet smell of their hair, the promise of who they are just beginning, who they'll become, bottled up in this tiny body. Babies remind me that good things grow from humble beginnings; that before we run, we crawl, then teeter, then walk. Spending this past year watching Lucia grow from a small, dark-haired, crying bundle to a bright-eyed, vivacious little person has been exactly what I needed as I worked my way toward opening the store.

"Everything looks wonderful, *älskling*," Mom says softly as I nearly walk right by her to lift my favorite succulent, Lorraine, out of Theo's reach. Theo's just a little over two and hell-bent on destroying everything these days. Why I thought it wise to invite tyrannical toddlers to my super-soft opening is beyond me. Well, I knew it wasn't wise; I just also knew it wouldn't feel right if my whole family wasn't here.

"Hey, you." Aiden swoops in quickly, lifting his son rather than the succulent, and deftly turning him upside down. It makes Theo erupt in belly laughter. "Hands off Uncle Viggo's plants."

Relieved that Lorraine's lived to see another day, I turn toward my mother. "That's nice of you," I tell her. "Thanks, Mom."

My mother arches an eyebrow, the same expression I see often on my oldest sister, Freya, with her wavy white-blond hair, Mom's twin in looks, twenty-five years apart. "It isn't 'nice,' Viggo. It's honest. Everything does look wonderful. I say what I mean."

"She's right," Dad adds. Bright green eyes he gave Axel, Ryder, and Ziggy. Red hair bequeathed to Ren and Ziggy, too. But now his hair is heavily streaked with silver so pale it's almost white. I swear it happened overnight. How many of those gray hairs did I put on his head?

I feel a pinch of anxious nerves as Dad squeezes my shoulder firmly and says, "We're proud of you."

My chest floods with relief, even as doubt lurks in the corners of my mind. I glance between my parents. I haven't always made things easy for them. I was a decent student, inclined to do well in subjects I cared about and the bare minimum to scrape by in the ones I didn't, but I also screwed around a lot—got myself into trouble and nonsense I shouldn't have. I'm the late bloomer of the family, the only one to merely dabble in, then abandon, college; the last to find their professional path. I've blown up Mom and Dad's kitchen with my baking side hustle for years, crashed in my old room at their house when my living situations went sideways. I've worried them. I want them to feel like all the hand-wringing and fretting, everything I put them through, was worth it. I want them to be proud of me.

I know they're proud of me, simply because they love me and I'm their son, but I want them to *really* be proud of me—to objectively see this place and think it's good.

I swallow my nerves as Mom clasps my hand and squeezes, too. "Thank you," I tell both my parents.

I glance around, trying to perceive the place with impartial eyes, to sift between what they're saying they see and what's there, without the bias of months of planning shaping how I perceive the store.

Late April's evening sun spills through the shop's windows, bathing the space in a butter-yellow glow. Floor-to-ceiling oak bookshelves teem with colorful spines, row after row of romance novels. Along the register is a reclaimed-wood bar that Ryder helped me build, dotted with tiny succulents, philodendron, ficus, pothos, and spider plants. Behind it are shelves stocked with my handmade mugs—pottery has been my latest love, giving my hands something soothing to do when my mind is whirring. A rainbow of coasters that I've crocheted sits stacked beside them, ready to hold hot cups of coffee or tea while patrons read their new purchases, hopefully while snacking on my baked goods.

I scratch at the back of my neck, my thoughts spinning. I need to hire people to do some of these jobs—make coffee drinks, serve baked goods, help patrons on the floor, not to mention handle unpacking and stocking inventory. But I've poured all my hard-earned money into making this place great, and I'm a little thin on the funds to compensate people right now. For a while, I'm just going to have to do everything on my own. Alone.

I have friends, and I have my family—I know any of them would, even with their limited free time, chip in and help—but I want to get this right on my own, to do things in a very certain way, *my* way, and not feel like I'm being intolerable with my demands.

A pang of loneliness hits me. If I had my person, they'd be the one who'd share this with me, who'd at least be the one I unburdened myself to. I don't want my parents to worry about me anymore. I don't want my siblings to hear how overwhelmed I am and feel obligated to help, when their lives are full with their work, their relationships, their kids.

"Viggo?" My dad's voice wrenches me from my worries, bringing me back to the present. His eyes narrow. "What's the matter, son?"

"Nothing." I force a smile. "I'm good. Fine."

Dad tips his head. "You sure about that?"

"Yeah!" I force my smile even wider, hugging both him and Mom. "Totally. Thank you for being here. Now go poke around some more. Make yourself comfortable, okay?" I tell them, pointing to the cozy corner at the front of the store, a handful of deep green velvet club chairs that I reupholstered myself, accented by pillows whose prints are mosaics of romance book covers.

Having successfully rerouted my parents, I take another glance around the store and do a little mental attendance check. Only an hour into being here, and we've put a massive dent in the food, some of which I made, some of which my family brought. Lids have been placed back over Mom's classic Swedish recipes, cookies and cupcakes, including gluten-free variations for Seb and Rooney's dietary needs. Dirty dishes are stacked neatly in the dish tub, waiting to be loaded into the compact dishwasher. Acoustic guitar covers play softly in the background, a soothing soundtrack as my gaze pans across the store.

There's Willa and Ryder, halfway down the historical romance section. Willa's browsing, easing books off the shelf. Ryder leans against a bookshelf across from her, a small stack of books tucked under one arm, watching her with a grin on his face.

Oliver and Gavin browse the sports romance section in the contemporary aisle, Ollie laughing at something Gavin mutters as he reads the back of a book in hand.

Frankie's got her eye on the Austen-retellings shelf, finger trailing along the spines, while Ren sits on the floor near the front of the store by the non-romance section, with Lucia in his lap as he reads her a baby board book. Pazza, their black-and-white Alusky, lies calmly beside them, never content to be far from the baby.

Nearby, at the edge of the coffee bar, Rooney and Axel sit side by side and pass each other books, a steady signing assembly line as they work their way through a tall stack of the children's books they've published together, written by Rooney, illustrated by Axel. Rooney's academic background is in science, and Axel's a painter. Three years ago, they published their first book about exploring nature and taking care of the environment. Since then, they've published three more, featuring a group of kids who go on adventures and learn about the earth—everything from marine life to native plant habitats, growing a garden to weather systems. I made sure my children's shelf in the non-romance corner was stocked with their titles, ready for them to sign before they came.

At the other end of the shop, Ziggy sits on the floor, long legs outstretched, her back to a fantasy romance bookshelf, her nose in an advance copy that I snagged for her, the first book in a new romantasy series the publisher sent me. One of the great perks of being a bookseller—early copies of highly anticipated titles.

"You're lucky I like you." Seb leans a hip against the coffee bar, arms folded across his chest. He jerks his chin toward where Ziggy sits, engrossed in her book. "Thanks to you, I'm now second priority."

I roll my eyes. "She tears through books, and you know it. You'll go back to being the center of her world in just a few hours."

"A few hours too long," he grumbles.

I feel that pinch of jealousy. *At least you only have to wait a few hours until you have your person*, I want to tell him. *I've been waiting and waiting and waiting, with no end in sight.*

I don't say that. I keep quiet about my loneliness. I hold tight to what I'm holding out for—an epic romance, a grand, once-in-a-lifetime connection with someone who turns my world upside down, who makes me feel that glorious thrill romance novels capture. I know good things take time, and love doesn't always knock on our door when we want it but instead when it's ready. So I'm trying to be patient.

I'm certainly not going to clue in my family to my desperation when, as I've mentioned, I've meddled and crossed the line plenty of times in their love lives. I'm in no rush to give them the green light to return the favor, because if I thought I was suffering now, their interference would launch me into a whole new level of misery. They all support my love of romance reading, some tolerating, others outright enjoying when I foist romance novels on them, but I don't think any of them understand what it is to want romantic love the way I want it—to walk around with this aching, gnawing want that feels like a sickness spreading through me the longer it goes untreated. I'm hurting enough as it is—I couldn't take them diminishing that, misunderstanding it, or worse, trying to shove some random person into my path to see if we click.

I'll know when I've found the one. Our eyes will lock. My heart will do that . . . *thing*, give me the signal that this is the person I've been waiting for.

Waiting. And waiting. And waiting.

An involuntary sigh leaves me as I adjust my ball cap and tug it low. Seb narrows his eyes, searching mine in concern.

Over the past year, since he officially joined the Bergmans when he became Ziggy's boyfriend, we've gotten close. As a professional hockey player for the LA Kings and Ren's teammate, Seb's busy, but he's good about texting, often up at late hours like I am. He's helped me out around the store with odd projects when his packed schedule allowed it. He's brought take-out meals when Ziggy was here, helping me decide on and then carry out my plans for shelving my inventory. And he's also sucked me into his world of tattoos. I now have three, thanks to his bad influence. Not that I think tattoos are bad, they're just damn expensive, and I shouldn't be spending money on tatts when I've told myself I can't even afford to hire a barista.

"What's wrong?" he asks.

"Nothing."

He slaps a hand on my shoulder, making me hiss in pain. That's where I have fresh ink, and he knows it. "You sure about that?" he presses.

"Thanks for the concern." I shrug off his touch and slap a hand over his chest, right where I know he has fresh ink, too, since we went together. "But I'm good."

Seb shoves my hand away. "You're full of shit."

"Am not."

"Are, too."

"Am not—"

A loud *ding* from the overhead bell interrupts our petty back-and-forth. The door nearly bangs into the wall as Charlie rushes toward me and wraps me in a hug while Gigi shuts the door behind her. "Sorry we're late!" she says.

I hug Charlie back. No, she's not a blood relative, but in the past year, she and Ziggy have braided more of their lives together— Bergman family dinners, game nights, birthday parties. Charlie and Gigi are family now.

"It looks amazing," Charlie says, stepping aside so I can hug Gigi, too.

"Seriously," Gigi tells me, "Viggo, everything is *stunning*."

I smile. "Thanks, you two. I'm glad you're here."

"Course we're here," Charlie says. "We would have been here sooner, but we were waiting for—"

"Hey, Char," Ziggy bursts in, breathless and flushed, book tucked under her arm. "You *have* to go check out the paranormal romance section. He has the newest in the alien romance series—"

"Say no more!" Charlie squeals delightedly, then hustles off, tugging Gigi by the hand so she'll follow. Gigi shrugs and smiles apologetically as Charlie drags her down the aisle.

I turn toward Ziggy. "What was that about?"

Ziggy takes a step back, clutching the beloved advance copy to her chest. "Uh. Nothing. I just wanted Charlie to see the alien romances."

Ziggy is a bad liar. She's up to something.

Before I can press her, my sister is gone in a flash of long red hair, headed for the paranormal romance section, where Charlie's poring through books, hazarding a quick, nervous glance my way.

I'm so confused. Frowning, I turn toward Seb. "*What* is going on?"

Seb seems to deliberate for a moment, weighing how to answer me. But we're interrupted before he can, as my niece Linnea runs toward him, yelling, "Catch me, Trouble!" He scoops her up, *Dirty Dancing*–style, then launches her into the air, making her erupt with laughter.

I scowl at them both. "That was *our* move," I tell Linnie.

Seb lowers her to the ground, then Linnie runs and barrels into me, wrapping her arms around my legs. "It's still our move," she says, peering up at me, wearing an extra-sweet smile, now that she's lost one of her front teeth. "I got lotsa uncles and aunts, Uncle Viggo. You gotta get better at sharing."

"I'm one of seven kids, Linnie. Growing up, I always had to share. Nowadays, I don't have to, and sharing comes to me about as well as eating only one slice of MorMor's *kladdkaka*."

Linnie looks thoughtful. I knew an analogy about my mom's chocolate cake would resonate. "It *is* hard to eat only one slice of MorMor's *kladdkaka*." She takes my hand and squeezes, pale eyes, just like mine, locked on my face. "What's wrong, Uncle Viggo?"

Dammit. What is it about my expression tonight that broadcasts discontent? Am I that obvious?

"I'm fine, Linnie."

Her frown deepens. She tugs my hand until I lower myself, crouching to her level. Then she steps closer and sets her palms on either side of my face. Her eyes search mine. "You're sad."

My heart pinches, but I force a smile. "I'm not sad. I've got all of you here. What do I have to be sad about?"

"Daddy says you can have good things and still be sad. He says there's room for all my feelings. Like when I had all of my Squishmallows, but I couldn't find my bunny to sleep with. I was happy I had my Squishmallows . . . but I was sad without my bunny. I was lonely for her even though I had lots of things around me. I needed bunny, to make it right."

"There you are," Freya says softly, her knuckle stroking Linnie's cheek. "I couldn't find you."

Linnie sets her hand on Freya's pregnant belly—baby Bergman-MacCormack number three is due this summer—and pats gently before she presses a kiss. "I'm here," Linnie tells her mother. "Just talking 'bout feelings with Uncle Viggo."

Freya smiles, watching Linnie affectionately. "Well, I'm sure he really appreciates that. Ready to go look at some books, now that you're done eating?"

"Yeah," Linnie says, doing a little twirl that ends in a jazz hands flourish just as the door dings again, signaling it's been opened. "Let's go," she says, taking Freya's hand.

"Coming?" Freya asks me.

I open my mouth to answer her, but Linnie beats me to it: "Don't think so. Looks like Uncle Viggo's got company."

I'm not expecting anyone else. Confused, I stand, glancing over my shoulder.

That's when I see Tallulah Clarke at the threshold of my store.

SIX

Tallulah

Playlist: "I'll Be Fine," Clairy Browne &
The Bangin' Rackettes

Considering how intentionally I've avoided him since our early morning coffee chat a year ago, I have *no* idea why I'm showing up to Viggo Bergman's bookstore for its grand opening.

Actually, I do have an idea—my sister, Charlie.

She gave me those big, sad puppy eyes, *pleaded* with me to come. I suck at saying no to her and she knows it. So, here I am, at Viggo's bookstore's grand opening. Though, as I look around and see only his family milling around the store, I'm starting to worry. This doesn't look like a grand opening at all.

My gaze flicks to my sister, hiss-whispering with Ziggy, who allegedly told Charlie about this "grand opening." Ziggy glances my way, turns bright red, then lifts a book to hide both her and Charlie from my glare. Gigi's beside them with a book in hand, too, which I think she's supposed to be "reading," except it's upside down. Slowly, heads lift and turn my way, warm greetings extended, but most of them express some form of surprise that I'm here.

Dammit. I've been duped.

Viggo strolls my way, surprise painted across his features, too. Same blue ball cap, even more beat-up than last year. Another T-shirt, this time sky blue, bearing a hard-shell taco loaded up with what I believe are historical romance book covers portraying half-naked couples in Regency clothes, arms twined around each other. Above it reads, *I like my romance novels like I like my tacos: extra spicy.*

My eyes flick up to his, and our gazes connect. There's something tight at the corners of that bright smile, like a storm rolling in at the edges of a sunny sky.

I take a deep breath to steady myself. I resent that this is how I keep bumping into him—Viggo on home turf, at ease; me in foreign territory, caught off guard. I resent that I've noticed there's something brittle in his smile, something indicating that he's not particularly happy to see me. I resent even more that I *care.*

"Tallulah Clarke." He stops a foot away from me, hands in his pockets. "To what do I owe the pleasure?"

"I was told tonight was your store's big opening event." I cross my arms over my chest, glaring around him at my sister, who stands at the other end of the store. She ducks behind Ziggy's book again.

Viggo peers over his shoulder, following my line of sight, then glances back, eyes on me. His smile warms. He's delighted by this. "Ooh, they got you good."

I glare up at him. "I'm glad you find this amusing."

"You know, Tallulah, I do." Viggo reaches past me for the door, bracketing me inside his body as he pushes it shut. He's close. So close I could make a fist around the fabric of his shirt and tug him closer.

If I wanted to.

Which I don't.

I peer up at him, eyebrow arched. "And why is that?"

"Because you're all ticked off that you're here, at my super-soft opening, when it sounds like you planned to come to the store's official opening, anyway. So you came when there's a couple dozen fewer people, big whoop." He shrugs. "You're here now, and there's a bunch of good books to browse, some snacks still, if you're hungry, people you seemed to like talking to, based on the last time you saw them. How about you just . . . enjoy it? Or is being in my presence *that* unpleasant?"

I swallow. "I don't find your presence . . . unpleasant."

He folds his arms across his chest, peering down at me. "So, after bumping into each other at the A-frame last spring, I didn't hear from you for a year, why, then?"

My stomach tightens. A little guilt, a little guilty pleasure that he actually seems put out I never took him up on his offer, never came by.

I didn't visit, I answer him in my head, *because I was struggling. Because I needed to get my shit together and take care of myself. But I thought about you. I wished you luck. I felt you wishing me luck, too.*

Shifting on my feet, I tuck a loose piece of hair back into my bun. "I was stressed, lots of moving parts, lots going on with the book, with . . . personal stuff. I wouldn't have been good company."

Something in Viggo's expression shifts. Softens. He leans against the wall, head tipped as his eyes search mine. "You could have come by, vented, talked it out. I would have listened. Maybe handed you a paintbrush, made you paint a wall while you were talking, but I would have listened."

My heart thumps hard inside my chest. How do I answer that? How do I tell him no one's ever done that for me? Offered to be the one who makes a safe space for *me* to fall apart? I'd have to admit that I'm not sure I even know how to fall apart, that I just keep pushing and going and grinding myself down.

"Wouldn't have been a very fair trade-off," I tell him quietly. "I'm a shit painter."

His mouth cracks in a grin. "Doesn't matter. That's what friends do, Lulaloo."

Lulaloo. No one's called me that goofy name, or any goofy names, for that matter, for twelve months. I hate that I've missed it.

"And I will remind you," he adds, ducking his head so a little of our extreme height differential is erased. His voice is soft, its warmth whispering over my skin, making goose bumps erupt in its wake. "Under the statutes of the Bergman Family Code, ever since you and I swapped secrets, we *are* friends."

I stare at him, warring with myself. Why is he so warm to me, when I'm so cold? Why is he soft when I'm sharp? Why do I feel this bizarre impulse to lower my guard, just say to hell with it, and enjoy how much I get a perverse kick out of his antics, his energy, his playful, poking jokes?

For twelve months, I've been struggling to move beyond operating in my default states: sad and stressed. For just one night, would it be so terrible to let myself enjoy this? Would it be so devastating to kick loose and hang out with his big, quirky family, which has wrapped its arms around my sister, made her feel loved and safe in a way my parents, my family as a whole, never have? Would it be the worst if I soaked up some time with this beautiful—albeit overly bearded—man who seems to see something about me worth leaning toward, even when I clam up, even when I snap, even if I have no idea what that is?

"Well then, *friend*," I tell him, shrugging off my bomber jacket. "How about you give me the grand tour?"

"This is Lisa." He points to another potted plant, a lacy, elegant fern. I'm no plant expert, but even I recognize that one. "And, last but not least, Beverly." He lovingly pats the ceramic pot containing an impressively tall, healthy-looking plant with giant, wave-edged leaves.

"What is that?" I ask.

"I said this is Beverly."

I roll my eyes. "Yes, I caught the name. What kind of *plant*?"

"Oh." He smiles. "A fiddle-leaf fig."

"Hmm." I touch the leaf softly, dragging a finger down its spine. "I like it."

A blush creeps up his cheeks. Viggo spins and gestures behind me. "This way next."

We've been all around the store, except for the front, across from the reading nook, where another row of bookshelves sits separate from the rest. A black-and-white Alusky that looks like it's getting up in years snoozes on a dog bed at the foot of the bookshelf, a bowl of water beside it. More plants hang from the ceiling above the sleeping pup, an aerial garden of leaves and vines, shades of green ranging from vibrant chartreuse to deep jade.

Viggo stops, then spins, facing me again. He looks perplexed. "What is it?" I ask.

"You didn't think it was weird that I've named all my plants."

I shrug. "You have strong plant-daddy energy; I'm not surprised."

"I named them for *romance* authors. Lisa Kleypas. Beverly Jenkins. Tessa Dare. Lorraine Heath. Courtney Milan. Cat Sebastian—"

"Again, I'm not surprised. You named your plants after authors you love. No knocks on that."

His gaze darts to mine. "Why are you being *nice* tonight? Do you feel bad for me? Is the place so pathetic that you're pitying me—"

"Whoa." I put my hands up. "Hold on."

Viggo sets his hands on his hips, peering down at me. "Okay. I'm holding."

The raw insecurity in his expression makes my stomach knot. "I'm not being *nice*. I don't pity you. I'm just . . . here. Responding to what I see. You did something big, Viggo. Something impressive. You opened up a damn store, and you have a lot to be proud of. I'm not here to take a shit on that."

He clears his throat, scrubbing at the back of his neck before he tugs his ball cap low over his eyes. "Okay."

I know he and I don't have the best history, but I hate that he's been walking around this whole time, talking my ear off, silently worried that I'm judging him, or worse, only humoring him. The intensity of my remorse makes me do something I never do, something I *hate* doing—explain myself.

"Listen," I tell him quietly, tugging down my sleeves to give myself something to do besides look into those striking, earnest eyes of his. "How I acted toward you, when we were in college, when I saw you last year, that's not a *you* thing. It's a *me* thing. Both in school and at the A-frame, you were welcoming and warm, and I was . . . closed off and cold. But that's just how I am. I'm that way with everyone. I've never looked down on you or thought less of you. I came to what I thought was your store's grand opening because you went after what matters to you, worked your ass off to achieve it, and that's worth celebrating, even if you are clearly overinvested in romance novels, and you might have a plant-hoarding problem."

He tips up his ball cap a little and meets my eyes, staring at me like I've shocked him. And then he smiles. "Thanks, Lu. That's . . . really nice of you to say. I'm uh . . ." He clears his throat, scrubbing at his neck again. "I'm glad you came tonight."

"I am, too." Uneasy about the warmth thawing through me, I shake my head a little and brush past him, toward the last bookshelf, which he hasn't shown me yet. "Now, what's here? Saving the best for last?"

"It's my non-romance section," he explains, standing behind me. "So, the best for last."

He gives me a playful glare. "Be nice."

I glance up at him over my shoulder and shrug. "I can't be *too* nice. Apparently, it raises suspicion."

He sighs, shaking his head, and redirects his attention to the floor-to-ceiling bookshelf. "These are handpicked selections that, while not romance novels, still lean into the hope of a happy ending."

"Hmm." I step closer, my gaze drifting along the spines. I recognize a handful that I've read, all of which I liked. I drift a finger down the spine of a book that made me cry like a baby, another one that kept me on pins and needles right up to the end, and then ...

My fingers slide off the bookshelf. I turn and face Viggo. I know immediately that he knows it's my book.

"Charlie didn't tell me," he says, reading my expression. "I figured it out on my own."

"How?"

He picks up a copy, turns it to the back, and clears his throat. "'Z.S. Ruhig writes weird, creepy stories because the world's given her plenty of disturbing material to work with. She doesn't pass out candy on Halloween, says bah-humbug at Christmas, and spends all her money on overpriced clothes and takeout. *Isochron* is her debut novel.'"

"You figured out it was me from my *author bio*?"

"Nah. The author bio was compelling but gave nothing away. When I read it, I just knew it was your writing. You have a very vivid style."

"You recognized my style from one semester of college, seven years ago, being peer partners twice."

He tips his head. "Very good memory. It *was* twice."

My cheeks heat. "I was approximating. I didn't remember exactly."

He smiles. "Uh-huh."

Sighing heavily, I turn back to the bookshelves and scowl. "I can't believe you put *my* book in your store."

His smile slips off his face. "Why the hell are you so mad about that?"

"Because ..." I flap my hands, aggravatingly lost for words. I'm a writer, dammit. I should be better at expressing myself. "Because ... I don't write happy endings."

Viggo snorts and leans against the bookshelf, arms across his chest, grinning. It's so condescending, I want to grab him by those biceps pressing against his shirt and shake him until he sees sense. "Tallulah, you do. You wrote about people healing together, rediscovering hope. That's a happy ending."

"I—"

"Lucia's hit her wall," his brother Ren says, wrapping an arm around Viggo while a baby strapped to his chest with dark, fluffy hair wails. "Sorry to interrupt," he says to both of us. "Just didn't want to disappear on you," he tells Viggo.

Viggo arches an eyebrow my way. "Nice to see *some* people don't want to do that."

I glare at him.

Turning, Viggo hugs his brother, then plants a quick, soft kiss to the baby's forehead, tenderly cupping her head as he does. A weird lump builds in my throat as I watch him.

The baby's cry dims and her eyes slip shut as Viggo swirls his fingers around her head, like a gentle scalp massage. He does it again, then another time. The crying stops. Her eyes flutter, then fall shut. Her mouth drops open for a tiny baby snore. She's out like a light.

Ren shakes his head as another Bergman joins the gathering, Viggo's brother Oliver. "I tried that just two minutes ago," Ren says in an indignant whisper. "It didn't work!"

Viggo grins smugly. "Must be the magic favorite-uncle touch."

"Hey!" Oliver hiss-whispers over the now sleeping baby. "*I'm* the one who came up with that soothing technique."

"*We* did," Viggo says. "And *I'm* the one who perfected it. Standard procedure."

Oliver blinks at his brother, then lunges around Ren for Viggo, swiftly getting Viggo in a headlock before going straight for what Viggo's muffled shriek reveals is his tickle spot.

"The baby!" Viggo squeaks into Oliver's torso. "I'm gonna wake her up!"

The sound is so high and strained, it makes me hide a smile behind a fist. I pretend to clear my throat.

"I'm gonna scream!" Viggo hisses, wiggling frantically, but Oliver's too quick, pinning Viggo's wrists in his grip.

"Should have thought of that before you ran your obnoxious mouth," Oliver whispers back, tickling him even more.

"You two." Freya, their older sister, jabs her fingers in the tops of their armpits, the exact same spot. They both yelp and tumble apart. "Behave yourselves."

They're both panting. Viggo shoves Oliver's shoulder. "Yeah, Ollie. Behave yourself."

"He started it." Oliver shoves Viggo back, planting a firm slap on his shoulder. Viggo whines in pain.

Elin, their mother, joins the fray. "Viggo Frederik. Oliver Abram. A truce, please. Now hug your mother goodbye."

Viggo and Oliver step dutifully into their mother's arms, letting her wrap them close, something whispered in words that sound like her native language, Swedish.

"Thanks for coming," Viggo says as his dad, bearing a box of food containers, a bag slung on his arm that his wife takes, pulls him in next for a hug and kisses his temple.

"Thank you for showing us this labor of love," his dad says, before stepping aside for a sleepy blond toddler draped across the shoulder of a dark-haired man with a beard and thick-framed black nerd glasses. Viggo's brother-in-law, Aiden, I recognize after a second. At least I think that's his brother-in-law. There are so many of these damn Bergmans, I can't keep track.

More family adds to the queue and files out, while Viggo stands right by the door with the stools to the bar on his other side, pinning me in the corner beside him with the non-romance novels. We stand in what feels eerily like a receiving line at a wedding.

Every Bergman offers me warm goodbyes as they stroll out the door, like they aren't fazed that I'm just standing there with Viggo.

"Bye!" the little girl with dark wavy hair—Linnie, I think?—tells me, skipping out the door. "See you Sunday!"

"Sunday?" I ask.

"Family dinner," Viggo's mother explains as she takes Linnie's hand before the little girl can run out into the parking lot. "You should come! Viggo will tell you details. Any dietary restrictions, just let him know. Always happy to accommodate them. Good night!"

"I . . ."

Rounding out the line are Ziggy and her boyfriend, Seb, who offer very quick hugs, then avoid Viggo's hissed whispers in their ears by yelling over each other, "Have to get going! Yoga early in the morning!"

Then come my sister, Charlie, and Gigi. Gigi hugs me, plants a kiss on my cheek, and dashes out. Charlie throws her arms around Viggo, then turns toward me and hugs me. I hug her back, keeping her pinned to my body.

"Thanks for that invitation to the *grand* opening," I mutter.

Charlie, darn her, might be tiny, but she's strong. She wriggles out of my hug, takes a hop toward the door, and smiles sheepishly, poised on the threshold. "Uh. Well. Seems I got my facts mixed up."

"Charlie—"

"Good night! Love you!" She blows me a kiss, then dashes out.

Suddenly, the place is eerily quiet. Viggo follows Charlie out, leaning a forearm against the doorframe as he watches his family get into their vehicles. I watch him smiling into the night, waving as they pull out and wave out their windows, too.

And then I realize I finally have a clear path—I can make a break for it, grab my stuff, get on the Vespa, and disappear.

Dashing behind Viggo, I scoop up my bomber jacket, then my purse, both slung over one of the green velvet club chairs. I turn, wiggling my jacket up my arms, purse clutched in one hand, ready to bolt. But then I freeze.

Viggo's wobbling dangerously on the threshold. He clutches the wood and shakes his head a little, as if trying to steady himself. But then he starts to sway again.

"Hey." I rush toward him, instinct guiding me to wrap an arm around his waist. He's leaner than I remember him being last year—not that I have very specific memories of what Viggo Bergman looked like a year ago. I can feel his ribs, his sharp hip bones, as my hand tries to get a tighter hold on him. "You okay?" I ask.

"Little dizzy," he mutters, dragging a hand down his face.

"When's the last time you ate?"

He frowns thoughtfully. "That . . . is an excellent question."

"Sit your ass down." I kick a foot at the club chair, making it spin on its swivel base so it faces us, then guide him into it. Viggo lands awkwardly and slumps into the chair, eyes shut. I root around my purse and pull out a mini peanut butter cup. I always have peanut butter chocolate in my purse for when my blood sugar gets low. "Peanut allergy?" I ask. "Any allergies?"

He shakes his head. "Nuh-uh."

"Eat this." I unwrap it and step inside the bracket of his open legs. Viggo's head lolls back. "Hey." I gently pat his cheek and cup his head, guiding it up. "Eat this."

He opens his mouth halfheartedly, and I drop the chocolate in. Dutifully, he starts to chew. I unwrap another one and slip it in his mouth. "That one, too."

"So bossy," he mutters, eyes shut, sighing heavily. "Can't you wait until I feel good enough to enjoy it?"

I roll my eyes. "Stop talking and start chewing."

He blinks slowly, scrubbing at his face as he chews. He seems a little more alert, the color in his face better. The chocolate is working its magic. "I meant to eat something earlier, but I just got so busy with making sure everything was perfect."

"For a, and I quote, 'super-soft opening.'" I cross my arms over my chest. "For your family to see your space. That you got so carried away, when it's only for them, does not bode well for when you officially open."

"I know," he says, his voice still a little bleary. I rummage around in my purse and find a small bag of fruit snacks. I rip them open, grip his hand, dump them in his palm, then bring his palm to his mouth. Viggo chews slowly, saying around his bite, "Thanks."

"You're welcome," I mutter, shoving the fruit snack wrapper back into my purse.

"Whew." Head still back, he blinks up at the ceiling. "I feel human again."

"Funny, how eating will do that for you."

Viggo drops his head, lifts his ball cap until his eyes can find mine, stretches out his legs. They're so long, they bracket mine where I stand peering down at him. "Did *you* get anything to eat when you came?" he asks.

"No. I wasn't hungry."

"Well, there wasn't much left, either, by the time you got here." His eyes search mine. "Why were you so late?"

Like hell am I going to admit that I was having a wardrobe crisis, much too preoccupied about how I looked for someone whose opinion of me and my appearance I definitely don't care about.

"I . . . had some inspiration strike for the book," I lie. "Had to get the words down before I lost them. I told Charlie and Gigi to go ahead without me."

He smiles. "Well, that's good, that inspiration struck. Is this your third book?"

Shame and frustration twist inside me. "The second one, still."

His eyebrows lift. Slowly, he sits up in his seat. "Aw, Lu—"

"Nope." I shake my head. "No pity parties here. I'm not pitying you and this badass bookstore you put together. You're not pitying me and my great book that I'm taking great time to work on."

Great books take great time.

My publisher didn't love Viggo's line, which I threw their way, but they respected it. I'm taking the time I need to get this book right. Even if I'm still struggling like hell to do it.

Viggo smiles softly. "No pity. Just . . . empathy. It's hard when the things we want take longer than we'd like to materialize. And respect—I'm glad you put your foot down."

"Yeah, well . . ." I shrug, adjusting my purse so it sits higher on my shoulder. "It was necessary."

For a moment, quiet hangs between us. I shift on my feet. I should go.

"Say, would you want to . . ." Tipping his head, Viggo peers up at me. He bites his lip. "Nah, forget it."

This is my moment. Whatever he was going to say, he stopped himself, withdrew the olive branch, whatever friendly offer he was about to extend. I should latch on to that. Leave. He's fine now. His super-soft opening went well. I showed up, congratulated him. My conscience is clear, the regret I felt for being so prickly to someone so softhearted erased, now that I've come here, done what I told myself I would. Now is when I walk out and never look back.

But instead, I watch myself, as if outside my body while it overrides my good sense, halfheartedly kicking his booted foot. "Would I what?"

Viggo smiles, slow and weary, slouched in his chair, ball cap knocked back. "I was gonna ask if you'd want to grab a bite to eat. I could go for a big pile of noodles. There's a great Chinese place not too far from here, about ten minutes down the road, driving. But then I figured, you probably don't want to do that."

Tell him he's right. Say goodbye. Walk out that door and just keep walking.

But what waits for me if I leave now? Going back to Charlie's, where I've been crashing the past week since my landlord very illegally gave me very little notice to move out because he'd sold the house I spent way too much money this past year renting all by myself, only to have to face Charlie and Gigi, who I'm deeply annoyed tricked me into this intimate gathering? Even if I drove around for a while and came back, I'd still have to face my sofa bed and a laptop with a Word doc bearing an accusatorily low word count.

I buy myself time by pulling out my phone, checking my CGM via the app. My sugar is in range, so I'm safe to drive, and I'll be good until I figure out what I'm going to eat.

I can say yes to grabbing Chinese. It can just be a simple shared meal, nothing more. I can nourish myself, clear my head, sneak back to Charlie's late enough that she and Gigi will already be sleeping, and avoid a conversation I'm definitely not ready to have with my sister about pushing me into something I don't want to be pushed into.

"Maybe you don't have me figured out after all, Viggo Bergman. Maybe a plate of lo mein sounds like just what I need."

A slow, sexy smile lifts his face, even hidden in that wild beard. I try and fail not to be annoyed by how satisfied he looks, how jauntily he springs out of his chair. "Well then, Lulaloo, let's get going."

SEVEN

Viggo

"Where is this place again?" Eyes narrowed, Tallulah frowns at the road as if the power of her scowl alone will reveal our destination.

I lock the store's front bolt with a satisfying *thunk*. "Just a quick five-minute trek down the road. C'mon, I'll drive." After strolling toward my car, I slip the key inside the lock. My car is so old, it doesn't have the capacity for a remote or keyless entry.

Tallulah takes one look at Ashbury and comes to halt. "I'm not getting in that death trap."

I widen my eyes meaningfully. "Kindly lower your voice. Ashbury will hear your cruelty."

She snorts, folding her arms across her chest. "*Ashbury* needs to hear the truth. He deserves a merciful end in the scrapyard."

"Tallulahloo, you're ripping out my heart. You can't talk about my car like that."

With a headshake, she turns toward a shiny bloodred Vespa parked a few spots down. I blink, more than a little surprised. She strikes me as the sensible, safe type—I expected a hybrid car with an immaculate interior, not a sexy-as-hell dangerous motorbike. Tallulah glances over her shoulder and throws me an aloof glance, eyebrow arched, full mouth set in a firm, serious line.

My body hums to life.

"You enjoy driving that junkpile strapped to an engine," she says. "I'm not getting in it. Just tell me where to go, and I'll meet you there. To be clear, I will *not* be riding behind you. I don't trust that clunker not to lose car parts."

I swing my keys around my finger, eyeing up the Vespa as Tallulah does an adorable little hop and swings her leg over it. With cool efficiency, she yanks out her bun. Ice-blue hair tumbles like a waterfall to her shoulders before she tugs it back into a low pony, then slides a glossy black helmet down over her face.

Guilt tugs at me as I peer back at my poor beat-up car, faded burnt-orange paint marred by gaping rust spots. I set a hand on the trunk and sigh. "Sorry, Ash. I'm a mere mortal. She's hot. And she's going to be even hotter driving an Italian *vroom-vroom*. I can't say no."

"Are you seriously talking to your car?" Tallulah calls.

"Would you mind?" I call back. "We're having a moment here. A heart-to-heart."

She rolls her eyes.

"You just rest easy." I pat the trunk again, then click the carabiner holding my keys to my jeans belt loop. "I'll be back in a little, old friend."

Turning, I catch Tallulah frowning at me. As I jog toward her, her frown deepens. "What," she asks, "are you doing?"

"Hitching a ride, of course." I ease onto the seat behind her and sidle close.

Tallulah's back goes ramrod straight. "I didn't offer to drive you."

"And yet you have a spare helmet hanging right here." I tear off my ball cap, shove it safely into my back pocket, then tug down the helmet.

Tallulah turns slowly, gives me a chilly, appraising once-over, then slams down her visor. "Well." Her voice is muffled inside her helmet, but her dripping sarcasm is impossible to miss. "Nice to see you haven't become any less pushy since freshman year."

I grin. "Nice to see you remember the details of my sparkling personality, even after all these years."

Tallulah slaps down my visor, then turns and faces forward. The engine roars to life. She grips my thigh *hard* and tugs, dragging me closer. I swear under my breath before all the breath I have rushes out of me. Tallulah takes my other hand, wraps it around her waist, across the soft curve of her hip and her belly. Heat bursts through me.

"Now do the same with the other arm," she orders.

Slowly, as if in a daze, I wrap my other arm around her waist, too. I'm curled around Tallulah, who's so short that her head, even with its big, sturdy helmet, fits neatly under my chin. She's so fierce and prickly, but she feels so sweet and soft, tucked close to me.

"Stop smiling," she growls.

"How do you know I'm smiling?" I'm definitely smiling. How could I help it?

"Call it a hunch." The engine roars even louder. "Now, hold tight."

I lift my arm in salute. "Yes ma'am— Shit!" The Vespa flies forward, and my arm drops instinctively back around her waist, hugging my body over hers. Her fantastic, full ass is tucked right up into my groin. My thighs hug hers, pinned close.

It would be, hands down, the hottest moment of my life, if I wasn't terrified I was about to die. She revs the engine noisily and does a couple of fancy swerves as we ease toward the main road.

"Tallulah," I warn.

"Viggo." Now *she's* smiling, the devious little menace. I can feel it, like I feel starlight before I glance up and find the sky filled with it.

"Enjoying my abject terror, you gremlin?"

"Immensely. But trust me, I'll get us there alive. Nothing's coming between me and my lo mein." With one fluid turn, Tallulah curves us around the parking lot and tears out onto the road.

———

"Tallulah Clarke." I yank open the restaurant's door and hold it for my almost executioner.

She strolls inside, twisting her hair back up into a bun on top of her head. "Viggo Bergman."

"That was a near-death experience."

"That truck," she says primly, releasing her hair tie with a *snap*, "needed to stay in their lane."

"Yeah, and much good your little duck horn did to remind them of that."

Tallulah flashes me a cold glare as I smile at the host and tell them just the two of us, and a booth, please. "Which is why I went around them," she says.

"And that's when I saw my life flash before my eyes."

She swats my stomach, earning my reflexive *oof*, before she steps ahead of me and follows the host. "I had it under control."

"Five years of my life shaved off in that moment, easy."

"You're just shaky from low blood sugar again." A mini peanut butter cup comes sailing over her shoulder.

I catch it, tear off the foil, and shove it in my mouth. "Chocolate can't solve all our problems, Lu."

Tallulah slides serenely into the booth, shimmying down the bench until she's tucked into the corner, purse wedged beside her. "Just eat and calm down."

"'Calm down,' she says," I mutter, yanking my ball cap low. "Like she didn't almost bring us to an untimely end on Venice Boulevard."

"You're just salty because I didn't let you drive me in your rust box on wheels."

"You," I tell her, pointing with my chopsticks still in their paper, "need to back off Ashbury. He's seen me through some tough times, and I'm a true blue, so I'm seeing him through his. I'm driving that car until he's . . ."

Tallulah raises her eyebrows. "Undrivable? Doesn't pass inspection? Falls apart? Sorry, bud, that ship has sailed."

I open my menu and scan it, even though I know exactly what I'm getting. "I'm moving on from this conversation."

"Of course you are—you can't talk your way out of it."

Our server approaches. Tallulah gives them the closest thing I've ever seen to a smile and politely orders. I order, too.

Tallulah sits quietly, hands folded on the table. I stare at her, a very aggravating blend of attraction and annoyance twisting tighter inside me. This is not what is supposed to be happening with my life. I've opened my store, made my dream a reality. Now I'm supposed to be keeping my eyes wide open for my perfect person, for that serendipitous moment we'll meet and my happily ever after begins.

Instead, I'm sitting, stomach so empty and hungry it's practically eating itself, across the table from a woman who manages to give me arctic glares but turn my body white hot. Who loathes romance novels and makes fun of my sweet old car and drives a Vespa like a bat out of hell.

"May I help you?" she asks primly.

"Yeah. You can explain what in God's name ever made you decide you were fit to drive a motor vehicle."

Tallulah bites her cheek, fighting a smile. I derive an unholy amount of pleasure from knowing I almost made her smile, even if I am perturbed with her.

"I enjoy the autonomy of a Vespa. It makes it very easy to travel efficiently, not to mention solo, and avoid unwanted passengers." Her eyebrows lift meaningfully.

Our server brings us two ice waters and we both thank them.

"Is it the thriller writer in you? Do you need periodic close brushes with death to keep you connected to your characters' fight-or-flight modes?"

"I am calm and cool, driving that Vespa," she says smoothly. "Adrenaline spikes complicate my already complicated health. I don't have time for them."

I peer at her, concern tightening my chest. "How, uh . . . is your health? You okay?"

She shrugs and pulls out a little device that looks like a small iPhone. It beeps as she types something in; then she slips it back into her purse. "Okay enough. I manage it well. Unlike *some* people, I take my blood sugar level seriously."

"Enough with the browbeating. I know I should have eaten. I just got busy and nervous and my medication kills my appetite. Hunger doesn't kick in until it wears off, right about now, when I eat enough to fuel a horse."

Tallulah tips her head, eyes narrowed. I can tell she's curious, but I also have a hunch she's not going to pry.

"ADHD," I explain. "Took a while to find a medication that makes me still feel like myself while improving my executive function and doesn't cost a fortune. Finally got one that's a pretty good fit."

"Besides the appetite suppressant," she says.

I shrug. "Besides that."

"Well, we do have these fancy contraptions called smartphones that allow you to set reminders and alarms. You could set them, then when they go off, choke down a snack if you can't manage a whole meal."

"Maybe," I concede. "But I can tell you, even with all the alarms in the world today, I was too focused and busy to stop."

Tallulah frowns. "You need someone managing this for you. Where was your staff tonight? Why didn't you have anyone there helping? You could have taken five, had a quick bite."

"I . . ." Clearing my throat, I scrub at the back of my neck. "I don't exactly have staff hired right now . . . per se."

"'Per se'? But you're planning on hiring them, right?"

I focus on looking at the Chinese zodiac symbols on my place mat. "Eventually."

Tallulah leans in, eyes wide. "Viggo! 'Eventually'? You're going to run yourself into the ground."

"If you and your Vespa don't first."

She glares at me. "You, sir, are real close to walking your ass back to that store when we're done here. My Vespa and I will enjoy the ride home without your snark."

I grin. "I'm just messing with you. Kind of. I wouldn't mind if we drove, like, ten miles per hour slower on the way back, but please don't leave me here to walk home with two pounds of lo mein in my stomach. I'm not honestly sure I can afford the cab ride back."

Our conversation's broken briefly as our food is served and we thank the waiter.

Tallulah picks up right where we left off, eyes narrowed, as she grips her chopsticks. "You had plenty of cash at one point, to make that store happen. Where did it go, that you have none left to hire staff?"

I shove noodles into my mouth so I don't have to answer her.

"Let me guess," she says, plucking up a noodle with her chopsticks. "All into the store."

"I couldn't cut corners. I saw everything it could be, and I didn't want to do anything by halves. I made and built from scratch as much as I could, did everything I could on my own—the mugs, the coasters, reupholstering the chairs, the bookshelves, the bar table— but still, raw material, supplies, demo and reno, and of course, all the books; it adds up."

"Wait." The noodles and chopsticks drop to her plate. "You *made* those coffee mugs?"

"Well, they're for tea, too. Pottery is very therapeutic. Ever tried it?"

I'm ignored. "You reupholstered the chairs?"

I shrug. "Yeah."

"*Sewed* the coasters?" Her voice is an octave higher.

"Crocheted, technically."

"What else did you do? Hand blow the light fixtures?"

"Nah, fire and I don't mix well. I tried my hand at glass blow- ing one summer up at the A-frame and nearly burned down Axel's art shed before he had his own studio. I have never run so fast in my life as I ran from that man."

She shakes her head, bewildered.

"I baked the pastries I'll be selling, too."

Her hands fly up, her arms lifted in a gesture of helplessness. "That's like five people's jobs."

"I'm aware. I've been doing them."

"And you're skin and bones," she snaps, poking my chest across the table. "You look exhausted, and you're not eating and . . ." She makes an aggravated little noise in her throat, stabs her noodles with her chopsticks, then shoves a bite of food into her mouth.

I smile, warmth blooming through me. "Tallulah Clarke. You sound an awful lot like you care about my well-being."

She wrinkles her nose, scowling at me. "I'm simply observing the facts."

I watch her, wondering what this new side of her is, a theory forming. Tallulah sure acts chilly and detached. But maybe she's not. Or, at least, not nearly as much as she lets on. Maybe Tallulah cares. Maybe she just doesn't feel comfortable showing it. Maybe she's afraid of what happens when she loses her cool, gets worked up, shows her cards.

I watch Tallulah poke around her noodles and knock a knee with hers under the table. Tallulah glances up, her expression guarded.

"You're right," I concede. "I messed up. I should have budgeted differently. And now it's biting me in the ass."

She shakes her head. She is appalled by this logistical nightmare. The evidence that she cares just makes me smile. "Now what are you going to do?" she asks quietly.

"Don't know." I shrug. "But I'll figure it out. I have before, and I can do it again. I tend to paint myself into tight corners fairly often, but I always find an out, one way or another."

Her eyes search mine. "Isn't that exhausting, though? To constantly be on that precipice?"

More than I can even explain.

I tug my ball cap down. "No mystery why I sleep like a rock."

This time her knee knocks mine. I peer up. "What about that big family of yours?" she asks. "The many friends I'm sure you have. None of them can help you?"

"They're all busy, Lu. They've got full lives, demanding jobs, kids. I couldn't ask them. Even if I could, I wouldn't. Because *I* did this. I put myself in this position. It's my responsibility to deal with the consequences."

Tallulah's quiet, fiddling with her chopsticks. And then she says the last thing I ever expected:

"*I* could help you."

EIGHT

Viggo

I choke on my noodles, coughing roughly. After I've managed to clear my windpipe, I take a deep drink of water.

Tallulah's glaring at me furiously. "Forget it."

"No, Lula!" I say hoarsely, knocking a fist to my chest as I clear my throat again. "I'm not *against* it. Just, the idea of you, ringing up books, taking latte orders . . ."

Tallulah's quiet. Her gaze dips to her noodles, which she stabs with her chopsticks. Her expression is ice, hard and frigid. That's the girl who stonewalled me in college. The woman who took a drink and disappeared on me last year at the A-frame.

I don't like it at all. I like the woman I saw glimpses of over coffee the next morning, the woman who showed up tonight and let me give her the grand tour of the store, who teased but never demeaned, who shoved chocolate in my mouth when I got lightheaded and gave me hell for neglecting myself.

I want that woman back. I have no idea how to do that, and it bugs me much more than it should.

"You think I'm too precious to work at a bookstore?" she says tightly.

My heart jumps. It's not much, but . . . it's her, speaking up, talking to me.

"Of course not, Lu. You're just a big deal, you know? You're an established, successful author. I should be rolling out the red carpet, hosting an event for you, not sticking you behind a counter to ring up books."

"Maybe I want to do that," she says, her voice quiet but firm. "Maybe I'm sick of staring at a computer screen, hating what I'm writing and hating that I feel stuck. Maybe I want to *do* something different and get out of my head."

"Well . . ." I lean my elbows on the table, bracketing my plate, chopsticks wedged in the noodles. "Maybe we can help each other, then. You want to help me with the store. Why don't you let me help you with the book? Talk to me. Tell me about it."

Tallulah freezes, chopsticks halfway to her mouth. Slowly, she lowers them back to her plate. "I don't see how telling you about it will help me."

"You ever done talk therapy?"

Her eyebrows lift. "No."

"Highly recommend." I lean back, stretching an arm across the back of the booth. "Talking with a therapist who echoes back to you what you're saying helps you gain a fresh perspective, insight into what you're dealing with. It can be very illuminating, talking it through with an expert."

"And you're an *expert* on thrillers?" she asks pointedly.

"I love books. I've read your thriller, a couple others that came highly recommended." I shrug. "Maybe that's enough. Humor me. Try it."

On a heavy sigh, Tallulah pokes around her noodles. She's quiet, and I can see she's deliberating before she finally says, "When the story starts, the main characters, a husband and wife, seem happily married."

"And then . . . ?"

She sighs again. "And then my editor said their relationship 'lacks a stitch of soul or sensuality.'"

I grimace. "Ouch."

"Indeed," Tallulah mutters, stabbing her noodles with her chopsticks. She unearths a snow pea and crunches on it.

"Can I ask, for being someone who doesn't seem too keen on romance, unless I'm wrong—"

"You're not," she says around her bite. "I am romance averse. In fiction and in real life."

I take a deep breath, then exhale. *Don't ask her why. She doesn't need you grilling her about her life and love philosophies right now.* "For being someone who's not big on romance, why are you writing a romantic relationship between your main characters?"

She's quiet for a minute, chewing. I watch her swallow, then reach for her water glass and take a deep drink. "Because I want to make a point. And that point won't be made if I can't write a convincingly intimate romantic relationship at the outset." Her eyes widen. "Wait. You *would* be the perfect person to help me with this book. I need someone who loves all that love stuff to help me sort out their dynamic. Who better than a romance reader?"

I smile. "I'd be honored to help you give your characters the happily ever after they deserve. Sounds great. A high-stakes thriller with a strong romantic subplot . . ." My voice dies off.

Tallulah avoids my gaze, swirling her straw in her water.

"Wait a second." My eyes narrow. "Are you going to leverage my background in romance only to murder their relationship along with whoever else you brutally off in this book?"

Tallulah is quiet. Abandons the straw. Fiddles with her bright blue hair in its twisted bun. "I mean, *maybe*—"

"Oh, hell no." I throw up my hands. "I will not. Cannot. C'mon, Lu, would it kill you to give them an HEA?"

She frowns. "An HEA?"

"A happily ever after."

Tallulah stares at me. "It's . . . complicated."

"Well, I've got another pound of lo mein to eat and a near-death ride home on a Vespa to delay, so I'll be here a while. Give me a chance to understand. Explain it."

Sighing, she leans in, elbows on the table. This position does great things for her very full, beautiful breasts, pushing them against the neckline of her black scoop-neck tee. I hold her eyes and tell my peripheral vision to stop working overtime.

"Listen," she says. "I don't . . . get the appeal of romance, this starry-eyed idea of love. I don't think it's real, though I understand it's real to many. Given that, I don't tend to write stories deviating from my mindset. But . . ."

"But?"

"But, I think, even with that, done right and with your help, you'd be okay with how this story ends."

I fold my arms across my chest. "Let's hear it, then."

Those big brown eyes nearly bug out of her head. "I can't tell you the ending! That spoils it!"

"I need to know what I'm getting myself into, Lulaloo."

Tallulah shuts her eyes and starts to massage her temples. "They're separated by the end, but . . . they're friends. Good friends. In fact, they're better friends than they were when they were married. Everything that unravels between them in the book, all that's revealed, makes you root for their happiness, and they get that—a happily ever after—just . . . not the one your books always portray."

I stare at her, sifting through what she's saying. How quietly she's said it, eyes shut, as if she's been bracing herself for the same kind of swift put-down I was bracing myself for when I pushed her just now to open up to me.

"Well . . ." I shrug a shoulder, picking up my chopsticks again and digging around, just to give my antsy hands something to do. "I can work with that. Sometimes happy endings end sooner rather than later. Doesn't mean they weren't beautiful or happy while they existed. And it doesn't mean there isn't more beauty and happiness to come."

Tallulah opens her eyes, and her gaze finds mine. "That's what I was thinking."

I smile. "Well then, Lu, I'd say we're on the same page."

She ducks her head, reaching for her lo mein with her chopsticks again, then plucks a carrot sliver from the noodles. "So," she says. "We can sort out the details, how you'll advise and help me, later on. For now, let's talk about how I compensate you. Is—"

"I don't want your money, Lula."

She blinks at me, confused. "But I have to pay you back somehow. And clearly, you need the money."

Sure, I could use the cash, but I'm too damn proud to take her money. This is part of what I've promised myself since I started planning for the store—this was going to be *my* success, my independent accomplishment. No dropping the ball and scrambling for people to help me pick myself up, no mismanaging my resources and having to crawl to someone to bail me out.

"Want my help at your store instead?" she offers. "I could 'pay' you that way?"

I swallow nervously. "Well, I don't think that's exactly a fair trade. The kind of help I need, it's more work than seems an even swap for a couple hours spent talking about the romantic nuts and bolts of your story."

"You are grossly underestimating what bad shape this draft is in. Second-book syndrome is real. Trust me, it's going to be an even swap."

I bite my lip. "I don't know. I have very specific ideas for how this place should operate, and I'm going to be a pain in the ass about it. I can be grating to spend extended periods of time around, especially when I'm fixated on a particular activity or outcome. I wouldn't want you to feel cornered into something you'd regret."

Tallulah frowns at me. "Says who?"

"Says who, what?"

"*Who*," she says calmly, but there's an edge to her voice, "says you're 'grating' to spend a lot of time around?"

"Oh . . ." Heat creeps up my cheeks. I clear my throat. "Just . . . most of the people who've spent a lot of time around me."

"Then fuck them," she says icily. "Fuck anyone who makes you feel like you're too much. If they feel that way, *they* aren't enough for *you*."

My heart's pounding, sweet, searing heat pouring through me.

"Tallulah," I say roughly. "You might want to stop . . . saying nice things to me."

She wrinkles her nose. "I'm not being 'nice,' I'm being logical. I'm making simple sense."

"You're definitely being nice, maybe even sweet. And now I'm really darn close to hugging you for it."

"No hugs." She points her chopsticks at me. "First, there's a booth and Chinese food between us and this is a very expensive, newly purchased top you could get food on."

"We could stand—"

"*And* with our height differential, my face would be smothered in your sternum—I don't need any more bitter reminders of how vertically disadvantaged I am."

I pout, slumped back against the booth. "Fine. I'll just have to accept your nice, sweet—"

"Logical—"

"—words, and let bygones be bygones."

She shakes her head as she bends over her lo mein again. I catch the tiniest hint of a smile tugging the corner of her mouth right up to her beauty mark.

Quiet settles between us as she takes another bite of noodles, as I sit, leaning against the wall, watching her. Generally, I'm not a fan of quiet. It makes me uneasy. It leaves me with my noisy, chaotic thoughts and an overwhelming sense of loneliness. But right now, I don't mind it so much. This kind of quiet feels . . . alive, like that moment's breath in a song between the final notes of a beautiful verse and the beginning of an epic chorus, full of promise and possibility.

Even so, after a couple of minutes, I hit my limit of stillness and silence, eager for what's next, ready to run headlong into it. I sit up, deciding on one more bite of lo mein. "So, uh . . . if we were to do this, let's talk logistics. Where are you living these days? Given your location, when would it be practical for you to come to the store, for me to help you with the book?"

Not that I've been keeping close tabs on Tallulah or anything, but last I heard through the grapevine, aka Ziggy via Charlie, she was renting a place in San Diego, living by herself.

Tallulah pauses chewing, then slowly resumes. "Oh . . . uh. Right now, I've been crashing at Charlie's."

"Charlie's?"

"My landlord was a dick," she says. "Had to move out quickly, but thankfully it was a furnished rental, so it didn't take long. Don't know where I'm headed next. I was thinking I'd stay in the area for now, given Charlie and Gigi's wedding plans are ramping up and I'm helping with them. I'm flexible. I can work around your schedule."

"You're sticking around here?" I ask. My heart beats a little faster. I like the idea of Tallulah sticking around, more than makes any kind of sense.

She nods. "At least until the wedding."

"Plan to rent again?"

"Probably." She peers up, meeting my eyes. "What about you—where do you live?"

"I live in the back of the store, actually. It's more spacious than you might think, plenty for one person. Open-concept kitchen, dining, and living room. One bath, two and a half bedrooms—that half bedroom is basically a glorified closet, small enough to fit some shoes, a desk, maybe a crib—not that I'm, ya know, welcoming kids anytime soon, maybe ever—"

You're rambling. Stop. Stop while you're ahead. Or less behind. Just stop!

"Not exactly sure I'm dad material," I prattle on. My mouth is a high-speed train that lost the brakes three sentences ago. "But anyway, yeah, what more can I ask for? Lots of natural light, plenty of bedrooms, short commute." I laugh, scratching at my jaw. Tallulah's looking at me curiously, and I'm looking at her, and then my brain does one of those things it does sometimes, when it just mashes up the last few inputs—*plenty of bedrooms! short commute! Tallulah!*

"Say, you could live with me if you wanted," I tell her. "Would you want to?"

Now it's Tallulah's turn to choke on her noodles. My heart rate spikes.

"Lula, can you breathe?"

Clearing her throat roughly, she nods, then croaks, "I'm okay." She grabs her glass of water and drains it in three long gulps.

I watch her, guilt and embarrassment twisting together inside me. "I'm sorry, Lu. I don't know where that came from—"

Her hand lifts, silencing me as she sets the glass carefully beside her. Clearing her throat again, she blinks away water that's pooled at the corners of her eyes. "Stop apologizing. *I* choked. You didn't make me do it."

"I surprised you," I counter.

"You did. But it's not your fault."

"Still—"

"Tallulah?" A low, rough voice breaks our conversation. Both she and I turn toward the person at the end of our booth, smiling at Tallulah. Mid-height. Bulky. Covered in tatts. It all feels vaguely familiar.

Tallulah's face smooths, her expression turning cool and unreadable. "Clint."

Recognition dawns. I know this guy. I've seen him at the tattoo shop where Seb and I have gotten inked. He works there. If he recognizes me, though, he doesn't show it.

His smile kicks up higher at the corner as he stares at Tallulah. At first I thought it was a friendly smile, but now I can see it has an edge to it. "What are you doing here?" he asks.

"Eating," Tallulah says, gesturing to our plates. "With my friend." I feel a little rush of pride. She called me her friend.

Clint huffs a breath as he throws a glance my way. "Aren't you going to introduce me to your *friend*?"

Tallulah blinks, peering my way. I see something now in her expression that makes my chest tighten, my heart twist. I recognize someone hiding when they're hurting. I've been doing it for years. Hiding when I'm lonely. Hiding when another person found me useful or funny until they decided I'd worn out my welcome. This guy hurt her somehow, and she's trying so hard to hide that.

"Right." She clears her throat. "This is—"

"Viggo Bergman." I offer the guy my hand, prepared for what's coming: a hard squeeze.

He's got a firm grip, I'll give him that. But I've been chopping wood and climbing, bouldering and building, since childhood. I have very strong hands. And I make sure Clint feels that.

His jaw flexes as I squeeze back, then release my grip. Whoever this guy was or is to Tallulah, I don't like how she dimmed as soon as he showed up. I don't like the hurt that she's barely hiding behind her cool facade.

"Clint Marwood," he says. As he shoves his hands in his pockets, Clint gives me an appraising once-over. His gaze lingers on my shirt. An empty laugh jumps out of him. "Wow, Tallulah, your 'friend' loves romance novels. How's that working out for you? And I thought *we* were a stretch."

"Clint," Tallulah warns. "Stop—"

"You've told him, right?" He plants his hands on our table's edge, dropping down. I smell the booze on his breath as he turns toward me. "She's told you, huh? She 'doesn't do love.' What she really means is, she's emotionless. Soulless. She lures you in with that untouchable aura, fucks you, then fucks you up—"

I'm out of the booth before I even know what's happening. Clint pushes off the table and takes a reflexive step back as I stare down at him, fire in my veins. "You can leave now."

He huffs a laugh, bathing my face in the smell of alcohol. "Who the fuck are you to—"

"Leave." I take a step closer as I glare down at him. "And leave Tallulah the hell alone, unless she tells you otherwise."

Clint glances over at Tallulah. She isn't looking at him, though. She's looking at me. I meet her gaze. "Do you want this guy bothering you anymore, Lu?"

She swallows, then shakes her head. "No. I want him to leave me alone." Finally, she looks his way. "Go."

He stares at her, then glances from Tallulah to me.

I hold his gaze, daring him to challenge me. "She. Said. Go."

Begrudgingly, he takes a step back. Then another. "Whatever." Then he spins on his heel and struts over to the counter, where they set to-go orders.

Tallulah drags her purse onto her lap and starts digging around. "I want to leave."

"Okay." I pull out my wallet, relieved I actually have a twenty in there, which I set on the table. I get the feeling Tallulah doesn't want to wait around to pay with a card. Tallulah pulls out way more cash than she owes, tosses it on the table, and snaps up her wallet before she slips it in her purse.

On the outside, she looks calm and cool, her movements serene, no rush. But I can tell she's upset. Very, very upset.

Slowly, Tallulah eases out of the booth. I turn my back to the asshole, a human shield protecting her from even having to look at him.

Her hand brushes mine as she starts walking—it's inadvertent, I think, but I feel how much she's shaking. I wrap my hand around hers, desperate to comfort her, to do *something* that shows her I'm here; she's not alone. I don't expect her to respond or squeeze back.

But she does. She squeezes hard. She holds tight. I use my free hand to push open the door and hold it for her, and Tallulah strolls ahead of me, then nearly drags me with her as I linger to hold the door for a couple behind us.

As soon as we round the corner, she tears her hand away, turns, and faces me. Something that looks scarily like tears is in her eyes.

I take an instinctive step toward her. "Tallulah—"

"Did you mean it?" she asks. Her voice is quiet, but something powerful lurks beneath its surface.

"Mean what?"

"Your offer, to help each other out—you, with my book; me, with your store—to be roommates."

I shake my head, disoriented. "Tallulah, I'm not worried about that right now, I'm worried about you—"

"Did you mean it?" she presses, stepping closer.

I search her eyes, asking myself that same question. *Did* I mean it?

As I stare down at her, a fierce pang of longing floods me. Every time I'm around her, I feel *so* much, none of which I can make sense of. No, she doesn't give me butterflies; the world didn't become brighter the first time I saw her stroll into our lecture. But I know

I feel *something* for her. I know that I'm fascinated by her—by the complexity of those chilly prickles and her quiet, concealed kindness. I think about waking up with her in the morning at my place, none of her artful black winged eyeliner or stylish updo between us. Seeing her in her pajamas, grumbling over coffee the way she was that morning at the A-frame. I think about having dinner and bickering good-naturedly like we have over lo mein tonight. And I like that idea.

A lot.

No, I don't think Tallulah Clarke is the one I'm destined to be with. But what if she's someone I'm destined to be with for a little while? A friend, a roomie, someone I can lean on and who can lean on me to make life a bit easier in a tough season.

I smile down at Tallulah, even as nerves tighten my stomach. What if she thinks my offer is ridiculous? What if she thinks *I'm* ridiculous?

Then again, *she* asked *me* if I meant what I said, when I offered to skill swap and cohabitate. She held my hand right back when I held hers. I think Tallulah's being pretty damn brave right now. I want to be brave, too.

"Yeah, Lula. I meant it."

She bites her lip, her eyes searching mine. "You're sure? We hardly know each other. I could be an axe murderer, for all you know."

I shrug. "I'm not too worried. I could wrestle an axe out of one of your little arms quite handily, if needed."

Her eyebrows shoot up. "First of all, besides my height, there is nothing little about me." She lifts one soft, full arm, the one bearing what a little covert research led me to learn is her continuous glucose monitor. I don't stare at the small oblong disc adhered to her upper arm. I'm aware of it, but my gaze is focused on something else—the dimple at her elbow that I want to nip with my teeth, then chase with my tongue. A dimple that makes me wonder where else there are deep, soft dimples on Tallulah that I could graze my teeth over, lick my way across.

Which is definitely not what I should be thinking about when proposing cohabitation to a woman who has demonstrated only the barest tolerance of my nonsense, who has never once looked at me the way every main character I've ever read in a romance novel looks at their love interest. Soft, aching longing. Heat in their cheeks. Gaze raking down their body. Tallulah's only ever given me exasperated glances and eye rolls. She's not into me. She wasn't in college, and she isn't now. There's nothing happening there.

I just need my body to get the memo.

"Second," she says, dragging my attention back from its horny detour. Making a fist, lifting her forearm, Tallulah flexes. "I'm a lot stronger than you think."

I smile, because goddamn, I can't help it. "Never doubted it, Lu."

Her eyes narrow. Her arm falls to her side. She stares up at me, and I wish so badly I could peek behind the curtain of her cool, unreadable expression. Those big, pretty brown eyes dart between mine. Her mouth purses as if she's thinking something through.

I wait quietly, patient and still, for once in my life.

And then Tallulah offers her hand and says, "Well then, Viggo Bergman. Looks like you've got yourself a roommate."

NINE

Tallulah

Playlist: "Walden Pond," Atta Boy

I'm barely holding it together. I had to push past the horror of bumping into Clint, straight to the logistics at hand. Because that's how I function. Focus on the facts. Ignore emotions. Just. Keep. Going.

Right up to the moment Clint showed his face, I was firmly prepared to turn down Viggo's roommate offer. I've already lived with someone who I was attracted to (and ended up sleeping with)—it blew up in my face *epically*. The irony, that the person with whom everything imploded was the very person who showed up and made me realize living with Viggo would be nothing like living with Clint.

As Clint crashed our meal and Viggo stood up for me, all I could think was, this person is good. And kind. And yes, he's also very hot and I'd thoroughly enjoy sleeping with him, which would otherwise immediately strike him from the list of eligible roommates, but I'm *not* going to sleep with him, not going to throw my emotionless-sex self at a die-hard romantic. In fact, agreeing to be roommates is the best way to avoid that temptation, *if* Viggo is even interested in sleeping with me.

Even if he is, Viggo is a gentleman. He won't hit on me while we're living together, while I'm working at his store and he's helping me with my book, while clear boundaries are in place. I'll respect those boundaries, too.

I'll be his . . . friend, maybe. And maybe he'll be mine. That will be enough. It'll probably be more than I've ever had in the way of support and consistency in my domestic life. I can simply be grateful for that.

Asserting my offer, I thrust out my hand even farther. Cohabitants. Coworkers. Friendly roomies. Nothing more.

Viggo stares at my hand, a smile tugging at his mouth. "We're gonna shake on this? Like a business deal?"

"It is a business deal," I tell him. "I help you with the store. You help me with my book; let me crash at your place until . . ." I wrack my brain. We need a clear end date—I have to finish this book already, and I can't live indefinitely with someone whom I'm this attracted to. "Until the wedding. Two months, then I'll be on my way. That's a deal."

Viggo bites his lip, staring at me.

"But we're friends, Lu." He slides his hand along mine, palm grazing palm, fingertips whispering over my wrist. "Doesn't that make this . . . a bit different from a business deal?"

I swallow nervously, unsettled by how turned on I'm getting when only his fingers graze my skin in light, lulling circles. I don't even think he knows he's doing it. He's just like this—touchy, talky, warm. "I guess . . ." I exhale slowly, getting my bearings. "I guess that's more than a business deal. It's . . . a mutually beneficial, platonic season of support."

His smile deepens. "I like the sound of that."

"Good." I nod once. Twice. I'm flustered. I shouldn't be, but I am. I'm riveted by his gaze, his hand holding mine, the flood of warmth that's lingered in my veins ever since he stood up for me in the restaurant.

"So," he says softly, "we gonna talk about how you're doing, after that asswipe in there harassed you?"

"Nope." I try to tug my hand away, but Viggo holds it, not so tight that I couldn't yank it out if I wanted, just enough to send a message.

Stay with me. Talk to me.

I'm so used to pulling back, shutting down, retreating. I've never had someone ask me how *I* feel, what *I* need. I'm the one who's done that for others. Who showed up for Mom when Dad broke her heart again, who answered Dad's texts begging for ideas about trips to plan, gifts to send Mom, whatever he could do to get back in her good graces. Who bailed out my brother Harry when he made a mess of things, cleaned up those messes with money and promises it wouldn't happen again. Who took care of Charlie, who's gone wedding-dress shopping with her and helped her make choices Mom and Dad should be helping her make, except they're both too absorbed in their own bullshit to see how much their daughter needs them. Who handled my friend group's rental finances, groceries, meal planning, upkeep, who was the quiet listener, the shoulder to cry on, the receptacle and vessel for what everyone else needed.

I don't have needs. Or feelings. I've never felt I could afford that luxury.

This past year, I've confronted that problem, at least abstractly. Reading, thinking, living alone. I'm trying to operate differently. Maybe, living with Viggo, I might actually get good at it.

"Clint was a friend I made in college," I tell Viggo, feeling my way through what it's like to open up. "We all got a place together, and then everyone left, and we sort of . . . ended up together . . . sexually. That was it. Just lots of cohabitational, unromantic banging."

We were just friends with benefits. I thought we'd made that clear. Until Clint said he loved me and I said I didn't love him, and then he yelled and threw things and kicked me out.

"It didn't end well," I add quietly. "That's it."

Viggo's jaw tightens—I can tell, even beneath all that beard. He's not happy with this answer. "Did he hurt you?"

I swallow thickly. "Not . . . physically."

Viggo's grip tightens. When he realizes how hard he's squeezing, he drops my hand. Then he steps closer. "Let me hug you, Lu?"

I bite my lip, tears welling in my eyes. I hate crying. I hate it so much.

"Lula," he says, opening his arms. "Please. You're killing me, standing there, sad and quiet and hurting. I've gotta do something—"

I throw myself into his waiting embrace, and his arms wrap around me, tucking me close. My head under his chin, his hand splayed across my back. This is like no other hug I've ever had. He's warm and strong; his shirt is cloud soft, and he smells like pure comfort. My arms twine around his waist. I bury my face in his chest and breathe deeply, trying so hard not to cry.

Viggo rests his cheek on my head. "Doesn't matter that it wasn't physical. He hurt you. I'm sorry."

I scrunch my eyes shut. Tears slip down my cheeks. "It's okay."

"It's not okay," he says fiercely, hugging me closer to him. "I wish pistols at dawn were still a thing."

A broken laugh jumps out of me. "What, would you call him out?"

"Hell yes. I wouldn't kill him, but I'd for damn sure scare the life out of him so he never so much as looked your way again."

I smile faintly against his chest. "I think you already accomplished that back in the restaurant."

He sighs, his hand circling my back. "But just think how much better I'd have looked, putting him in his place in the early morning mist, skintight buckskin breeches hugging my fabulous legs."

Another laugh leaves me, hoarse and loud, straight from my belly. "This is a very developed fantasy you have."

"I've read four hundred and ninety-one historical romance novels, Tallulah. I have lots of Regency-era fantasies, and this is probably one of the more 'normal' ones."

My smile deepens. I burrow into his chest, hiding it, and sigh, overtaken by a kind of exhausted peace I haven't felt in . . . maybe ever. "For some inexplicable reason, I have to admit, I'm looking forward to hearing more about them."

"When we're roomies?" Viggo asks.

I nod, my arms tight around him. "When we're roomies."

The Vespa ride home—at a markedly slower speed out of deference to Viggo's delicate sensibilities—is uneventful. I pull into the back of the store and kill the engine, trying very hard not to stare at my future roommate's ass while he walks up to his door and unlocks it. There are plants everywhere back here, creeping, flowering vines marching up a trellis, across a tall wood fence obscuring what I'm assuming is his patio. A light is on inside, and when he opens the door, the woodsy sugar-spice scent that never leaves him hits me tenfold.

Lust crests through me. I'm going to have to invest in some new, seriously sturdy vibrators if I'm going to survive living with that sexy scent surrounding me every day for the next two months.

"Wanna come in?" Viggo asks, holding open his door. "Poke around? Take measurements?"

His eyes are bright, his smile wide. I think he enjoyed the Vespa ride this time, a little more familiar with the experience, our speed more his pace. There's something intoxicating about his smile, his excitement. He's got his hands in his pockets and this . . . glow warming his gaze, his skin, his whole face—well, what I can see of it, with that overgrown bushy beard.

Dammit, I have a soft spot for him. For that eager, bright smile, the excitement vibrating through his whole body. For the way he stood up for me and held me hard and cared. It's contagious, that energy, that warmth. I feel like I was outside in a rainstorm, getting pissed on by the sky, and then the sun just elbowed its way in, wiped away the gloom, dried every drop of misery clinging to me.

I take a free, deep breath. The air seems tinged with possibility, with hope.

I'm going to figure out this book. I'm going to keep holding better boundaries with my parents and brother and stay good for Charlie, who's inundating me with all things wedding, bouncing between wild excitement and wide-eyed terror. I'm going to help Viggo make his store thrive.

I'm going to be a faithful friend, a reliable roomie. I'm going to do and enjoy something good for *me*.

"Lula?" Viggo steps closer, studying my face. "What is it?"

His fingertips brush mine, calloused, rough, sending sparks across my skin. It's the most unideal part of this plan—how horny I am for him. But I'm not going to cross that line. I'm not going to risk ruining this good thing. I'm going to lock down my libido and use some state-of-the-art vibrators to keep the edge off so I can coexist with Viggo while not falling into the trap of trying to seduce him.

Not that I'm sure he'd even be seducible. I have no idea if he sees me that way. He's flirty—he was a flirt in college, and a year ago, and he is now—but I get the feeling he's flirty with everyone. I'm nothing special to him.

And that's how it's going to stay.

"Lula?" he asks, frowning. I've been quiet for too long. "You okay?"

Clearing my throat, I meet his eyes and pull myself into that familiar place—a cool, placid pool of water, where fears and wants and worries are sucked under, silenced, lost. "I'm fine. Just a long day."

He nods thoughtfully. "You alert enough to drive back to Charlie's? I've got a bed in the spare room. It's going to be yours anyway. You could crash there—"

"I'm okay. Promise." I squeeze his hand in reassurance. "I'll come by tomorrow, if that's all right, take a look around, make sure I know what I need to bring when I move in."

"Text me when you get home, then, so I'm not worried you're a blue-haired, cute-as-a-button pancake on the highway."

I roll my eyes. "You're such a drama llama."

Viggo pulls out his phone as I pull out mine. We exchange numbers. He sends me a GIF of an animated historical romance cover, a guy who looks like Fabio in Regency clothes wiggling his eyebrows at the viewer with a come-hither stare. I send him a GIF of Alexis Rose saying, "Ew, David!"

Viggo snorts a laugh, then pockets his phone.

"See you tomorrow," I tell him. I step back onto the Vespa and slip on my helmet.

Viggo stands in the doorway, watching me. "Good night, Lulaloo."

I turn over the engine and roll forward, knocking up the kickstand, before I pull onto the road. For the first time in a very long time, it really does feel like a good night after all.

TEN

Tallulah

Playlist: "Anti-hero—Acoustic Version," Taylor Swift

"You're doing *what*?" Charlie blinks at me owlishly. Like mine, her dark hair is a bird's nest. She grips her coffee cup so hard, her knuckles are white.

I sip my coffee from the other end of her sofa, my makeshift bed the past week, and raise my eyebrows. "Don't tell me you're displeased by this turn of events."

Charlie blushes and buries her face in her mug, taking a long gulp of coffee.

"I know exactly what you were doing last night," I tell her, "tricking me into going to the Bergman family gathering at his store, running out of there afterward with your tail between your legs. You're trying to set us up."

My sister lowers her mug, revealing that familiar guilty look, those big pleading puppy eyes. "Not exactly set you up, but . . . you know, nudge you toward him?"

I huff a laugh. "Semantics. You're gunning for us to get together. And it's not going to happen."

Charlie's expression dips to a pout. "So you're moving in with him . . . why?"

"For practical reasons. I need my own place."

"Tallulah, we love having you here—"

I hold up a hand. "Charlie, you are the sweetest person in the world. You're going to tell me I don't need to get out of your and Gigi's hair, and you'll mean well, but that doesn't mean you're making sense. You two need your space. You're getting married in two months, and there are a lot of moving parts, lots of stressors coming at you—you need to come home in the evening and snuggle on the couch with your fiancée as long as you want, not worry about leaving it so I can go to bed. You need to be able to screw each other six ways to Sunday on whatever surface you want and not have to be mindful that I could walk in the door any minute. You need . . ." A lump catches in my throat because, saying this, I'm realizing, it's finally hitting me—my baby sister is getting *married*; she's got her own family now; she made it through the emotional shitstorm of our upbringing and found happiness.

I swallow, then meet my sister's eyes. "You need space to live your life."

Charlie bites her lip, eyes searching mine. "So you're moving in with Viggo just for somewhere to stay? That's it?"

"Well . . . no."

My sister emits an irritating self-satisfied hum. "I didn't think so. Otherwise, you'd just find another rental."

"We're doing a skills swap, of sorts. He's going to help me iron out the kinks in my book—"

"'Iron out the kinks,' eh? Is he going to help 'fill your plot holes,' too?"

I thwack her with a pillow. "It's not like that. Our arrangement is just business. He'll help me with the book. I'll help out around the store. It's easiest to do that if we're living behind the store, in the same space."

Charlie grins and nudges my foot with hers. "Sounds like quite the arrangement."

I shove her foot back. "Stop smiling like that."

"I'm just saying, maybe you don't think you're relationship

material for each other, but I still got something right, dragging you to his store yesterday. You came out of that with hope for your book that's been giving you a hard time and a really good new living situation."

My heart kicks against my chest as I confess my worry, wrapped in a question: "You think it'll be good, us living together?"

Charlie's smile deepens. "Of course it will be. Viggo is a *blast*. He's like . . . the opposite of how we grew up—talkative, affectionate, playful. Every time I see him, I'm happier. He's the human embodiment of serotonin."

"You sure you don't want to throw *yourself* at him?"

She rolls her eyes. "I'm a happily engaged woman. I just like him. He's my friend. And a good person, Tallulah. I know he'll be a good roommate to you."

"Yeah, well, just don't get any ideas beyond that." I sip my coffee and give her a stern look. "This is going to be a purely practical, platonic arrangement."

Viggo's home is exactly what I expected; at least the main living area is, which is all I've seen so far. There are large posters of historical romance covers blown up big enough to fill chunky wood frames. Plants everywhere. A sunshine-yellow couch long enough for someone as tall as Viggo to stretch out on, covered with fluffy pillows inside colorful crocheted covers. Perhaps the only unexpected aspect is that it's immaculately clean. He's a single guy, and most single guys I've known are on the slob end of the tidiness scale. I also remember what the inside of his open book bag looked like crammed between us in recitation back in college—pure chaos. Not that people can't change, but I just had the sense that he's one of those guys who has to rummage around to find just about anything.

I glance around, taking in the space, while Viggo stands a few feet away from me, hands on his hips as he watches me. He's flushed and breathing heavily, like he was when he answered the door a minute ago, as if he'd been exercising.

On a particularly winded breath, he reaches for a mason jar on the side table filled with ice water and drains half of it.

"Doing okay?" I ask. "Did I interrupt a workout when I arrived?"

Viggo sets down his water a little clumsily, then dabs his mouth with the collar of his shirt. This one bears a haphazard stack of books, their spines reading phrases like *enemies to lovers*, *bluestocking and rake*, *fake dating*, *grumpy + sunshine*, *only one bed*. I frown, trying to make sense of them. And then my gaze dips down when I notice that lifting his shirt has revealed a thin band of tan skin, a line of chestnut hair arrowing down beneath his jeans slung low on his hips.

Heat rushes through me. I glance away.

"No workout." He exhales heavily again. "Just got myself sweaty moving stuff around."

"I hope that wasn't on my account."

"Nah." He waves a hand. "I needed to do some rearranging anyway."

"Hmm." My eyes narrow as I stare at him. "You're a bad liar."

"Okay, so I cleaned up a little, too. Sue me for wanting to be considerate of my future roomie coming by. And I'm a great liar, by the way."

"Wow, that's what you want to hear from someone you're about to cohabitate with."

"Tallulah," he growls, tugging down his ball cap and marching toward the kitchen end of the open space. "Stop being ornery."

"Can't. It's in my DNA."

"Well, then it skipped your sister. Charlie is as sweet as can be."

I shrug. "The exception proves the rule."

Viggo opens the fridge, pulls out a glass container sealed with a clear plastic lid, and sets it on the counter. "Maybe this will get you to reconsider your orneriness."

I walk tentatively toward the container as Viggo unsnaps the lid. Now I can see what's in there. "Brownies?"

He smiles. "All for you."

My stomach flips. "You made brownies . . . for me?"

His smile deepens. "Course!"

"You . . . didn't have to do that."

He shrugs, glancing down at the brownies, spinning the container a quarter turn. "I like baking. I'm still tweaking the recipe, but I think I'm getting close. Who better than my new roomie to taste test them? The recipe is low sugar and"—he rummages in his pocket and pulls out his phone, eyes on the screen as he taps and scrolls before turning the screen so I can see it—"I calculated the carbs in each serving. That's helpful, right?"

I stare at him, trying to process this, trying to find something to say. I'm being too quiet. I know that, but I don't know how to respond.

This might be the most considerate thing anyone has ever done for me. It's going to spoil me, make me want things like this, even when I'm gone and this is over. And I'm so scared to want anything from anyone. All it's ever done is hurt me.

I can't tell him that. So, instead I tell him, "I'm not a big brownie gal."

Viggo blinks like I've slapped him. Then he tugs his ball cap low, hiding his eyes. Heat creeps up his cheeks. I've embarrassed him.

I want to kick myself.

"Come on," he says, turning and starting down the hallway. "I'll show you your room."

I follow him after a beat, warring with myself. I'm terrified to latch on to this level of kindness from someone I'm determined not to sleep with. But I'm sick to my stomach, knowing I made him feel bad.

"Viggo—"

"This," he says, either not hearing me or, more likely, ignoring me, trying to push past the damage I've caused, "is your room. I'll give you some space to check it out."

I've just made it to the threshold when he turns and steps out at the same time I try to step in.

I'm a thick girl. I take up space in a doorway. And while Viggo's lean, he's broad—wide shoulders, wider stance—and he's not turned sideways, unprepared for my entrance during his exit. His elbow knocks into my boobs, making me hiss in pain, sending me bumping back into the doorframe. I try to steady myself as I lurch sideways and trip over his foot.

Viggo lunges and wraps his hands around my shoulders to stop me from falling. "Shit. Lula, I'm sorry."

Instinctively, I lift my shirt so I can see my stomach and check the state of my pod, which delivers insulin to my body, a welcome upgrade from my old pump and tubing setup. It could have come loose when we bumped torsos. Feeling along the adhesive, I'm relieved to find it's still secure.

Viggo's hands fall from my shoulders. "God, did I hurt you? Did I mess something up—"

I drop my shirt and put a hand on his mouth, which requires more of a reach than I'd like, reminding me how damn short I am and how tall he is. But I'm glad I've stopped him, that I have his attention. Viggo's quiet, his eyes searching mine.

"You okay?" he asks against my fingertips. "I really am sorr—"

I press my fingers harder, and he sucks in a breath. It takes a second for me to find my words, to orient myself. I'm not used to talking this way, and I'm definitely not used to someone like him standing so close, steadying me.

He smells like sweat and woodsy soap, a wisp of cinnamon sugar. His hard body presses right up against mine. My boobs are smooshed against his chest. His thigh is wedged between my legs. He stares down at me, jaw tight, as I lower my hand from his mouth, telling my body to calm the hell down. But it really doesn't want to. It wants to sink into him, my fingers deep in his hair, my hips working against his.

Aching lust thuds, sharp and low, in my belly, right between my thighs. Viggo's grip on my arms tightens a little, then slides down. His thumbs hit my elbow dimples and press, then circle, like he's soothing me, maybe soothing himself, too.

"I'm okay. I just had to check my pod, because we bumped into each other and it could have made it come loose."

His eyes search mine. "Your pod?"

"It's the device that sends insulin to my body. So, pretty important."

He swallows nervously. "And . . . it's okay?"

"It's okay."

"I really am sorry," he starts, but I interrupt him.

"Please stop apologizing. We bumped into each other, it was just an accident, and I'm fine. *I'm* the one who should be saying sorry," I tell him quietly. "I . . ." My voice sticks, and I force myself to swallow, to wet my throat and find my courage. "I'm sorry I didn't . . . respond well to the brownies."

Heat hits Viggo's cheeks again. "Oh, it's fine!" He steps back, shoving his hands in his pockets. The deprivation I feel, losing his touch, is concerning. "I get it. They looked like moose turds, honestly—"

"Stop." I push off the threshold, get right in his space, and grab a fistful of his shirt, because, dammit, he needs to listen to me. "Please just . . . let me apologize. I panicked, and I lied. I *do* like brownies, and it *was* helpful that you counted the carbs per serving, though they don't even need to be low sugar; just knowing the carbs is enough, so I can bolus the right amount of insulin. I'm just . . . not used to people doing things like that, Viggo. It caught me off guard. I don't think well on my feet. I do better with a laptop in front of me, time to figure out the right words, and . . . hell, I'm sucking at even that right now. So, just . . . please, *please*, promise you won't take my fuckups personally. It's me. *I'm* the problem."

Viggo grins. "We're a Swiftie, are we?"

I narrow my eyes. "You are annoyingly good at deflecting."

His grin deepens, but then it slips as he registers my undeterred gaze, pinning him in place. "I, uh . . . I just don't want to make you uncomfortable," he says. "I made those brownies because I wanted you to feel welcome. But I get that it was too much. I do that. I do too much. I *am* too much—"

"It wasn't." I press my fist into his chest, right over his heart. "It wasn't too much, and *you're* not too much. Don't assume other people's problems are an indictment of you. Don't take on their shit, especially mine, and make it yours, or I swear to you, this arrangement is off."

Viggo blinks at me like I've stunned him.

"I will get used to this . . . courtesy," I tell him. "I will probably be awkward about it a lot of the time, but don't you dare internalize that as anything to do with you, least of all anything bad or wrong. And I'll try to get better at how I respond, okay?"

Viggo blinks at me some more, then finally opens his mouth, but just as I think he's about to speak, something thuds inside the closet across the hallway, followed by a muffled curse.

My head snaps toward the sound, my heart racing. Viggo . . . does not seem nearly as surprised by this as I expected him to be.

In fact, Viggo only seems deeply annoyed.

Curious, I turn toward the closet, reach for the handle, and turn it.

"Tallulah—"

Out tumble three very large men, tripping and bumping into each other. It takes a second before I recognize them—Ren, Viggo's older brother; Oliver, his younger brother; and Seb, his sister Ziggy's boyfriend.

Oliver gasps for air, lifting his hands in praise. "Sweet, fresh oxygen. Thank you, Jesus."

Seb, looking peeved, rakes a hand through his disheveled hair. "Remind me never to hide in a closet with you ever again. You are the least quiet or still person *ever*."

"I don't like confined spaces," Oliver says defensively. "Besides, *you*—"

"Tallulah!" Ren smiles wide and seems to be trying for a casual lean against the closet door, which doesn't work out too well—it just makes the door swing back and smack Seb in the shoulder. "Fancy seeing you here."

"Christ," Viggo mutters, scrubbing his face.

I turn toward Viggo. "Why were you hiding your brothers in a closet?"

"We," Seb says, pointer finger darting between him and Viggo, "are not related. Thank God."

Viggo shoves Seb. Seb shoves him back. Ren wraps an arm around Seb's neck, breaking up the skirmish, and grins at him affectionately. "Seb, you're in way too deep now. It's called honorary Bergman status."

"It's too early for earnest feelings, Ren," Seb pleads. "I can't choke up before noon; it's a policy I have."

"Come here, you big secret softie," Ren says, tugging him in for a hug.

"We'll just be going," Oliver says, doing a little moonwalk past us, flashing me a smile. "Have a great day!"

"What is going *on*?" I ask.

Oliver pauses mid-moonwalk. Ren and Seb freeze in the throes of their hug.

Viggo sighs and massages the bridge of his nose. "I might have panicked to them that my place was a mess and you were coming over. And then these fools decided that meant they needed to show up and *help* me."

Seb rolls his eyes. "How *cruel* of us."

Viggo scowls at them. "I didn't ask for help."

"But he clearly needed it," Oliver says out of the side of his mouth.

Viggo lunges at Oliver, fencing style. Oliver parries with his arm, then ripostes with a poke to his ribs. Viggo yelps and spins away.

"Twelve months younger, but who's got a two-inch-wider wingspan?" Oliver lifts his arms in triumph and does a celebratory jazz square as he says, "This guy right here!"

"I hope you pull your groin box-stepping out of here," Viggo grumbles.

"Excuse me," I tell them. "Cute as this cuddle slash tickle fest is, I believe we've gotten off topic."

"Oh, right," Oliver says. "So we helped Viggo make his house not look like a bomb went off in it, and as a token of thanks, he shoved us in a closet."

I frown at the three of them, confused. "And you . . . went . . . willingly?"

Viggo turns toward me. "I didn't see your text that you were on your way until you were literally ringing the doorbell. I panicked and told them to hide." He glares their way. "Which worked out *so well*."

"Seb poked my tickle spot!" Oliver says.

Seb sighs. "It was an *accident*."

"Now, guys," Ren says diplomatically, "let's just take a breath and—"

"While I deeply appreciate your unsolicited help," Viggo says, herding the three of them down the hallway, "please, *please*, just go."

I bite my lip, fighting a laugh as they turn and say their goodbyes. Oliver squeezes Viggo in a hug that Viggo listlessly returns, patting his back. Seb kisses his fingertips, then brings them to Viggo's cheek, which Viggo swats away. Ren gently tugs Viggo's ball cap low and grins, saying, "Turn that frown upside down, brother."

"Yeah, yeah," Viggo mutters, following them out as they traipse through the main living area toward the door.

"Bye, Tallulah!" they all call.

Oliver throws Viggo an exaggerated wink. Seb wiggles his eyebrows. Ren gives Viggo two thumbs-up.

Viggo sighs as he shuts the door behind them, then turns toward me. His cheeks are bright pink. "Well. That was humiliating. And awkward. I'm sorry about that."

"Nothing to be sorry for," I tell him. "It's nice that you have family who are so supportive."

"It's invasive is what it is." He turns the lock emphatically on his back door.

"That accomplishes nothing!" Oliver yells from outside. "You gave me a key, remember?"

"Get out of here already!" Viggo hollers at the door, before tipping his head back, staring up at the ceiling. He sighs despondently as he yanks off his ball cap, rakes a hand through his hair, then tugs it back on. "The worst part is, I deserve it."

"How so?"

Viggo drops his head. His eyes meet mine. "I *might* have overstepped a little bit over the years in the area of my family's love lives—well, their lives in general, honestly—and now my chickens are coming home to roost."

I don't know what it is about this moment, whether it's just how damn cute the past five minutes have been, how endearing I find his pink-cheeked embarrassment, how funny it is to think of Viggo being all holier-than-thou with his romance-novel wisdom, and now finally, he's getting a taste of his own medicine, but I feel it, bubbling up from deep inside me, the unfamiliar tug of a wide, delighted smile.

I throw my head back and laugh.

ELEVEN

Viggo

Playlist: "Wish I Knew You," The Revivalists

For a second, I'm too annoyed that I'm being laughed at to process what's happening.

Tallulah Clarke isn't just laughing, and I mean, really laughing—she's *smiling*.

And holy hell, does it transform her. Those dimples pop in her round cheeks, even deeper and more luscious than the dimples that my thumbs found at her elbows. Smiling lifts the rosy apples of her cheeks, brightens her wide, dark-lashed eyes like sunlight spilling through amber.

And suddenly, my brothers and Seb wholeheartedly embarrassing me, Tallulah's schadenfreude showing in the face of my confession that I'm reaping what I've sown, doesn't matter.

All that matters is that Tallulah Clarke is standing in my living room, laughing straight from the heart of her, smiling from ear to ear.

My heart thuds inside my chest. I'm not sure what's happening, why it's doing that. Maybe it's the victory that, even at my expense, I made her smile. Maybe it's that it was unexpected, earning her unadulterated delight, and I fucking love surprises.

It's so damn confusing. This woman, what she makes me feel, is *so* damn confusing. It isn't butterflies in my stomach, more like ants under my skin. It's not that light-headed, delirious magic I've been holding out for, but instead a tightness in my chest, a knot in my gut.

Considering everything I know about love from what I've read in romance novels, what I've seen in my family, I'm not falling for Tallulah Clarke. But I'm certainly not unaffected by her either.

Is it just the lust talking? I know I'm physically drawn to Tallulah, but I've been physically drawn to people before. This feels different. This feels *more*, not a fleeting itch I can scratch, but a bone-deep, grating, nagging *something* I can't put my finger on.

I just don't know what it is. But maybe I don't have to. Maybe I can just . . . enjoy it. Tallulah certainly seems to be enjoying herself, considering she's *still* laughing.

"Okay, pipsqueak." I fold my arms across my chest. "It's not *that* funny."

Tallulah stops laughing abruptly, fire in her eyes. "*What* did you just call me?"

I have two sisters. I know the look of murderous fury in the female gaze, and I am well trained to put as much distance between myself and that as humanly possible. I take a reflexive, life-preserving step back, placing a club chair between me and Tallulah, then tell her, "I called you 'pipsqueak.'"

Her gaze narrows. "I will *not* be answering to that nickname."

"I'll workshop it. We'll find a good one for you."

"We will not." She folds her arms across her chest, mirroring me.

"Mmm, we will. Nicknames are mandatory for roomies."

She rolls her eyes, dropping her arms. "I'm beginning to think that's going to be your excuse for a lot of things, Viggo—'it's what roomies do.'"

I grin, happy to be in familiar territory, reminding Tallulah I'm just as capable of getting under her skin as she is at getting under mine. Even though I feel a twinge of regret that her gorgeous smile has vanished.

Maybe more than a twinge.

I console myself that I've got time to earn it, the next two months we're roomies, and under less self-deprecating circumstances. I'll get her to smile again.

"This isn't a one-way street, Tallulahloo," I tell her. "You're welcome to bring your own mandates for roomie life."

Another laugh leaves Tallulah, but this one's soft and low in her chest, a little sinister. She sweeps up her purse and walks toward me, flames still dancing in her eyes. "Oh, trust me, I will." She pokes my chest. "Just you wait."

I grin down at her. "How long will I be waiting?"

"Twenty-four hours," she says breezily, strolling toward the door. "I'll be here, same time tomorrow, ready to move in." With a pause, she spins, hand on the doorknob. "When I show up, I'd appreciate it if you weren't stashing any more family members in the closets. I've got a lot of clothes. I'm going to need all the room I can get."

———

"A lot of clothes." Talk about an understatement. Clothes might just be the only thing Tallulah owns, judging by the fact that she's *two hours* into unpacking and she's still strolling between all the available closets, hanging things up, muttering to herself as she works.

I am not allowed to help. I was told that very firmly, after I brought in the eighth garment bag that was delivered. Tallulah hired movers. For her clothes. I laughed so hard after she tipped them and shut the door, I nearly pulled a muscle.

That may be why I've been banished to my living room, forbidden from helping her unpack.

"Sure you don't need any help?" I call from the couch.

"No!" Tallulah calls from her room. "Lest I be called a precious princess again for accepting *help* in moving my very expansive, expensive wardrobe."

"I didn't call you a precious princess."

Tallulah pops her head out of her room, glaring at me. "It was implied. You laughed so hard at my movers, you squeaked."

"Wheezed," I correct.

The glare intensifies. "No wonder you and Charlie are friends. Semantics. All you do is play with words."

"Tallulah." I spring up from the couch and stroll toward her, down the hall. "Let's have a reset."

"A reset, huh?" She's clutching a dress to her like it's a shield, glaring up at me. The iridescent material shimmers, shifting from bronze to amethyst to turquoise, an oil spill spread across the fabric's silky surface. I can picture that dress poured down Tallulah's lush curves. The bronze would bring out her eyes; the turquoise, echo her hair; the purple, pop against her golden skin.

"That's a lovely dress, Lu."

Her eyes narrow to distrustful slits. "It's going to take more than complimenting haute couture to make me forgive you."

I sigh, leaning against the doorway. "I'm sorry, all right? It's just . . . kind of adorable bordering on absurd, how many clothes you have. It tickled me that you had all your other worldly possessions contained in a backpack you rode over with, but you needed a U-Haul to move your clothes. C'mon, you're a writer—you know that's funny."

Tallulah arches an eyebrow. Her mouth quirks a little, as if she's trying not to smile. "I like my clothes, okay?"

I sense a shift in her, that arctic anger thawing. Warmth hums through me, and I reach for the dress, drifting my finger down its satin smoothness. "I can see why. You have very pretty clothes."

She sniffs as she stares down at the dress. "Thank you."

"I'm sorry I laughed at your wardrobe's . . . volume. I swear I wasn't making fun of you. I was just a little surprised, mostly de-lighted by it. But I shouldn't have laughed. I apologize."

Tallulah peers up at me beneath those thick, dark lashes, the eyeliner she always wears winged out from her eyes, accentuating them. "That's okay. I'm sorry I laughed at you yesterday. It was the same thing . . . I wasn't laughing at you. I was just . . . entertained by it, the dramatic—"

"Irony," I finish for her.

"Yeah." A soft half smile lifts her mouth, not nearly as full as the one she let loose yesterday, but it's a triumph all the same, the best kind of triumph—not a victory *over* her, but *with* her. This moment feels like a little win for both of us.

Tallulah clears her throat, and I blink, realizing I was staring at her. She's flushed, tiny ice-blue hairs stuck to her cheeks, the nape of her neck. A lone tendril clings to her clavicle, drawing my gaze to the dewy skin revealed by her scoop-neck blue tank top. Heat rushes through me. I glance away and clear my throat.

It's warm. *I'm* warm. Tallulah looks warm, too, judging by her flush. It's hard work, unpacking, and the sun's beating down on the house. I should turn on the AC so it's more comfortable for her. Tallulah is obviously used to nice things, and I'm sure that in-cludes a living space that isn't hot as hell.

Pushing off the threshold, I take a step back. "I'm gonna turn on the AC, then whip up some lunch for us. How's that sound?"

Tallulah opens her mouth, then closes it, like she's debating with herself how to answer me. Finally, she says, "That . . . would be great. Thanks."

"Sure thing, Tallulahloo."

Just as I'm starting down the hall toward the main room, the doorbell for my house rings. I frown. I'm not expecting anyone.

"Oh!" Tallulah calls. "That's the movers with my shoes. Hope you have some more closets tucked in this place, because I'm definitely going to need them!"

———

I do not, in fact, have more closets for Tallulah's shoes, and when we realized we needed some way of storing them, there was only one solution: IKEA. Besides the A-frame and a well-stocked romance-only bookstore, IKEA is my happiest happy place. It is not, apparently, Tallulah's.

"What's with the face?" I ask her.

Tallulah frowns up at me. "This joint smells like mass-produced meatballs and hoodwinkery."

I snort. "Hoodwinkery?"

"They hoodwink you. They show all their furniture assembled, then make you go buy it in pieces and put it together."

"Well, Lula, some people *enjoy* putting things together."

"Well, Viggo, this gal enjoys paying people to put things together."

I come to a dead stop. Tallulah turns and peers my way, fake potted succulent plant in hand. "Tallulah, we are *not* paying someone to assemble your Ställ shoe cabinet."

"You're right." She slips the fake succulent into her IKEA bag and tucks a loose piece of blue hair back into her bun. "We're paying them to assemble my Ställ shoe cabinet*s*. I need at least three."

I choke on my disbelief as Tallulah spins on her heel and marches off. I jog and catch up to her in three strides. "Lu, I'm half-Swedish. I can*not* allow for a single piece of IKEA furniture in my home to be assembled by some . . . some stranger, when these two hands are perfectly fit, when my genetics are *designed* to do this."

She rolls her eyes. "That's absurd."

"It is not. I will not back down on this." I reach inside her bag, pulling out the fake succulent, and set it on a stand of bulk-packaged votive candles. "And I will not back down on this either: no fake plants."

Tallulah gasps. "Hey! That's for *my* room. It's the only kind of plant I can keep alive!"

"Lula, I got some tough news for you, but you deserve to know the truth—it was never alive to begin with."

She growls in frustration, then lunges for the fake plant, shoving it in her bag again. "But I want plants in my room!"

I yank the fake plant out of her bag again and slam it back down on the candle stand. "Then we'll get you some!"

"I'll *kill* them!" she yells.

"I won't *let* you kill them!" I yell back.

A couple with a few kids trailing behind them gives us a concerned look.

Tallulah reaches for the fake succulent, but I swipe it up, holding it over my head. "No. Fake. Plants. Tallulah. For the love of God."

"You're *so* rude!" She scowls at me. "Using my height disadvantage against me."

"Desperate times, pipsqueak."

She stomps on my toe. I hiss, hopping as she storms away. "Fine!" she yells over her shoulder. "We'll get real plants! We'll buy the flatpack cabinets and assemble them! But I'm warning you, you're going to regret it."

Turns out, Tallulah's right. I do regret my decision when, two hours later, I find myself halfway through assembling the first of *four* Ställ shoe organizers. While I consider myself a nonviolent man, I am about to break something.

"That's wrong," Tallulah says, standing over me, pointing at the first half-assembled shoe organizer. "We definitely put it on backward."

I glare up at her. "Tallulah, would you let a man put a shoe cabinet together in peace?"

"Nope." She plops down beside me. "I get to participate. They're my shoe cabinets. I paid for them."

"I offered to pay for them," I mutter between gritted teeth.

"With what money?" she asks.

"Credit card debt would have been well worth it to spare myself this torture."

She rolls her eyes. "When I move out and leave them here, you can reimburse me, but for now, they are my purchase, and I am helping ensure their successful assembly."

"'Helping,'" I grumble sourly.

Tallulah sits back, an evil little smirk lifting her lips. "I told you you'd regret it."

I shake my head, taking a deep breath as I refocus on the furniture. It's that or scream into a pillow, and I can't let Tallulah know how much she's getting to me.

"Maybe having them assembled *wouldn't* have been so bad after all," she whispers, leaning in. Her breath is hot on my neck, and a shiver rolls down my spine.

"I swear to God, Lula." Turning my head, I'm about to glare at her in warning, but she's right there, her mouth a few flimsy inches from mine. I stare at her, fighting the impulse to grab that bun, wrench her head back, and kiss her so hard, so long, until she stops driving me up the damn wall. Her gaze dips to my mouth, then flicks back up. A swallow works down her throat.

Tallulah's phone beeps, breaking the moment. She blinks away, then picks it up, silencing the sound. Then she stands, brushes off her hands, and says, "Dinnertime."

TWELVE

Tallulah

Playlist: "I Think I Like You," Donora

Viggo does not join me for dinner, despite the alarm I set to make sure he'd stop working and eat something. I didn't have the courage to harass him into eating when he didn't follow me out of the room, even though I think it might have helped improve his mood. I know it improved mine. Between the work of moving, unpacking, and shopping at IKEA, I got a little low, and I feel better now, having eaten. Even so, I can't blame my behavior solely on my blood sugar drop, though it likely played a minor role in my moodiness. Because I know I willfully pushed him. I've been willfully pushing him since the moment we walked into IKEA, side by side, bickering about cutting through the store straight to the organizers (my preference) and walking through the whole display floor (his), when I realized what it looked like, what it felt like:

Like we were an *us*. Like we were a unit, Viggo and Tallulah, steps in synch, his stride politely shortened for my sake as we begrudgingly compromised and agreed we'd browse the living room and bedroom sections before heading toward the shoe organizers.

It scared the hell out of me. Because it felt—it *feels*—easy, familiar, being this way with him. His woodsy sugar-spice scent, his arm brushing mine as we walk, the way he holds open doors for me and calls me goofy nicknames; how he rolls with my snark and gives it right back, all with a warm smile on his face that's begun to thaw my icy edges.

And we're just getting started. I have two *months* of cohabitating with him to make it through.

I'm not deluded enough to think I'm incapable of caring about someone, wanting them—I just don't call it love, because I don't believe love is real. What I do believe is real is vulnerability, its power to draw you in, lower your defenses, teach you that you're safe to rely on this person you've opened yourself up to. It's so easy to get hurt then.

I'm not a therapy girlie—I just can't imagine pouring myself out to a stranger—but I have tried to understand myself a little better this past year, picked up a couple of books about family dysfunction, about attachment theory, and about how and why different people react to intimacy: anxiously, avoidantly, securely.

I'm avoidant. I know this. I'm averse to opening myself up to people. There's this powerful grip around my chest that tightens when I try with Viggo. It's too appealing already, to trust his goodness, to crave more time with our feisty wordplay, that energy that sparks between us, to lean toward every part of his body that my body wants. When I'm around him, I feel profoundly out of my depth. I felt that way especially today.

So I pushed. I bickered not in the fun way but the petty way; I broke his concentration and criticized our IKEA shoe organizer assembly. Because that made me feel safe.

Now I just feel like shit.

I'm better than this. I'm *braver* than this. No, I'm not experienced in living healthily with someone, without sex or passive aggression gluing us together. No, I'm not practiced at letting anyone help me with anything the way he has and will, but it's two measly months, and yesterday, today, they're going to be the exceptions, not the rule. Soon Viggo will be busy with his fully opened store. I'll be busy working there quietly in the wings, and when I'm not, I'll be writing and revising. This is just a . . . tricky moment. I can make it through without being a jerk to him. I can and I *want* to.

Carefully placing the bread on top of his sandwich, I add a generous handful of potato chips, a thick dill pickle spear. It's nothing fancy like the fresh pesto avocado chicken salad Viggo made for us at lunch that I noticed he ate very little of, but it's a meal nonetheless. It's the best I can do.

I grab an ice-cold seltzer from inside the fridge door, shut the door with my hip, then lift the plate from the counter, armed with my peace offering.

I just hope he'll accept it.

THIRTEEN

Viggo

Playlist: "Along the Way," The Hunts

I'm in a foul mood when Tallulah walks in. My back is to her, but I hear her footsteps, feel her silence weighted with something enigmatic, something I can't begin to decipher. There's nothing about this woman I can decipher—how I feel about her or how she seems to feel about me. The past hour spent assembling these shoe organizers, the mindless distraction of following the instructions to build the first one, replicating the procedure as I began the second, has settled me somewhat, but not as much as I'd like.

I can't stop fixating on Tallulah, how twisted up I am by my frustration with her. This—the two of us being roommates, working together—wasn't supposed to be another hard thing to tackle. It was supposed to be simple, easy-breezy, swapping skills, rooming together for a couple of months, then parting ways.

Right now, two months sounds like a very long, exhausting time.

"You missed a screw," she says.

I shut my eyes and exhale slowly, calming myself. "Not now, Tallulah."

A ceramic plate lands gently on the floor beside me with a quiet *clink*. I turn, just enough to inspect it, and feel my heart do a weird kick. Soft, thick-cut sourdough bread. A few juicy slices of tomato on top of arugula and thin-sliced turkey. Beside it, a towering pile of kettle-cooked potato chips, a chunky dill pickle spear.

My mouth waters and my stomach grumbles. My body's just realized how hungry it is. Perhaps part of my shitty mood can be explained by the fact that it's—I glance at my watch—seven in the evening, and I've hardly eaten today.

"I was trying to make a joke," she says, lowering to the ground a few feet away from me. I'm already reaching for the sandwich, taking a bite that puts a hefty dent in it. "About the screw."

"Hmph." I stare at her, chewing slowly as I watch her crack open a seltzer can and set it beside my plate. Goddamn, this is a good sandwich. Lots of whole-grain mustard, just how I like it, and plenty of mayo. There's something else I can't place, something unexpected, but it's good. It makes everything taste . . . more.

"Italian seasoning." Tallulah nods her chin toward the sandwich. "That's what you're tasting. And lots of black pepper."

My eyes narrow. How did she know I was wondering that?

"You looked perplexed," she explains, once again apparently reading my mind. "I reasoned you were trying to figure out what was on it that was unexpected."

I take my time chewing, then swallow. After picking up a chip and crunching into it, I take a bite of dill pickle spear. Having left her hanging long enough, I tell her, "It's good. Thanks."

Tallulah's staring at me, her gaze unflinching. She doesn't say anything, and it's annoying. She's so good at staying quiet, holding the upper hand.

"That was another brownie moment," she finally says.

I lift my eyebrows, then take another bite of pickle. I'm quiet. She can have a taste of her own medicine.

"I panicked," she continues. "I don't know how to live well with someone like you."

"Like what?"

She huffs, but she doesn't seem annoyed, more like . . . stumped, as if she's searching for the right words. "Friendly. Emotionally well-adjusted. Determinedly helpful."

Helpful.

My stomach sours. I've been "helpful" to a lot of people over the years. I like to be helpful. But I've also learned what often comes after I'm helpful, when the way I'm simply trying to be useful seemingly becomes too much—when *I'm* too much. Unaware that I'm doing it, I push and shove my way around, take it too far. Say more than I've been asked to. Suggest more than I should. That's when people pull away. They like me for my helpfulness, until how I'm helpful bothers them, then they don't. Then they're done.

Not everyone's done that, not my family, not some good people over the years who've shown me they like all of me—loud, chatty, inquisitive, curious me—and stuck by me, but enough people have to make me wary.

And I think that's why I'm so pissed off. Because here I am again, with Tallulah Clarke, who already has a history of being all high-and-mighty, leaving me once more feeling like an asshat.

"I do appreciate the help," Tallulah adds, her brow furrowed as if she's confused, uneasy about how quiet I'm being.

See, Tallulah? Two can play this game.

"I'm just . . . unfamiliar with it," she continues. "I don't handle it well. And I coped by being petty. My blood sugar got a little low, too, which isn't an excuse, just a context. I get moody and irritable when it's low. So . . . I made you a sandwich by way of apology, and I know I keep saying sorry, but I promise, I'll do better."

I stare at her, turning her words over, glancing back down to the sandwich that she made me. I can't remember the last time someone made me something to eat, except for Mom at family dinners, and more often than not, I'm right beside her cooking in the kitchen, happy to be there, but still . . . this is . . . rare.

It feels good.

And now, as I take another bite of my sandwich and weigh how to respond, having eaten most of it at this point and feeling remarkably more human, I can see that I wasn't blameless in this situation either. I projected my way of doing things onto Tallulah—I wouldn't budge on leaving the fake succulent when she confessed she just wanted a plant in her room that wouldn't die on her; I insisted on us assembling the shoe organizers.

I was a bit of an asshole.

I was pushy. Not my low-level, good-natured, excusable pushiness, but my full-throttle, inconsiderate, steamrolling pushiness.

Chewing my last bite of sandwich, I brush my fingers off over the plate. "I'm sorry, too," I tell her. "I was a pushy asshole back at IKEA. About the fake plant. About assembling the shoe organizers. We wouldn't have been squabbling over the shoe organizers if I had just let you do what you wanted and pay to have them assembled."

Tallulah peers at me intensely, head tipped. "I mean, yeah, you're right. But that doesn't cancel out my bullshit. I messed up. You messed up. We both did."

Slowly, I push the plate toward her. "Truce?"

Leaning forward, she reaches not for a handful from the mountain of potato chips still left, but for the last juicy bite of dill pickle spear. Of course she does.

She pops it in her mouth, then says, "Truce. Now, you sit and eat your potato chips. I'll chip away at this organizer."

My stomach sinks. She doesn't want my help anymore.

"Then," she adds, spinning the instructions so she can see them, "you join me when you're ready, and we'll work together. How's that sound?"

A smile that has no business being so wide breaks across my

face. I duck my head, tugging down my ball cap, hoping I've disguised just how pleased I am. "Sounds great."

Tallulah stands, arms raised in triumph, bright-eyed and rosy-cheeked. "We did it!"

I smile up at her, then glance toward the four finished shoe organizers neatly lined along her bedroom wall. "We did."

"And we didn't kill each other." She bends and offers me a hand.

I high-five it, my smile widening. Hyped-up Tallulah is too damn cute.

"This," she says, "deserves a celebratory drink. Whiskey?"

I frown. "I don't have any. I've got some beers, though."

She waves a hand. "I brought some. You can have a beer if you want, but I have earned myself a nice, neat pour of Lagavulin."

"Laga-what-a?" I spring up, following her out of her room, down the hall.

"Lagavulin," she says over her shoulder. "My favorite whiskey. When my book hit the bestseller list, Dad got me a bottle . . ." Her voice trails off.

I want to follow up. I'm a curious guy, and Tallulah's family is largely a mystery to me but for the occasional tipsy statement Charlie throws out about her "fucked up family."

Since Charlie came back into Ziggy's life in adulthood, my sister has only painted me the broadest picture of the Clarke family's dysfunction, and I haven't felt like it's my business to inquire any further. Except now, I sort of do. I watch Tallulah roll her shoulders back like she's trying to shake off something bad, and there's a knot in my chest. I want to know. I want to understand. I want to be there for her.

*She's your roommate. Your barely friendly roommate. And she'll
be gone in two months. Settle down. Don't. Push.*

That voice of reason inside me is right. I have no right to push,
no reason to. I can care about Tallulah and not know all her business, especially the complicated, messy nuances of her family. If
she wanted me to know, she'd tell me.

"It's a good whiskey," she says, turning into the kitchen area.
"Smooth, rich, smoky. You're welcome to try it."

I shrug. "Sure. I'll give it a whirl."

Tallulah frowns, scouring the kitchen counters. "Well, I'd offer it to you, but I don't see it anywhere. I swear I left it right here."
She points to the right of the range, where the olive oil sits in a
large green glass bottle with a pouring spout.

"Oh." Suddenly, my memory is jogged. Tallulah dumped a number of things on the counter when she got here this morning, taking all of it with her down the hall except a tall bottle whose label
I didn't bother to read but figured was liquor. I swept it up without
thinking and put it in the liquor cabinet. "That's my bad," I tell her.

Reaching, I open the cabinet above the fridge, then pull down
the bottle I stashed there this morning.

Tallulah frowns, hands on her hips. "That's not going to work."

I hand it to her and watch her walk down the counter until she
spots the glass-front cabinet revealing the small mason jar tum-
blers I have. "What do you mean?"

"I can't reach that," she says. "In fact, I don't know what I *can*
reach in this kitchen."

I scratch the back of my neck. "Sorry about that. During reno,
I installed the cabinets higher than is typical."

I frown, remembering Axel, the tallest in our family, saying in
his deep, quiet voice, "You should install them standard height.
Someone else might want to use these cabinets one day, and they
probably won't be as tall as you."

I hate when my brother's right.

Tallulah opens the cabinet door and huffs, reaching on tiptoe. I rush her way, reaching over her back for the glasses she seemed to be going for. "Here you go," I tell her.

Tallulah glances up, and suddenly I realize how close she is, inside my arms, how good she smells, something expensive and quietly alluring, deceptively rich and floral. She glances away as I set down the glasses, her eyes on the task of pulling out her whiskey bottle's cork.

I take a step back and open the fridge, letting the ice-cold air knock some sense into me. I have to stop doing this, letting my lizard brain override my good sense whenever I get close to her. But, shit, is it hard. She smells so good. She's sexy and soft and my hands ache to touch her and learn her, to drag her hands down my body so she can touch and learn me, too.

Roommates. We. Are. Roommates. Nothing more.

Cooling myself down, settling my thoughts, I take longer than strictly necessary finding a beer that appeals to me, then pop the top off against the counter.

"Okay, Viggo." Tallulah turns and faces me, holding two mason jars, one filled with a hefty glug of whiskey, the other with just a sliver. "We survived me moving in. We made it through IKEA in one piece. We assembled furniture and didn't kill each other. This is a victory." Eyebrows lifted, the barest coy smile softening her mouth, she raises her glass. "I say we get a little sauced."

———

"This," I tell Tallulah, setting down my whiskey glass, "tastes like a bonfire in my mouth. And that is not a compliment."

She sticks out her tongue. Fuck, it's cute. "You," she says, pointing with her glass, "have no taste."

"Excuse me!" I slap a hand to my chest. "I have impeccable taste."

"Not when it comes to whiskey you don't."

I take a deep drink of my beer, washing away the ash and soot taste of the whiskey. Blech. "Let's move on. We called a truce, remember?"

Tallulah nods, leaning forward, pouring herself more whiskey. Dusk bathes the living room in a cool blue glow, and the candles I lit flicker around us, warming the shadowy corners with fading gold light. Her hair's fallen out of her bun, ice-blue waves crashed against the shore of her shoulders, the twisty old telephone-cord-looking hair tie she was using discarded on my couch. I pick it up and wind it around my finger.

"So." I lean into my corner of the sofa.

"So." Tallulah leans into her corner of the sofa, glass in hand.

"I have a buddy, Wesley, who rescued a cat last month." I drain my beer, needing to wet my throat. "Turns out, Wesley's rescue cat was pregnant, which now means he has a litter of rescue kittens, too."

She peers my way, eyebrow arched. "And?"

"And I was, uh . . ." I scratch at the back of my neck. "I was going to adopt all of them."

Her eyes widen. "*All* of them?"

"Well, there are only five."

"*Five!*" she yells, leaning forward.

"Five," I confirm. "They're weaned, eating food, using a litterbox; they won't be high-maintenance to own."

She snorts into her glass. "Oh, sure. Just what you need. A handful of 'not-high-maintenance' kittens on top of a brand-new bookstore you have to singlehandedly run."

"I'm not running it singlehandedly," I remind her, smiling. "I have you, too."

She sighs. "Was there a point to this feline anecdote?"

"There was. I wanted to make sure you aren't allergic before I brought them home."

Tallulah peers at me, eyes narrowed, biting her lip.

My smile widens. "You're seriously considering lying about an allergy so I won't get them, aren't you?"

"Maybe," she admits. "But we called a truce. This probably applies."

"Definitely applies."

"Well then, if that applies, say I buy more IKEA furniture, the truce applies to letting me pay to have it assembled."

I make a pained noise in the back of my throat. "Damn, you drive a hard bargain. Fine."

"Five cats," she mutters into her whiskey glass. "To be clear, baby-sitting those little needle-clawed furballs is not part of the work I've agreed to. And so help me God, if they get their paws on my wardrobe."

I know I'm practically beaming at her, but I can't help it. Tallulah clearly hasn't had much exposure to kittens, because they melt even the frostiest of hearts. I can't wait to see her fall head over heels for them.

"Great. Good." I crack open a new beer, then take a swig. "So, next order of business. Just confirming, you haven't developed a dog allergy since Gertrude Stein the sheepdog?"

Her eyes widen to saucers. "Seriously? You're getting a dog?"

"Just two," I reason.

"Oh, *hell* no."

"C'mon, Lu, be honest. Dog allergy?"

She sighs. "No. I don't have a dog allergy. But you cannot really think adopting two dogs in addition to five kittens is a good idea right now."

"They're old sweeties. They just need a quiet corner to sleep in, a couple walks a day, and some food and water. I can't leave them at the shelter anymore. If you took one look at them, you wouldn't be able to either."

Tallulah stares up at the ceiling and sighs again. "This is going to be a freaking animal menagerie."

"Isn't it the best?"

"The best," she says dryly.

I stare at her, dying sun and candlelight bathing her in soft, dwindling light. Everything about her glows, and in her blue tank and skintight faded jeans, she looks so fucking gorgeous, I can't help but drink her in.

Tallulah tips her head, noticing me staring at her. "What is it?"

I bring the beer to my mouth, then take a long pull. "Nothing."

She arches an eyebrow. "And yet you're staring at me."

I am staring at her. I feel the beer warming my body, loosening my lips. "Twilight suits you, Lu. That's all."

Tallulah's quiet for a second, blinking, before she tips back her whiskey glass and drains it. "I know."

I laugh, hard and right from my belly.

"Suits you, too," she says casually.

My laughter abruptly dies away.

"At least," she adds, "it would, if three-fourths of your face weren't hidden behind the remnants of Bigfoot's last trip to the hairdresser."

I gape. "Ex*cuse* me!"

"Your beard," she laments. "It's out of control. You're a pair of eyeballs, a strong nose, and a beard."

"What's wrong with that?"

Tallulah sets her whiskey on one of the crochet coasters adorning my coffee table, then leans forward, crawling across the sofa, landing up on her knees right beside me. Her hands clasp my face and frame it. Gently she smooths down my beard, tracing the contours of my jaw. Her thumbs sweep the perimeter of my mouth, as if she's searching for my lips.

She's quiet, her face tight with concentration. Inching closer, she lifts my beard and feels along my throat, beneath my jaw. My breath catches in my lungs, and my brain short-circuits, processing all the places she's touching me, how good it feels—her knees pressed into my thigh, her fingertips grazing my skin through my beard, her thumbs tracing my jaw.

Her eyes meet mine. "What's wrong is that you're *hiding*."

I swallow roughly. "I'm not hiding."

But in a sense, she's right. I am. I'm hiding my loneliness, my fear of failure, my exhaustion from years of hustling, scrimping, and saving, my ache for someone who wants to see and love *all* of that.

"You," she whispers, leaning in, clutching my jaw between her hands, "are hiding a hot-as-hell bone structure beneath all that beard. It's a tragedy."

Suddenly I don't know what to do with my hands. I plant them hard into the sofa, my palms crushed against the woven linen. "I don't know about that."

"Do *not*," she says, leaning closer, her mouth a breath away from mine, "even try to tell me you don't know you're a smoke show."

I try to swallow again, but it's so hard to think, to do the simplest thing, while she's touching me like this, calling me hot, that I almost forget how to do it. "How do you know I'm a smoke show? Last time you saw me clean-shaven, I was eighteen."

"Yeah. And you were hot back then."

My eyes snap wide. "You thought I was *hot* in college?"

She laughs. Laughs! "Of course I did."

"Why the hell is that funny?"

"Viggo, *you* knew you were hot back then."

"I did *not*. If I did think anyone thought me hot, it certainly didn't include you."

She waves that away like my logic is a gnat, just as easily brushed off. "Nonsense."

"Not nonsense," I tell her emphatically. "Not nonsense in the least." My heart's pounding, my head spinning. It's one thing to have had an unrequited crush on Tallulah. It's a whole other thing for her to have had a crush on me, too.

Then again, she just said she thought I was hot back then, not that she had a *crush* on me. There's a difference, at least to me. And I have to know if there's a difference to her.

"You thought I was hot," I tell her. "Does that mean . . . did you have a crush on me?"

Tallulah drops back, palms settling on her thighs. She's not as close as she was, but she's still close enough, I could lean forward and kiss her in a heartbeat, if I wanted to.

If *she* wanted me to.

Gracefully, Tallulah leans sideways into the sofa, untucking her legs, letting them dangle, her knees brushing mine. "Define 'crush.'"

I narrow my eyes, suspicious of this. "*You* define crush."

Tallulah shrugs, then pulls her phone from her pocket. After opening it, then typing, she says, eyes on her screen, "According to Merriam-Webster—"

"I don't want Merriam-Webster's definition," I tell her. "I want yours."

She peers at me intensely, quiet for a minute, before she tosses her phone aside on the sofa and says, "I thought you were cute, handsome even. But I don't think I ever let myself know you well enough to develop a crush."

It doesn't escape me that she still hasn't defined "crush." But I'm too taken by what she's said to call her on it. I stare at her, heart thudding hard against my ribs. "Why do you say it that way? That you didn't *let* yourself know me?"

She's quiet as she peers at the back of the sofa, an irregularity in the linen where the fabric is bunched into a knot in the weave. "Because it was a choice, not to know you. Because, if I had . . . I would have had a crush on you. And I didn't want to."

"Why not?" I press. "You're still not really answering me. You haven't even told me what 'a crush' means to you."

Tallulah glances at me sharply. "You and your damn questions. Fine. I define 'a crush' as wanting someone unattainable. Okay? Now, your turn. Did you have a crush on *me*?"

My brain whirs; my heart sprints in my chest as I stare at her, more of those "damn questions," as she calls them, flying through my thoughts.

Why didn't she want to have a crush on me?

Given how she defined crush, why was I unattainable to her?

"Viggo." She nudges my knees with hers. "Do what you do best. Talk."

Biting my lip, I drum my fingers on the couch. My fingertips are barely an inch from hers. "I thought you were stunning, sophisticated, so put together. You were mysterious and quiet, always bringing in those thick books with their bloodred covers."

Her mouth lifts at the corner.

"I was distracted by you," I tell her. "I swore you were doing it on purpose somehow, trying to sabotage my grade in that class, get a leg up on me."

A huff of a laugh leaves her. "Oh yeah, my entire personality and appearance were designed solely to fuck with your GPA."

"I didn't say it was rational." My fingers brush hers. Her fingers brush mine, too, then slide between them, up over my knuckles.

"You were distracted by me, huh?" Her eyes meet mine. "What does that mean?"

I stare at her, heat flooding my cheeks. The tiny, sober part of my brain is screaming at me that this is *not* what I should be doing with my platonic roommate, but the vast majority of me is *not* sober and does not give a single shit. "I thought about you a lot back then, Tallulah. I'll admit that."

"Thought about me . . . how?" She bites her lip. "Physically?"

I try to hold out, but I can't help it. I nod.

Her eyebrows lift. A soft, tiny smile tugs at the corner of her mouth, accentuating her beauty mark. "Reeeally?" She sounds annoyingly pleased.

I'm too turned on to care that she might be reveling in having the upper hand, too relieved to finally have admitted it.

A sigh leaves me as she slides her fingers over the backs of my hands to my wrist and says, her voice smoky and quiet, "Go on."

"Lu, I don't want to make this uncomfortable—"

"It's not for me," she says softly. "If it isn't for you either, tell me."

I swallow roughly and shift just a bit on the sofa, lifting my leg enough to hopefully hide what the command in her voice, what talking about this, does to me. "I thought about what it would be like to touch you. Kiss you. Taste you. Make you come undone. To have those big, beautiful eyes holding mine while I did it."

Her breath hitches. Her fingers curl around my wrist. "Did you ever . . . touch yourself to the thought of me?"

"Fuck, yes." I flip my hand and glide my palm along hers, savoring her shiver when I curl my fingers along her wrist. "So much. I tried not to, but you were all I could see when I closed my eyes, Lula, when I'd get myself off—"

A soft moan leaves her as Tallulah tugs me by the shirt, drawing me near. Our mouths are so close, I feel her breath and catch the trace of smoky whiskey. "I did that, too," she whispers.

A groan rumbles up my throat. It's a hell of a fantasy, but I don't believe it. No way did the chilly, close-lipped girl get herself off to the thoughts of a guy she wouldn't even acknowledge. "Yeah, right."

"I did." She drags her hand up my shirt, toward my neck, and pulls me closer, her breath hot on my ear as she whispers, "I made myself come all the time, thinking about you. I thought about your hands on my tits, your face buried between my legs, fucking me with your tongue. I was obsessed with you, your body, your hands, your mouth. It was infuriating."

"Shit," I moan, dropping my head to her shoulder. "You hid that very well."

"So did you," she whispers.

Her fingers slip so softly through my hair, I almost miss the sensation. Except that goose bumps dance across my neck, down my back. I turn my head, and my lips brush her collarbone. My hand grazes her waist, dying to wrap around her, drag her against me, and finally ease this ache. Her thumb trails down my ribs to my hip. I jerk reflexively, arching toward her touch.

Tallulah's head dips as I peer up at her. We stare at each other, breaths sawing, rough, out of our lungs.

"And that," she says, her voice as smoky as that whiskey she's been drinking, "is why I think the beard is a tragedy. I know what a face like yours inspires. At least think about giving it a trim."

Without another word, she slowly eases up off the sofa, then tugs my ball cap low, teasing, unexpectedly sweet. I tip back my hat and watch her walk straight down the hallway, shutting the door to her bedroom behind her.

And then I lie there on the sofa, unmoving.

For a very. Long. Time.

FOURTEEN

Tallulah

Playlist: "invisible string," Taylor Swift

I am never drinking with Viggo Bergman. Ever again.

My head pounds and my stomach is queasy, but the latter has very little to do with drinking too much alcohol, and thankfully, neither are due to my blood sugar being out of whack—I checked; it's always the first thing I check when I feel off. I'm nervous about bumping into him this morning, trying to survive this interaction without my trusty coping mechanism: avoidance.

Avoidance is not the healthiest way to live, I know this. But I'm still crossing every digit as I walk down the hall from my bedroom, hoping Viggo's sleeping off his hangover so I can get myself coffee without having to face him or what we did last night.

Or maybe, more accurately, what we did *not* do.

What we both clearly wanted to do and didn't.

He's attracted to me. After last night, I know that. And while, on the one hand, it's hot, exciting, gratifying—it's bad news for my commitment not to try to get in his pants.

As I round the corner into the kitchen, I throw out a silent plea to the uncaring universe, hoping it sticks anyway: *Let him still be asleep. Please let him still be asleep.*

When I enter the kitchen, my hopes are dashed.

There stands Viggo, mass-market historical romance in one hand as he pours hot water with the other, swirling it over a carafe filled with ground coffee beans. Like last year, out on the deck of the A-frame, he's working a romance-lover T-shirt (this one says *Unapologetic Romance Reader*) bed-head hair, and plaid slippers. This time, though, instead of sweatpants, he's wearing a threadbare pair of gray athletic shorts that do nothing to disguise the fact that Viggo either deals with significant morning wood or he's hurting from last night's unresolved lust as much as I am.

I scrunch my eyes shut so I won't stare at that formidable outline pressing into his shorts. Healthy or not, avoidance sounds pretty great right now.

Viggo doesn't seem to have noticed my arrival. I can take a few steps backward, turn the corner, and slink back to my room and wait him out, eat a snack from my nightstand, and read for an hour, however long it takes for him to disappear into a different part of the house to get dressed for the day, maybe take a shower—

The image of Viggo's naked body, what I imagine it might be, floods my mind. Those hard, strong arms flexing as he put together my shoe organizers last night. The peek of his stomach and his hips, as his shirt lifted the first day I came by, only to find him winded and sweaty. The sight of his long, muscular legs this morning. Every visual fragment I have of him coalesces into a filthy fantasy. Viggo, lean and hard and wet beneath the shower's spray, sudsy water sliding along his tan skin, droplets drifting down his taut stomach, those sharp hip bones, lower, where he's—

I grimace, eyes scrunched shut even harder, trying to banish the horny visual. When I take another careful step back, the floor beneath me lets out an outrageously loud *creeeeak*.

My eyes snap open. Viggo's romance novel lowers, just enough to reveal pale blue eyes, one arched eyebrow. "You that dependent on coffee, you can't walk forward or with your eyes open till you have it?"

I grumble under my breath, storming back into the kitchen, past him, toward his pullout pantry cabinet.

Viggo grins, his gaze darting over me as he sets down the kettle. "Coffee will be ready in just a minute."

"Thanks," I mutter, grabbing a breakfast bar from its box, the same one I eat most mornings. I pull out my PDM—personal diabetes management—device, a little iPhone look-alike that makes diabetic life a bit simpler than it used to be back when I had to manually calculate my insulin needs based on the carbs I'd eat, and enter the carbs in my breakfast bar to bolus the correct amount of insulin. Then I tear off the wrapper and take a big bite.

Viggo is quiet, leaning against the counter as he reads. It reminds me of last year on the deck, watching the sunrise, the way he sat still and watched the sun spill light across the ground, the treetops, his gaze drinking it all in.

Chewing my breakfast bar, I let myself do the same. I stand still and just . . . drink in the moment. I'm aware of how rare it is, how long it's been since I was fully present to the moment I was in and *felt*.

Cool morning air whispers through the open windows, rippling the curtains until they billow like ship sails. The coffee slides through the filter and lands in the glass carafe in a steady, soothing *drip drip drip*. Viggo drags his finger beneath the paper's edge of his romance novel, chased by a faint *shush* as he turns the page.

I feel hyperaware of every detail, nearly overwhelmed by the beauty of it. And I feel like I've been here before, like I've woken up from what I'd sworn was a dream that wasn't a dream after all. A shiver ripples through me. Déjà vu weirds me the hell out.

Plopping onto one of the kitchen island stools, I take another bite of my breakfast bar, surrounded by the rich aroma of percolating coffee, Viggo's visceral presence, soft clothes draped over his hard body, as he turns, sets down the novel, and pours a cup of coffee, then another.

I stare at him, so . . . torn, so confused.

Why do I feel this draw to him? Why can't I contain it like I have with plenty of other people? Put it in a box with discrete boundaries and points of contact in my life, my thoughts, my feelings?

What do I do about that?

Viggo turns and sets my coffee in front of me, then slips onto a stool on my other side. Our arms brush and I flinch, drawing back, hoping I hide the movement by lifting my mug to my lips and bracing my elbows on the counter.

Viggo sips his coffee. I sip mine. It's not boiling hot this time like it was at the A-frame, and I wonder if he remembered that I burned myself, how he managed to make it just right for me. Then I see the ice cube floating in the middle of my coffee cup, dissolving rapidly.

My heart thumps. I tip back my mug and gulp a third of its contents.

Viggo watches me as I lower my cup. Then he says, "Now that you're somewhat caffeinated, I want to talk about last night."

My eyes widen. I set down my coffee cup and stare into its contents' smooth, dark surface. "Okay."

Slowly, he turns my way on his stool. His knee knocks into mine. "I want to apologize for the direction I took things."

My head jerks up, my eyes finding his. "Viggo, I was right there with you. Hell, I started it."

"But you're my guest. You're helping me out, you're staying here, and it was shitty of me to talk about . . . *that*," he says delicately, "when we're going to be working together, living together. I never want you to feel cornered or uncomfortable—"

"Viggo." My voice is firm. I turn and face him, too.

This guy. I want to shake him. I want to kiss him. He is so different from any other person I've known. He so far outstrips anyone

I've ever met, so much thinking, feeling, worrying, the energy he expends, torn about doing what's right, about doing right by me, when we're barely even *friends*.

He swallows, his eyes searching mine. "Yes, Lula?"

Gently, I wrap my hand around his and squeeze. "You did nothing wrong. I wasn't uncomfortable. I'm sorry if I made *you* uncomfortable—"

"No," he says quickly, leaning in, his knees brushing mine again. "No, you didn't."

Our eyes search each other's. "You sure? Because you seem a bit . . . *uncomfortable* right now, if you know what I mean."

His eyes narrow as he seems to try to figure out what I mean. I point downward. He glances at his lap, then his head snaps up, heat high on his cheeks. "Tallulah Clarke!"

"What?" I laugh. "My dude, how was I not going to notice that?"

Viggo glares at me, scooching himself closer to the bar, which does very little to hide that he's still hard inside his shorts. "Our discussion was vivid last night, and its impact hasn't exactly . . . diminished."

"There is definitely nothing 'diminished' about that."

Viggo shakes his head, a smile breaking across his face, before he sips his coffee. "I also may have been reading a steamy scene when you walked in."

My jaw drops. "Wait. Romance novels do that to you?"

"Mm-hmm," he says, throwing me a glance over his coffee mug. "Now romance novels have your attention, don't they? Ten bucks says you pick one up before the week is over."

"Ten bucks? We've got a high roller, folks."

"I'm hedging my bets with you." He sips his coffee again.

I stare at him, fascinated. "They really give you boners?"

Viggo splutters into his coffee, wiping his mouth. I think I've scandalized him. "Tallulah," he chides.

"Oh, come on. Let's not be squeamish about you having an erection this morning, me waking up soaking wet—"

Viggo drops his coffee mug. It spills everywhere. "Christ, Tallulah." He grabs a rag from the other side of the counter and starts mopping up coffee. It's not really working, just painting the butcher block chocolate brown.

"What? There's nothing to be ashamed of." I leap off the stool, grab a rag from the oven handle, and wet it a little, add a squirt of soap, and chase his haphazard mop job with actual cleaning power. "It's just hormones and pheromones," I tell him. "We're two people who are attracted to each other physically and we talked about sexual desire; you were reading a sexy book; I had a vivid dream—"

"Tallulah," he warns.

I toss the rag aside. "That's going to affect us, is all I'm saying. Simple biology."

He turns his head, abandoning the coffee-soaked rag on the counter. His eyes search mine. "You really think that's all it boils down to? Hormones and animal impulses?"

"I won't generalize. Attraction and arousal aren't universal experiences, and people have all sorts of frameworks for them. But for me, for my body, my perspective, that is what it boils down to, yes."

"So what, then," he asks, leaning in, hands braced around his mug, "love is a lie?"

"A construct. And, as I said, that's just *my* perspective. I respect that you feel differently."

Viggo nods, staring down at his coffee. "So this . . . pull between us, our chemistry, you'd chalk that up to pheromones? And if . . ." He peers up, searching my eyes. "If one day you felt like something more existed between us, that would just be some hormones making you feel warm and fuzzy about me?"

I shrug. "A hormonal response because of an evolutionary adaptation that makes me predisposed to bond to people who make me feel good, yes."

"Hmm." He stares down at his coffee.

"How do you see it?"

Viggo's quiet for a minute, turning his coffee mug gently back and forth on the counter. "I see love as . . . elemental, something so deeply woven into everything that makes life feel *alive*. And I'm not even talking exclusively about romantic love. Love takes so many forms. Love for ourselves. Our surroundings. Strangers. Friends. Family. Partners. To me, to reduce it to only an animalistic impulse does it a profound disservice. I think—" He clears his throat, scrubs at the back of his neck. "I think love is . . . wrapping your arms around every emotion, even the hard ones, even when being numb seems so much safer. Love is hoping, even after disappointment has taught you not to. Love is that bone-deep hum of peace through your body when you're hugged hard, when you're listened to well, when you're not left alone in your sadness. Love is stubborn and persistent, an indomitable weed that springs up in those slivers of soft soil in our concrete-jungle existence. It's like . . ." He leans closer, wedging our legs together like puzzle pieces. "You remember, in high school science, we learned about subatomic particles, how they behave, that it means we don't *actually* ever truly touch each other?"

I frown, not sure where he's going with this. "Yes," I tell him slowly. "Electron repulsion."

He opens his hand on the counter. Hesitantly, I set mine on it. Viggo stares at our hands, clasping mine gently. I feel every callus on his palm, the heat of his skin. His thumb sweeps along the tender space between my knuckles, and warmth spills through me. I pin my thighs together.

"That's how I see it," he says quietly, "that both things can be true. Science is right. And so is this. We're not touching; that is proven. But we are *feeling*, and that is just as real. I'll never know what it's like to be you, Tallulah . . ." He peers up, those pale eyes even more striking in the soft morning light. "What's your middle name?"

"Jane," I whisper.

He smiles. "Tallulah Jane Clarke. I'll never know exactly how, emotionally, mentally, the world presents to you, how you experience it, in the same way I'll never actually physically touch you, no matter how close I might try to get . . . *But*, that proximity, that touching-yet-not-touching. . ." His fingertips graze down my hand, making me shiver. He turns it over, tracing the lines of my palm, swirling up and down. "That . . . charged, impenetrable space between two people who feel *so* close—their hearts, their minds, their bodies—yet never truly touch, that place of mystery, *that's* real. And I think, it's that reach to feel and know and connect to every part of each other, in spite of the distance between us . . . I think that's love, in so many beautiful, mysterious iterations."

I stare at him, a lump in my throat, my eyes burning.

I have no words. No way to explain how deeply I respect the conviction of his belief, even when I am so empty of corroborative experience to embrace it. Listening to him talk, I feel glimmers of what he's known, how he's encountered love and intimacy. But mostly, what I feel is a profound sense of how far my life experience has been from what he knows. Sadness washes over me.

"I think . . ." Carefully, I pull my hand from beneath his, then turn and glide my fingertips over his knuckles. "I think that is beautiful."

"But you don't see it that way," he says after a beat.

I shake my head. "No." Lifting my head, I hold his eyes. "I do, however, look forward to picking that very eloquent brain of yours when we start working on my book couple's dynamic."

He blinks. "You . . . think I'm eloquent?"

"Did you just hear yourself?" I take a deep drink of coffee, then stand from my stool and grab for the coffee carafe, refilling his mug, topping off mine. "You are incredibly eloquent when you talk about this, Viggo. I'm surprised you aren't itching to write a book yourself."

He frowns down at his coffee. "Nah. I'm a reader. Not a writer. I just want to enjoy it, not make it my job, beyond pushing books I love on people."

"Fair enough." Easing back onto my stool, I sip my coffee, then put it down. "So . . . this was good. We cleared the air, acknowledged we're attracted to each other . . ."

Our eyes hold. Viggo's throat works roughly with a swallow. "Yeah, we are."

Heat spills through me as I sit beside him, knees brushing, so close I can see the pale silver slivers in his irises, auburn glittering in the wavy depths of his hair. It would be so easy to take his coffee from his hand, press him back against the counter, slip my fingers beneath his shirt, glide my palms up his hot skin, and kiss him until he was moaning, begging for more; to drop to my knees, yank down his shorts, and make him come right there, hands braced on the stool's edge, his head thrown back, hips working—

A car backfires outside, snapping me out of my lusty fantasy. I clutch my coffee cup hard, clench my jaw, breathe through it. Viggo's staring at me like he's read my mind. Like maybe he's been indulging in a fantasy of his own. Heat is high on his cheeks; his eyes are bright. His gaze keeps darting to my mouth, and he rolls his shoulders back, like he's trying to shake off the urge to lean closer, to touch me.

I have never felt this intensely drawn toward someone, never so sure that they're just as drawn to me. There is no doubt in my mind that we'd have incredible sex. There is also no doubt in my mind, given the circumstances in which we find ourselves, living under the same roof, that it would be terribly irresponsible of us to do it.

Viggo and I hold each other's gaze, bring our coffee to our mouths, and take twin long, slow drinks.

"But . . ." My voice is so thick with lust, the word comes out faint and cracked. I clear my throat, straighten my spine. "While we're attracted to each other, we absolutely are not going to fuck."

Viggo chokes on his coffee.

I whack him on the back.

"I'm good," he croaks, then clears his throat. "I'm fine."

"Why'd you choke, then?"

His cheeks are red. "You just . . . talk about it so matter-of-factly."

"I see it as a matter-of-fact thing."

"Yeah." He glances down at his coffee.

"And you see it as something . . . emotional?" My gaze darts to the romance novel he was reading, then back to him. "Something you share with someone you . . . love?"

His eyes meet mine. "Yes."

And that's not you. That's the unspoken truth that hangs in the air between us.

It shouldn't sting—it *shouldn't*—because dammit, I don't believe in love, I don't *want* him to "love" me or want romance with me. And yet something inside me twangs sharply, like a plucked string reverberating on a sour note, gratingly off pitch.

I shrug, expression cool. "There you have it, then. Since my last roommate-with-benefits disaster, I don't sleep with people I live with. You're a romantic who wants to sleep with someone you love.

We can just . . . acknowledge the physical attraction is there and move on."

His eyes search mine. His fingers drum across the counter. "Don't you feel like it's a bit trickier than just . . . 'moving on'?"

Yes.

I stare at him. "How so?"

Viggo leans in, elbows on the counter, eyes searching mine. "I can't explain it. The way I want you, physically, the way I respond to you, it's like an itch I can't even reach, let alone scratch. I don't think that's just . . . going to go away."

"That would be the unsatisfied lust talking. Wanting what you haven't had."

"It's not that simple. Dammit, Lu."

"So, if it isn't that simple," I press, "if it isn't just biological, how do you explain being attracted to me so . . ."

"Intensely?" His voice is sandpaper rough.

Desire spills, hot and quick, low in my belly, between my thighs. I roll my shoulders back and try to shake it off. "What else besides biology? You don't love me. You hardly know me. How do you explain that?"

"I can't." The intensity of his gaze pins me in place. "I don't know. What I do know is it drives me up the goddamn wall."

"Well"—I raise my mug—"sympathies. You think I appreciate being horny for a high-handed IKEA-furniture-assembling, plant-hoarding, romance-loving, rescue-animal-adopting pushover?"

Viggo laughs, clinking his mug with mine. "I'll try to keep my pheromonal allure as under wraps as possible. You do the same, huh?"

"You got it," I tell him. We both take sips of our coffee. "But listen, even if it stays like this, we'll be okay," I reassure him, reassure us both. "We're reasonable people. We have an understanding we'll respect. We can make it through unscathed. It's only eight weeks."

"Psh." Viggo waves a hand. "Eight weeks is nothing. We'll be so busy. It'll fly."

He shifts on his stool as I do, and our bodies brush—his knee wedged high between my legs, my thighs pressed against his. We both draw in deep breaths.

Both pick up our coffees and sip in silence. Cheeks hot.

I try to ignore the nagging worry that, at least when it comes to this, eight weeks is *not* going to fly by, at all.

FIFTEEN

Tallulah

Playlist: "Riptide—Ukulele Version,"
Acoustic Guitar Revival

Viggo and I *might* be tiptoeing around each other. Just a little bit.

Okay, a lotta bit.

For the past week, I've done what I could to minimize unnecessary interactions outside of his helping me learn my way around the bookstore. We've decided to divide and conquer. I will ring people up and take food and drink orders. Viggo will fulfill food and drink orders, unless he's helping patrons on the floor, in which case I'll step in. I've learned what I've needed to, his point-of-sale software, the curated coffee drink menu he's offering, how to warm the baked goods. Otherwise, I've kept to myself as much as possible without making it awkward.

I declined the invitation his niece extended, that he extended again, to Bergman Sunday family dinner. I ordered tacos and started a Karin Slaughter reread that is a fucking masterpiece. I didn't watch the clock, wondering when he'd be back.

Too much.

I ripped off the Band-Aid and gave him my book to read—the draft I have so far, at least. I emailed it to him Sunday night, after I heard him park his car, and I scrambled to the safety of my room, then had a stern talk with myself about acting like a scaredy-cat.

I made him swear not to say a thing about the book until I asked him. My ego is bone-china fragile.

Every morning since then, it's gone like this: I lounge in bed, stewing about how terrible my book is, how humiliating it is that Viggo is reading what I've written of my terrible book. Then I do my morning finger prick to check my blood sugar, scowling out the window about my terrible book as I suck my prick spot. I take my insulin, a delayed extended bolus, entering the carbs I'll eat at breakfast into my PDM.

I do all this while listening to Viggo lumber around the kitchen. The kettle's *scrape* when he lifts it off the range, right as it starts to whistle. The soft *thud* of the refrigerator door after he pulls out ingredients to make himself breakfast.

Then, once I hear him traipse down the hall to his room, I sneak out, pour a mug of coffee, grab a breakfast bar from the pantry, then slip back into my room. I sit at my desk, eat the breakfast bar, gulp my coffee, and make myself work on revising the terrible book until lunch.

I'm still fully ignoring the couple's romantic arc, whose shoddy structure is absolutely screwing up the first third of the book, maybe all of the book. I'll deal with that later, once Viggo's read what I've written so far and my ego can handle hearing how awful he thinks it is, too.

My alarm goes off at noon sharp, which is when I force myself to (or, more often, sigh with relief that I can) wrap up writing and revising, the afternoon reserved for any help Viggo needs with the store. I check my blood sugar again, this time via my CGM, bolus insulin, then wander into the kitchen to make one of my go-to meals whose carbs I know by heart and can enter into my PDM.

Usually, while I'm meal making, Viggo joins me.

Like he does today.

The door leading from the store to the house shuts, and I glance up. My stomach twists as I allow myself a moment to drink him in.

Viggo's a little sweaty, hair curled up and damp at the nape of his neck, beneath the usual beat-up blue ball cap. He plucks at the fabric of another romance-lover T-shirt, fanning himself. This one bears a raised fist clutching a fanned-out handful of romance novels. Above it reads, *Read romance. Fight the patriarchy.*

A smile tugs at my mouth. I duck my head, focused on assembling my chicken salad sandwich.

"Afternoon, Tallulahloo," he says.

"Afternoon, Viggo." I add one more leaf of butter lettuce, then place the other slice of bread on top. "Come eat."

Viggo sighs. "Lula, I've got so much to do."

"Which I'll help you with. It can wait for a chicken salad sandwich." I point to the plate beside me.

He passes me to reach the sink, careful not to so much as brush elbows, then starts washing his hands. "Bossy pants," he mutters.

I smile wider because I can with my back to him, inordinately tickled by those little moments he gets grumpy with me, when our roles reverse.

When he drops onto a stool at the counter across from me and tugs off his hat, I slide the plate his way.

"It seems disingenuous," he says, bringing the sandwich to his mouth, "to thank you for force-feeding me. But I'll say thank you all the same."

"You're welcome," I tell him, before crunching into my sandwich.

Viggo rolls his eyes, then bites into his sandwich. A sigh leaves him as he chews. "Rude."

"What's rude?" I ask around my bite.

"That this tastes so damn good."

"Food that someone else made you always tastes better."

Viggo peers at me in that way I've caught him a handful of times the past week, when we're together—cleaning up from dinner, sitting on opposite ends of the living room, reading quietly—well,

I'm quiet; Viggo hums to himself, sways in his creaky rocker, audiobook blasting in his headphones as he knits what looks like a blanket. Sometimes I'll glance up and catch him staring at me like I'm a word scramble he's trying to sort out.

That's how he's looking at me now.

"What?" I ask. I take another big bite of my sandwich.

He shakes his head, then bites into his sandwich again, chewing thoughtfully as he stares off. After he swallows, he chugs the remaining half of his mason jar of water, then sets it on the counter with a hollow *clunk*. "Just wanted to say, I really appreciate you doing so much to learn the ropes of the store and help me out this week."

I shrug as I chew, then swallow. I told him I'd do it. He doesn't need to thank me for doing what I promised. "Sure thing."

"I'm almost done with the book," he tells me, holding my eyes. "Lula, it's—"

"Don't tell me," I blurt. "Just . . . let's . . . get through the soft opening. Then we can circle back to the book."

He frowns. "But—"

"Please?" I beg.

He sighs. "Fine. But if you change your mind before then, tell me." He shoves the last of his sandwich into his mouth and chews, a thick chipmunk wad in his cheek.

"You don't need to rush reading it," I tell him. "You're so busy right now."

"It hasn't come at the cost of my work. I've been listening to it at night while I putz around with the pottery wheel, thanks to Microsoft Read Aloud."

"Are you even sleeping right now?"

"Not much," he concedes. I watch him rake both hands through his hair, eyes shut. "Trust me, I haven't rushed reading it. I've needed a distraction by the end of the day, Lu. I try to go to sleep, but my brain is running in circles."

Staring at him, I notice for the first time what I now recognize has been there all week—shadows under his eyes, anxiety pinching his brow, tightening his shoulders. His leg is bouncing so hard on the stool, I feel its movement shaking the floor.

"Hey." I toe his foot beneath the counter.

He peers at me, hands frozen in his hair.

"You've got this, okay? We've got this. I won't let you down when you open."

A smile lifts his mouth. "Yeah. I know. Thanks, Lula."

I pop the last of my sandwich in my mouth, then clean my hands with my napkin. "All right. Want to walk me through anything else in the store this afternoon?"

He smiles sheepishly. "Well . . . not so much walk you through. More . . . introduce you."

I narrow my eyes. "Viggo Bergman. What have you done?"

———

"Jesus. Christ." Sighing, I fold my arms across my chest. Two Labrador retrievers, one brown, one black, both gray at the snout, doze, curled around each other on a plush dog bed placed in a patch of thick, hot sunlight that spills through the bookstore's large front window.

"Not even close," he says, pointing. "That's Romeo. And that's Juliet."

My gaze flicks toward Viggo. "You're kidding me. *Those* are their names?"

"I'm trying not to let it bother me," he admits.

I stifle a laugh. "This is hilarious. The guy whose bookstore is devoted to happily ever after gets two dogs named for the main characters of the most famous tragic love story."

"Pff." He waves a hand. "Not that. I've got a whole section in the store devoted to *R and J* retellings with happy endings. *That* doesn't bother me."

"Then, what does?"

He sighs. "They're brother and sister."

A snort sneaks out, then a cackle. I bend over, laughing so hard my stomach hurts.

Viggo glares at me. "Seriously, that's messed up. I've got open arms for all sorts of 'taboo' romance tropes, but incest is not one of them. And they're so old, it's not like I can change their names; they'd never answer to them. I'm stuck."

Now I'm wheezing, slapping my thigh.

"Oh, yuk it up, pipsqueak."

Goddammit, that nickname. My laughter dies off abruptly. I poke Viggo's side, right where I remember Oliver got him after I found him, Ren, and Seb in the closet. Viggo yelps and hops away, betrayal in his eyes. The dogs perk up, observing us curiously.

"Hands to yourself, ma'am," Viggo says sternly.

"Stop. Calling. Me. Pipsqueak."

He grins. "You know that just makes me want to call you that even more, right?"

I roll my eyes, bending and offering my hand to the brown one, Juliet, who's more alert. She rolls over, shamelessly begging for a belly rub.

Viggo crouches beside me and rubs Romeo's side, patting his flank in that way dogs love.

I smile to myself when Romeo pushes up and noses in under my hand, greedy for affection from me, too. Viggo reaches over me and gently scratches behind Juliet's ears. Her eyes slip shut as she leans into his touch. Relatable content.

Not that Viggo and I have been touching. The past week we have been very pointedly *not* touching at all, as if, having said what we did the night I moved in and we both got drunk, having acknowledged the next morning our attraction to each other, even the most chaste and platonic of touches is fraught with risk.

But it doesn't even matter. I still remember that hug outside the Chinese restaurant; I've gotten myself off to *that* memory more than to any filthy fantasy involving his wet hands working a pottery wheel, his rough fingertips gliding down just-watered plant leaves, every flexing muscle and animal grunt as he put together IKEA furniture.

I haven't even needed my vibrator the past week. Just my hand slipped beneath my underwear, where I've had an ache so sharp by the end of each day, it's only taken a few swirls of my fingers before I'm going off like a firework to the memory of his hard, lean arms tight around me, the heady scent of his skin, that soft shirt against my cheek, my ear pressed to his heart hammering inside his chest.

It's bad news.

"Well," he says quietly, wrenching me from my thoughts. He nods toward the dogs. "What do you think of them?"

"They're sweet," I tell him, unable to stop myself from smiling at the pups as they scramble for my attention. As I sit beside him, Romeo leans in and licks up my chin. Juliet noses in and plops her head on my arm. "Especially for rescue dogs. They usually have a lot of baggage. I was braced for it to be tougher than this."

"Me too," he says. "But we have a bit of a history, these two and I."

"Oh?"

He nods, easing down to sit, legs crisscrossed. Romeo flops back onto the dog bed and sets a paw on Viggo's thigh, sighing contentedly. "They showed up at the shelter about six weeks ago. At the time, I knew, as adorable as they were, it was not smart to get them. I didn't have much money, and I had even less time."

"Why were you there, then?" I ask. "At the shelter?"

"For the better part of the past year, I've gone to walk the dogs early in the morning and late in the evening. It helps me clear my head, and they always need volunteers to keep the animals exercised. Once I met these two, I figured they'd be gone soon, given how cute they are, even if they're getting up there in years. I braced myself for them to have been adopted every time I showed up. But they never were. They were there every time I came, and every time, even though they assigned walkers randomly, I kept getting paired with them. They were skittish for a while—Juliet growled at me pretty consistently, and Romeo wouldn't meet my eyes for weeks."

My heart pinches. "And then?" I offer, once again drawn in by his way with words, with telling stories, that makes me so curious to know what comes next.

"And then . . . I just kept walking them. Talking to them. Giving them treats. Hoping that would help them feel safe, ready for that someone who was going to show up and love them. I decided that even if I couldn't have them, I was going to help them be ready for their perfect match. I started looking forward to those walks so much, I shamelessly asked for them every time I came."

"What made you decide to adopt them? It's not like the timing or finances are any better than they were a month ago, right?"

He tugs his ball cap lower. "Yeah, you're right. But it got to a point where, one day, I just couldn't leave them. I realized they had me wrapped around their furry little paws. I was pissed at first. Why did I have to find the perfect pups now, when I wasn't ready for them?"

"And . . . ?" I lean in.

He smiles down at the dogs, rubbing both their heads. "It just . . . dawned on me, strolling with them down the sidewalk, past people going about their lives, through the trees, beneath the sun, all of this beauty that began from absolutely gorgeous, utterly random chance: I didn't have to know, didn't have to make some profound sense of *why* they were put on my path when they were, for me to love them. I could just . . . love them. That was enough."

My heart's pounding. My eyes are wet. It feels like every word he's said has sawed, jagged, hot, right down my chest, and cracked me open.

And that is when I do something foolish. Something wild. Something unstoppable.

I clasp Viggo Bergman by the face, and I kiss him.

SIXTEEN

Viggo

Playlist: "You Taste Like Wine," The Collection

For a split second, I'd swear I've left my body. And then I realize I've never been so fully *in* it. My heart thuds in my chest. Air swells in my lungs. Every atom of my skin that Tallulah touches is on fire— her fingers splayed across my face, her mouth as it moves with mine, her lips soft and searching.

Oh God. This. *This* is like nothing I've ever known.

I've kissed and been kissed before. Not many times, I'll admit. I used to try it, hoping that was what I needed to feel a spark with someone. It never worked. Never felt right. Romance novels did it better. They always did it better.

Until now. Until her.

Tallulah's lips are velvet smooth, slanted against mine, pressed hard and sure, such a perfect fit, it makes my hands ache, my fingers curl into the fabric of her skirt, which has spilled onto my lap.

I suck in a breath, drinking in this moment, the perfection of her mouth against mine.

Tallulah tears herself away, eyes wide, hand shaking as she brings her fingers to her mouth. "Oh, God, Viggo. I'm sorry. I'm so sorry—"

"Don't." I tug her close, and she comes willingly, splayed across my lap, knees on either side of my hips. "Don't you dare apologize, not if you wanted to do that."

She stares at me, blinking, like she's stunned. "I . . . wanted to."

"You don't regret it?" I ask roughly.

She shakes her head. "No. I don't."

"Then, hold tight, Lu." I sink my hand into her bun and tip her head back, earning her gasp. I wrap an arm around her waist and bring her closer. And then I give her everything I have.

Our mouths brush, soft, once, twice. Tallulah melts in my arms, clasping my face as I sink my fingers deeper into her hair, coaxing her mouth to open for mine. My tongue strokes hers. I groan as I taste her, as our tongues meet, sweet, velvet hot, slow and tender.

I deepen our kiss, fuse my mouth to hers, take it the way I want to take *her*—deep, desperate control riding the razor's edge of abandon.

I'm not wildly experienced. She's probably done this lots more than I have, but it doesn't matter. That's not what this is, abstract technique—it's the simple rightness of her and me, our bodies moving, her hips rolling into mine as I rock beneath her, pressing my hand down her back, over the full, soft curve of her ass, until she's tucked even tighter with me.

She knocks off my ball cap, presses up on her knees so my head's no longer bent down to her but thrown back as she looms over me. Her fingers rake through my hair as she wrenches her mouth away from mine and kisses my cheek, my forehead, the corner of my smile, before she crashes back down on me. Tongues dancing, gasped breaths, moans and murmurs. I clutch her hard, my hands gliding up her back, splayed wide. I want every inch of me touching every inch of her.

We fall onto the floor, Tallulah cupping my face, my hands everywhere. Her ass, her waist, her hair, which I yank out of its tie, until it spills, cool water blue around us, turning the world dark and peaceful, nothing but us.

I'm so hard in my jeans, every rub of her hips is aching torture.

She's teasing me, feather-soft kisses to my lips, her breasts smashed into my chest. I can feel her nipples, hard and tight inside her shirt, chafing against mine. I want to push her onto her back, ruck up that skirt, and sink into her, feel her tight and wet and hot, wrapped around me, hear her moaning my name as I fill her and please her and learn everything there is to know about how to make Tallulah feel so damn good.

And yet. Alarm bells sound in the back of my head. My body's getting ahead of me—both our bodies are. Just a week ago, we acknowledged that we are worlds apart in how we view sex, intimacy . . . love.

I know myself. I know that when I do this with someone, I need to love them, need to know they love me. I need that reassurance, that trust, that safety net below me when I fall from such a terrifying height, because there is no other option for me. I do nothing halfheartedly. When I finally have sex, make love, I'll be throwing all of myself into it, and I sure as hell need love to catch me when I fall.

But God, does she feel good, smell good, taste good. She feels perfect in my arms, all her soft, delicious curves right up against me.

One more kiss. One more kiss, then I'll put a stop to this. Of course, as I've made this resolution, Tallulah undoes me. She slows our kiss, deepens it. Her hips grind against mine and her breath stutters. A smile lifts my mouth against hers. I understand that sound, somehow know it means she's close, she's getting herself off on me, and hell, I am not far behind her—

Arf!

Romeo's loud dog bark startles us apart, sends Tallulah scrambling upright, hands on my hips as she stares down at me, wide-eyed, messy blue hair, breathing harshly.

Slowly, I sit up, too, searching her expression for some clue as to how she feels about what we just did. I can't read her at all.

She seems wary, careful. Slowly, she reaches for my hair, smoothing it back.

I clasp her wrist, stroking it with my thumb as I search her eyes. For once, I'm quiet, too. Because . . . what's there to say? She's made her position crystal clear. As I've made mine. They're divergent, our views on what this is or could be. This is a battle I can't win. But I'm too stubborn, too foolishly drawn to her, to withdraw entirely either. So here I am, pinned beneath her, yet trying to hold my ground. I won't retreat, but I won't push for more than she's already given me. I couldn't take her, of all people, responding to that how so many already have:

It's too much to ask, to want, to expect. You're *too much.*

Peering down at me, she bites her lip. "Sorry. I . . . kind of kiss-tackled you. And then got very carried away."

The reminder that Tallulah initiated this does great things for my plummeting mood. I grin because I can't help it. "I already told you, there's not a damn thing to be sorry for."

Slowly, she slides off of me and stands, smoothing her skirt. Doubt creeps up inside me. Is *she* sorry? Does *she* regret it?

Staring down at me, Tallulah offers her hand. I take it but hardly tug, using my legs to spring upright. She's still so quiet, staring up at me, hands turned to fists by her sides.

She *is* sorry. She does regret it.

My heart sinks lower and lower by the second.

Our gazes hold. I feel the tension in the room swell like a balloon about to burst.

Tallulah's phone buzzes in her skirt pocket. Now that I'm fully aware of my surroundings, my senses expanded to their normal perception from their telescoped state, in which nothing existed but Tallulah's mouth, hands, body, scent, I realize it's been buzzing for a while.

Tallulah unearths her phone, frowning as she reads the screen.

Her expression tightens, then smooths. I want to ask her what's wrong. I want to wrap my arms around her.

And I have no idea what she wants.

She pockets her phone. "I have to go," she says quietly.

Dread seeps through me. She's leaving. Because of what we did? Because of whatever she just read on her phone?

I don't have answers. I'm not brave enough to ask the questions that might earn them.

But before I can panic anymore, spiral any further, Tallulah leans in, reaching up on tiptoe. Her hands clasp my arms, and she pulls me close. Then she gifts me with the softest, sweetest press of her lips to my cheek, before she whispers, warm against my ear, "Best kiss of my whole damn life."

SEVENTEEN

Viggo

Playlist: "I Won't Give Up," Noah Guthrie

The pups and I are on our second walk of the evening. Romeo and Juliet seem less enthusiastic about this stroll than the first, but I just couldn't sit around the house, waiting to hear from Tallulah, worrying about what made her leave, wrestling with this gut feeling that something's wrong.

At the intersection, we stop and wait our turn to cross. Romeo plops onto his stomach with a weary sigh. Juliet takes one look at him and plops onto her stomach, too.

"Come on, now," I tell them. "Don't give up on me. It's breezy out, not too hot. It's the perfect night for an evening promenade."

Romeo cocks his head, skepticism written all over his doggy face.

"Yes, I said, 'evening promenade.' Don't give me that attitude, old man. I like my historical romances—expressions like that are going to slip out from time to time, so you better get used to it."

Romeo blows out a doggy *hmph* and glances away.

Juliet whines.

I crouch and pet her, soft, steady strokes from her snout up over her head. "I'm sorry I made us go out again. I'm just worried about Lu—"

My phone rings in my pocket, the *Bridgerton* theme song's string notes bursting through the road noise nearby. I stand so I can reach my phone in my pocket, fumbling for it as it rings again. My heart drops to my feet when I see it's Tallulah. Something's happened to her; that's the only reason she'd call. No millennial in their right mind calls unless something's seriously wrong.

I'm about to accept the call when it ends abruptly. Immediately I tap Tallulah's number, trying to call her back. It goes straight to voicemail. Maybe Tallulah's lost her key and she's locked out. Maybe she's home, wondering where I am. Maybe she's been in an accident on that death trap of a motorbike. I tug gently on the dogs' leashes. They're all too happy to turn around and head home.

I try to call Tallulah again, but again, it goes straight to voicemail. Panic tightens my chest. I hustle the dogs along, as fast as they can go without having to break into a jog.

When I get home, Tallulah's Vespa isn't outside, no sign of her as I start to walk the place, calling her name. Just as I'm pulling my phone from my pocket to try her again, I get a text from her.

> Sorry for calling. Meant to text instead.
> Something came up that I have to take care
> of. I'll be back the day after tomorrow, in time
> to help with prep for the soft opening.

I stare at her message, worry tugging my brow tight, my mouth into a frown. Taking a deep breath, I type my response back.

> Don't worry about the soft opening. I've
> got it under control. Take the time you need,
> Tallulahloo. I'll be right here when you
> get back.

She doesn't respond. But my phone immediately shows my text has been read. That's a consolation. She knows I'm here. That I care. Even if she doesn't know how to respond to that.

Half an hour later, a text-alert sound dings in my headphones, interrupting my audiobook as I sway in my rocker, knitting this blanket in progress. I pause Mary Jane Wells's god-tier narration and feel my pulse quicken as I unlock my phone.

A smile lifts my mouth. It's the smallest thing, but it feels so damn big.

Tallulah's responded to my message with a sunshine-yellow heart.

"Wow, brother." Oliver stands, hands on hips, staring down at the mewling kittens twining around him. "You truly do nothing by half measures. All *five* of them."

I scrub the back of my neck. Five kittens in theory was cute. Five in practice is . . . a tad overwhelming. "I just couldn't break up a big brood of siblings. It didn't feel right."

Oliver crouches and pets the kittens. "At least they're cute."

They're also loud. The main room of the house echoes with tiny kitten meows.

Crouching, I join Oliver on the floor.

"So," he says casually, "where's Tallulah?"

I clear my throat. "Not here. Something came up that she had to deal with, and she said she'd be gone a couple days."

Oliver watches me closely as I scoop up one of the kittens with fluffy gray fur and big golden eyes. "How are things going so far, with her living here?"

Oh, swell. It's just been a week and change of sexual tension, bickering, and making out on the store floor.

I shrug. "Okay."

"You've got a thing for her, don't you?"

I focus on the kitten. "Define 'thing.'"

"A crush."

"Yeah, I do. She's sharp and chilly, but she can also be sweet and warm, when she wants to be." I frown at the kitten as she nips me. "Sort of like a cat. She's sexy as hell. It's just a physical thing. You know how it goes, sometimes."

Oliver lifts his eyebrows. "I do. I felt that way about Gavin."

I jerk my head his way. "I don't feel *that* way about Tallulah."

"I didn't feel *that* way about Gavin, either," he says. "Not at first. Not for a while. He pissed me off for a long time, but that didn't make him any less attractive to me."

The hairs on my neck stand up. I roll my shoulders back, picking up the black-and-white kitten with green eyes. "I'm debating getting tiny kitten harnesses so we can all go for walks together."

Oliver rolls his eyes. "V, you're so bad at changing the subject—"

"That's not us, okay, Oliver?" It comes out sharper than I mean it to, but I do mean what I say. "Tallulah and I . . . we've got chemistry, but we're not . . . we're not going to be more than that. We are strictly platonic roommates. She doesn't want romance, doesn't believe in love, isn't looking for it. And if that doesn't tell you enough about how incompatible we are, when I'm with her, I don't feel those feelings I'm waiting for."

Oliver's quiet, petting the orange kitten who crawls across his lap. "What feelings are those?"

"*Don't* make fun of me," I warn.

He raises his free hand, which isn't occupied with petting a kitten. "I won't."

Scratching the black-and-white one's chin, I tell him, "Those . . . butterfly feelings. That sense that I've found my best friend, my perfect partner. The puzzle-piece-slipping-into-place click of rightness."

Oliver's quiet. I glance his way, surprised to see him frowning in thought. Oliver doesn't frown often.

"What?" I ask.

He hesitates for a moment, like he's weighing his words. "I just wonder if maybe you're possibly relying a *little* too heavily on romance novels to shape your expectations. Don't get me wrong—there's a lot in romance novels that speaks to real life, and beautifully, for that matter, but . . . there are also parts that are maybe a bit . . . unrealistic?"

"I do recognize, to my profound disappointment, that romance novels don't comprehensively reflect reality, but I still think there's something to be said for feeling the magic of finding your person, knowing they're right for you. I'm someone who needs that, who's hardwired to hold out for that epic kind of love. I think that's why I love romance novels the way I do, why I've gone this long, meeting so many fun, attractive people that I have a good time with, but never want to go further than a date or two, even though I'm actively looking for that kind of connection."

Oliver tips his head, biting his lip. "All right, well, you know yourself best. If that's what you think you're looking for and why you're looking for it, I respect that, V."

As he says that, the white and calico kittens crawl onto my lap, then up my thighs, before they tumble into a ball of play-fighting fur.

"Hey, look," Ollie says. "It's us."

I laugh.

"So, have you named them?" he asks.

I don't tell him that I was waiting for Tallulah to come back and help me with that task. That, when Wesley dropped them off yesterday morning, the first thing I thought was that the gray one's eyes were the same shade as Tallulah's—sunlit amber.

"Nope," I tell him.

"Well, I'd be glad to assist." Oliver picks up the orange one, inspecting her face. "How about we name you . . . Cheddar."

"Seriously, man? Cheese?"

"This one . . ." He scoops up the white kitten. "Brie."

"Absolutely not. We are not naming my cats for cheeses. I don't care how color coordinated their names are."

"Iberico." He points to the black-and-white kitten, next the gray one. "Tyrolean." He scratches the calico's chin. "Mimolette."

"Enough! You have a disturbingly unhealthy obsession with something that literally destroys your stomach."

Oliver smiles sweetly, batting his eyelashes. "Fine. Then name them yourself, already."

"I was getting around to it," I grumble.

"It's just very unlike you. I mean, Ashbury's keys weren't even in your hands yet, and you already had that car named. Your *plants* had names before we'd driven off the lot at the nursery. This delay is"—he clucks his tongue—"dare I say, uncharacteristic?"

I glare at my brother. Generally, I love how close we are. Right now, I am deeply resenting how well he knows me.

"Wonder why he hasn't named you," Oliver croons to the kittens as they congregate toward him, meowing, pawing over each other for his attention, "when he's had you for almost two days, hmm? Wonder if it has anything to do with his 'strictly platonic roommate' being absent since your arrival?"

"That's it," I tell him. "Get out."

"I'm good staying right here," he says breezily, lying back on the rug, letting the cats crawl up his chest. "Thanks, though."

I groan, jumping up from the floor. "Fine. I will excuse myself to the bookstore, then."

"I'm happy to cat-sit while you work," my brother calls as I open the door to the store. "I'm sure you're busy with prep for the soft opening. When's the *grand* opening, again?"

I scrub at the back of my neck. My chest feels tight when I think about opening the store. I know I keep moving the goalposts back, but I keep telling myself I'll know when it's time. Until then, a soft opening feels like the safe next step. "Not sure."

Oliver's quiet for a beat. "I see. Will there be a semi-grand opening next, before the grand opening? A demi-grand opening as well?"

I stop on the threshold of my home and the store, a prickling sensation running down my spine. Turning, I stare at my brother.

His expression is no longer teasing.

Mine is no longer amused.

"You got something to say, Oliver, I suggest you say it."

Ollie sits up slowly, gaze searching mine. Finally, he gently extricates himself from the kittens and stands, hands in his pockets. "Okay, I'll say it."

"Great. Lower the boom."

He's unusually quiet as he walks past me into the store, glancing around, before he turns and faces me. His hands leave his pockets, arms wide. "What the hell are you waiting for?"

My stomach knots. "What are you talking about?"

"This place, Viggo . . ." Oliver looks around. "I'm no expert on running a bookstore, but it's ready. It's *been* ready since the night the family was here. Your inventory is bursting off the shelves. You have your pastry recipes down to a science, a coffee machine that practically makes the drinks itself. Your plants have flowered since we were here!" His voice is louder now, his cheeks pink. He's fired up. "What are you waiting for? Why don't you just open those damn doors and let yourself succeed already?"

"Because I don't *know* if I'll succeed!" I yell.

His eyes widen.

"Because," I tell him, my voice shaking, "I've never done this, Oliver. Never poured this much of myself into one thing, and I'm fucking scared I'll fail. I am a 'diversify your existential portfolio' kind of guy, and I just went all in on this place. If it fails, *I* fail . . ." My voice breaks. I cover my face with my hand, exhaling heavily. I'm dangerously close to crying.

Oliver's arms wrap around me, tight and reassuring. His chin rests on my shoulder. "This is *not* going to fail," he says, confident, calm. "And even if, somehow, it didn't work out the way you hoped, *you* would not be a failure. You would grieve and then pick yourself up, brush yourself off, move forward." He's quiet for a second, hugging me harder. "It's not going to fail, though."

"How do you know?" I croak.

Oliver smiles. I feel it in his cheek against my ear, the upswing in his voice. "Because everything you do, Viggo, you do excellently. Because as long as I can remember, I have known that my brother could do any damn thing he set his heart on, and do it spectacularly. Because I'm looking around here, at this dream you've built, beautiful and intentional, on the brink of wild success, and I know the only thing stopping it from already being that is your lack of faith in yourself. Open its doors wide and believe in yourself."

My jaw clenches. I blink away tears. "It's . . . scary."

He pats my back. "I know. But these books we're surrounded by, that you've voraciously read, isn't that what they're all about? Being brave enough to take risks to have the life we want and love? Be brave for yourself, Viggo. You deserve it."

I swallow roughly. "Thank you. Love you, brother."

"Love you, too."

We pull apart. I wipe under my eyes and clear my throat, peering around the store, knowing Ollie's right. It's time to open the place already and stop dancing around the inevitable, letting fear hold me back.

"I see those gears turning," Oliver says. Arms folded across his chest, he watches me closely.

"Yeah." I slide my hand along the bookshelves, the smooth polished wood that my brothers helped me install and finish. My gaze drifts across the store. The green velvet swiveling club chairs Freya called me about when she saw them on the curb just waiting for some reupholstering TLC. The fantasy romance section Ziggy lovingly curated and organized. The historical romance section, which is where this all began, years ago—because my parents kept the A-frame well stocked so Dad could read to his wife at night, because I picked one up while wrestling with feelings for a woman who wanted nothing to do with me.

Maybe I'm still wrestling.

Maybe, even though romance novels have given me a vocabulary for so many feelings, I'm still trying to make sense of what *she* makes me feel.

Maybe Oliver's right, that I cling too tight to my romance novels because I want the security of this idea that if my heart's journey echoes that of a perfectly crafted path to happily ever after, I'll be okay—I won't get hurt, won't get rejected, won't throw myself at the wrong person and get my heart broken.

But maybe there isn't some crystal clear sign that *this* is the right moment, *this* is when it will all work out. Maybe, like the store's success, my heart's happiness can't be guaranteed, even with all the time and preparation in the world. Maybe all I can do is trust myself and throw its doors wide open.

How wise. How absolutely terrifying.

"Whenever you open, however you open," Oliver says quietly, setting a hand on my back, "I'll be here, rooting for you, okay? We all will."

I nod, offering him a faint smile. I feel off-kilter, dizzy from the implications of my brother's tough love. "Thanks, Ollie."

Oliver peers at me. "You look a little wiped. Hungry? Want to grab a bite to eat?"

I open my mouth, then shut it, weighing my words, how to answer. I am hungry. And for the past two days, anxious about Tallulah, missing her high-handed demands that I consume actual meals, eating well or grocery shopping has been the last thing on my mind. I've been distracting myself with rescue pets and fixating on my store.

Trying not to worry about Tallulah.

She said she'd be back in a couple of days. Tonight would be exactly a couple of days. I want to be here when she gets back—*if* she gets back.

Biting my lip, I wrack my brain for a plausible lie in place of the truth. Oliver would read way too much into my honest answer.

Kitten meows on the other side of the door offer me the perfect excuse. "Nah. I should stick close to home, with the kittens. Thanks, though."

"Good point," he says, following me as I open the door to the house and gently scooch back five meowing kittens with my boot. "How about takeout instead?"

Before I can answer him, the purr of a Vespa breaks the silence, growing louder by the second, closer to the alley and the door to my house.

Oliver's eyes widen. He hops back, tugs the curtains away from the window, just enough to peek through, then drops them like they're a hot potato. "You know what, totally forgot. We've got poker night with the guys. Gotta run."

"Ollie, wait—"

I'm panicking. I don't know if being alone with Tallulah, with all these feelings my brother's kicked up, all the worry for her I've been carrying around for two days, is a good idea. Not if I don't want to make things even messier between us than they were before she left.

"Love ya!" he calls, jogging through the store, making his escape. "I'll lock the door behind me!"

The door to the store shuts behind him, just as the door to the house opens with Tallulah's entrance.

Helmet-mussed ice-blue hair. The same clothes she was in two days ago. No sight of the always put-together woman I know.

I stare at her, my heart aching. So much feels tumbled, tangled inside me. So much I don't know. But I do know this:

Tallulah's hurting. And I'm hurting for her. I don't have to understand everything about this woman or what she makes me feel to know I want to care about her and know whatever she'll let me, even if just for this small time that she's here and I'm here, under this roof, together.

I want to stop holding myself back for fear of the unknown. I want to trust that what comes will come, and I'll make it out on the other side, no matter what. I want to open my heart wide, my arms, too, and wrap them around this enigma of a woman.

Tallulah walks toward me, eyes holding mine. The kittens prance toward her, meowing, rubbing against her ankles, hopping over her boots.

"Hey, you," I tell her, searching her eyes for some clue as to how she is.

She doesn't smile. But her eyes are bright, glowing like embers about to burst back to life, into a full-blown fire. "Five. Kittens."

I grin. "This is what happens when you leave. I get lonely."

Her mouth twitches, the faintest hint of a smile. She rolls her eyes. "Let me guess." She turns, shrugging off her jacket, sliding it down her arms as she walks toward the hall leading to her room. "You named them for peers of the realm."

My eyes widen. "Hot damn, Lula. Now, *there's* an idea!"

EIGHTEEN

Tallulah

Playlist: "Singin' My Soul," Gin Wigmore

I take a long hot shower that turns my skin pink. I wash off two days of grime and grit.

And then I put on my softest, comfiest clothes, not a stitch of makeup. My hair is wet, dripping on my shoulders, as I walk down the hall into the main living space.

Viggo sits in his rocker, swaying steadily, back and forth, headphones on, knitting needles clacking. The dogs lie at his feet on their side, dozing. They're unfazed by the kittens that paw around them, swatting at their tails, hopping over them to pounce on Viggo's yarn.

My heart clutches.

Two days. I spent two days driving, burning gas, crashing at filthy motels just long enough to sleep a few hours so I could keep riding safely. I rode for two days, processing the conversation that followed after I saw my mom's text message and did what she asked: Call me please. We need to talk.

My parents' voices on speakerphone, their words, played on a loop in my mind as I rode:

We're divorcing. This time, we hold no hope for an eventual reconciliation.

We love each other, but we don't love each other well.

We've both been working on ourselves, and that work made us see we need to go our separate ways. For good.

Dad's moving to New York, to focus on live theater. Mom's selling the house and moving up to Santa Barbara to live with your grandmother.

You'll be welcome at both our places. We'll see each other soon, at Charlie's wedding.

We know we've hurt you kids, through the years, with our ups and downs, and we're sorry. We really are.

I got on that Vespa and just kept going because I couldn't face Charlie's sadness, knowing I couldn't fix it. I couldn't handle whatever destructive response Harry was going to come up with. Lying in those crappy motels, exhausted, drained, all I kept thinking was, *I want to go home.* After just a little over a week, when I pictured *home*, it was this place. Here, with Viggo.

It scared the shit out of me. It still scares the shit out of me. Because I feel raw and unsure, scared and needy. My parents' divorcing yet again isn't what's thrown me. It's how they told me, what they said.

We love each other, but we don't love each other well.

Those words are a burr stuck to the fabric of my thoughts. The past two days, I've tried to tug them off, but the harder I tried to disentangle myself from their impact, the more those words snagged and tore through me, until I unraveled, until I was left with a rip right down the middle of my conviction that what I know to be true *is* true.

Maybe the truth isn't that love is disproved by how poorly I've seen it born out, but that I've just wanted it to be. Because then I could protect myself from its complexity, its vulnerability. What if love is like anything else humans strive at—something you can fail at spectacularly, and, by contrast, by some mysterious, terrifying chance of sharing it with the right person, through hard work and hope, something you can also do spectacularly well?

I feel naked without my old confidence, exposed to the elements of a wider world, a bigger picture than I've ever let myself see. I have never felt so in need of something, some*one*, to wrap around me and shield me while I stitch myself back together.

But I can't ask that of Viggo. I won't. Not after how far we took it, well beyond our defined boundaries, before I left. I can't ask Viggo for any more than I already selfishly have.

I have to suck it up. Push through. Handle my struggle on my own. Like I have before. Like I will again.

I'm far from being able to force even the faintest smile as I walk into the kitchen and grab a seltzer. Sinking onto the sofa, I set the can on one of Viggo's crocheted coasters, then pick up my e-reader. We'll read quietly. The animals will lie around us, and I will soak up that comfort until my eyes get tired and I can finally sleep deeply, in my bed. In my home, for now.

But Viggo seems to have other plans. He glances up, does a double take when he sees me on the sofa, then tugs off his headphones. "Hey there."

A smile is still beyond me, but I lift the corner of my mouth, trying my best. "Hey."

Viggo taps his phone, pausing his audiobook, then pulls his headphones off his neck and sets them on the coffee table. The gray kitten meows loudly and he picks it up, holding it on his chest. "How you doing, Lu?"

I bite my lip as a lump thickens my throat.

I will not cry. I will not cry.

"Eh." I shrug. "Not great. But I'll be okay."

He rocks steadily, petting the kitten. "Want to talk about it?"

"Not all of it," I say quietly, my gaze drawn by the white kitten, who makes the leap up onto the sofa and prances toward me, onto my lap. I pet her gently. Her fur is fluffy and soft, her tiny body so delicate. "But . . . a little."

Viggo angles the rocker my way, tiny scooches that rotate him toward me, careful of the dogs' tails and the three other kittens milling around. "I'm all ears."

"My parents . . . I'm assuming you know their history?"

"Just the bare bones. Multiple marriages and divorces. Messy."

I huff an empty laugh. "'Messy' is the word."

Viggo is quiet, watching me, waiting.

"I had a call with them," I tell him. "After . . . I left the book-store. They told me they're done for good. I believe them. And, uh . . . well, I was expecting to be relieved, just so ready to have it done and over, no more mess. But, turns out, it still made a mess of things." I swallow thickly, trying to steady my voice. "Inside of me."

Viggo stands with the kitten, joining me on the sofa. Not too close, but closer. "I'm sorry, Lula."

I shrug. "That's okay. Life is messy. I don't like it to be, but it is." I shut my eyes so tears won't spill over. "I'm not surprised my parents are finally calling it quits for good, but how they talked about it, just . . . hit me hard. It's got me reevaluating things, reassessing the . . . direction of parts of my life. I think that's all I want to say for now."

His hand wraps around mine, warm and sure. "You're brave, you know that, right?"

I bite my lip. Keep my eyes shut. Tears leak out anyway. "How?"

"Because," he says quietly, "not everyone has a day like you had two days ago and ends up where you've ended up—willing to let something hard not harden you but instead shape you for the better."

The cat curls up in my lap, and I stare down at it, so small, so trusting, so vulnerable. I curve my hand gently down its bony spine. "Thank you."

Viggo smiles. He squeezes my hand, then lets go. "You know how I talked last year, about us being accountability partners—me with the store, you with the book?"

I nod. "I certainly didn't hold up my end of the bargain."

"Not my point, you stinker. Listen up."

I glance his way, and I'm riveted by those beautiful pale eyes, locked on me. "I didn't," he says, "exactly hold up mine, either."

I frown. "What do you mean? We're living in your dream brought to life."

"Well . . ." He draws out the word, settling lower in the sofa with the gray kitten. The orange one jumps up and joins the cuddle fest, too. "Sort of. But, the truth is, I've dragged out this process much longer than I needed to. I've hemmed and hawed and fussed because it was safer to stay in limbo, telling myself I was pursuing my dream without actually putting it out there for anyone to see, to possibly disparage; to watch it fail if it didn't do well, a prospect which obviously terrified me."

I blink at him, processing his words, stunned by them. "You just . . . seem so confident about all of this. Your dream. Your future. Your romance books. Everything."

"I was, until I started trying to live it all. Now . . ." He peers down at the kittens curled up on his chest. "Now I just feel like all this buildup, creating something I believe in, has led me to a height I didn't realize I'd be so afraid of. So, I've stalled. Because I'm scared to jump. Just like, I think, maybe you've been scared to jump, too."

It's not the first time he's said this, implied I'm afraid of something. But for once, I don't disagree with him. Because he's right. I am afraid. "Yeah," I whisper.

He peers my way again and holds my eyes. "You and me, Lu. We'll be brave together. Little bit by little bit, okay? No pressure to do or be something by a certain date, no shoulds or judgments or deadlines. Just you and me, trying our best, cheering each other on. How's that for a deal?"

For the first time in two days, a smile lifts my mouth. Small, halting. But there. I hold out my hand, palm up, resting on the sofa. Viggo glances from my hand to me, a smile brightening his face, too. Slowly, he rests his hand on mine, wrapping it in his warm, steady grip.

I hold his eyes when I make my promise, to him, to myself.

"Deal."

NINETEEN

Viggo

Playlist: "Running for Cover," Ivan & Alyosha

I walk into the kitchen the next morning, scrubbing a hand over my face. Fill the kettle, set it on the burner, turn the dial, clicking on the gas. The flame swooshes to life.

When I reach for the coffee beans, I catch a reflection in the cabinet's glass—a person in my kitchen. I scream as I spin around, frantically reaching for a weapon from the crock of utensils I keep on the counter. I come up with a rubber spatula.

My brain finally processes that I'm not about to be murdered. This is just an unusually early morning appearance by Tallulah.

She wiggles a finger in her ear, grimacing. "Hell of a shriek you've got, Bergman."

Hand over my pounding heart, I glare at her. "Hell of a scare you gave me, Clarke."

"Sorry." She brings a glass of orange juice to her lips, takes a small sip, then a bigger one.

My glare melts to a worried frown as I watch her set down the glass. Her hand is shaking. My gaze snaps up to her face. "What's wrong?"

"Woke up low," she says. "I'm fine."

My chest is tight. I watch her slip her shaking hand beneath the counter, hiding evidence that she is definitely *not* fine. "Tallulah."

"Viggo." She reaches quickly for the bag of fruit snacks sitting on the counter, scoops up a handful, pops it in her mouth, and returns her hand to beneath the counter.

A few fruit snacks fell out of her unsteady grip, scattered across the counter. I lean in on my elbows, then sweep them my way. Picking one up, I pop it in my mouth and chew. "Let's try that again," I tell her. "What's wrong?"

She chews her mouthful, taking her sweet time. Finally she swallows. Her eyes narrow as she sips her orange juice. I watch her shaky hand the whole time, before my gaze returns to her face. "Woke up with low blood sugar." She sets the empty glass on the counter. "Don't feel great right now. But the orange juice and fruit snacks are helping. I *will be* fine. Happy now?"

"Not happy you don't feel great, but happy I know what's going on."

"Well, if you're happy, then my work is finished; I can go back to bed. My sole purpose for the day has been accomplished already."

I snort. "Smartass."

Tallulah smiles, revealing those dimples deep in her cheeks. Right as she does, the room brightens, the morning light ratcheting up. I feel like that light has seeped right through my skin.

Our eyes hold. Tallulah glances away first. "Thanks for asking," she says. "But you don't need to worry. I have a lot of practice managing this."

"I respect that." The tea kettle starts to whistle. I turn the flame low. I want the water to stay hot, but I still have to grind the beans before I can start our pour-over. "I just . . . care about you, Lula. I want to know when you don't feel good and be there for you, however I can."

Tallulah swallows thickly but stays silent.

I pour the beans into the grinder, snap on the lid, and hit the button. The satisfying sound and scent of crushed coffee beans fill the air. I try to focus on that, not the pinch in my chest, as I think about how much more I want to know about this disease she lives with, how inadequate my initial research feels now. While she lives with me, I want to know more—I *should* know more. It's simply . . . responsible roommateship.

I open my phone and set a reminder to do some reading on it tonight. If I don't set a reminder, it'll slide out of my head, even though it's important to me. My brain doesn't just keep every ball in the air that I want it to, even when all those balls matter deeply to me. Reminders are my best friend for staying on top of priorities.

"So." Tallulah clears her throat. "How are we looking for the soft opening?"

I invert the grinder, pouring the coffee grounds into the filter resting in the carafe. "Change of plans. No soft opening."

A perplexed frown tips her mouth down. "No soft opening?"

I think back to my conversation with Oliver yesterday, the hours I spent lying in bed last night, turning over his words. "I don't need it. I've just been dragging my feet. Time to rip off the Band-Aid and open the damn place."

Tallulah's eyes widen. "What, like, now?"

"God no." I pour water over the grounds. "But soon. Two weeks from now, I think. Use the time between now and then to hype it up on social media, in the community, get the word out. How's that sound?"

"Doesn't matter how it sounds to me. It's your store."

I peer over at her. Tallulah's stacking fruit snacks, eyes narrowed in concentration. I smile. "I know that. But I value your input."

Her fruit snack tower tumbles. She sighs. "Then I'd say, I think, based on my limited knowledge of what, logistically, you need in order to be ready, you're ready. Go for it."

I nod, turning back to the coffee, pouring more water over the grounds.

"But . . ." she says.

I turn back. "But?"

She shrugs, stacking the fruit snacks again. "But I also think, if you're nervous about jumping straight from only having your family here into a grand opening, there's a middle ground that isn't all the hassle of a soft opening, either. How about a group of friends?" She peers up and gives me a pointed glance. "People who you'll actually let buy something from you?"

"I wasn't gonna let my family *buy* stuff."

"Fair. But if you get some people in the store who'll be paying customers, it gives us some practice using your point-of-sale software. And for that matter, juggling food and drink orders. Invite people who'll be hungry and thirsty, who'll have an armful of books and bookish merchandise they'll want to buy. You'll work out the jitters, we'll get some experience under our belts, then you're ready for your grand opening."

An idea tickles in the back of my brain. "Hmm."

Tallulah frowns at me as I pour the last of the water through the grounds. "Hmm what?"

"I think that's a great idea. And I agree to it, on two conditions. One, if you do it with me."

Her frown deepens. "Course I'm doing it with you. I'm working the damn place for the next six and a half weeks."

"Excellent." I smile, leaning back against the counter, arms across my chest. "And two, we finally talk about what you sent me of your book, which I finished, day before yesterday, and *loved*."

That frown becomes an adorable scowl. "Ugh. Must we?"

"We must. Or I can't let you help me in the bookstore anymore. In fact, how about we start today? I've got some errands to run this morning, but after that, my day is clear. Think you can pencil me in?"

She sighs. "Fine, you big, bossy Swede."

"Half-Swede, pipsqueak." I pour her coffee, then slide it across the counter. "Now, drink up. We've got a big day ahead of us."

"So." I scroll through the document on my laptop, to chapter 2, the first place I left a comment. "Right here, after the first chapter in the wife's point of view, we're in the husband's head now."

Tallulah nods beside me. We sit on the floor, laptop on the coffee table, legs crisscrossed, knees touching. I am unnaturally aware of a kneecap touching mine.

Because it's hers.

Blowing out a breath, I turn a little, facing her. "This first scene from his point of view, it's all about his perspective on his wife. You set up a scene whose environment and circumstances parallel their meet-cute."

She blinks. "Meet-cute?"

I groan. "You're killing me, smalls."

She pinches my arm, right above the elbow. An expert sibling retribution move. "I'm not small."

Rubbing my arm, I tell her, "The meet-cute is when they first meet. Presumably it is—"

"Cute," she provides.

"Right. Of course, many romance authors play with that idea of 'cuteness,' invert it, make it comedic, make it a meet-disaster, but I digress. The point is, that first meeting matters. Drawing your reader into it, taking your time with that moment, invests them in the idea of these people as a couple, by *showing* the reader their chemistry, their snap and sizzle and draw toward each other."

She frowns in thought, peering back at the document. "So . . . instead of him saying this parallels their first meet-up, I could . . . show it? A flashback maybe?"

"You could. You could also just have him relive it a little. Notice things about the way this scene is unfolding that take him back to that moment. You want your reader to see this man loves his wife; that's how you complicate their suspicion of him later on—brilliantly done, by the way, I still have no idea if he's a shit-hole or actually a good guy."

Tallulah beams. "Thank you."

I blink at her, stunned. That smile is . . . Jesus, it's breathtaking. Bright teeth, deep dimples; the full, rosy apples of her cheeks.

Her smile falls. "What?" She sounds defensive. Which is understandable. I just stared at her for ten seconds in total silence.

I shake my head. "Sorry. Thinking."

Her brow furrows.

"Anyway." I scroll farther down the chapter. "I think this is the first of a number of moments where you should play with either brief flashbacks or slowing down the pace to describe tactile, emotional parallels that connect to their past. You could, theoretically, jump in time between past and present, but I'm guessing you want to—"

"Distance it from the time-loop element of my first book, correct."

"Got it. Moving on." I scroll farther down, toward the end of the chapter, a tense, charged moment in their kitchen. Or, it has the potential to be tense and charged. Right now it's . . . well, it's flat in the chemistry department. "Here," I tell her. "You have a chance to once again *show* the reader their connection, not simply tell them."

She rereads the paragraph, then peers up at me. "How?"

"You want to describe . . ." I scrunch my eyes shut, trying to think how to explain it. "You want them to feel, when they're there, in the kitchen, like . . . He should . . ." I groan in frustration. "Sorry, I'm a kinesthetic learner. Seems I'm a kinesthetic teacher, too. Mind if we hop into the kitchen and I show you what I mean?"

Tallulah's still for a beat, frowning in confusion. "Okay?" she finally says. It comes out slow and hesitant, but it's an affirmative, and I'll take it.

I spring up from the floor, holding out my hand. Tallulah clasps it and lets me help pull her up. I grab the laptop, then lead the way into the kitchen side of the main room. "So." I set down the laptop. "You stand where she is, roughly. I know my kitchen might not be exactly how you pictured theirs."

Tallulah seems to think for a second, then turns and stands, facing away from me, her hands braced on the counter. Just like the wife in the story.

I back up, then stroll in from the hallway. Just like the husband.

"He walks in," I tell her, "and he spots her, right? Sees her standing with her back to him, with that excellent dancer posture, chopping speedily. You have this great creepy line, where he thinks about how vulnerable her neck looks, the way he pictures the vertebrae in her spine stacked like dominoes, about peeling back her skin to watch her spinal column at work, its speedy connection to those arms and hands that move so dexterously."

"Nod to *Gone Girl*," she says.

"Flew over my head. Never read it."

Tallulah gasps. "It's a classic!"

"Oh, don't get all indignant with me about unread genre masterpieces. I have easily thirty romance novels I could throw at you if we started down that path."

Tallulah sighs. "Carry on."

"So, after that very creepy thought, you have him reflect on how they just had sex, before she came down to start making dinner, while he was up to whatever we don't know about yet. You have him think about how good the sex was. Then you jump right back to action and dialogue between them. But you didn't spend time in his feelings about their sex, his desire for her, those lingering..." I clear my throat, feeling my cheeks get warm. "Those lingering postcoital warm fuzzies."

Her mouth twitches. "'Postcoital'? I don't think I've heard that term since tenth-grade health class."

"Hush up, Clarke, I'm trying to be helpful here."

A tiny smile peeks out. "So sorry. Please continue."

"Thank you. So, if the goal in this revision is to find more moments for your reader to latch on to that romantic connection between the husband and wife, this is one. You show him *acting* on how he says he feels about their sexual intimacy, rather than breezing by it."

Tallulah frowns, turning my way. "I don't . . . I don't know what you mean by that."

"What do you mean you don't know what I mean?"

"I mean," she says impatiently, "I don't know how I would . . . describe that happening."

I stare at her, trying to piece together understanding from the fragments she's giving me. Tallulah said flat out she had sex with that asshole Clint, for years, so I'm not sure why she doesn't know what I'm referring to, unless . . .

Unless they never indulged in postcoital warm fuzzies.

I am both ridiculously pleased by the thought that Tallulah unromantically banged his lights out, and thoroughly annoyed that I have to think about Tallulah blowing that jerkwad's mind in bed for years, even if they never cuddled afterward.

"Viggo?" Tallulah frowns up at me. "You okay?"

I feel the tension in my face, my brow drawn tight, my jaw hard. I force my expression into a breezy smile. "Yeah. All good. Just thinking. I make weird faces when I do it."

"I'll say," she mutters.

"So . . . I think I have to show you what I mean. Is that okay?"

She shrugs. "Fine by me."

"Turn around, then, if you please."

She does.

I take a step back, at the threshold of my hallway into the kitchen. "He walks in, looks at her. Insert creepy, *Gone Girl*–homage thought."

Tallulah smiles. I catch it in her profile, just a peek of it lifting the apple of her cheek.

"How you have it now, he thinks about their sex, then moves on to helping with dinner. But if we stretch out this moment by revisiting their desire, reflecting on their intimacy . . ." I cross the kitchen, stopping right behind her. "He comes here. Right to her."

Tallulah swallows. "Okay. Then what?"

"Then . . ." I swallow, too. "Then he touches her."

She's silent for a beat, before she says, "Show me?"

I stare down at her, the back of her neck, fine ice-blue hairs kissing her tan skin, fallen out of her bun. I breathe in and smell that rich yet subtle perfume of hers—something warm and luxurious, softened at the edges by the scent of flowers. "You sure?"

She nods. "Yes."

I bring my hand to her neck, fingertips trailing down her vertebrae. Goose bumps bloom across her skin. "He touches her . . . gently," I whisper. "He's just been satisfied, right? There's nothing desperate in his touch."

"Makes sense." Her voice is quieter than normal, breathier.

"But just because he's had her doesn't mean he doesn't want her again, doesn't feel that fundamental desire for her, as steady as his pulse."

Tallulah blows out a slow breath. "And then what?"

"Then . . ." I bend, just enough, until my nose brushes her earlobe. Tallulah shivers. My hand curls around her waist and she leans into me, her head falling back, a satisfying *thump* against my breastbone.

My body's hot, aching. I know this is getting away from me, but it feels like all I do is try to smother the fire inside me that burns for Tallulah, and for once, being able to give it air feels so fucking good.

It's gratifying, too, knowing what I know, what she's admitted to me—that I'm not alone in this. That Tallulah burns just as much as I do.

"He holds her," I whisper, nuzzling behind her ear, my hand growing bolder across the soft curve of her stomach, bringing her tight against me. "The knife would fall from her hand, because it feels—"

"So good," she whispers.

I nod. "And she can't hold it any more. She has to let it go—the knife, and everything the reader will associate it with, further in the book."

"Solid symbolism," she agrees.

"He has her in his arms," I continue, wrapping my other arm around her waist, tucking her against me. Sweet Christ, she feels good, her full, soft ass nestled into my thighs, her waist, snug inside my arms, her head resting heavy on my chest.

I have to think about the time Oliver and I got in some petty fight, and Ollie swapped salt for sugar when I was making myself brownies from scratch with the promise that I wouldn't share any with him; I ate them like it didn't bother me one bit, like I hadn't tasted the difference, determined not to give away how miserable he'd made me. I wanted to vomit every bite I took. And I did, afterward. Violently. That memory is the only thing that keeps my body in check. And it *barely* keeps it in check.

"Then what?" Tallulah asks.

I clench my jaw, steady my breathing, trying so hard to keep myself in line. She's been through hell the past few days, and before that, we went wild on each other in the bookstore, an event we have yet to talk about. Though, what would we even say? *Hey, yeah, still super attracted to each other. Still both agree we want different things from a sexual partner and shouldn't have sex.*

There's no point in dredging it up, especially when she's so raw. But I do feel a responsibility—to her, to myself—not to let this go where I could see it heading. Me, spinning her around, Tallulah clambering back onto the counter as I hiked up her skirt and found her wet and tight, made her come with my fingers, my tongue, again and again.

The thought of tasting her, making her fall apart, has my body rapidly losing the battle to hide its response to her.

I press a soft, savoring kiss to her neck. "And then, even though the last thing he wants is to let her go," I whisper against her skin, "he does."

Slowly, I pull my arms away. Slowly, Tallulah turns. She stares up at me, eyes wide, skin glowing. "That . . ." She licks her lips, then clears her throat. "That was . . . very informative. Thank you."

I nod. "Glad I could help."

We stare at each other. Tallulah's gaze dips to my mouth. Mine dips to her rock-hard nipples inside her shirt.

Jesus Christ, this woman has the most beautiful tits in the world, and I'm never going to touch them. It's a tragedy I can't even begin to reckon with.

"I'm just going to go . . . write that, then," she says, taking a step back, picking up her laptop from the counter. "Give me a holler if you need anything, with, you know, the store, the animals, et cetera."

"Sure." I take a step to the side, conveniently placing me behind the bar-height chairs and hiding the evidence of how all of this has impacted me. "Good luck."

"Thanks," she says tightly, breezing by me. "I think I'm going to need it."

TWENTY

Tallulah

Playlist: "No River," Esmé Patterson

Well, it was inevitable. I'm rooming with a romance reader in a house connected to a romance bookstore owned by someone who runs a romance book club—it was only a matter of time until I got ambushed by romance lovers.

And here I am. Thoroughly ambushed.

Viggo's book club buddies mingle around the store, genre terms and phrases humming in the air that I have only abstract familiarity with, from their presence on Viggo's vast rotation of romance reader T-shirts. I sit behind the counter, chin in hand, facing my *fifth* interrogation from a customer, another member of Viggo's romance book club.

"So what's your favorite trope?" Tad—they/them, according to their name tag—asks. Everyone is wearing name tags, which strikes me as odd, given they all seem to know each other pretty well. I have a sneaking suspicion Viggo did it for my benefit, which would be considerate if I was trying to connect with this heart-eyed crew. Which I'm not.

"Not a trope gal," I tell them.

Tad's eyebrows shoot up. "I'm sorry, *what*?"

"Not a romance reader," I clarify.

Tad looks like I shot their dog.

"Can I take your order?" I ask them.

Tad blows out a breath. "Uh, sure. I'll take the..." They frown, browsing the menu overhead. "*Semlor.*"

"Good choice."

I serve Tad their baked good, direct them to use the chip reader to pay, and send them on their way. Glancing around, I see everybody has a baked good, drink, or both in hand. Some of them are starting to take their seats in the front of the store, where Viggo has moved the club chairs aside and set up a circle of IKEA folding chairs with little cushions on all of them. He 100 percent crocheted those cushion covers.

I'm concerned for that man's joints. And sleep habits. When does he do all of this?

Relieved to see no one else is here to accost me with more romance-related inquiries, I sit back on my stool behind the counter and sip my grapefruit seltzer. I spot a lingering book club member—name tag indicates she is Steph, she/her—who licks buttercream off her fingers before reaching for a book on the shelf. I clear my throat loudly. Steph startles and glances around, then catches me glaring at her.

Smiling sheepishly, she retreats to the circle of chairs.

"Damn right," I grumble.

"Easy does it, Tallulahloo. You're gonna scare away patrons with that scowl."

I whirl around and spot Viggo smiling at me, ball cap reversed, so I can see much more of those lovely gray-blue eyes. They're even lovelier under the store's lights, removed from the shadow of his ball cap's brim. Pale as ice, yet not nearly as cold. Not cold at all, actually. They're warm and happy, lines crinkling at the corners as he smiles at me. His smile falls a little when I don't return the gesture.

Reaching for his water, he sucks a deep drink through the straw, brow crinkled as he analyzes my expression. An expression I am trying very hard to mask behind my usual cool, unruffled poise.

It falters a little when he leans to set his water down and his free hand brushes mine.

I hate that I love the feel of those calloused fingertips on my skin. I hate that I have spent the past week trying not to think about how I loved his hands on me when we did that first workshop on my book.

We have not done another hands-on workshop. We've spent three mornings since that first time talking through more of his feedback in that same vein—show the connection, don't tell; slow down, stretch out moments that tie their romantic past to its crumbling present, revealing for the reader how their relationship has shifted.

Each time, Viggo's kept it to words only, no offer to demonstrate his meaning. I reassured him that I could extrapolate from his advice, based on what he showed me that first morning. He seemed relieved.

Which bothered me. And it shouldn't. His relief should relieve *me.* Then again, lust is part of the lizard brain—it is primitive, irrational, and driven by my libido. Expecting it to behave logically is absurd.

So I've been ignoring it. Well, trying to.

In the end, I've just been using my vibrator a lot.

Viggo's staring at me. I poke his chest, right in the sternum, snapping him out of it. "I know Elin Bergman taught you not to stare."

"What can I say? I'm a rebel child." Viggo's concerned brow pinch morphs to a bright smile as he steps closer. "C'mon, Lu." He sets his fingers at the corners of my mouth and gently lifts. "Turn that frown upside down."

"One day," I tell him, as I clasp his fingers and remove them from my face, "I'm going to write a thriller about a woman who snaps when one more person tells her to smile."

Viggo gives me a comically exaggerated grimace. "Uh-oh. Have I just put a target on my back?"

I take a swig of my seltzer, hiding my smile. "How are you feeling about everything?"

He smiles. "So far, so good. Everyone's a big fan of how the books are arranged by subgenre. Rave reviews of both baked goods and coffee drinks, in particular."

I make a theatrical bow. I insisted on making all the coffee drinks tonight so he could rub elbows and be social. "Glad to hear it."

His smile deepens. "About to get started with book club. Would you, uh . . . want to stick around? Could be some good material for your book. The nuts and bolts of relationships come up a lot when we discuss what we've read. You might pick up something you could use."

"Oh . . . um." I clear my throat and decide to focus on picking invisible lint off my jeans. "I think you're giving me all the guidance I need, honestly. But . . . if you *really* wanted me to, I could stay, otherwise I was just going to—"

"I want you to."

I peer up. Our gazes meet. I see it now, the nerves tightening the corners of his eyes, his mouth. I frown. "What are you nervous about?"

He blinks. "Me? Nervous? Psh."

"You are nervous. Why?"

Viggo darts a glance to the circle, then back to me. "It's our first historical romance. And a lot of people were dragging their feet about reading it. I'm nervous they hated it, and then I'm going to have to disband the group, kick them out, and lose a bunch of friends."

I roll my eyes. "You goofball. They probably loved it. And even if some of them didn't, I'm sure they'll be respectful about it. You can disagree on things and still be friends, can't you?"

I hear how desperate my voice turned on that last sentence. How invested I sound in its answer.

Because I can't have Viggo the way I want—his body, his closeness, his intimacy—not when he wants so much more than I am remotely capable of giving him. But, when this is over, I wouldn't mind having him in my life. Someone I can talk books with while playing with the dogs and cats I'd see when I paid a visit to his bookstore. Someone I could grab Chinese with and shoot the shit, whom I could see when our lives continued to overlap—our sisters' parties, milestones, birthdays—and share . . . comfort, familiarity. Even if I never find my way toward seeing love, romance, happily ever after, the way he does. Even if we never truly agree on what all this—sex, intimacy, relationships—really means.

His eyes dance between mine. "Friends can disagree," he says. "They absolutely can. You're right." He shakes his head, glancing away. "I'm being silly."

"You're not being silly. You're being nervous." I clasp his hand and squeeze tight. "It's okay to be nervous. But you've got this. Go have fun. And if they can't appreciate the allure of a broody duke in skintight breeches, you send them my way." I shake a fist. "I'll handle it."

Viggo laughs, squeezing my hand, then pulling away. I shouldn't feel like it's a loss, but I do.

"Thanks, Lula." He smiles. "So you'll stick around, then?"

I nod. "Back here, but yeah. I'll stick around."

Watching him round the counter into the throng of excited people, who light up as he joins them, I feel a sad sinking sensation. I don't like watching Viggo step into a world I'm not a part of.

And that's not supposed to happen. I'm supposed to be okay with me here, him there, with plenty of our lives, outlooks, never overlapping.

I stare at him, stomach twisting, heart pounding. I think, I'm starting to realize, I'm not okay with it at all.

———

I'm drowning in a sea of wedding dresses. Thankfully, the painful part is over. Charlie chose her dress months ago. Now is her first time trying it on after the first alterations were made. I sit quietly, sipping my coffee while Charlie and the seamstress discuss details of the dress. They have this well in hand.

Charlie glances in the mirror, meeting my eyes.

A smile lifts her mouth.

I try to smile back.

It's a bit tense. Charlie and I haven't talked since our parents delivered the news of their divorce. Charlie didn't reach out, and I didn't reach out either. I felt selfish relief that Charlie didn't need me, when I wasn't sure I could give her anything, when I felt so lost and spent myself. I felt bitter guilt that I couldn't muster the emotional strength to let her know I was there for her. There's so much unspoken between us, and I don't know how to navigate it. Charlie doesn't seem to, either.

My sister's gaze slips to my thermos, which reads, *I like my coffee like I like my dukes—hot and rich*. God forbid Viggo have a normal to-go mug.

"Nice mug," she says.

I raise it in cheers, then take a swig. "The joys of living with a romance reader."

Charlie laughs softly, then peers down at her dress. The seamstress finishes pinning its hem, since the dress turned out to still be a little long. Then she steps back.

"Ready for the veil?" she asks. "So we can see if we like how that's lying, lengthwise, with the dress?"

Charlie nods.

Just as we're left alone when the seamstress walks out, a buzzing phone cuts the silence. Both of us check our purses, extracting our phones. Charlie smiles, then starts typing. My screen is blank. Nothing from Viggo. Not that I'd expect it. We don't generally text.

But I guess I wondered if he'd let me know where he was this morning. I woke up a little late, after having tossed and turned in bed for hours last night, listening to the sound of voices and laughter lingering in the bookstore, even after book club wrapped up and I slipped out, seeing Viggo's wide smile, his relief. The book club loved their first historical romance. He'd successfully sold them on the subgenre, opened up the place to a group of people, sold books, drinks, pastries, bookish merchandise. He didn't need me anymore.

When I came into the kitchen this morning, there was nothing to signal that Viggo had been here and was gone already except a carafe of coffee waiting for me and the absence of his keys from the little *Home, Sweet Home* key hook by the door.

I pushed past the disappointment that I'd missed him. Drank my coffee, ate my breakfast bar, and rode the Vespa to Charlie's wedding dress fitting.

"Tallulah?"

I jerk my head up, wrenched from my thoughts. "Sorry, yes?"

My sister stands with the veil on her head. Somehow, I was that zoned out, I missed the seamstress returning, placing the veil on Charlie's head.

She looks perfect.

"Well?" My sister's eyes search mine.

Pushing up from my seat, I walk closer, a real, wide smile lifting my mouth. "Char. You look . . . stunning."

Charlie blinks. Sniffles. And then she bursts into tears.

The seamstress's eyes widen. I turn toward her. "Would you mind if we just had a minute?"

"Of course." She's out of there in no time, leaving us alone.

I wrap my arms around Charlie, who buries her face in my neck and sobs. I do what I have so many times before, when she's fallen apart. Slowly, I sway her, rubbing her back. "It's okay, Char. It's okay."

"I'm sorry," she sobs.

"Shh, no sorries from you."

"I'm such an emotional mess."

"You're getting married," I tell her. "It's understandable to be emotional—"

"No. Not that. I mean, yes, that, but it's just Mom and Dad. I'm relieved. I'm angry. I'm tired."

I'm about to do what I always have. Swallow my own feelings, focus on hers. Reassure her, tell her she'll be okay. But then I remember what Viggo said earlier this week, earnest and kind.

We'll be brave together. Little bit by little bit.

"Me too," I whisper. "I'm feeling all of that, too."

Charlie pulls away, frantically wiping beneath her eyes. "You are?"

Taking a deep breath, I clasp my sister's hand. "What do you say we grab ourselves some ice cream?"

TWENTY-ONE

Tallulah

Playlist: "You're Not Special, Babe," Orla Gartland

While my favorite place I've ever lived was up in the cool, moody beauty of Washington State, there are definitely perks to calling LA home. Fashion. Great weather. And a plethora of kick-ass ice cream shops.

Charlie and I sit beside each other, ice creams in hand, facing the Pacific, toes in the sand as we watch waves break on the shore.

"I really needed this," my sister says before taking a big bite of her rocky road.

I lick my mint chip and nod. "Me too."

The silence that follows isn't uncomfortable, but it isn't easy, either. We're in new territory, outside the roles we've always occupied. I think we both feel a little lost.

Charlie glances my way, her eyes searching mine. "So," she says. "What you told me, back at the dress shop . . . Can we talk about it?"

I clasp her hand and squeeze. "I want to try."

She nods. "Okay."

I stare at my sister, debating how to talk about this. "I'm just . . . trying to feel my feelings, Charlie, silly as that sounds. I'm realizing everything with Mom and Dad messed me up more than I wanted to admit. I might not be very good at talking through this, but I want to work on it."

"Haven't you . . ." Charlie bites her lip nervously. "Haven't you talked to your friends about this before? I figured you just didn't talk to *me* about it."

I lick a drip of my ice cream from its waffle cone, then shake my head. "No. I haven't."

"Why not?" Charlie asks.

I never told my siblings the extent of my loss when Clint kicked me out. He didn't just take my home; he took what was left of our friends. He told them I'd broken his heart, used him, coldly shut him out.

I never promised him anything more than a friends-with-benefits situation; he never asked me for more. Until he did, at the end, and I told him gently nothing had changed for me, from how things had started. And then he got quiet, sulked around for days. Then asked again. When I said no *that* time, he raged at me, threw things, and kicked me out.

That's what really happened. His lie isn't even the part that hurts the worst, though. It's that my "friends" believed his version of the story over mine.

"Oh, you know." I shrug. "Everyone moved away, moved on. Got jobs, found partners. Even a couple of them are starting families. We're in different places now. And when they were around . . . I didn't realize, didn't see what I see now."

Charlie frowns. "I'm sorry. I didn't know."

"It's okay. I've been busy," I tell her. "My career's had my focus. I haven't exactly had time to miss friendship. But now I do see that keeping all this to myself hasn't been for the best. So I figure, this is a good place to start, the two of us, talking. And Harry, too, if he's ever open to it."

"It is a good place to start," Charlie says. But then she goes quiet. The kind of quiet that I know means she's biting her tongue.

"Just say it," I tell her.

"Go to therapy!" she blurts so loud it startles the seagulls hovering near us, angling to mooch for the tiniest bit of food that might fall from our hands.

"Had a feeling you were going to say that."

"You did?"

"I did." I lick my ice cream. "How did you do it?" I ask her. But my eyes are on the ocean. "Take that leap?"

"On what? Therapy?"

"That and . . . everything. Reading those books Viggo gave you. Opening your heart to Gigi. Figuring out what you believed, what you wanted?"

Charlie takes a bite of her ice cream, frowning out at the ocean. "Well . . . it was gradual. But it began when I got mad."

I turn and look at her. "Mad?"

She nods. "So fucking mad. Ziggy and I, you know how we reconnected when I started at USC."

"I remember."

"Well, she invited me to their Sunday family dinner. I came. I was feeling really anxious and emotional, overwhelmed. Lonely. I hoped sitting around a familiar group of people, a happy family, would make me feel better. But it just made me really fucking mad."

A twinge of recognition echoes inside me. "Why?"

"Because they have something we'll *never* have. Because that lack messed me up so bad, Tallulah. It messed us up, you, me, and Harry. And I felt so . . . helpless. I didn't ask to be born to Mom and Dad. I had no choice in how dysfunctional they were and how that fundamentally shaped me."

I bite my lip as tears prick my eyes. Charlie's saying everything I never knew how to put into words, never knew how deeply I felt.

"I kept it together until after I left dinner. I went for a run, so fast and long, I puked up dinner, right on the sidewalk. And on the sidewalk nearby was this small tree branch. It had fallen out of the tree above me, probably. About the size of a walking stick. I picked it up, lifted it over my head, and just smashed it into the sidewalk, over and over again, screaming at the top of my lungs."

My eyes widen. "Seriously?"

She laughs. "No one even called the cops on me. Nothing fazes people here. I love it." Turning, she meets my eyes. "It felt good, Tallulah, to get mad. Because that anger cleared the way for me to feel other things. I released my anger that I couldn't change my past and focused on the fact that I sure as shit could change my future. Step by very little step." She shrugs. "Now here I am. In love. Engaged. Ready to get married."

"That's quite the journey."

"Our parents' journey is not ours, Tallulah. Therapy helped me figure that out—that what they showed us, in what they called 'love' and 'marriage,' does not define those terms for *me*. What I have with Gigi . . . whatever you might want with someone, someday, *we* get to say what that means. No one else." She licks her ice cream. "But that's really only possible after a shit ton of therapy to unlearn all the bullshit we internalized growing up."

I stare at my little sister and realize how very grown she is, how wise, how brave.

"You're incredible, you know that, right?" I clutch her hand. "I admire you, Charlie. So much."

My sister glances my way. She seems stunned. "You do?"

"So much. I'm sorry if I haven't shown you that."

"Tallulah, don't be sorry for a thing. You've been so much more to me and Harry than you ever should have had to be." She squeezes my hand back. "I'm where I am in so many ways because of *you*. I have always admired your strength, your confidence. I've learned to believe in myself because of how you believed in me, because of how you showed me, if I put my mind to something, I could be successful."

I tug her close, wrap my arm around her, and hold my sister. We sit in silence, temple to temple, watching the ocean.

"I love you, Tallulah," Charlie whispers. "You don't . . . have to say that back. I know you don't like that word."

I swallow against the lump in my throat. I haven't said it since we were little. Since I started hating that word so much. It sits on my tongue, sharp and daunting, the word I haven't said in so long. But, staring at my little sister, I know I feel a bond to her unlike anything else—that I'd kill for her, die for her, take on any pain to protect her. If there's one kind of "love" I can get behind, it's that. And she deserves to know it.

"I love you, too, Charlie. I'm sorry I haven't said it. I should have. That kind of love, family love, that's not what I've taken issue with. That kind of love, it's different."

My sister smiles up at me, eyes glittering mischievously. "Is it?"

I give her an arched eyebrow and attack my ice cream, indulging in a big, cold bite. "Don't push it."

Her laugh dances on the sea breeze, so loud, it outstrips the waves' roar. Mine joins hers, softer, not as strong, not as bright. Not yet.

But I think there's a chance that, one day, it will be.

———

Killing the Vespa's engine, I frown. I'm looking at a soccer field full of kids. Cones, small nets, balls flying through the air.

This is . . . not what I was expecting when I got Viggo's SOS text: Ashbury won't start.

After parting ways with Charlie, watching her pull out, I was just tugging on my helmet when I felt my phone buzz in my pants pocket. I checked it, took one look at Viggo's text, and texted him back, asking where to pick him up. Then I gunned it for the dropped pin he'd sent me.

I didn't think anything of the details of the destination. I was too focused on getting there. Now that I'm here, I am thoroughly confused.

Viggo stands at the edge of a field, wearing white soccer socks bunched down at his ankles, yellow athletic shorts, and a white T-shirt. The weirdest part of this isn't that he's in soccer gear, surrounded by elementary school kids—it's his T-shirt. It says nothing about romance but instead, *Bergman Northwest Outfitters— Bringing the outdoors to everyone.*

I squint against the sun, walking toward him. This is bizarre.

"Thank God you're here," he says, pulling me into a hug, like he's on a ship about to go down and I'm his lifeboat.

I pat his back stiffly. "You okay?"

"Never been better."

A soccer ball flies toward us. Viggo spins with me still in his arms, shielding us from the live fire. He takes a shot to his back and curses under his breath, hot and right in my ear. It makes longing rush through me, imagining a very different scenario, in which Viggo would be holding me tight, hot and sweaty, swearing into the crook of my neck. A scenario in which his long body was pressed into mine, rocking into me, making me gasp and beg for harder, faster—

Another soccer ball *thwacks* into his back, snapping me out of my dirty thoughts. I pull out of his arms. "What is going on?"

Viggo steps a smidge to his left, adjusting for my movement, shielding me still. "Mutiny," he says darkly.

I frown. "Viggo—"

Another ball smacks him, and he spins around. "Okay, now, that one was my butt. Cut it out."

I move past him just as another ball sails our way. I catch it tight in my hands, my old goalie reflexes returning. Viggo's head snaps my way. He blinks, stunned. "Damn, Clarke."

"Oooh, Coach Viggo swore," a kid says, pointing up at him.

Viggo turns bright red. "I—"

"A dam is simply a human-made or animal-built barrier that stops water from flowing," I tell the kid, staring down at them sternly. "Coach Viggo was referring to my goalie skills at stopping the ball the way water is stopped by a dam. Now, run along, urchin, before he makes you run sprints for your impudence."

The kid blinks, gaping at me, then runs off on a shrill scream.

Viggo bites his lip. "Wow, Lu. Didn't know you had it in you."

"What? A backbone? Everyone's too soft on kids these days. They can handle a firm talking-to, here and there."

A wide smile breaks across his face. "I was actually referring to the goalie skills. You play soccer?"

I shift on my feet, setting the ball on my hip. "Used to."

Soccer used to be one of my few happy places. It gave me a community in high school, where my brutally competitive, cold determination was an asset, something that actually earned me friends. I got to escape my parents and their drama, traveling for soccer. It helped me find community in college, a competitive co-ed league. But it was also where I met Clint and most of our friends. Another thing that dissolved slowly as people moved away. I haven't been able to find my way back to it since.

"You play?" I ask. "And . . . coach?"

Viggo sighs. "Yeah, I play. I got a little busy with the store to play on my team this past session, though."

"And yet . . . you had time . . . for coaching . . . kids?"

He grimaces, scrubbing at the back of his neck. "Long story. For now I gotta get these kids into some kind of organized chaos. Practice will be over in thirty."

"You're not done? I figured you were trying to leave and you realized the car wouldn't start."

"No, I realized Ashbury wasn't feeling like himself when they took their first water break and I took two to cool off in the car. He wouldn't turn on. I'm sorry to make you wait—I just didn't know how soon you'd get here, and I didn't want to be stranded any longer than absolutely necessary."

Beyond him, a dozen or so kids are bouncing around each other, kicking balls, screaming, like feral animals.

I squint up at him. "You were going to make a break for it, weren't you?"

"No," he says way too emphatically.

He was definitely thinking about it. I don't blame him.

I swallow a laugh. "Is it just you? No co-coach?" Growing up, playing soccer, I always had a couple of coaches running my practices and games.

His expression turns the closest to angry I've ever seen. "I *had* a co-coach. Until that traitor, Jeff, up and quit on me."

A ball flies toward the back of Viggo's head. I lunge and catch it. "Gee, I wonder why."

"I'm screwed," he says bleakly.

I drop the ball at my feet and set my pristine white street sneakers on it. I'm not giving those kids any more ammunition. "Why in the hell, with all you have going on, are you coaching kids' soccer?"

"Jeff begged me to help," Viggo explains. "And I suck at saying no."

"Who is Jeff?"

"A guy whose bike I fixed last fall. I passed him on the trail and offered to help. He bought me a beer in thanks afterward, and while we were drinking at the bar, soccer was on the TV. We started talking about the game, realized we both played. I invited him to join my co-ed league, since we were short on numbers that session. This spring, he invited me to coach his kid's soccer team with him."

I blink. "You, my friend, were bamboozled."

Viggo laughs emptily.

"Wait, if this is Jeff's kid's soccer team," I ask, "where is *he*? And his kid?"

"Max broke his foot two weeks ago, jumping on the trampoline, so he's out. Jeff was still coming and coaching, but . . ." Viggo glances out at the kids, now pelting balls at each other in the net. "He texted me this morning and said he's out. Apparently, their spring calendar 'suddenly got very full.'"

"Very full," I mutter, rolling my eyes as I shrug off my jacket.

Viggo frowns at me as I hand it to him. "What are you doing?"

"Fixing this," I tell him, stepping closer until I can reach the whistle hanging around his neck. "I suggest you plug your ears."

TWENTY-TWO

Viggo

Playlist: "House We Share," Chance Emerson

Watching Tallulah Clarke coach kids' soccer is a glorious thing. She stands, eyes narrowed against the sun, hands on her hips, sporting a white T-shirt that features a black-outlined tiger, hair piled high on her head, and my whistle in her mouth.

Its shrill tone cuts across the grass as she watches the kids dribble with their balls around the cones, practicing their inside and outside cuts. "Now back the other direction!" she yells.

"Hey." Dan, our league coordinator, steps up beside me. Tallulah's on my other side, and I think his decision is strategic, placing as much distance as he can between him and her formidable presence.

"Hey, Dan." I offer my hand, which he takes. "This is Tallulah Clarke, my new co-coach."

She nods, eyes still on the field. Her whistle drops from her mouth as she yells, "Faster!"

Dan and I both jump. Dan looks at me. "She have her clearances?"

Tallulah unearths her phone and hands it to me. I swipe it open, hold it up to her face for facial recognition, then hand it to Dan so he can see the photos she showed me five minutes ago.

After I told her she'd need them to be able to help and she showed me she did, I didn't ask why Tallulah, a solitary twenty-six-year-old thriller writer, has her child abuse and FBI criminal record clearances. I'm not looking a gift horse in the mouth.

Dan shrugs. "Good by me, then. Nice to meet you, Coach Clarke."

"Likewise," she says to him, eyes still on the kids.

Dan walks off, hands in his pockets, leaving us alone.

"Why *do* you have your clearances?" I ask.

"Brief stint in a Unitarian Universalist church this past year. I volunteered in the preschool and toddler rooms. I got lonely. It was something to do on Sunday mornings."

The idea of Tallulah with a bunch of kids my niece's and nephew's ages, finger painting, reading books, and playing goofy games, makes something warm settle beneath my ribs.

She glances my way. "What? I don't strike you as the church-attending type? Tighter cuts!" she calls to the kids.

They're stunningly quick to follow her orders.

"Nah, I wasn't thinking that."

"What were you thinking, then?" She only hazards a half-second glance my way before her eyes are back on the team.

"I was thinking there's a lot I don't know about you, Lula." I swallow, nerves getting the better of me, tightening my throat. "But I'd like to know more."

Tallulah blows the whistle, then yells, "Two-minute water break! Then scrimmage until practice ends!" She turns back to me and smiles. "Funny. I was just thinking the same thing about you."

———

From my spot, stretched out on the couch, I watch Tallulah walk down the hall, hair brushing her shoulders, wet from her shower. A heather-gray T-shirt dress drapes beautifully down her body, swinging at her knees. Barefoot, bright blue toenails that match her hair. No makeup on her face. She looks relaxed. Content.

At home.

That warmth is back like it was as I watched her on the field, spilling through my chest, reaching farther through my limbs, to my fingertips, my toes.

I watch her come to a stop at the edge of the kitchen and take a deep drink of water from the mason jar she has in hand. When she lowers it, she looks at me, brow furrowed. "How you doing?"

"What do you mean?"

She gives me a puzzled look. "Ashbury being in the shop. I figured, given your emotional attachment to him, you'd be upset."

It hits me like a bolt of lightning. All at once. I sit up on the sofa, anxiously scraping my fingers through my shower-wet hair. Panic builds inside me.

This . . . warmth filling me, when I look at her.

Watching her here, this sense of . . . rightness.

My beloved car has been towed to what will probably be its final resting place, and I'm not falling apart. I've had more important things to think about: riding home on the Vespa while clutching Tallulah's waist, breathing her in, soaking up the warmth of her skin seeping through her clothes. Showering so I didn't stink to high heaven, trimming my beard a little to make it look less scraggly.

This is not normal. This is . . . different. More.

Oh God.

"Viggo?" she presses.

I blink, shaking my head. "Sorry." I clear my throat. "I'm okay. Donnie at the shop will take good care of him. Ashbury will live to drive another day. I have faith."

I don't. But the old Viggo would, and that's the one Tallulah needs to think is still sitting here, talking to her.

Because the new Viggo is a man who is . . . changing before his very own eyes. This new Viggo texts not one of his three local siblings or parents or friends when his car doesn't start—he texts

Tallulah. This new Viggo isn't lonely and antsy on a Saturday after-noon, putzing around his house, trying to find something to do—he's sitting here, counting down the minutes until Tallulah comes out of the shower.

This new Viggo . . . is quite possibly falling for his roommate. Quite possibly has been falling for her since the first time he watched her walk into his classroom seven years ago, looking for her since the day he walked out of the world they shared, until they stum-bled back into each other's paths, seven years later.

It can't be that, can it? All this waiting and wanting, yet not finding a single person I clicked with . . . was it because I already knew what I wanted, *who* I wanted? She just wasn't . . . here?

It can't be that simple. That cruelly simple.

Maybe what I'm feeling is just the familiarity we've started to build after a few weeks of living together. Maybe it's simply the pleasure of getting comfortable around each other, working on her book, working on my store, sharing meals, hanging out with the pets. Maybe this is how being friends feels with her.

I stare at her as she strolls into the kitchen. "I hope he can fix up Ashbury for you, too," she says. "If not, I'm going to be stuck hauling you all over Los Angeles on the Vespa, driving ten miles under the speed limit."

The familiar teasing eases the tightness in my chest, cools my brain's overheating thoughts. I smile.

She smiles back. After a beat, she asks, "Did you trim your beard?"

I bring a hand to it, equal parts satisfied and self-conscious. She noticed. "Just a little."

Her smile deepens. "It looks nice."

More warmth spilling through me. You'd think she told me the sun rose when I did, given how good it feels. "Thanks, Lula."

"You missed about four inches, though. And you used the wrong tool." She makes a buzzing noise and mimes dragging a razor along her jaw.

"You leave my beard alone, Clarke. It gives me character."

She laughs, straight from her belly, and I grin like a fool. "You have character aplenty without a woodsman beard, Bergman."

Romeo barks, chiming into the conversation. "See," I tell her. "He has my back."

Juliet makes a whiny groan and rolls onto her back. "And *she* agrees with me," Tallulah says, "don't you, Juliet?"

The dog hops up and wanders over to Tallulah, brushing her snout into Tallulah's hand. Tallulah pets her and mutters something quiet and sweet. "What about you, Romeo?" she calls.

My traitorous dog trots her way. "There you go," she tells me. "Three to one. The beard goes."

"Like hell it does."

She gives me a coy smile, then turns and opens the fridge. "Okay, food time. Let me guess. You didn't eat."

"I was waiting for you."

She glances over her shoulder, her eyes holding mine. "You didn't have to do that."

My heart's thudding harder in my chest, tightness creeping back in as I feel a new weight to what I'm about to say. "I wanted to wait for you."

A soft, perplexed smile lifts her mouth. "Okay. Well, you want me to make something?"

"I thought . . . maybe we could go out. Treat ourselves. It's been a busy week. We've been busting our butts. I think we earned it."

Tallulah turns fully and shuts the fridge door. She leans against it, her eyes searching mine. "Sure. That sounds nice."

Relief floods me. Why, I don't know. It's just a dinner date. That is, dinner together. Not a date. Just two roommates, coworkers, co-coaches . . . friends. Eating a meal.

"Want to take the dogs?" I ask.

"Definitely. How about that new Korean place? I'm craving bibimbap."

"Perfect." I push up off the sofa, ready to grab my ball cap, keys, wallet, and go.

I tug on my ball cap and turn, catching Tallulah watching me in the hallway, a pinch in her brow. I want to smooth my finger over that. And I shouldn't. Not if I just want her physically, not if this is just the case of unsatisfied lust that I've told myself it is.

"Gotta hit the restroom before we go," I tell her. "Chugged a bunch of water when we got back from the mechanic—"

Her hand is on my chest, stopping me. Tallulah peers up, her eyes dancing between mine. No eyeliner, just wide amber eyes. She's breathtaking like this, bare and unguarded. I want to walk her back, press her into the wall, kiss her, and kiss her some more. And then I want to walk her right across the hall to her bedroom and lay her down, make her come, give myself relief, finally scratch this damn itch, so I can clear my head, stop confusing lust and another, much more daunting L-word.

Her hand slips from my chest. "No rush. Take your time. I have to get ready first."

"Get ready for what?"

She lifts her eyebrows. "To go outside."

"You're clothed, Lu. Grab some shoes, and we're all set."

She rolls her eyes. "I need to put on makeup. Fix my hair."

"No, you don't. I mean, you can, of course, it's your body—"

"Glad we cleared that up." It's her usual bristly retort, but her voice is teasing and warm, no icy edge to be found.

"I just meant . . ." There's a blue hair stuck to the edge of her jaw, and I can't help it. I reach for that strand and slide it back, my fingertip tracing along her cheek, behind her ear. Tallulah shivers. "You look beautiful, with or without makeup, hair done or undone. So, you know . . . if you don't want to make a man wait any longer for his bulgogi, you could just slip on a pair of shoes and we'd be out of here."

Her gaze narrows. But a smile lifts her mouth. "Fine," she says, breezing past me, back toward her room. "I'll just get a pair of shoes. Might take me a while, though. I'm very choosy about my footwear."

"Tallulah," I warn.

She laughs, a bright, bubbly sound that echoes down the hallway. I stare at the dogs, who've settled at my feet, eyes up, waiting patiently. "I don't know what to tell you. The woman likes her shoes."

"Just kidding," she says, walking briskly back my way, a pair of sensible sandals on her feet. Her hand clasps mine and tugs. "Come on. I'm starving."

TWENTY-THREE

Tallulah

Playlist: "Baby Where You Are," Mountain Man

For once, a week does fly by. Viggo and I exhaust ourselves with tasks. The final, perfecting touches on the store, social media blasts, and flyer distribution. Baking, plant propagating, mug making, and coaster crocheting (Viggo). Writing, revising, writing some more (yours truly). Together, we walk the dogs, talk store logistics during meals, and plan our next soccer practice, strategizing for the team's upcoming first game.

I'm grateful for the busyness, the distraction that keeps us from lingering in the soft, cozy start of the day that we've settled into, sipping coffee side by side at the counter, Viggo reading while I crunch on my breakfast bar, blinking awake, setting out our plans for the day.

After a successful team practice this morning and a disciplined day of writing (me) and final inventory (him), we treated ourselves again to the Korean place we tried last weekend and loved.

I sigh contentedly, sated, relaxed among the fragrant blossoms and winding vines that make up Viggo's little outdoor patio oasis, and tell him, "I surrender." Groaning, I snap on the lid of my to-go container of bibimbap on the table, then slump back in my chair.

"Same." He dabs his mouth with a napkin before tossing it onto the table, too.

He has some rice in his beard. Leaning in, I brush it away. Our faces are close, so close I can see the clouds reflected in his eyes.

"Stragglers?" he asks.

I nod, letting my hand fall.

Viggo smiles. His gaze dips to my mouth, then away. He sits back on his seat. "Thanks for looking out for me."

"Happy to."

He tips his head, smile deepening.

"What?" I ask.

"Just . . . had one of those moments. Déjà vu."

A thrill runs through me. "I've had déjà vu with you, too."

His eyebrows lift. "Really?"

I nod. "First morning I was here."

His smile fades. I stare at him. A very strange need creeps up inside me. All week, since talking to Charlie, mulling over what we talked about, it's been building—this need to feel close to him. To touch him, smell him, burrow close.

I don't want sex with him. Well . . . maybe it's more accurate to say that I don't want sex with him *right now*, not just yet. I want something in between. Something I've never wanted before.

Viggo holds my eyes as he sips his seltzer. I feel nervous and needy. Unsure.

We'll be brave together. Little bit by little bit.

"Viggo?"

"Hmm?"

I swallow, then take a deep breath. "You know how we've . . . acknowledged we're attracted to each other? How we've acted on that a couple times."

He swallows, too, then sits up, setting down his seltzer can. "I do, Lula. I've actually been thinking . . . maybe we should talk about that."

My heart pounds. Anxiety spins through me, scattering my courage. "I have, too. But . . ."

His eyes search mine. "But?"

"But before we do, I was wondering, if you're comfortable with it, and obviously, it's totally okay if not . . . if we could . . . cuddle."

A soft, surprised smile lifts his mouth. "You want to cuddle?"

My voice is shaky as I knit my hands together so tight it hurts and tell him, "I've never done it before. But from what I've heard about cuddling . . . it sounds like something I could use right about now."

Viggo's expression blanks. "You've never *cuddled*?"

I shake my head quickly. "Parents never did it. Maybe I've cuddled Charlie before, when she was little and she was upset? But . . ."

"No one's ever cuddled *you*," he says quietly.

I nod.

His gaze holds mine. Slowly, he reaches for my hand and clasps it. "Then I'd say it's high time we fixed that."

Viggo tugs me up to standing, reaches, and opens the door for me. I grab our leftovers in my free hand, watch him shut the door behind us, and follow him inside.

He takes the food from me and sets it on the counter, dragging me with him. Glancing over his shoulder, he smiles. "You couldn't have asked a better person. I am the cuddle king."

That sours my stomach. I don't like thinking about all the people Viggo's cuddled. My distaste for this news must show in my expression.

Viggo tips his head. "What's that face about?"

"Nothing."

"'Nothing.' Hmm." He sits on the couch, then swings his legs up before spreading them wide. "Right here. C'mere, Lulaloo."

"Right where?"

He pats the space between his legs.

I eyeball it skeptically.

He smiles. "Cuddles involve being close. That's what you want, right? If not, we can just sit here on the sofa, side by side—"

"This is fine," I blurt. Then I kneel on the sofa, spinning until I rest against him, my back to his front. I'm stiff, awkward, holding myself halfway through a crunch. Viggo feels it.

"Relax into me," he says quietly, his breath warm, rushing over my ear.

I fight a shiver. "I'm heavy. My weight will be on you."

"That would be the point." He pulls me back. "Lean back on me."

I do, at least more than I was, trying to believe him. Gently, he wraps an arm around me, across my collarbone, coaxing me into him.

"Trust me, Lu. I can hold you."

Finally, I relax fully, the way I would into a bath. Viggo rests his head against mine, his jaw to my temple, and sighs deeply. "There."

I shut my eyes, soaking up the rush of warmth, sweet and soothing, spilling through my veins. He smells like his woodsy soap, which I sometimes pick up, bring to my nose, and smell in the shower, like a lust-addled weirdo, the whisper of cinnamon sugar that I've traced to his beard oil. His arm is heavy, his bicep round and hard, straining against his shirt. I lift my free hand and trace a vein just beneath the surface of his skin.

He shivers.

"Sorry." I drop my hand.

He picks up my hand and puts it back on his arm. "That was a good shiver."

A smile tips my mouth. I'm glad to have my back to him. It feels safer this way. I wonder if that's why he arranged us like this. I'm sure there are other approaches to cuddling that involve facing each other, but this . . . it feels like a good way to learn the cuddling ropes.

"How you feeling?" he asks. I glance up and catch our reflection in the TV. A rush of self-consciousness that he could see me after all ebbs when I notice his eyes are shut, a peaceful smile on his face.

"Good," I tell him, resting my head back on the curve of his shoulder. "You could be a bit squishier, but we'll work on that. Give me some more time to make sure you eat lunch every day, and we'll fill you in."

"Be nice. Maybe I'm insecure that I'm not bulky."

I roll my eyes. He's gorgeous, and he has to know it.

"Stop rolling your eyes at me, Clarke."

My gaze snaps up to the TV screen and our reflection, where I spot his eyes on me. He grins.

"Stop spying on me, Bergman."

His grin widens. "Not spying. Just watching . . . trying to figure out what you're thinking."

I hold his eyes. "I was thinking you're beautiful. That your body is perfect."

His grin slips a little. Our eyes hold. His grip on me tightens. Mine tightens on his arm, too.

We are on the precipice of something I promised myself we wouldn't cross over before I was honest, before I told him how I feel about trying to be someone who lives beyond her tightly se-cured walls and ideology—scared, curious, inexperienced.

I have to put the brakes on where we're headed, because I need this first—this safe, caring touch, this comfort with him. Our gazes still hold in the TV reflection. An idea takes hold.

Viggo tips his head. "What is it?"

"Want to . . . watch a movie?"

His brow furrows. I've surprised him. But then he gives me an-other sweet, soft smile. "I'd love that."

One movie down—my choice. One to go—his.

"Rest in peace, Heath," Viggo says, as the end credits of *A Knight's Tale* start to roll. I lift my mason jar of water in solemn agreement, then tip it back for a long drink.

"Heath was a great actor," I tell him.

Viggo nods. "Brilliant. Man, I love that movie."

I smile. "One of my favorites ever."

"Why do you like it so much?" he asks, peering down at me.

I frown in thought. "Because . . . it's about reaching for a life beyond what you've been born into, about how hard it is, not just to reach that place, but believe in yourself as you try. Plus the fun anachronisms—old clothes, modern music and dance—and of course, Heath Ledger and Shannyn Sossamon are great eye candy."

"Those two, their characters have a cute little romantic sub-plot," Viggo says, eyebrows wiggling.

I glare up at him playfully. "Emphasis on *sub*plot."

"Just for that, I'm making you watch the sweetest, romanciest flick I've ever seen."

I let out an exaggerated groan.

"You heard me." He pats my hip in a way that makes me wish it was about twice as hard and right on my ass. I try to ignore that, bring myself back to where I've been the past two hours—cuddling, safe, unsexual closeness. "Make some popcorn," he says, "then get back here and get ready to cry."

"*You* make the popcorn. I can't reach it."

He tips his head as he peers down at me, then gently taps the end of my nose. "With the new stepstool in the kitchen you can."

"Since when is there a stepstool in the kitchen?"

"Since this afternoon."

I narrow my eyes at him. "You built me a stepstool."

His cheeks pink a little bit. "Who says I built it?" He scratches behind his ear. "I could have run to IKEA."

"When? After midnight, when I finally heard you go to bed, and before eight a.m., when I woke up to you making coffee? We've been together all day since then."

He smiles sheepishly. "I chipped away at it over the past few weeks. Couldn't sleep two nights ago. That's when I finished the varnish. It's dry now."

I sigh. "Viggo. Would you please stop being so considerate? And sleep more?"

His gaze holds mine. "Sleep is overrated—"

"False."

"And I like thinking about you, Lu. You're my roomie. I want you to be able to get whatever you need around here."

His roomie. That's all I am right now. A valuable reminder. Platonic cohabitation is our boundary, until we discuss it being other than that. Which we haven't. Because *I* asked to cuddle first.

"Fine. Popcorn it is." I ease up, clutching the sofa and kneeling to stand. When I'm upright, I glance over my shoulder. Viggo's gaze is fixed right on my ass. "Enjoying the view?"

His gaze snaps up to me guiltily. He bites his lip. "I'm just a man, Tallulah."

"That's how the guy who wears a 'Read romance, fight the patriarchy' shirt justifies objectifying me? Toxic masculinity?"

He grimaces. "Human, I should have said. Who, I might add, only just now gave in to the temptation to look."

I fold my arms across my chest and stroll toward him, until my dress brushes his bent knee. He stares up at me. I stare down at him. "This is your *first* time checking out my ass?"

His cheeks pink. "I mean . . . I might have rounded down. A lot."

I lean my knee into his hand where it rests on his thigh. His fingers brush my knee, once, gently. Our eyes hold as I lean my knee in harder. His fingers trail higher, up my thigh, beneath my dress, skimming beneath the hem, grazing my skin.

We're playing with fire. But hell if I care that I'm going to get burned. I want him. And he wants me.

Talk, Tallulah! You're supposed to talk!

"I don't think we should make popcorn just yet."

Viggo swallows. "No?"

"No." Slowly, I reach for his thigh, pulling it wide, until there's space for me to sit again. I ease down, one knee drawn up, the other leg hanging off the couch, and hold his eyes. "I think we should talk."

TWENTY-FOUR

Tallulah

Playlist: "Nobody," Bess Atwell

"Talk." Viggo blinks as if I've stunned him.

I smile nervously. "Caught you off guard with that one, didn't I?"

"I mean . . . a little." He sits up straighter on the sofa, his hand reaching for mine. I lace our fingers together. "But I'm here for talking."

"Good." I clear my throat, nerves tightening my voice. "Because I want to tell you about what's going on, since my call with my parents, since I went for that ride last week and came home. I want to talk to you about a lot of things. And I want to talk about"—I gesture between us—"this."

He swallows, nods. "Okay. I'm listening. And . . . I'm ready to talk, too."

I draw my hand from his and clutch mine together, take a deep breath. And then I tell him—more than I've ever told anybody. About my family, my parents, my siblings, our dysfunctional dynamic. I give him the bullet-point, boiled-down version, a crash course on my life, from childhood up through high school, college, the fallout with Clint, the steady loss of my friends.

When I'm done, I peer up from where I've held my gaze fixed on my clasped hands.

Viggo stares at me, his brow furrowed, his mouth tight. "Lulaloo," he says quietly.

I bite my lip, trying not to cry. And then I realize . . . I can cry. Because I'm feeling deeply, scared but also brave. I feel raw and naked, like, all this time, I've lived wrapped in layer after layer that dimmed sensation, dulled light and sound and scent, and now that I've unwrapped myself, I'm inundated by all that I'm feeling. It's *so* much.

Slowly, Viggo leans closer, sliding his hands over mine, which are still knotted tight. He holds my eyes. "Thank you."

"For what?" I whisper tearily.

He raises his eyebrows. "You just trusted me, Tallulah. With so much tough shit. That's . . . wildly brave and vulnerable and . . ." He swallows roughly. "I don't take it for granted, that you trusted me with all of that."

I shrug. "Gotta start somewhere, I guess."

He laughs softly. "Then you are one hell of an overachiever, for just getting started."

His thumb skates over my knuckles. His eyes search mine. "Would it help if I did that, too?"

"Did what?"

"Trust you? Tell you about my tough shit?"

"What tough shit?" I pull my hand away, dabbing at my nose, which has started to drip.

Viggo pulls out a hankie from his pocket. I laugh tearily. Of course he's got a hankie. It's probably hand stitched.

I look closer as he hands it to me. Sure enough, it is embroidered with tall, spindly blue flowers, and in the corner, the initials, *VFB*.

"You are too much," I mutter before blowing my nose.

Viggo scrunches one eye shut, bashful. Adorably bashful. "I went through an embroidery phase shortly after I left USC. Thought it was a very romantic idea, to have an initialed hankie I'd give someone if they needed it, if they cried in front of me."

I stare at him, that word ringing in the air, frightening the living daylights out of me.

Romantic.

He peers down at his hands, clasped over mine still. "That's what happens when you're a *teensy* bit emo and lonely and reading too much historical romance."

A laugh jumps out of me. I sigh, staring at the handkerchief. "I think it's sweet. Can I keep it? Or is . . . that too . . . intimate?"

Viggo's gaze jumps up to mine, pale eyes pinning me in place.

"Because . . ." I exhale shakily. "If you wanted it to be . . . romantic, I couldn't guarantee . . . I'm not sure what it would mean, if I kept it."

I hope he hears what I'm saying without saying it, as much as I know I should be bolder, braver, tell him straight out, *I want to try and give you everything you might want with me—if you want anything with me—but I have no idea what I know, what I can do, what I can be with someone else. I've never tried. I've never thought it was even possible.*

Viggo squeezes my hand. "It can mean whatever you need it to, Tallulah. So long as you know it means I . . . care. So much."

He does know what I'm saying. I'm relieved. Grateful. I want to be able to say more, but I've said so much that's so hard already, and I don't have anything left in me. Not today. Not yet.

"You're sure?" I ask quietly. "You don't mind it being . . . unclear? Undefined?"

He tips his head, his expression serious as he gazes at me. "I've started to realize, Tallulah, that life, people, connection, most of it is unclear and undefined. I love that romance novels break it down into these linear, straightforward steps. But . . . that's not how life works, not how people or relationships work; not how you feel about someone, how healing and growing and taking risks, works."

"You don't think?" A tiny glimmer of hope sparks inside me, flickering delicately, so faint, it could snuff out at any moment.

He shakes his head. "I *wanted* it to work that way. But life is meandering side trails, accidental shortcuts and detours, dead ends, turning back. It's not just a path rolled out before you; I wanted it to be. And that's because . . . I've struggled for a long time to find my path. To find my place. I've made friends and lost some, tried things that I thought would fill that ache inside me, make me feel better about myself. When I've come close to failing those things, I've turned around, taken new trails, found something else I was sure I'd be better at, that would finally make me feel like I was walking the path I was supposed to be on, make me feel good about myself, at peace with who I am and where I'm going.

"I haven't wanted it all to be so . . . messy, for myself or the people I love. Life's chaos makes me worry that the people I care about won't be okay, makes me anxious and unsure of myself. And so I've clung to my happy stories, to this idea of a formula for my and others' happiness—my own kind of ideological rigidity."

I lift my eyebrows. "Your 'own kind'? Are you implying *I* have an ideological rigidity?"

He shrugs, a grin brightening his face. "Just a bit."

I slide my fingers into his and lock our hands tight. "I'm trying to be . . . flexible. I want to be. All that's happened, the past few weeks, it's made me realize I want to be open to change, to believing new things. A lot of work lies ahead for me to do that, but I want to grow. I really do."

"I want to grow, too," he says softly. His fingers graze my palm as he stares at me. "It's not . . . *just* you, but you do make me want to grow, Lula."

My heart races. "I do?"

He nods.

I squeeze his hand, pulling him closer, pulling myself closer, too. "That's how you make me feel, too."

Viggo's gaze roams my face. He lifts his hand, cups my cheek. "Want to try . . . together?"

Air rushes out of me. I tip my face up, resting my hand on his thigh, anchoring myself. "I do, but I'm a mess, Viggo."

"Makes two of us."

"It *will* be messy."

His thumb sweeps along my cheek. "Define 'it.'"

I swallow roughly, squeezing his thigh harder. He's pushing me, just a little. But hasn't he given me so much, telling me he wants to meet me where I am, to open himself up to what's happening, unclear and hazy as it is? Hasn't he walked so far across that bridge between us? Can't I take a few steps, too?

"By 'it,' I mean . . . 'us.'" A slow, shaky breath leaves me. "What's between us. Whatever it might turn out to be."

His smile deepens. His eyes search mine, tender, warm. "Lula."

I peer up at him, my voice shaking. "Viggo."

"Can I kiss you?" he asks roughly.

I nod, silent, cupping his face, that thick, dense beard tickling my hand. I draw him close until we brush mouths, soft, slow.

Air gusts out of his lungs. Viggo leans in, chasing the end of our kiss, beginning another. This one deeper, savoring.

I sigh with happiness.

"You taste so good, Lu." He whispers it against our kiss, open-mouthed, searching for more. I give it to him, my tongue stroking his, my hands in his hair.

We fall back onto the sofa, and I feel him, already hard inside his shorts, wedged right up against me. I moan. "You *feel* so good," I whisper.

He smiles against our kiss. "So do you."

Viggo's hips shift against mine, pressing deeper as our kiss deepens, too. I feel their proximity to my pod, adhered to the left side of my stomach, and set my hands on his shoulders to stop us.

"Sorry," he whispers, staring down at me, concern in his eyes. "Too fast?"

"Just my pod." He saw it on move-in day, when we bumped bodies, so I don't bother lifting up my dress to show him. "It's on my left side. It can't get bumped or rubbed, because that could make it come loose or fall off."

He nods. "Okay. I'll be careful. Do you want to show me how . . . the best way . . ."

I press him onto his back and he takes my cue, drawing me over him, cradling my neck. Our gazes hold as he pulls back, searching my eyes. "I want to make you feel good, Lula."

"I want to give you that, too."

"You first," he mutters. His hand slips into my hair, cups my head, and we fall sideways, my thigh climbing up over his hip. His free hand skates up my leg, splayed wide, possessive, up over my ass. He groans. "What kind of panties are these?"

"The expensive kind."

He grips the lace tight in his hand and sighs. "You're gonna kill me."

"I better not. We have unfinished business."

"Yeah, we do."

He presses me back on the sofa, propping himself up on one elbow. I stare up at him as his fingertips trace the line of my panties, high above my hip, down my pelvis. I arch into his touch.

His eyes hold mine, as one finger, then two drift over the seam of my panties, right where I'm wet and aching, dying for his touch. "I've wanted you like this since the moment I saw you."

He rubs right over my clit, a light, swift circle. I gasp. "I wanted you, too."

"Fuck, Lu." He bends and kisses me, tender, featherlight, chased by a swift bite of my bottom lip that's gone before I've even processed it happened. "You drove me wild," he whispers.

"Well then, you're getting your vengeance now, because this is torture."

He smiles; his eyes search mine, questioning. "Good torture?"

I nod, shake my head. It feels incredible, but I'm so desperate to feel all of him, his skin on mine, giving me the relief I crave. "More," I whisper.

He holds my eyes, another circle over my panties, before his fingers hook around the fabric and tug it aside. Cool air kisses where I'm hot and aching.

I'm panting, shamelessly needy as his fingers glide over me, slick and slow.

His mouth falls open. "Fuck, you're wet."

I nod frantically.

"God, Lula." He shakes his head, wonder in his eyes as he circles my clit, steady, light. I cant up my hips into his touch. "Tell me," he says quietly. "Tell me how to make it good."

"Just a little more pressure and faster."

"As the lady wishes."

I smile as he kisses me. His touch shifts how I've asked, and he watches me, studying me. A moan rolls out of my throat when he gets there—just how I like. "Perfect," I gasp. "Oh, please don't stop. Viggo, please don't stop—"

"I won't." He bends his head again and kisses me, urgent, deep, wild, teeth clacking, tongue stroking my mouth. Sweat blooms on my skin as heat seeps through me, pools tight and low in my belly, between my thighs where he works me steadily.

My legs start to shake. My foot scrambles for purchase on the sofa as I roll my hips into his hand. Every corner of my body sings, a plucked string vibrating, pleasure humming through my limbs.

This is nothing like I've known, clothed but laid bare, touched by someone who wants to see *all* of me, who I'm letting see so much more than I ever have.

Our eyes lock as moans leave me—broken, jagged sound I have no control over.

Viggo smiles down at me softly, one hand bringing me so much pleasure, stroking, swirling. When he glides a finger inside me, I cry out, clutching his shoulder.

His palm, calloused, rough, rubs right over my clit as he curls another finger inside me and strokes, slow and deep.

"Yes," I plead, my hand clutching the fabric of his shirt, drawing him down into a messy, begging kiss. "Yes. Oh, God, Viggo."

"I have you, Lula." His voice breaks on my name as he feels the first promise of my body's release, tightening around his fingers. "Let go. Come for me, Lu."

Release slams through me, a molten tidal wave obliterating every sensation but his hand, his fingers, his mouth serenading mine, swift, hungry strokes of his tongue, his hips rocking against me.

I call his name again and again, as he wrenches every drop of that white-hot wave, until it ebbs, finally soft, finally stilled.

I stare up at him, breathless and broken open, held in his arms.

Viggo smiles softly. A rough swallow works down his throat. "That was the most beautiful thing I've ever seen."

Warmth floods my cheeks. I shake my head. "Nonsense."

"No, Lula." He kisses me sweetly, brushing his nose with mine. "That's the honest truth."

Sighing, I drift my hand down his chest, over his pounding heart. "My turn."

He stares down at me, another harsh swallow. "There's no rush. Just relax."

I frown, searching for hidden meaning in those words. Does he not *want* me to touch him the way he's touched me?

Worry itches at my thoughts. He wants this kind of intimacy

with someone he loves. He's told me that. But he also said he wanted to be . . . flexible, to move beyond how he used to think about things. He told me that, too. Does this apply?

I take a deep breath, fortifying myself, finding my courage to ask him, when the doorbell rings.

Viggo's eyes widen to saucers. Mine do, too.

"Shit," he hisses, snapping upright on the sofa, untangling himself from me. I feel absurdly bereft. Self-conscious, I tug down my dress, straightening my underwear as he scrambles over me for his phone on the coffee table. I watch him swipe it open, tap his calendar, scroll down.

"Fuck."

I sit up slowly. "What is it?"

"My niece and nephew." He leaps off the sofa, takes one look down at his massive erection, and tries—unsuccessfully—to tuck it away. "I invited them over to come meet the animals. "Freya and Aiden, they have some fancy dinner to go to, and I said not to bother with a sitter, I'd have them here to hang out and meet the pets. Shit."

"Okay." I smooth back my hair. "Well, I can make myself scarce if—"

"What?" Spinning around, he stares at me. And then all traces of his anxiety vanish. He grips me by the hands, tugging me up. I tumble into his arms and he clutches me to him, pressing a hard, sweet kiss to my temple, breathing me in. "I want you here. I don't want you to go. I just . . . have tiny people about to come into my house, when I have a raging boner and all I want to do is lay you down and make you come again."

Relief whooshes through me. "There's time for that," I whisper. "Later."

He sighs against my hair, then pulls back, cupping my face. "Yeah. You're right."

I peer down at his shorts and the very significant problem he's still dealing with. "Tell your dick to get the memo."

He groans. "I can't. You're here, all flushed and sexy. I have you all over my hand."

"Viggo Bergman!"

A grin lifts his mouth. "Wow, *I* finally scandalized *you*."

"Wash your hands," I tell him, stepping back, smoothing my hair. "I'll handle the tiny humans for now."

I start past him, but Viggo stops me, his hand clutching mine, pulling me close. A swift, hard kiss. He smiles down at me. "Thank you."

I smile up at him. "My pleasure. In more than one sense of the word."

Groaning, he rushes past me, jogging toward the bathroom. Only after the door clicks shut do I realize I'm laughing. Loud, happy, satisfied.

Like I've hoped, wanted, waited to.

Smiling to myself, I walk toward the door. "Coming!"

TWENTY-FIVE

Viggo

Playlist: "Mess Is Mine," Vance Joy

I figured Tallulah would be good with my niece and nephew. She's voluntarily spent time with little kids at the church she used to attend. She's handled my unruly U-10 soccer team twice now, like a pro. She was, according to Charlie, more of a mother to her little sister than their own mother was.

But watching it unfold is entirely different from abstractly knowing it. It's a thousand times better.

I sit on the sofa, stretched out, Theo sprawled in my lap as he crunches sleepily on handfuls of dry Cheerios, mesmerized by the entertainment that is Tallulah and Linnea making up a handshake, an effort that has Linnea bursting into fits of giggles.

"No, Lula Blue!" Linnie yells.

Romeo's ears go back. Juliet whines as she burrows her snout beneath her brother's head. The dogs were all about Linnea's enthusiastic pets when she first got here. They are not, however, big fans of her volume level.

"What did I do wrong?" Tallulah asks. Her eyes are comically wide. A deep smile brightens her face, making those gorgeous dimples appear.

Making my heart ache.

I'm in deep shit.

Linnea sighs dramatically, crawling into Tallulah's space, where they sit on the floor, leaning against the other end of the sofa. She grabs Tallulah's hand and guides it through the steps. "Like *that.*"

"Ohhh," Tallulah says dramatically. "Man, this is complicated."

"Just keep practicing," Linnie tells her. "Some things take lots of practice to get better. Like . . . riding a bike without training wheels. But good news—once you get it, you're all set, your muscles remember and you can always hop on a bike and do it after that, isn't that cool? It really is hard to learn, though, and I get mad when I keep trying and I still can't do it. But Mommy says I can do hard things. She says what's hard about hard things isn't often the things themselves but believing in ourselves when we try."

Tallulah's expression falters a little bit. "Your mom is very wise, Linnie."

"Thanks!" Plopping beside Tallulah, she smiles up at her. "I like you, Lula Blue."

"I like you, too, Linnie Loo."

"Linnie Loo!" Linnea laughs. "That's a funny name."

"Well, you gave me a funny name. I owed you one."

My niece crawls up to her knees and sinks her hands into Tallulah's hair.

"Linnie," I say gently. "You have to ask before you touch someone, remember? 'May I please . . . ?'"

Linnea cranes her head until she's right in Tallulah's face. "Lula Blue. May I *please* touch your hair?"

Tallulah throws me a quick smile, then meets Linnie's eyes. "You may."

"Thank you," my niece says primly, raking her fingers through Tallulah's hair. "So. How'd you get it blue? Markers? Paint?"

"I dyed it," Tallulah tells her. "With chemicals. Well, I paid someone to dye it, with chemicals."

"I want blue-hair-dye chemicals," Linnea says. "That's what I'm gonna ask for, for my birthday."

Tallulah clears her throat nervously. "Well, that's something your parents might want you to wait to do until you're older. You have to bleach dark hair like ours first, *then* add the color. It's hard on your hair, dries it out, and damages it. You have such pretty dark waves."

Linnea frowns, her eyes on Tallulah's hair. "We'll see," she says, in that way that makes her sound even older than she is, that makes me remember how much she's growing—a smart, highly verbal, clever kindergartener. "You know what?" Linnie lifts a chunk of Tallulah's hair. "Your hair is the same color as my eyes."

Linnie picks up my phone, unlocks it, because that tech-savvy little mischief-maker learned my passcode eons ago, and opens the camera. With a tap of her finger, she reverses the camera's direction and snaps a selfie, then hands my phone to Tallulah. "See?"

Tallulah peers at the photo, blinking rapidly. She clears her throat. "Wow. Go figure."

"It's the same color as Uncle Viggo's eyes, too!" Linnie yells.

"You want a snack?" Tallulah asks her, popping up from the floor. "You passed on a snack earlier, and Uncle Viggo said Mommy's and Daddy's rules are bedtime snack by eight o'clock. It's almost eight."

Linnea glances between us. "Did you get hair to look like Uncle Viggo's eyes, Lula Blue?"

Tallulah blushes. Spectacularly. I have never seen her blush like this. She clears her throat, smoothing down her dress. "I . . . had blue hair before I met your uncle Viggo."

I tip my head, smiling. "Not true, Lula."

Her eyes dart to mine, blinking rapidly. "College doesn't count."

"Doesn't it?" I hold her gaze, reminding her with my slow, knowing smile what I said just a few hours ago, when she was falling apart beneath my touch. *I've wanted you like this since the moment I saw you.*

Reminding her what she said in return. *I wanted you, too.*

Tallulah's blush deepens. She tears her gaze away. "How about that snack, Linnie?"

"I'm hungry now. Let's go, Lula Blue!" Linnea yells, clasping her hand and dragging Tallulah toward the kitchen. "Snack time! Then we gotta name the cats!"

"Good night, Percival!" Linnea whispers, though her whisper is other people's natural speaking volume. She blows a kiss to the gray cat, which sits on the sofa's edge, watching her, its head cocked. The rest of the kittens hop along the sofa's back and cushions, chasing each other around. She blows them kisses, too. "Good night, Penelope! Good night, Pascal! Good night, Pearl! Good night, Paisley!"

Aiden grins, clasping her hand and drawing her toward the door. "All right, Linnie. Time to go home, sweetheart."

"But the kitty cats!" she whines. "They need me. I'm their mama now. I can't just name and *leave* them."

Freya laughs softly. "Those are quite the names. I see we're putting our study of the baby-name book to good use."

"Oh, did we ever," I tell her, shifting sleeping Theo in my arms. "Want me to bring him out to the car?"

My sister waves me off. "Nah, I've got him."

I frown. Theo's a big two-year-old. And Freya's well into pregnancy. "You sure?"

"I'm sure." She lifts him effortlessly from me and settles him in her arms, straddling her belly, his cheek smooshed against her shoulder.

"I don't want to leeeeeave," Linnea cries.

Freya grimaces. "And that's our cue to go home and get this sleepyhead to bed."

"I'm not sleepy!" Linnea howls.

"Thank you, you two," Aiden says, scooping Linnea up into his arms. "They were both very excited to come over."

"We had a lot of fun," Tallulah says, smiling as she rubs Linnea's back. "See you soon, Linnie Loo. We'll do this again, okay?"

Linnea picks her head up from where she buried it in her dad's neck while crying. She wipes her eyes, her bottom lip trembling. "Promise, Lula Blue? Again and again?"

Tallulah nods solemnly. "Promise."

Linnea smiles. I'm smiling, too.

Again and again.

I like the sound of that. More than I should. But God, is it easy to draw out this picture, months into years, Tallulah and I coaching soccer, Tallulah and I playing with my nieces and nephew. Tallulah and I cuddling, watching movies, putzing around the bookstore, walking the dogs. Tallulah and I . . .

That's a complete statement. That's what I picture. Tallulah and I.

Taking a slow, calming breath, I will the panic away.

We stand, she and I, on the threshold, waving, watching them pull out.

As soon as I close the door, the contrasting silence, after hours of Linnea and Theo's delightful noisiness, is almost shocking.

Tallulah peers up at me, smiling softly. "They're adorable."

I nod. "They are."

"You're good with them," she says.

I swallow, heart racing. "You are, too."

She shrugs. "Despite what you've seen at soccer, I'm just one of those people who clicks with kids."

"I loved what I've seen at soccer."

She laughs as she strolls past me into the kitchen. "That's because I whipped them into shape for you."

I follow her, trying not to stare at her wide, swaying hips and failing miserably. "I know I sort of begged you to help me again this week, but would you want to keep helping me coach them . . . for the season?"

Tallulah pauses, a bunch of markers gathered in her hand. She glances up. "You want me to?"

I want whatever you'll give me, Lu.

"Of course I want you to."

She smiles, eyes back on her task as she sets the markers in their container, then snaps it shut. "That sounds fun, yeah."

"Good." I shuffle together the unused papers scattered across the counter, separating them from the ones Linnea drew on, which I'll stick on the fridge. There's a picture I hadn't noticed before—she was coloring with Tallulah for a bit while Theo and I read books on the couch. I stare at it, my heart thudding.

Three stick figures standing on green grass, all of them smiling. One tall, with a huge brown beard and brown hair and a dark blue ball cap. One short, with ice-blue hair and a triangle dress. The last one, biggest, in the foreground, wearing a rainbow triangle dress, bright smile, blue eyes, black squiggly hair. Me, Tallulah, Linnea. Red hearts dance all over the stick figures, floating up to the big sun overhead.

Stick-figure Viggo and Tallulah hold hands, two overlapping circles.

Tallulah steps beside me, peering at the paper. "Kids don't miss a thing."

I peer down at her, aching for her. I want to lay her down and make her feel so fucking good. I want to cuddle and kiss her senseless, until I'm dizzy from the need to breathe.

Turning, Tallulah peers up at me and brushes my wrist with her knuckles. "Speaking of missing things . . ." She steps closer, her hand skating up my arm. "You missed out on a return favor, earlier."

I swallow nervously, panic that's been my frequent companion this past week creeping through my body. I'm feeling so much, so much more than I ever thought I would about the woman standing before me. The woman who once swore that my idea of love, of everything I believed would hold together me and the person I wanted was a lie. The woman who now says she wants to try to see it differently, to open herself up to possibilities she'd never believed possible before.

I'm scared she'll change her mind. I'm scared she'll change her mind about *me*. I'm scared to give her my body when so much remains unanswered. But I don't want to push her away, either. I don't want to tell her no. I want to tell her . . . not yet. I hope she can hear what I'm saying, what I'm asking, what I need.

I cup her face, my thumbs sweeping along her cheeks. "You don't owe me anything in return for what we did earlier."

Tallulah frowns, her mouth pulled tight. "Why?"

I exhale unsteadily, stepping closer, dragging my knuckles against her cheeks. "What we did, there's no scoreboard. I'm not keeping a tally. I did that for you because I wanted to."

"And I want to do that for you, too," she says earnestly.

"I know."

Her eyes search mine, understanding seeping in. "You're not sure . . . if you want *me* to."

How to explain something so complicated? How to tell her I want more than she may want to give me, that I'm afraid to finally give myself to someone this way, only to have it possibly mean so much less to her than it would mean to me?'

"I . . ." Exhaling slowly, I hold her eyes, find my courage. "I've . . . never . . . done this before, Tallulah."

She tips her head. "Intimacy outside of a clearly defined relationship?"

Heat creeps up my cheeks. I shake my head.

Tallulah blinks once, twice. "Wait. You've never done it . . ."

"Ever," I whisper. My face is bright red. I am my father's son in this aspect—no red hair like Ren and Ziggy's, but a solid auburn streak and their same capacity to turn the color of a beet when thoroughly embarrassed.

"Viggo," she breathes, clasping my hand. "God, I'm sorry. I feel so thoughtless. I should have asked. I didn't know—"

"Don't be sorry," I blurt. "There's nothing to be sorry for. I could have told you. I wasn't even thinking about anything at the time, except making you feel good, Tallulah, and I loved what we did. I wanted to do it. So much."

She's silent for a beat, searching my eyes. "But it's different, the concept of it . . . being reciprocated?"

I nod. "Yeah."

When did we reverse roles? When did Tallulah become so adept at talking, filling in the blanks, and I become so inept?

Peering up at me, Tallulah clasps my hand and squeezes hard. "We'll slow down."

Self-consciousness swarms me. "We don't have to, for you—"

"*Don't* finish that sentence." Another firm squeeze of my hand. "It's not just you. It's me, too. For me to explore this, I also need to table that kind of intimacy. We'll pump the brakes. There's a lot we can enjoy while we figure this out."

"You sure?"

She smiles, holding my gaze. "Absolutely. We'll keep it to . . . cuddles?" she offers.

"Definitely. Kisses, too. I think those seem reasonable."

She bites her lip. "I won't say no to kisses. Hugs?"

"Implicit in cuddling, Lulaloo. Obviously."

Laughing softly, she tugs me toward her by my shirt. "Then come here and cuddle me good night."

I wrap her in my arms. Her hands slip around my waist. Her head to my chest. My chin on her hair.

It feels so right. Like a puzzle piece slipping into place on a *click* that echoes through me.

I hope she feels that, too. Even if not now, not yet . . . one day.

TWENTY-SIX

Viggo

Playlist: "So Tied Up," Cold War Kids, Bishop Briggs

I am a nervous wreck. Up until about half an hour ago, I've been grateful for my consuming anxiety the past week about the store's grand opening, because it was the only thing that kept me from spiraling about Tallulah. About how much I want her, how much I'm afraid to admit she means to me, after one short month of sharing life and work and a home with her.

Focusing on taking deep, steady breaths, I stand, rooted to the floor, in the middle of my bookstore, whose doors I'm finally about to open. Over a year's hard work poured into this place. A super-soft opening, a romance book club kickoff soft opening. Two weeks of social media blasts, old-school flyer distribution around the area while walking the dogs. One month of Tallulah's steady, calm, practical presence beside me, while I tweaked and rearranged and finally said it was time.

Now it's here.

The door from my home to the bookstore opens, swinging wide. In walks Tallulah, stealing the breath from my lungs. Glowing golden skin. Ice-blue shoulder-length waves. Dark liner winging her amber eyes. A blush-pink sundress with a plunging neckline that flares out at her full, soft hips, fluttering just past her knees. Matching strappy blush-pink sky-high heels.

For the millionth time in the past two weeks, I want to punch myself in the face for pumping the brakes. Desire burns through me, hot and fierce.

The only thing stopping me from pouncing on her right now—besides my store opening in fifteen minutes—is the reminder that Tallulah said she was right there with me, firm in her conviction that, in order to explore what we could share beyond physical attraction, physical intimacy needed to be set aside.

Well, at least, certain kinds of physical intimacy.

I think back on this afternoon, when making lunch in the kitchen became making out. I remember how good she felt, even with my touch held safely at the curve of her waist filling my hands. My cock twitches in my suit pants.

Tallulah smiles, bright and dazzling. A whistle leaves her. "Wowy, Bergman. You clean up real nice."

I shrug, hands in my pockets. "Shucks, Clarke." My gaze holds hers, then dips down her body, back up to her eyes. "You're stunning, Lu."

"Gee, thanks." She shrugs, then does a twirl that reveals a peek of lacy blush-pink panties. A whimper catches in my throat.

"Oops." She pats her dress down. "Accidental Marilyn Monroe moment."

I shake my head. "Better be the last one of the night. I've got people about to enter this establishment."

She grins. "Would it bother you if those people got a show?"

"Hell yes," I growl.

Her eyebrows shoot up. Her mouth parts. "Oh."

"Sorry." I rake my hands through my hair, blowing out a breath. "Got a little intense there."

Tallulah saunters my way. I can tell she doesn't even mean to be sexy about it, but she is. She's wearing her practical, no-nonsense expression as she steps up to me and smooths her hands across the fabric of my light blue dress shirt rolled up to my elbows, paired with charcoal gray suit pants, brown belt, brown chukka boots. Professional but approachable.

"It's going to go perfectly," she says quietly. Her hands squeeze my shoulders once, hard, then fall to her sides.

"How do you know?"

She smiles up at me, rosy round cheeks, deep dimples. "Because you've built much more than a store, Viggo. You built a community and now you have a place for it. Believe in yourself. *They* all do. See for yourself."

Frowning, I glance over my shoulder. Tallulah tugs up the rolling blinds, revealing the big front window, then the other. My mouth falls open.

There's a *crowd* outside. The sidewalk is filled with people.

"Told ya," she whispers, winking. She struts to the counter, then steps behind the register. "Ready when you are."

I hold her eyes as I take a deep breath. Exhaling slowly, I turn and face the door, take one step toward it, then another, then another, until my hand hovers over the doorknob.

I grip it tight, take one more breath, then open that door wide.

———

Ten minutes before closing, the place is still full of patrons milling around the rows of bookshelves, crammed into the club chairs, the built-in window benches, every stool at the counter.

I'm sweaty and my stomach grumbles with hunger, but it barely registers beneath the roar of my happiness, buzzing and electric, coursing through me. Tallulah looks about as worn-out as I do. But she also looks just as elated. A smile lifts her mouth as a patron talks to her, leaning their elbows on the counter.

Tallulah laughs at what they say, wiping crumbs off the counter, clearing away their mug and plate.

My eyes narrow. That smile. That laugh. They're not supposed to be for other people. They're supposed to be for *me*.

"Told ya." My brother's voice makes me spin around.

Ollie stands, hands in pockets, beaming as his eyes scan the place, filled with people, the success he promised me he knew it would be.

"You're the second person who's said that tonight, and I'm not sure whether I love it or hate it."

Ollie wraps me in a hug. "I have a guess who else said that to you."

I peer over my shoulder as we step apart, staring at Tallulah. That patron is *still* there. She is *still* talking to them. A frown tugs at my mouth.

My brother clears his throat. I spin back around, facing him. He's grinning from ear to ear. "Hooo, you've got it bad."

"You hush. I do not." I tug at my collar, knocking it open one more button. I'm too damn hot. "I've got it just the right amount. Same as her."

Oliver snorts. "Okay, brother. Well, I'm heading out. I just wanted to say congratulations again, and I'm so proud of you."

I smile, reaching out, squeezing his arm. "Thanks, Ollie. For everything. Cheering me on. Coming tonight. Bringing half the soccer team."

He lifts his hands. "Don't look at me. They *asked* to come. I just told them about the store. Same with Ren, Seb, and the hockey team. You shouldn't be surprised. How many of them have you turned on to romance over the years?"

Tallulah's words dance through my thoughts, and I smile, pride and contentment filling me.

You built a community and now you have a place for it.

Even knowing the number of guys on my brothers' soccer and hockey teams that I've pushed romance novels on, I'm still trying to wrap my head around how many professional athletes were in here from their teams, from Ziggy and Charlie's team, too, buying romance and proudly walking out into the night.

With one more hug goodbye, I see Oliver off, waving to Gavin, who gives me a tip of the chin and a wry smile before they both slip out the front door. They were the last to leave of my local family, all of whom came *again*, which meant so much, given that I already had my super-soft opening for them.

A couple of guys from the hockey team are still hanging by the sports romance section, laughing it up with their partners. Romance book club members sit on the club chairs and built-ins, leaning close, talking animatedly. A dozen people I don't know at all browse shelves, drink in the space as they sip from their mugs, inspect scented candles, bookmarks, stickers, keychains, the tiny potted plants I decided last minute I'd sell, too, in the section at the front with bookish merchandise.

"Hey, you!" A familiar voice makes me spin around.

"Charlie!" I wrap her in a hug, and Charlie hugs me back hard. She smiles wide, her short dark hair smooth and shiny. She's wearing a cropped electric-green tank and matching wide-leg pants. She's glowing.

"Impending nuptials suit you, Char."

Her smile deepens. "I love when you talk like a historical romance novel. And thank you."

I laugh. "Thanks for coming by. You really didn't have to." I drop my voice. "I know you don't love publicity. That's part of what the super-soft opening was about, giving you and my hotshot siblings privacy. You doing okay, being here now?"

Charlie's smile softens. "You're sweet. That . . . fear of publicity, it's something I'm working on. Baby steps, right? That's why I'm not here long, but very happy to be here."

"Back door is yours to use if it gets to be too much, okay?"

Charlie squeezes my arm. "Thank you, Viggo. You're a gem. Now. I have someone for you to meet." Turning, Charlie gently grips the elbow of someone who stands near her, leaning away and crouched for a photo with a patron. She signs a piece of paper in their hand, then smiles brightly as they dart off. It takes me a second, but finally I place her.

"This," Charlie says, "is Nat. She's—"

"Your goalie." I nod. "I remember. Welcome!"

Nat is tall and strong, bleached-blond hair, tan skin, bright blue eyes. Classic SoCal looks. She radiates confidence and energy as she beams a smile my way and wraps me in a sudden hug that surprises me. "Congratulations on your grand opening!" She pulls away and laughs. "Sorry, I'm a hugger."

"No, that's okay." I force a smile, confused by how unsettled I am. I don't normally think twice about hugging or being hugged. I'm an affectionate guy, always comfortable with friendly physical touch. At least, I have been. But now I feel something odd, a tug to find Tallulah, yank her into my arms until she locks her hands around my waist, sets her cheek on my chest, and sighs. The way she has so often the past few weeks.

"Thanks for coming, Nat," I add, realizing I'm being rudely quiet.

"Are you kidding?" she says brightly. "I *love* romance novels. When I heard Ziggy's brother was opening a romance bookstore, I was all in. Wouldn't miss it for the world."

Charlie grins. "Well, I'm going to go say hi to Tallulah. I'll leave you to it."

A frown tugs at my mouth. I'm a bit perplexed by Charlie off-loading her teammate on me. It's almost like she's . . . trying to set us up. After what she and Ziggy pulled, tricking Tallulah into coming to the super-soft opening, dragging her back into my life again, I could have sworn Charlie would be the first person rooting for *us*, or at least not trying to actively put other prospective partners in our paths.

I watch Charlie over my shoulder as she rushes toward Tallulah at her post behind the counter, *still* talking to that damn patron. They're leaning even closer now, their fingers tracing figure eights on the counter as they hold Tallulah's eyes. Shamelessly flirting with her.

My hands clench in my pants pockets. My stomach knots sharply. I feel like I swallowed battery acid.

Tallulah glances up when Charlie approaches, then peers past her sister as they hug. Her eyes meet mine, then dance to Nat, who stands beside me. One eyebrow arched. Hard-set mouth. She looks . . . displeased.

Pleasure flies through me. I arch an eyebrow, subtly nodding my head toward the patron at the counter. I want Tallulah to know I'm just as aware of people flirting with her as she is of people paying attention to me.

"So . . ." Nat says.

I spin back, guilt hitting me. I'm being rude. "So sorry! Just making sure we were all good at the register."

"No, that's okay!" She smiles warmly. "So, I'm a big contemporary rom-com gal; I've never read historical romance, and I want to give it a try. Charlie said you will have *the* best recommendations. Mind showing me where to start?"

"Absolutely." I use the pretense of stepping aside to guide Nat to the historical romance section as an opportunity to glance over at Tallulah one more time.

She's leaning in on the counter now, Charlie seated at a stool next to the other patron, who's making no effort not to stare down Tallulah's dress.

Red. I see *red*. My jaw clenches.

Tearing my gaze away, I face Nat and plaster on my widest smile. "Right this way."

I lock the dead bolt on the shop's front door, flip the sign from *Open* to *Closed*. When I turn around, Tallulah's standing in the middle of the store, her dress starting to slip off one shoulder, heels dangling by their straps from her fingertips. I stare at her, my pulse pounding.

She stares right back.

Reaching for the light switch, I hold her eyes. Then I flick it off. Darkness fills the store, leaving only soft pockets of light from the dim, warm lights mounted at the tops of the bookshelves.

"So." Tallulah's voice is soft, smoky at the edges, hoarse from talking. Talking to so many people that weren't me, people like that patron I had to barely restrain myself from booting out by the ass when I announced we were closing, half an hour past the end of official store hours.

"So," I reply, slipping my hands into my pockets. They're tight fists. My fingers ache with the need to touch her.

"That went well, I think," she says, shifting her weight onto one hip, shoes swaying.

"I think so, too."

Our eyes hold, a stare down so intense, it feels like electricity arcing in the air.

"Thanks for all your hard work tonight," I tell her. "You did great with the customers. One in particular. How many coffee drinks did they order? Three? They'll be up all night."

The light is a faint yellow glow in the store, but my eyes have adjusted, so I don't miss it, that arched eyebrow, the small tip of her mouth. "He ordered decaf. And I might say the same to you. You and Nat really hit it off in the historical romance section."

My hands flex in my pockets. Tallulah's grip tightens on her shoes.

Her gaze dips to my mouth. Mine dips to hers. I can't stand the distance one more second.

I take a step toward her. She takes a step toward me.

My hands leave my pockets. Her shoes clatter to the floor. We rush at each other, collide fierce and fast, my hands dragging her by the waist against me, splaying wide as they skate up her back. Tallulah sinks her hands into my hair and tugs my head down. Our mouths crash against each other's, rough, hungry. Tongues battling, teeth bumping, openmouthed, panting, so fucking desperate.

A groan of relief rumbles in my throat as she presses her soft body into mine, wedging my rapidly thickening cock right between her thighs. "I wanted to grab that fucker by the scruff," I mutter between kisses, "and throw his ass out of the store."

"I wanted to take that Barbie by the hair"—she gasps as I bend and bite her neck, chasing it with a hot lick of my tongue—"and drag her out the way she came."

"Fuck, Lula." I shudder as she sinks her teeth into my shirt right over my pec and bites. Hard.

"Sorry," she whispers.

"Don't you dare apologize." I grab her hair in a fistful and kiss her neck, lick my way up her ear. She moans. "I loved it. I want you to do it again."

She smiles, head back, throat exposed to me. I kiss my way down it, over the swell of her breast. "Wait!"

I pull back, breathing heavily, staring down at her. "Lula?"

"We promised." She sighs miserably. "We promised we'd take it slow."

I nod, swallowing roughly. "You're right."

Her hands slide up my chest. She clasps me by the jaw, her thumb tracing my lips. "But I want you so fucking bad."

"I want you, too."

She bites her lip, her eyes drifting down my body. "We could . . . play with semantics."

I arch an eyebrow, my hands wrapping tight around her waist, over her big, lush ass. "I'm listening."

"You could . . . touch yourself." She peers up at me beneath her lashes. "I could touch myself. We could do that . . . together."

Heat pulses through me, turning my cock rock hard. "Hands to ourselves. But not our eyes."

"Exactly," she whispers.

I crash down on her again, a hard, hungry kiss. "Fuck yes."

"I want that woman erased from your memory," she mutters, tugging me back with her, toward the club chairs.

"She was never there to begin with, Lu. I want you to forget that flirty fucker ever existed."

She laughs. Laughs! "Please, I was not interested. He's got neck tatts. After Clint, I'm over people with tatts for life."

I pull back, breathing roughly, as I undo one button of my shirt, then another. "Then I've got bad news for you, Clarke." I shake off my shirt hastily, tossing it aside. "Because I've got ink."

Tallulah's mouth falls open. "Fuuuck," she groans. Her hand comes to my shoulder, to the mountains and evergreens, the water running through it, spilling toward my pec.

"Deal-breaker?" I ask.

She shakes her head quickly. "Never mind. Tatts are fine. Great, actually."

I drag her back into my arms and kiss her, taking her mouth with my tongue the way I want so badly to take her with my cock, deep and slow. Tallulah pulls away, panting, and says, "Sit down."

I smile down at her. "Yes, ma'am."

She pushes me gently by the chest, hand splayed right over my pounding heart, and I drop with a *thud* into the club chair. It swivels with the force of my landing, but I plant my feet wide to steady myself, then go right for my belt buckle.

Tallulah hooks a foot in the nearby chair, drags it closer, then drops onto it, rucking her dress up her thighs. She drapes one leg over the arm of the chair, revealing the faint outline of her lace panties.

"Who the hell turned off the lights?" I mutter sourly.

Tallulah laughs, shrugging the sleeves of her dress down off her shoulders, past her cleavage, revealing a matching blush-pink bra that barely covers her nipples, dark and pointed beneath the lace.

"Jesus Christ," I groan, my hips lifting reflexively as I unzip my pants and press my palm down my pulsing cock. "You have the most magnificent tits, Lu."

She smiles and slides her fingers beneath her panties. I swear under my breath, drink in the sight of her rubbing herself.

Her eyes fix on the bulge at my briefs. "Why, thank you," she says.

I shove my briefs down, spit on my hand, then grip myself. Her smile wipes clean off her face. "Oh God," she whispers, watching me.

"Touch your tits, Clarke."

She bites her lip. "Don't tell me what to do."

"Tell me you don't want to."

Her back arches as she groans in frustration. "Asshole." Her hand goes to her breast, overflowing her grip. She plucks at her nipple. My hips rock up as I watch her, making myself go slow, torturously controlled strokes into my fist that make my molars grind.

"Touch them," she orders, eyes down at my balls, drawn up tight.

"Shit," I groan, doing as she says. I won't even pretend I don't want to—be ordered around by her or do what she's told me.

Tallulah's hand is moving faster beneath her underwear. She growls in frustration, lifts her hips, and yanks off her panties.

"Fuck," I moan, eyes fixed on what I can see, which in the dim light isn't much, but it's a hell of a lot more than I've ever seen, even in shadow. Even from here, I can see how wet she is. "You're gonna kill me, Lula. I'm so fucking close."

"I am, too," she pants, rubbing herself in earnest now. "Oh God, Viggo."

"That's it," I grit out, pumping myself. "Rub that pretty pussy for me, Lula. Make yourself come."

She cries out, watching me as I jerk myself in earnest now, panting. "Fuck, Lu. You're so beautiful. You make me so fucking hard."

She arches up in the chair, eyes holding mine. I watch her legs shake, her breath stutter, my name on her lips.

That sight, that sound, sets me off, sends lightning soaring through my veins, pulsing through the base of my cock. I groan her name, hips jerking as I work myself through it, hot, thick, ropes of come all over my stomach.

She gasps, rubbing herself still, her eyes fluttering. She's getting herself off. Again. The sight of it intensifies my pleasure, dragging out my release so long, so hard, my breath catches in my lungs until I start to see stars and drag in a desperate tug of air.

Tallulah cries out, high and hoarse, and slumps back in her seat.

I can't take a second longer, either. My hand falls away. I slump back in my chair, too, winded, panting.

Tallulah's head lolls to the side as she breathes heavily, her eyes holding mine. A wide, satisfied smile brightens her face.

I stare at her, breathing roughly, a smile lifting my mouth, too.

She sighs as she eases her leg down off the chair, then tugs up her dress over her bra. I pull a hankie from my pocket, wipe my stomach clean, tuck myself back inside my briefs. Slowly, Tallulah stands from her chair, then sashays my way. She stands between the bracket of my legs, just like that first night, a month ago, when she showed up here, when I least expected her to.

Planting a hand on either arm of the chair, she leans in.

Tenderly, softly, she kisses me and breathes in. "Now, *that's* what I call a good opening night."

I laugh against her kiss as I cup her neck, sinking my hand into her hair. "I'll say."

Slowly, she stands, then grazes her knuckles along my cheek. Her eyes hold mine. "Sleep well, Viggo."

I watch her scoop up her shoes and walk toward the door leading to the house, arms swinging lazily, wide swaying hips. Hunger burns through me. I just came and I'm already dying for her again. Dying for more.

"Sweet dreams, Lula," I call.

She turns at the threshold and smiles coyly. "I'll be dreaming, all right. But I guarantee you it won't be sweet."

TWENTY-SEVEN

Tallulah

Playlist: "Can't Buy Happiness," Tash Sultana

I wake up rested and relaxed. In a much better mood than I was last night, watching Charlie's teammate be all chummy with Viggo.

The delicious details of what came afterward rush back to me as I stretch, blinking up at the ceiling, smiling to myself. God, that felt good. Really, really good. It makes me nervous, though. If what we did was that good, how much more intense, satisfying, hot, will it be if we get to the point where we're doing more?

My smile slips. I'm halfway through my time here. One month down, one to go. Just four weeks until Charlie's wedding, until I promised myself the book would be done and Viggo promised himself he'd be in a place to run the store without my help. Four weeks until we agreed I'd move out.

I know Viggo said there was no need for timetables or shoulds as we figured this out, but *I* have a timetable. *I* have a should. Because I'll be damned if this roommate situation ends with me being where I've been before, caught off guard, hurting and being hurt, everything good that we've built and shared going up in flames.

I want to be healthier, to work through all my shit that drives my fears, tightens my chest, constricts my throat, when I think about trying to open my heart wide, to pursue a life I didn't know I could have, a person I told myself I shouldn't want.

Whipping back the sheets, I sit up. Start my morning routine, finger prick, blood sugar check, take insulin, enter carbs from my impending breakfast bar into the PDM. Staring out the window, I frown, thinking. I want a plan. I need one. Where do I even begin?

My gaze slips to my laptop. It blossoms in my thoughts, the beginning of an idea for the last act of my book, a radically different ending...

A happy one.

But how to write it? Believe it? Do it justice? More importantly, how to do that for myself?

My sister's voice echoes in my head. *Go to therapy!*

Sighing, I ease up from the bed and stroll over to the laptop, the place where I've lost myself to words and worlds, an escape, a catharsis. Opening it, powering it on, I sit. I open a web browser, typing in the word *therapist.*

Time to stop avoiding the unavoidable. Time to get to work.

Charlie said I might have to shop around before I found a therapist who was a good fit for me. I didn't like the sound of that. I worried that with each failed attempt, I'd lose my nerve and chicken out. Thankfully, I had no need to worry. My therapist, Linda, the first one to email me back after the handful of contact forms I filled out two weeks ago, had an opening the very next day.

She's maternal in the way I imagined maternal would be but never knew myself. She's softspoken, silver-haired, always bundled up in a cardigan and thick socks, even though it's hot as hell as we start to crawl our way through June.

After our first session, she gently suggested we meet three times a week. I didn't balk, didn't blink. I know I'm fucked up. I'll take all the help I can get.

Linda has early appointments, and I now hold her eight a.m. slots on Monday, Wednesday, and Friday. It's the hardest thing I've ever done, opening up to a stranger and sharing my deepest pains, allowing her to guide me into uncovering even more pain that I didn't even know I had repressed, trusting her to help me feel safe in processing all of it.

But I do it. I feel braver, stronger, almost fearless.

Almost.

Because once I step out of that quiet room and cool air-conditioning, into the blaring, blazing-hot reality of life, my confidence dips. It's one thing to do what I'm learning to do in therapy. It's a whole other thing to do it with people I care about. People who matter to me. People who I want to be close to.

The shop opens at ten, so I have time to collect myself before working.

Viggo is always around when I get home, lingering in the kitchen, fresh coffee waiting, another delicious treat on the counter, carbs calculated per serving, scribbled tidily on notepaper, so I can bolus the correct amount of insulin before I eat them.

That's where I find him as I shut the door behind me, feeling drained yet unburdened. Hip leaning against the counter, nose in a romance novel. He lowers it just a little, his eyes meeting mine. "Hey there, Lulaloo."

"Hey." I hang my keys on the *Home, Sweet Home* hook, then bend to greet Romeo and Juliet, who offer me happy barks in greeting, lolling tongues and wagging tails as I pet them. I give them both hugs, soothed by those warm, sweet bodies, their steady, loyal affection that always makes me feel better.

I stand, the dogs following in my wake, and stop by the sofa, where the kittens sleep, like little ants on a log, snoozing across the length of the sofa. I slide a hand down each of their backs, feeling soft, fluffy kitten fur, tiny purrs rumbling their ribs. Pet greeting complete, I stroll into the kitchen.

Viggo sets his book aside and opens his arms. I step into them, wrapping myself around him until my fingers clasp low on his back and my cheek rests on his chest.

"How ya doin', Lu?"

"Exhausted."

He nods. "Therapy is exhausting. Proud of you."

"Thank you." I smile against his chest and sigh, savoring the comfort of his embrace.

The past two weeks, since the grand opening, we've been on our best behavior, kept our touch safely to hugs and the occasional movie-night cuddles. Every day, the store is busy from open to close. I work on my book early in the morning and all evening, while Viggo bakes and restocks the store. We haven't kissed once. Haven't made out. I tell myself it's because we're too busy, but that's not really true. We have quiet moments in the morning like this, on the couch in the evening, before we part ways for bed. We don't take advantage of them. I think, by some unspoken agreement, we've recognized and decided to respect that, until we figure this out, figure out who we are, we're both too fragile to risk going where kissing seems to take us.

My gaze slips down to the historical romance he's reading, the couple's longing clear in their embrace. Not for the first time since that night, since I woke up the next day, determined to get this fix-my-shit show on the road, I battle a profound wave of insecurity. In going to therapy, in the way I'm writing the last of the book, I'm trying first and foremost to make myself healthier, to open myself to healing. But I am also definitely trying to be someone who can have a healthy intimate relationship. With him.

Except Viggo's not just some ordinary person who wants an emotionally open partner. He's a romantic who has so many ideas, feelings, hopes, for something I'm entirely ignorant of. How can I ever meet his expectations?

"New recipe," he says, reaching with one hand for the plate of cookies. "Peanut butter chocolate chip and oatmeal breakfast cookies. You said you were craving something with peanut butter and chocolate."

I scrunch my eyes shut, battling a sudden rush of tears. He's so damn sweet.

"Those look great," I whisper, hoping it hides the lump of emotion thick in my throat. "Thank you."

He nuzzles my head with his chin. "You're welcome, Lu."

I'm quiet again, holding him tight. I know I need to let go, to move forward into today, tomorrow, the next two weeks. But it feels harder, every time I hug him, to let go.

Viggo is unfazed by my behavior. Six sessions in, he's learned to expect my quiet when I get back from therapy. He stands there patiently, holding me tight, breathing slow and steady, as I cling to him, silent, my mind racing. I take a deep breath and try to calm myself, settle my thoughts. I can't worry about what might happen between us when I reach my goal, my destination. I have to focus on where I am on the path right now.

One step at a time, Linda reminds me often. I remind myself now, as I pull away and peer up at him.

He smiles down at me, tinged with that familiar vibrant energy, but this feels like more. Like he's got a secret he can't wait to share.

"What is it?" I ask.

Viggo reaches for his laptop and spins it so the screen faces us. "Those are my sales so far, the first two weeks."

I lean in, scanning the spreadsheet. A smile lifts my mouth. "Viggo. This is *incredible*."

"Yeah." His smile deepens as he leans in and knocks shoulders with me. "Thanks to you."

I roll my eyes. "Hardly. It's your store. Your vision brought to life. Don't you dare blame me."

He laughs. "C'mon, Lulaloo. You've made a big difference. If these sales continue, when I round out the first month, there's no way I'll have made that money if I'd had to pay staff. Free labor's not nothing."

"It's not free labor. It's a trade-off. You've invested time and expertise in my book. You're letting me live here for free, when you and I both know what splitting rent on a place like this would cost me." I clasp his hand, squeezing hard. I have to get this through his thick skull. "Stop downplaying what you've achieved. You deserve to celebrate it, not minimize it."

Viggo's smile slips. He stares down at my hand, his thumb skating over my skin. "Ah, but if I diminish a joyful moment and lower the high, it's not such a painful drop when disappointment and failure inevitably come."

I frown. "I find that . . . deeply relatable. But I'm going to tell you what Linda told me: that's not a healthy way to look at the good in your life."

"Well, my therapist agrees with yours and has told me that many times, too." He shrugs. "Doesn't mean it stuck. I'm working on it, though."

"That is . . . relatable, too."

Viggo squeezes my hand back. "Works in progress, right?"

I nod, smiling faintly. "Works in progress."

"Speaking of," he says, bringing a cookie to his mouth and taking a hearty bite, "when do I get to read the finished draft?"

"Mmm, these look good." I tug my hand away and use it to pick up one of the cookies, inspecting it with way more intensity than makes any kind of sense.

"Lula," he pleads.

I drop the cookie onto the plate. "Eventually, I promise. Just . . . not yet."

Viggo chews his cookie, eyes narrowed playfully at me. "Fine."

"Now, if you'll excuse me," I tell him. "I have a busy day at the bookstore to get ready for."

"Wait, Lu." Viggo pops the last of the cookie in his mouth, dusts off his hand, then reaches for an envelope. "This came for you."

I stare down at the envelope, seeing my publisher's name and return address . . . My breath catches, looking at my name above *his* address. My chest tightens. The sight of that feels so . . . right. And strange. And good.

I bite my lip, turning it over.

"I was surprised mail came for you," Viggo says, leaning his hip against the counter, giving me a respectful distance to open my mail in privacy. "You haven't gotten any before this."

I shrug. "Didn't really have any. No utilities. No student loan statements—Mom and Dad paid my tuition, which is a massive luxury, I know . . ."

Viggo shifts his weight. "Sure is. But it's one that comes with complicated strings, I'd imagine."

"Gotta love when your parents try to buy absolution for your toxic upbringing." I tear open the seal. "Everything else I pay for, I went paperless. Except this. I gave my agent your address in case they wanted to send early copies to read for blurbs or financial stuff. I hope that's okay."

Viggo's quiet. I peer up. He's watching me intensely. "Of course it is, Tallulah, you're living here."

Not for much longer, I think. *Unless I get the nerve to ask to stay.*

He shifts. "Actually, about that, Tallulah. We should talk. I know you said—"

I clasp his hand, squeezing it tight, and mercifully, he goes quiet. I know we need to have this conversation, that avoiding it is un-healthy. But I tell myself this isn't avoidance. This is . . . a pause. I'm raw from therapy, battling my demons that whisper how badly trying to have something good in my life is going to end. I want to have what I need to talk about our plan regarding when and how I leave, but that conversation is inextricably tied to *us*, and that is a conversation I know I'm not yet prepared to have.

"We should definitely talk about it." I hold his eyes, hoping he sees what I mean. "Just . . . not yet, please?"

Viggo searches my eyes. Finally, he nods. "Okay."

"Thank you." I squeeze his hand again, then draw it back, tugging the paper from the envelope. I unfold it, then spin it around. And then I blink at the number I'm staring at.

My royalty check for *Isochron* . . . it's massive.

"What's wrong?" Viggo asks, his gaze darting frantically over my face as he tries to decipher my expression.

Good luck to him. I have no idea what my face looks like, no idea what I'm feeling, either. Shocked? Stunned?

Holy shit.

I've always had the privilege of living with financial security, thanks to my wealthy film-star parents, which, with a disease like diabetes, has been an immense relief. Both my parents' insurance, which covered me when I was younger, and the insurance I then bought on the marketplace have periodically denied coverage of my CGM, my pod, the type of insulin I use until my doctors get through to my insurance, but thanks to that financial security, I've been able to afford what I need to stay alive—a luxury many with my disease don't have.

I've never lacked what I need. College was paid for, my parents gave each kid an obscene amount of money upon graduating, and then my book broke out, so I didn't have to wait long for a royalty check. The first few checks were solid. But this check . . . as cliché as it sounds, it's a whole new world.

"Tallulah, you're scaring me."

Viggo's voice wrenches me from my trance. I fold the paper

tight, then slip it back into the envelope. "Good publishing news that I wasn't expecting."

His expression morphs from deep concern to a wide, beaming smile. "Lu, that's great!" He wraps me in his arms, and I hug him back hard, squeezing tight, scrunching my eyes shut. Happy tears. The first time I can remember ever crying them. I hope it's not the last.

Pulling away, I peer up at him, a smile lifting my mouth.

Happiness.

I feel it, lighting me up. Yes, I'm grateful for this check, the success it signals, the even greater financial security it brings me, but what makes me smile, what fills me with this fizzy, sparkling warmth, is the joy of sharing this moment with him.

Viggo brushes back a hair stuck to my tear-wet cheek, his eyes holding mine. "I really am proud of you. I admire your hard work, your success. But most of all . . . I'm happy to see you happy."

My smile deepens. "Thank you."

"That smile," he whispers. His gaze fixes on my mouth. "That is a beautiful thing."

His head dips. Mine tips up. Our noses brush as I press on tiptoe. This unspoken no-kissing agreement is about to go out the window.

But then his phone rings, startling us both.

I clutch my chest, heart pounding.

"Sorry," Viggo says, reaching for his phone in his pocket. "Freya's not due for eight more weeks, but I worry—"

"Take it, please."

Viggo peers at his screen, his expression blanking.

Now it's my turn to be worried, to be wringing my hands, trying to read his expression. "Viggo? What's wrong?"

He swallows. "It's Donnie. He's . . . calling. He normally just texts."

Six weeks ago, I'd probably have made some snarky dig about how serious he was treating an update on his car in the shop. But now I know that over the past month, while Viggo's waited for word from Donnie on what parts could be found, what could be done to save his car, his worry has built the longer he's gone not hearing news. I now know that Ashbury is much more than just a car he's sentimental about. This is the car that drove him up and down from Escondido while he built a dream in that beautiful brain, while he delivered orders from his baking hustle, to odd jobs during the day, to his parents' late at night and early in the morning to bake some more, so he could save and save, working steadily toward making his dream come true.

"Answer it," I tell him. "I can give you space, if you want."

I'm already backing away when Viggo grabs my wrist, holding it tight. "Stay, please."

I freeze, then take a slow step toward him. "Okay."

Viggo's fingers lace with mine. He answers his phone with the other hand, bringing it to his ear. "Hey, Donnie."

I can't hear what Donnie says. But I watch Viggo's face fall. Watch him catch it and force a reassuring smile my way.

I stare up at him, still holding his hand as he thanks Donnie and hangs up, knowing it's bad news. The worst news.

He swallows thickly as he pockets his phone. I squeeze his hand. "Viggo," I say quietly.

I don't have to say any more. He knows that I know. I think he's grateful that he doesn't have to spell it out for me. Maybe it makes it easier for him to pretend he's fine, when he's clearly not. I'm about to press, to push, to tell him that it's okay to cry that his car is dead, not coming back, that for once *I* can be the one who holds him while *he* falls apart.

But he steps back before I can find my courage. "Store's open in five," he says. "I should head over there. Get things ready."

"Okay. I'll be right there." I clasp my hands in front of me, watching him go, Romeo and Juliet trotting after him through the door to the shop, before he closes it with a quiet *click*.

I bite my lip, my heart aching for him. I'd do anything to make him feel better, to fix this. But you can't fix an unfixable car.

Unless . . .

I pull out my phone and open up my web browser, searching for Donnie's shop and phone number. Donnie answers, and after explaining who I am, why I'm calling, my suspicions are confirmed.

Ashbury's not unfixable. He's just beyond expensive to repair, when it comes to the parts it would take to make him run again.

"I feel terrible," Donnie says on the line. "I'm such a chickenshit. I've known for two weeks that this was the case, but I kept trying to find a way around it. I know how much he loves that car, and listen, he's been nothing but a prince of a guy for as long as I've known him. I wanted to be able to help him. He deserves it. I owe him so much."

I frown in confusion, then remember Donnie can't see me. "What do you mean?"

"He used to live in the apartment next to my dad. I was busy with a bunch of updates to the shop at the time, wasn't around as much as I should have been. My dad had a heart condition he hadn't told me about, too proud, didn't want to need help; but he had doc appointments he needed to be driven to, meds he needed to have picked up. Viggo drove him around in Ashbury, everywhere he needed, till he was hospitalized, then passed."

A lump settles in my throat. "Sounds like Viggo."

"We connected at Dad's funeral, swapped numbers. I offered him a tune-up for Ashbury as a gesture of thanks. He wouldn't hear of it, but I insisted. Tune-ups became grabbing a beer, having him over for dinner. Then, when my wife had her accident, he helped me around the clock with all the reno and modifications to make the house accessible. I'd do anything for him, even fix it for free . . ."

"But the parts," I fill in for him. "They'd be prohibitively expensive."

His sigh is heavy through the line. "Yeah. I feel awful. I was hoping, if I had a good month, I could swing it, but I just can't."

"That's sweet of you, Donnie, but Viggo would never want you to do that for him."

"Doesn't mean he doesn't deserve it," Donnie says roughly. His voice is thick with emotion.

My gaze dips to the envelope sitting on the counter. The envelope containing my royalty check.

"Say, Donnie, mind telling me what parts and labor would cost?"

"Parts, I'll tell you, but there's no way under God's blue sky I'm letting someone pay for me to service Viggo Bergman's car, so you can forget about that."

I smile. "Parts, then. What would it be?"

Donnie tells me a number whose impact on Viggo's facial expression I now very much understand. It's a lot of money to pour into Band-Aid fixes for a car that's destined for the junkyard.

But aren't all cars eventually destined for the junkyard? And who's to say what kind of new lease on life is possible, with some time and love and elbow grease? Nothing's unsalvageable. I have to believe that. For Ashbury. For myself.

"Donnie," I ask, tapping the envelope on the counter, a smile warming my face, "how much more, not just to fix that car, but to make it like new?"

TWENTY-EIGHT

Viggo

Playlist: "Cherry Wine—Live," Hozier

I can't sleep. I've never been a very deep or long sleeper, my brain often waking me up at night, bursting with ideas, my body humming with the need to do something about them. The past two weeks, though, have been unprecedentedly rough.

I've barely slept at all, even with how exhausting the days have been—the bookstore busier than I'd ever let myself hope it would be; coaching kids' soccer practice on Wednesday evenings after the shop closes and games before the store opens on Saturday mornings; waking up early to bake and prepping for the next day late at night; all of it with Tallulah by my side, in the store, on the field, on the couch, typing steadily on her laptop.

It doesn't matter how exhausted I am, because my brain can't stop fixating on what's coming, what I've been dreading—the end of our agreement, being roommates, coworkers, sharing life and home.

And Tallulah isn't ready to talk about it.

The past two weeks, I've woken up halfway through the night, staring at the ceiling, trying to remind myself what I promised her, what we agreed to, when we both said we wanted to try, together, to see where this would go—no shoulds, no timetable.

But, I'm learning the hard way, sometimes things sound good in theory, while in practice, they suck.

Insomnia having struck again, I sit in the main living area's two a.m. darkness, knitting baby Bergman-MacCormack number three's blanket, swaying in my rocker, headphones on for a reread of one of my favorite historical romances, one side half-off so I can hear the dogs down the hall in my room, if they start barking at something in the middle of the night, which they occasionally do. I don't want them to wake Tallulah, who has been wearing herself out, working at the store all day with me, writing all evening, waking up early with me in the morning, sharing coffee and plans for the day. For *our* day.

"Chapter twenty-two," Mary Jane Wells reads.

I swear under my breath, tapping the rewind arrow on the app. I've zoned out. I missed the whole last chapter. That's been happening a lot lately. This is how bad I have it. I can't even focus on a romance novel.

I'm a mess.

Just as the chapter begins again, Juliet trots into the room, Romeo following her. She whines and jogs down the hall toward Tallulah's room.

I frown, setting down my knitting needles and blanket in progress, tugging off my headphones. That's when I hear what must have drawn Juliet, a faint, high-pitched beep coming from Tallulah's room.

My heart races. I know what that beep means. I've seen Tallulah's phone go off, the app on her phone, which she explained is connected to her continuous glucose monitor, beeping to alert her that she's too low or too high. She's told me if I hear that beeping in the night and it doesn't stop, that I can come bang on her door and make sure she's awake before she gets too high or too low.

The beeping stops, which is a small relief. I realize I'm holding my breath, so I force it out, force myself to take a deep, slow breath in, then breathe out. I count seconds, listening closely, trying not to worry. She only said to make sure she's awake when the beeping keeps going, but what if it malfunctioned? What if she's still not okay?

I'm emptying my lap of my knitting materials, tugging off my headphones from where I set them curved around my neck, when I hear the muffled sound of crying—Tallulah crying. I bolt out of my rocking chair, rush down the hall, past the dogs. I knock hard on Tallulah's door. "Lula? You okay?"

Her voice answers right away, but it's faint and hoarse. "Y-yes."

I press my forehead to the door, exhaling heavily. I'm relieved that she answered, that she's well enough to tell me she's okay. But I'm also struggling so hard, anxiety pulsing through me. It doesn't feel like enough, to stand here with a door between us, with only that shaky reassurance to hold on to.

"Lula," I say loud enough so she can hear me through the door. "Can I . . ." I swallow roughly, then take a deep, slow breath. "Can I come in?"

There's a beat of silence, then another hoarse, unsteady "Yes."

I open her door instantly, speeding into the room. She lies curled up on her side in bed, blue hair fanned out across her pillow, tears streaking down her cheeks as she clutches a juice box and sucks steadily on the straw. My heart plummets to the soles of my feet.

"Lula." I rush toward her.

She sniffles as I kneel beside her. I want to touch her so badly, do something, help somehow, but I'm unsure what would feel good, what might make things worse.

"I'm okay," she mutters. The bubbly sound of the last of her juice disappearing through the straw echoes in the room.

I stare at her, my hand moving across the sheet toward hers, which rests limply on the bed. "Can I . . ." I search her eyes. "Can I do anything? Can I help?"

Her pinkie brushes my fingertip, then hooks around mine. Wearily, she tips the juice box my way. I take it from her, then set it on her nightstand.

Tallulah gropes for her phone on the mattress, then opens it, peers at the app, and sighs. "Fruit snacks?" she asks quietly. "In my nightstand drawer?"

Relieved to have something to do, some small way to help, I turn to open the drawer and pull out a pack of fruit snacks.

"One more," she says quietly, then adds, "Please."

I pull out another fruit snack bag, then set both of them on her bed. I tear one open and hold it out for her. She reaches inside, cups the bag's entire contents inside her hand, then drops them into her mouth. Her eyes shut as she chews, and a heavy sigh leaves her. She seems so . . . weary. So tired.

My heart aches. Gently, I unhook my pinkie from hers and wrap her hand in mine. "This feel okay?" I whisper.

She answers me with a faint squeeze. Soft doggy whines emit at the door. I glance back to see Romeo and Juliet, obediently waiting at the threshold, eyes pinned on Tallulah.

Tallulah opens her eyes and sees them, too. She smiles faintly, then lifts her hand, beckoning them to her. They rush her way and clamber over me to rub their snouts on her hand, licking it.

Lula starts to sniffle again, her weary smile fading as fresh tears crest in her eyes.

"Lula, what can I do? More fruit snacks?"

She nods. I tear open the second bag, and her hand leaves the dogs long enough to dive in like last time, emptying all the fruit snacks into her mouth. She shuts her eyes again on another sigh, chewing steadily.

The dogs whine, sniffing the empty fruit snacks bags, me, Tallulah. I pet their heads to calm them.

Tallulah swallows, then sighs as she eases onto her back. The dogs seem to relax as Tallulah does, settling onto their bellies, letting out their own contented sighs.

Slowly, Tallulah turns her head my way and meets my eyes. "Thank you," she whispers.

Still clasping her hand, I stroke her knuckles with my thumb. "Don't thank me for that, Lu."

Her eyes slip shut. But her grip tightens. Her eyes open again, fixed on mine. "Stay?" she whispers.

She doesn't have to ask me twice. From being up on my knees, I start to lower down to the ground, ready to sit against the bed and simply stay by her side, but she tugs my hand. "Here," she says, nodding toward the empty side of her bed. "If you don't mind."

I glance from the open space on the far side of the bed to her. "You sure?"

She nods, eyes shutting again. "Mm-hmm."

I crawl onto the bed carefully, settling on top of the sheets. I lie on my side, propping my head on my bent arm, watching her. Tallulah turns toward me and cuddles in, setting her head on my arm, too. "Hold me?" she asks.

I wrap an arm around her, rubbing gently over her back. "Feel okay?"

She nods.

I feel her tears before I realize she's crying. She's so quiet, so still inside my arms. I stop my hand's circling over her back, and I pull away just enough to be able to look at her, to bring my thumb gently beneath her eyes and wipe away her tears.

"Lula," I whisper. I want to say more, to tell her I'm sorry she has to go through this, to ask if she's all right, to tell her it kills me to see her cry, that I wish I could take away all that she carries every day with this disease and bear it myself. I pour everything I feel into those two syllables—*Lula*—whispered in the darkness, and somehow I know she knows.

She peers up at me, sighing shakily, more tears filling her eyes. "I just get so fucking tired," she whispers. "Tired of my stupid pod coming off and fucking things up. Tired of waking up low. Tired of going too high when I'm having a perfectly good day and there's no goddamn reason for it. Tired of trying to do everything right and this stupid disease still manages to pull the rug out from underneath me. It's claustrophobic, just inescapable. And it's lonely, so fucking lonely, when I'm the only one who understands, who's carrying the weight of this disease, the unpredictability of it. I'm so tired—" Her voice breaks, and she burrows into me.

"I'm so sorry, Lula." I rest my cheek on her head, rubbing her back again. "I can't imagine how hard it is, how exhausting. I know . . . I'll never understand what it's like to be you, to live with this disease, but . . . if there's any way I can carry a little of it, if telling me more or showing me or, or . . . depending on me more might help, I . . . I want to do that. I'd . . . be honored to do that."

She sniffles and presses her forehead to my sternum. "It helps, just . . . talking about it sometimes, like this. It helps that you're not freaking out right now, seeing me low; you gave me what I needed to eat, you stayed, you're . . . still here."

"Of course I am." I hold her close, my arm wrapping around her waist, and she jumps.

"Watch my pod." She jerks back, lifting her shirt.

"Shit, I'm sorry, Lu." Panic knots my stomach. Have I knocked it loose? Made things worse?

Her hand goes to the disc adhered to her stomach. She runs her fingers along the adhesive. Then she leans back, pulls her PDM from the nightstand, and clicks through it. "All good. It's okay."

"You're sure? I'm really sorry, Lu, that's the last thing—"

Her hand clasps mine. "It's okay. Promise."

"Your blood sugar, too? Is it okay now?"

Tallulah's checking her phone, opening up the app. She glances at the screen, frowning in concentration. Her expression clears slightly before she turns and sets both her phone and her PDM back on the nightstand.

She eases toward me again, staring up at me. "Blood sugar is good, too." I hold her eyes as she takes my hand, until we're close to her pod. Gently, she guides my finger along the edge of the adhesive. "All safe and sound," she whispers. "You didn't knock it loose."

I swallow roughly, flooded with emotion as she settles my hand on her hip and nudges her thigh between mine. Our eyes hold as I glide my hand slowly from her hip along her back, a soothing circle. I'm relieved I didn't hurt her. I'm overwhelmed by this trust and honesty she's given me, telling me how hard this is, showing me an entirely new level of this part of herself and her life.

"I wish I could do something," I whisper. "Anything to make it better for you, Lu."

Tallulah stares up at me and smiles faintly. She blinks away tears. "You are. I told you, this makes it better, you understanding, helping, being here."

"Doesn't feel like enough," I mutter roughly, blinking away my own tears.

"It is," she whispers. And then she's quiet for a moment, her eyes searching my face. A faint smile lifts her mouth. "Your hair is a sight to behold."

I don't move my hand from her hip, don't check to feel how goofy it must be. "Headphone hair. I was listening to an audiobook."

She frowns. "Couldn't sleep?"

I shake my head.

Uncertainty tightens her expression. "Maybe you want to go back to your audiobook now. I shouldn't . . . I shouldn't keep you."

I stare down at her, my hand gliding across her lower back again. "You're not keeping me. It's a reread anyway. So . . . I could stay. If . . . you wanted me to." Nerves get the better of me, make me ramble, afraid if I'm quiet, she'll say what I'm dreading—that she doesn't need me, doesn't want me, that I've overstepped. "Besides, it's been a while since I slept on the right side of the bed. I like to mix it up, which side I sleep on. Lately, I've been on a left side streak. The left side of the bed has a very specific kind of energy, know what I mean?"

A soft laugh huffs out of her. "You're rambling."

My cheeks heat as I grimace. "I am."

She brings a hand to my hair and softly combs through it. "You do that when you're nervous."

"Unfortunately, yes."

Her eyes hold mine. "I'm a little nervous, too. I've never shared a bed with someone. But . . . I want to, with you. If . . . *you* want to."

I beam down at her. "I do."

"Just don't get too attached to the right side of the bed," she says as she shuts her eyes and snuggles into me.

My stomach drops at the implication. That she won't want this again, that this is just a onetime thing—

"I have to switch sides," she says, her voice quieter, her breath sweet and warm against my neck. "When I rotate my CGM and my pod to the other side of my body, I have to sleep on the other side of the bed."

A ridiculously wide grin lifts my mouth. I shut my eyes and rest my cheek on her head. "Well, then, lucky for you, to have found such an expert cuddler who appreciates the merits of both sides of the mattress."

Who wants to hold you and comfort you for as long as you'll let me.

I feel her smile against my skin, soft and sleepy. "Lucky for me indeed."

"Ready to go?" Tallulah calls from the kitchen.

"Almost!" I yell from my room, dragging my soccer shorts up my legs.

"We're going to be late!"

I frown, peering down at my phone. "No, we're not!"

Tallulah storms down the hall and knocks. I open my door. She takes my breath away. Like always. Lightweight gray athleisure capris, a yellow team T-shirt tight across her tits and soft stomach, hair up in a messy bright blue bun. "Yes, we are. Our game is at nine this week, not ten."

"Shit." I lunge past her, to where my turf shoes and soccer socks sit in a pile on my dresser.

"We'll be okay," she reassures me, hands on hips. "We just need to keep moving."

I feel the familiar shame and frustration of losing track of my schedule, of time, that's plagued me for as long as I can remember. "I know, but it's my fault we're rushed now."

"Hey." Her voice makes me pick up my head and glance her way. Tallulah strolls into my room, ignoring my odd piles of stuff that are tidy enough but bizarrely organized. She clasps my hand. "Take it easy on yourself. It's our first nine a.m. game. You've been incredibly busy lately; it's easy to lose track of changes like that when you've got so much going on. Plus, I threw off our schedule this morning."

"Lula, no—"

She sets a finger against my mouth. "I did. I'm not judging it. Just pointing out a fact. You . . ." She searches my eyes. "You very sweetly took care of me last night. And then we both slept in. That threw us off our typical early morning routine of coffee and sorting out the day."

I stare down at her, my chest tight, my hands aching to touch her, draw her close, kiss her deeply.

"Thank you again," she says. "For taking care of me last night."

I smile softly against her finger. "Thank you for trusting me to take care of you."

As her finger falls away, our eyes hold the way they did this morning, when I blinked awake and saw her doing the same, dark lashes fluttering, amber eyes lit up by the morning sun. We lay there for silent seconds, just staring at each other, until Tallulah slowly sat up, squeezed my hand, whispering, "Thank you," then slipped out of bed toward the bathroom before I could even answer.

"You're a good one, Viggo Bergman." She cups my cheek, her thumb sweeping along the line of my beard. "Even if you don't know how to use a razor."

I laugh quietly, staring down at her. "Back off the beard."

"Never." She smiles, sweet and feisty, a coy glint in her eyes. "Now, let's go. We've got a game to win."

———————

We won last week's game, which we made *just* on time. And we're about to win this one, too, I can feel it.

"Let's go!" Tallulah yells inside her cupped hands before she claps them together. "Two more minutes, yellow. Leave it all on the field!"

I bite my lip, smiling down at her.

Messy blue bun, aviator sunglasses, whistle around her neck. Bright yellow shirt that makes her look like a ray of sunshine.

She's perfect. Here, in this moment. In every part of my life.

My smile slips. Because this is it. Charlie's wedding weekend. The end of our agreement. And still, she's said nothing.

I'm about to implode from the waiting, the not knowing, the fucking agony of wanting this woman, knowing she means so much to me, that I want to mean that much to her, and not knowing where she stands.

Even if so many things make me hope.

Quiet nights, toes tucked under my thigh while she scowls at her laptop, revising and revising. Smiles over coffee cups and swift kisses to my cheek when she leaves early in the morning for therapy. Promises of *again and again*, for my niece, *fall session* for our little soccer team, *next month* for the romance book club she hovers on the edges of.

I hold tight to that hope, but it feels like such a small, delicate thing to keep me afloat in the sky-high swells of all this unknown.

"Coach Viggo," Joaquin says beside me on the sideline, winded from his stint out on the field.

I peer down at him. "What's up, Joaquin?"

"Thanks for bringing Coach Tallulah. We needed her."

I smile. "Coach Tallulah brought herself; I can't take the credit. But I agree, we needed her."

"That's it!" Tallulah yells, walking past me down the sideline as Cooper dribbles the ball up the field. "Pass it," she mutters, eyes on the field, tracking Maddison, who runs into open space like we taught her, careful to stay onside, not running past the last defender. "Pass it to her."

Cooper and I have had words about his reluctance to pass. He was not swayed by my talking-to. Tallulah stepped in later that practice, crouched to his level, and said something that had him wide-eyed, nodding vigorously, then sprinting off. I think she got through to him. I hope so. Because the other team knows Cooper likes to hog the ball and shoot, so they're marking him. And Maddison is *wide* open.

"Pass it," Tallulah grits out, hands clenched by her sides.

"Coop," I yell, hands cupped around my mouth. "Be a team player, buddy!"

He picks up his head, having heard me, gets one look at Tallulah staring at him across the field, then goes wide-eyed again, takes a touch on the ball, and kicks it toward Maddison.

I clutch Tallulah's arm, shocked that it worked, riveted by how this is unfolding.

Maddison gets a great first touch on the ball, passing it to herself a few feet ahead, then running on to it.

"Low and in the corner," Tallulah mutters, grabbing the hem of my shirt, staring at Maddison. "Shoot low and in the corner." She chants it again and again as Maddison draws close to the goal, then kicks it past the defender who's coming toward her.

"Prep touch, plant your foot, power through," I whisper, the three steps I've taught them over and over for a clean strike on the ball.

Tallulah's grip slips to my hand, curls around it, and squeezes tight.

Maddison takes a touch, plants her right foot, and strikes with her left, low and into the corner. It rolls over the line, past the goalie.

"YES!" Tallulah screams, jumping up, dragging my hand with her.

The whistle blows from the ref. Time done. Game over. We won.

"Yes!" Tallulah yells again, running out onto the field toward the kids, who swarm around her, jumping up and down, shrieking, hands high, smiles as wide as the field.

I don't normally support excessive celebration. Mom ingrained it in us to be calm, cool winners, but this team we were up against has played a dirty game of late hits, trips, and shirt tugging, and their coach is a jerkface. I don't feel too bad about celebrating.

I rush out onto the field and join them. A cluster of kids screaming happily between us, I smile at Tallulah. She beams at me, flushed, happy, the sun shining in her eyes. I want to kiss her so badly.

The high of our victory lasts while we do our postgame roundup, praising the kids for their hard work, their sportsmanship, then throw hands in for a final time, chanting our team name. I watch the kids disperse with their parents and caregivers, pack up our gear into my coach book bag—tiny goalie gloves, onetime-use ice packs, first aid kit, pinnies for warm-up, a few extra water bottles.

When I stand straight, Tallulah's watching me, eyes shielded against the sun.

"What's up, Lu? We on time to catch our flight?"

She smiles. "Yeah, we're fine on time."

I smile back. These moments, they're the ones that fill me up and keep me going. Shared plans, rides home, a flight together to the wedding. It feels so good. So right.

Even if it doesn't have a name to it yet.

"Let's get going, though," she says. "I want to make a quick stop on our way to the airport."

"You want to head there now? I don't mind, if that's easier."

"No!" she blurts, before smoothing her expression.

I frown, confused.

She smiles again, slipping her water bottle into the holder on the side of my bag, pulling out her keys from its front pocket. "First, I want to go home."

I stare after her as she starts walking toward the Vespa, the word ringing in the air, warming my heart.

Home.

TWENTY-NINE

Tallulah

Playlist: "Without You," Lana Del Rey

Here we are, back at the A-frame, full circle.

The house hums with life that's turned quieter, now that little ones are being tucked in, doors shut quietly, lights dimmed, voices hushed. It's peaceful and content, floors creaking, dishes clattering gently as they're washed (to my profound annoyance, I was, as sister of the bride, forbidden to help with cleanup). A window is lifted open; someone laughs softly.

The sounds of a family wrapping up the day.

I can see why Charlie and Gigi wanted to get married here, beyond the nostalgia of this being the place where they got engaged. Surrounded by a family that's become their own, in a home filled with love and memories. It feels like an invocation, a hope, for their own future, Gigi and Charlie's, to begin married life in a place like this.

Groaning, I stretch my arms up, one side, then the other, trying to work out the kinks from flying. Viggo and I came straight from the airport into setup mode for the wedding tomorrow, followed by the rehearsal, which was brief and went smoothly, then dinner afterward, which was delicious, noisy, chaotic, and absolutely perfect. This is the first time since we got here that I've felt like I could catch my breath, knowing that my sister has everything she needs, everything the way she wants it for tomorrow—I've triple-checked. I feel a unique responsibility, not just because I've always been protective of her, but because I'm the only member of our family here right now.

Harry has, to my relief, checked himself into rehab. We've been emailing, ever since he first wrote me, sharing his struggles, an apology for the ways his behavior hurt and scared me. I've opened up, told him my own struggles, too. We talk about therapy being hard, about how raw it is, healing those parts of ourselves we'd hardened to protect ourselves.

Mom and Dad aren't here either, but they will be tomorrow. Charlie told them they were welcome to attend the wedding, but not be part of it. I can't say I'm excited to see them tomorrow, given where we left everything, but I've started to learn hard things always have to start somewhere, even if they're small. Just seeing them tomorrow, sharing Charlie's day, I think that's about all I'll be able to handle. I hope that's all they'll ask of me, because if not, I'm going to have to draw a firm boundary around that—a skill I'm still very much working on.

But that's a problem for Tomorrow Tallulah. For now, finally, I feel like I can slow down and just . . . be.

In need of some quiet to think and process, I walk the hallway of the first floor, soaking up the family photos. Viggo and Oliver, dark and light hair, same pale blue eyes, knobby skinned knees, and bright smile; Ziggy with her red hair and freckles wedged between them, green eyes squinted as she grins. Elin and Alex, Viggo's parents, on their wedding day; Elin, white-blond hair, ice-blue eyes, sultry Mona Lisa smile; Alex, red hair, bright green eyes, beaming like a man who hit the jackpot. Freya, tallest, with her mother's coloring; Axel, brown hair, his father's green eyes, lanky and nearly his sister's height; Ren, shorter, stockier, ice-blue eyes, freckles and wide smile; Ryder, windblown blond hair, bright green eyes, shovel in hand, all standing on the beach, eyes narrowed into the sun, an epic sandcastle in the foreground, Elin in the background, softly out of focus, her belly round . . . with Viggo.

I touch the glass covering the photo, trace the curve of her stomach. That's where he began, *how* he began—from love, so much love.

I swallow past the lump in my throat, moving down the hall, and come to a stop, a candid of little-boy Viggo, up in a tree, leaning against its trunk, long legs dangling off the branch he's sitting on, a book in hand.

Tears well in my eyes.

Here, in this home, with all his family, the night before my baby sister gets married, I'm feeling so much. For once, I don't resent it. In fact, I crave it, like I've been living my life holding my breath, drawing in only the bare minimum necessary to survive, but now the air is clear and clean, free for me to breathe in deep.

"Hey, Tallulah."

I spin around, startled. Rooney. Tall, honey-blond hair drifting past her shoulders, blue-green eyes, and a wide, sunny smile. "Sorry I surprised you," she says. "Just on my way back from the bathroom, and I saw you here. Figured I'd see how you were doing."

I smile faintly. "That's nice of you. I'm okay." I turn a little, glancing at the photo wall. "Just . . . taking it in."

Rooney steps beside me, hand going to the soft swell of her stomach, which I'd bet, based on her otherwise slender frame, is a baby bump, even though I haven't heard anything from Viggo. I'm not saying a word. I get asked enough when I'm due that I am a firm believer that under no circumstances should a person ask another if they're pregnant. That's news you let someone share with you.

"It's a lot," she says, gaze roaming the photos. "To take in."

I glance her way. "Was it for you?"

"Oh yeah." She laughs softly. "I mean, I craved it, their family's love, their closeness. But it was bittersweet sometimes, a reminder of all I didn't have. They were so welcoming, and I always felt so at home with them, but I still used to worry that I'd never truly feel like one of them."

"You did?" I turn, facing her fully.

She turns and faces me, too. "Absolutely."

I swallow, trying not to let tears spill down my cheeks. "And that fear . . . went away?"

"It did." She smiles. "Little by little."

"How?" I whisper.

She peers back at the photos, a close-up of a boy I'm pretty sure is Axel drawing at the dining table, his tongue stuck out in concentration. "Time. Opening up to them. But mostly time. Until one day . . . I realized, to the Bergmans, I already *was* one of them. That they'd opened their arms and hearts to me, and once they do that, they do it fully, without reservation. I had nothing to prove, no place to earn. Their love, that belonging, it was right there the whole time, waiting for me to see it."

"I second that." We both startle, glancing over our shoulders, toward the voice that's joined us. Willa, Ryder's wife, wild brown waves pinned up on her head, a powerful, compact soccer player's physique, shimmies closer, smiling sheepishly. "Sorry. Couldn't help but overhear. Just wanted to chime in." She clutches my hand, touch that even just a few months ago I'd have balked at, but after months of sweet, caring touches like that from Viggo, I lean into it. I squeeze her hand back. "Rooney's right," she says. "You have nothing to prove. But I'll say that, from my own experience, it can take time to trust it, to feel safe in it. Be gentle with yourself along the way. That comfort will come."

"Third that," a new voice adds. We all spin and turn.

Frankie, Ren's wife, stands tall, dark hair swept back in a ponytail, a sleepy baby in one arm, her cane in the other hand.

"Lucia!" Rooney coos, opening her arms, taking the baby from her mother.

Frankie takes a step closer, then leans her back to the wall, cane between her legs. "We're missing a few members presently, but welcome to the dysfunctional section of the Bergmans."

"Frankie!" Willa snorts.

"What?" Frankie shrugs, holding my eyes. "It's true. This is what they do, love people who've got baggage and hang-ups. The Bergmans are different. We're different from them, no judgment, just a fact. They don't see love like we do, with conditions and clauses, end dates and disappointments, and it's a mindfuck at first. We get it. You're not alone. If you ever think you are, we're here."

Willa and Rooney nod, smiling encouragingly at me.

I glance between the three of them. "That's very nice of you, but . . . Viggo and I, it's not . . . well, it's not exactly . . ." My voice dies off.

They stare at me, confusion painting their faces.

I bite my lip. "I mean, I *want* it to be."

Willa's grins deepens. Rooney's smile turns wider. Frankie's mouth tips up at the corner. "But . . . ?" she offers.

"Ba!" Lucia yells.

I offer the baby my finger, which she clasps tightly, her wide green eyes locked on me. I look at her, because it's easiest to confess this to a tiny person with no judgment, no expectations. Just curiosity and innocence. "But . . . I haven't quite worked up the courage to tell him how I feel. I even had a grand gesture planned, before our flight, but then I realized it was all wrong."

Frankie frowns. "How so?"

I tell them about Ashbury, my plan for us to stop by Donnie's on our way to the airport, how I panicked on the ride there and made up a fib when we got to the airport about forgetting about my errand.

It was the wrong timing. That was something you do *after* declaring your feelings for someone, not before. It felt too dangerously close to doing what my parents would—throw money at an issue rather than talk about it, buy affection with gifts. I want Viggo to have his car, his happiness with it, but I don't want him to think I've done that for him with some expectation of his feelings tied to it.

Willa sighs dreamily. "That's so romantic."

I blink at the word, my heart pounding. "Really?"

"Definitely." Rooney wipes beneath her eyes. "Damn hormones. I'm a watering can."

Frankie smiles knowingly at her sister-in-law, then glances my way. "I think you made the right call. Take it easy on yourself. It's nerve-wracking, but you'll figure out the right way and time to tell him."

"Lula?" Viggo calls.

"Shit!" Willa hisses as she spins and ducks into the bathroom, shutting the door behind her. Rooney squeaks, rushing after Frankie with the baby. They melt into the shadows, exiting through a door down the hall I didn't even know existed.

I spin around just as Viggo steps from the kitchen into the hallway, a towel on his shoulder, plaid flannel sleeves rolled up to his elbows. "There you are."

He's so beautiful. Soft, tender smile. Suntanned skin. Those tiny creases at the corners of his ice-blue eyes. His beard looks extra full tonight, which would normally frustrate me, but I'm attached to the familiarity of it now. I think he looks handsome, but I still want to tug it flat and see his jaw, his mouth, kiss every inch of it.

A nervous smile tugs at my mouth. "Here I am."

He glances past me. "See you found the family photos."

"I did." Turning, I peer at them again, my gaze drifting to even more pictures that I haven't had the chance to look at closely, that I might not even get the time to revisit.

We're not here long—this evening for the rehearsal dinner; to-morrow, Sunday, for the wedding; then a flight back on Monday, so the store isn't closed too long and the sweet couple from romance book club, Arturo and Lee, don't have to spend too many days dog- and cat-sitting for us.

Us.

I've hoped so many things today. That we'd be an *us* when we came back to the store, flicking on its lights, taking down the sign on the glass that Viggo made, saying, *Closed this weekend for the best reason—a wedding!* That when I walked through that back door to the house, it would be to a home, my home with him. That down the road, I'd have all the time in the world here at this A-frame, to poke around its corners, look at old photos, browse its bookshelves, learn its secrets and memories.

That hope holds steady as I stare up at Viggo, as I clasp his hand. He smiles down at me, eyes searching mine. "The bride-to-be is looking for you." He glances over his shoulder and calls my sister. "Found her!"

Charlie rounds the corner, smiling wide, buzzing with energy, like a kid awaiting Christmas. "We're off to bed!" she says. Gigi waves from the landing. I blow her a kiss.

"Sleep well," I tell my sister, squeezing her tight.

"I'll be lucky if I sleep at all," she says. "But I'll crash eventually. You sleep well, too, Tallulah."

Officially exhausted, having said my good nights to everyone, I follow Viggo a few minutes later as he leads me up the stairs, carrying my suitcase ahead of me.

I frown, confused, when I process what's missing. "Wait. Where's your suitcase?"

"Downstairs. I'm crashing on the couch."

I stop, halfway up the stairs. "Absolutely not."

Viggo backtracks, takes my hand, and tugs me up the steps with him. "Lu, I love sleeping on the sofa." He clears his throat. "And our room only has one bed."

"So? We'll sleep in it."

He shakes his head. "I'm not making you share a bed with me."

"You wouldn't be *making* me; I'm offering, you goofball."

"Because you're nice," he counters, leading me down the hall. We stop in front of a shut door. "Since when?"

"Tallulah, you're nice to me. You're being nice now."

"Because I . . ." I swallow nervously. "Because you matter to me, despite your despicable disregard for modern shaving methods. Now, go get your suitcase."

"No."

"Fine." I yank my suitcase from his hands, then start back toward the stairs. "I'll sleep on the floor in the living room."

"Tallulah Jane Clarke, I swear to God—" He groans, hustling after me, beating me to the top of the steps. He spins around two steps down and faces me. "Lu, please."

I peer down at him, my heart pounding. "Tell me you don't *want* to sleep in that bed tonight, and I'll let it go."

Viggo bites his lip, eyes narrowing.

"And *don't* you dare lie to me," I say icily.

He swallows. "Fine, okay? Go get unpacked. I'll be up soon with my bag."

I'm a ball of nerves, sitting up in bed, e-reader in hand, not processing a word. The door opens, and I glance up to see Viggo standing with his back to me, hanging his towel on one of the hooks mounted to the wall. Bright yellow athletic shorts and a plain white T-shirt, hair wet from his shower, curled up along his neck. Happiness hums through me at the sight of him.

He turns, shutting the door behind him, and smiles nervously. "Hey."

I stare at him as my mouth falls open. His beard is . . . almost gone. Shaved to a tight shadow along his jaw. I can't even process how beautiful his face is, revealed more fully, the faint hollows in his cheeks, the sharp, lovely line of his jaw. That lush, soft mouth.

"Oh my God," I whisper.

Viggo sets a hand to his face, clearly self-conscious. "You don't like it?"

"Like it?" I shake my head. "I . . . It's . . ."

I can't even find the words. Yes, in a way, I miss the familiarity of what I've known, that full, bushy beard. But I'm riveted by the luxury of seeing so much more of him. I'm glad he didn't shave it clean, like I spent the past two months heckling him to. He still looks like the Viggo I know, but now also a little more like the young man who scared the life out of me seven years ago, kind and curious, sitting beside me in class.

He's so handsome, it hurts.

"You look incredible," I finally manage.

Viggo's smile broadens and brightens. My mouth lifts reflexively, because that's what happens now, like there's a glowing, golden string connecting the corner of his mouth to mine. When he smiles, I smile.

"Thanks," he says quietly.

I set my e-reader aside and watch him traipse past the bed as he tips his head, shaking it once, twice, wiggling his finger in his ear, working water out. He opens the closet door, checking that his clothes are ready for tomorrow.

"What made you do it?" I ask.

"Shave?"

I nod.

He glances my way. Heat pours through me. I want to lick his jaw, feel that stubble scraping across my skin. "Figured the brides deserved not to have a Bigfoot impersonator as their celebrant, front and center in the wedding photos. You really think it looks okay? I feel naked without it."

"I really think it looks much more than okay," I tell him quietly.

He throws me another faint smile, a blush on his cheeks. "Well, good. That . . . that matters to me."

We just . . . stare at each other, eyes locked, soft silence and night air mingling in the room, the hum and buzz of bugs outside our quiet chorus.

I bite my lip as my throat grows thick, fingers curling into the sheets, knowing it's happening, inevitable, terrifying, beautiful—my heart pounds, affection, delight, joy, possession, desire, need, longing, coalescing, spilling through me, a kaleidoscopic flood that fills my heart, my thoughts with one crystal clear thought:

I love you.

Tears fill my eyes, a smile breaking across my face as I watch him turn back toward his clothes, brow furrowed in concentration as he smooths his shirt down. He's nervous for tomorrow, to fill the role of celebrant that Charlie asked of him. Of course he's nervous, not because he has anything to worry about, but because he cares. He's done his online application so he can legally officiate their marriage. He's practiced what he's going to say countless times—I've heard him, pacing in his room, his voice low and cadent.

"How's the minister feeling this evening?" I ask softly.

Viggo glances up again, his eyes meeting mine. His smile is bashful as he shuts the closet door, scrubbing at the back of his neck. "Nervous."

"You'll be perfect."

His hand falls as he stares at me, his throat working. He really is nervous. I open my arms. "Come here. Come to bed."

He doesn't hesitate, just crawls right up the mattress, into my arms, resting his head on my chest. I sink my hands into his hair, combing through gently. "I love how much you care. I love how you love my sister."

I love you.

I kiss his hair, breathing him in. I want to say it so badly, but, God, what if he doesn't want to say it back? What if he doesn't feel that way yet, doesn't think he'll ever feel that way? What if the way I say it is unromantic, anticlimactic, a disappointment? And then how the hell will I get through the wedding tomorrow, staring at the man I've fallen for, who's given me a home, a place to grow and flourish? How could I handle sharing this day with someone who taught me to love but doesn't love me in return?

I swallow the words, clutching him tight, rubbing circles over his back.

Viggo sighs. "Thank you, Lula."

I shut my eyes, savoring the feel of him, that clean woodsy scent, the trace of cinnamon sugar. I feel Viggo reach past me, turning off the light, then settling back in, arm curled around me, nestling his head on my boobs.

I laugh softly. "Getting comfy there?"

"Mm-hmm." He nuzzles me, his nose brushing my bare skin, his chin grazing my nipple through my shirt. I bite my lip, my grip in his hair tightening, eyes falling shut again. Quiet settles between us again, the whir of insects outside the screen, the cool evening breeze whispering through it.

Viggo's grip around my waist tightens. His thigh slips over mine. "Lula," he whispers.

I drag open my eyes, blinking as they adjust to the darkness, only soft moonlight illuminating the room. Peering down at him, I catch his gaze as he stares up at me, eyes bright, a flush splashed across his cheekbones. "I need . . ." he whispers. "I need you."

"You have me." I cup his cheek, stroking it tenderly with my thumb. "I'm here."

He shakes his head. "I need to touch you. I need you to touch me. If . . . if you want."

Understanding dawns. I melt toward him, kissing his forehead. "'*If* I want you.' Of course I want you. I just . . . want to respect what you need—"

"I know you do," he says roughly, cupping my neck, drawing me closer. "It means so much that you've respected that, Lu."

I smile down at him, smoothing his wet hair away from his face. "Lie back."

He frowns. "Why?"

"Because I want to touch you."

A soft, uncertain smile lifts his mouth.

Sitting up, I gently press his shoulder until he falls back onto the pillows. I crawl over him until I'm straddling his waist, up on my knees. I reach for the hem of his shirt, my fingertips skating across his stomach. It shudders under my touch, muscles jumping. "Take off your shirt," I tell him.

Viggo sits up quickly, gripping his shirt by the back of the collar, yanking it off, and throwing it aside. I smile and press him back again, until he's flat on the bed, staring up at me. His hands go to my hips, tugging me toward him.

I relax my legs, let myself settle over him. He groans as his hands glide up my back. I bend and kiss him, light, soft. Then I part his mouth with my tongue, earning his gasp as I grind my hips against his.

He sinks his fingers into my hair, his mouth falling open, hips moving up into mine. My hand drifts down his chest, tracing the tattoo, the landscape of this place he loves. My hands dance lower, over his ribs, which bear a black line tattoo I couldn't see in the dark of the bookstore that night. I trace across fluttering pages of open books, nestled among hardy vines and peony flowers.

He drags an arm from around my waist, reaching for me, where I ache between my thighs, but I catch his wrist.

"Lula?"

Slowly, I lift it over his head, pinning it back to the pillow. I take his other wrist and do the same, kissing him once more, slow and deep. He sighs into my mouth, tongue seeking mine, urgent, needy. "Just let me make you feel good," I whisper, rocking my hips over his, kissing him tenderly and teasing.

Viggo groans, his fingers linking through mine as I pin them back over his head. His hips arch beneath me. He's breathing hard and fast. "This is torture."

"Good torture?" I kiss the corner of his mouth, his cheekbone, behind his ear, the hollow of his throat.

He nods. "Yes."

I start to kiss my way down his hard chest.

"Wh-what are you doing?" he asks, voice tight.

I lick at his pebbled nipple, making him gasp, his hips lurching up into me. "Touching you. Trust me?"

He peers down at me, then nods, another soft, uncertain smile. "I trust you."

"Good." Gently, I kiss my way along the waistband of his shorts, then, hooking them with his boxers, start to drag them down his hips.

Viggo's breath turns rougher as I pull them off his legs, dropping them to the side of the bed. I can't see perfectly clear in the darkness, only faint moonlight on the cloudy night, but I can see enough. His cock is tall and thick, and I grip him at the base, bringing him to my mouth.

"Oh God." He throws back his head, his hand going to my hair, sinking in.

I hum happily around him, loving his taste, how he feels—hot and hard, yet smooth and soft.

Going slow, I work him with my mouth, trace with my fingertips the flock of birds tattooed high across his thigh onto his hip,
swirling my touch to the V at his stomach, over his pelvis.

He pants, his grip tightening in my hair. "Lula," he breathes.
"Feels so good."

I stare up at him, stroking up and down, swirling with my
tongue, learning what makes his hips jerk up, makes his breath
turn rougher, faster.

I love you, I tell him with my touch, my eyes fastened on his. *I
love you.*

Viggo stares down at me, mouth open, jagged breaths, chest
heaving. "Lula, oh *fuck*." His head falls to the pillow again. Reaching back, he grips the bed frame as I take him deep in my mouth,
stroke his thighs, between his legs, right behind where he's tight
and drawn up, rubbing, teasing.

"I'm gonna come." His voice breaks. His legs start to shake.
"Oh God, Lula, please."

I watch him as I move faster, take him deeper. His hips roll.
His knuckles turn white as he grips the bed frame. His mouth falls
open as he gasps my name again and again, and then he throws his
head back, turning it, burying his face in the pillow as he shouts
my name and I feel him spill into my throat, as I work him through
every rough jerk of his hips, every cry of my name.

On the next gentle stroke of my mouth, he shudders and gasps.
"No more. I can't."

I smile, crawling up his body, falling to the side, tucked close,
my thigh thrown over his, my hand circling over his heart, which
beats wildly against his ribs.

Slowly, I bend and kiss him. *I love you*, I tell him with my lips'
serenade to his. *I love you*, I tell him, my hand resting over his heart.

Viggo blinks up at me, a darling, dazed smile brightening his face. He blinks slowly, sated, exhaustion all over his face. "Lula," he breathes.

"Viggo," I whisper, kissing his forehead, pulling back, smiling down at him.

His eyes slip closed. "You killed me dead."

"Death by orgasm. Not the worst way to go."

He smiles, eyes shut. "Just a metaphor, Clarke. I'm not going anywhere." His words are slurred with sleepiness.

My smile deepens. "Good. I want you around for a long time."

"Hmm." His smile fades, sleep smoothing his expression. A soft snore rolls out of him.

I bite my lip, smiling so wide it hurts. Tears settle in the corners of my eyes. I could stare at him, watch him sleep like this, naked and peaceful beside me, forever.

If things go the way I want them to tomorrow, I just might get to.

Carefully I reach for the foot of the bed and bring up the soft knit cotton blanket, covering him. I settle back into the pillows, and I watch him sleep, moonlight casting deep shadows on his lashes, the long, straight line of his nose.

When I've had my fill, at least for now, I turn, careful to be quiet and slow. I reach for my e-reader on the nightstand, power it to life, and turn the brightness down. Blowing out a steady breath, I stare at the screen, my finger hovering over the title.

One of his favorite historical romances, according to the adorably detailed "Bookseller's Favorites" index cards he's written and perched around titles he loves shelved across the store. I downloaded it before our flight. Finally, I tap it and watch the book open up.

I settle in beside the man I love, a story he loves in my hands.

THIRTY

Viggo

Playlist: "From Eden," Hozier

Sunlight wakes me, warm on my skin. I blink, disoriented, bone-deep calm weighting my body to the mattress. My hand slides across the bed, eager to feel Tallulah, to touch her and draw her close.

But the bed is cool. Empty.

I jackknife upright, heart pounding, as last night rushes back to me. Tallulah's hands on me, her mouth. Her slow kisses and tender touch making me fall apart. The most intense orgasm of my life, which knocked me back, left me spent and peaceful, my mind blank, my body sated, in a way it's never been.

I remember kissing her afterward, cuddling close. And then . . .

Oh, sweet Jesus. I fell asleep. After that incredible intimacy she gave me, I didn't reciprocate, didn't take care of her the way she'd so lovingly taken care of me.

Lovingly.

The word echoes in my head. I rake my hands through my hair, panicked, my breathing shallow. It felt loving, her touch, her kiss, her eyes holding mine. But what if that scared her? Worse, what if she did that for me, gave that to me, but she still doesn't know, believe, think, love is something we could share?

Love.

I've been holding that word at bay, locked away deep inside myself, always in the corner of my thoughts, telling myself it's not really *real* if I don't drag it out into the light and name it, face it head on.

But it's no less true.

And it's terrifying.

I love her. I love Tallulah. And falling in love looked . . . nothing like I believed it would. It wasn't sudden or showy, clean-cut or clear. It was uneven and unexpected, creeping quietly, a vine that began as a small, delicate shoot winding its way through me, until one day it was everywhere, twined through my heart, my mind, my life, every corner of it.

God, I love her. And I don't know if she loves me, if she even believes in love itself.

I groan, heart aching, eyes wet. I can't breathe, can't think, can't process what to do with myself anymore. Tearing out of bed, I drag on clothes distractedly, then rummage around for my phone. No text from Tallulah. I scour the bed. No note.

I whip open the door, rush down the stairs to a houseful of family. No Tallulah to be seen. Panic blanks my thoughts, leaves me standing in the entranceway of the house, chest heaving, struggling for breath. "H-has anyone seen Lula?"

A sea of frowns, heads glancing around, murmured nos.

"I'm sure she's here," Willa says. "Maybe with Charlie?"

My mom shakes her head. "I just checked on Charlie. She wasn't there. But I'm sure there's an explanation."

I run toward the front of the house, peering out the windows, searching for some sign of Tallulah. Nothing. I turn back, my chest tightening, my throat thick.

Linnea frowns at me from her bowl of cereal. "You okay, Uncle Viggo?"

I shake my head. "I need . . . I . . ." My voice cracks.

Oliver puts down the knife he was holding, hovering over chopped herbs, and starts toward me. "V, you're okay. Take a deep breath."

"I can't," I gasp, falling into my brother as he wraps his arms around me.

There's a quiet murmur of voices, chairs scraping, cups being set down. A door opens. I'm guided by my brother's strong arm down the hall to an open door.

That's when I realize where I am, what's happening.

I stand at the threshold of the basement, watching my brothers trundle down the steps, knowing what I'm about to face, what's been coming for me for years, what's finally here.

My own Bergman Brothers Summit.

―――

"Welcome, Viggo," Oliver says quietly, "to your very own Bergman Brothers Summit."

I sit, slumped over on a plastic storage bin, head in my hands. "Go ahead, gloat. Tell me I had it coming. It's what I deserve, after what I've put you all through over the years."

Silence rings in the basement. I pick my head up, trying to breathe properly, to steel myself to face them. I'm met by solemn faces, not a trace of triumph in their expressions.

"Well, technically," Ryder says, "I have yet to earn a Bergman Brothers Summit."

Everyone stares at him sharply.

Ryder grimaces. "Sorry. That was not, uh . . . that was not helpful, right now."

"Not at all." Oliver smacks his shoulder.

Ryder scowls. "I said I was sorry."

Tears well in my eyes.

Aiden rushes toward me, dragging me up and into his arms.

"This is not what I pictured," he mutters, "when I envisioned relishing this moment."

"Sorry to disappoint," I mutter into his shoulder.

His hand comes to my neck, clasping it gently. "That was my attempt at lightening the mood."

I huff an empty laugh against his shoulder, blinking away tears. Slowly I pull away and wipe my face dry.

Ren peers up at me from his seat on a big cardboard box, his face serious. "Why don't you tell us what's going on, Viggo?"

Sighing heavily, I drop back onto the plastic storage bin, accepting the black stuffed animal cat Seb's been hugging. I hug it to my chest. Axel steps up beside me and squeezes my shoulder.

"I don't even know where to begin," I whisper.

Gavin clears his throat, then stands and offers me a tissue, a firm squeeze of my other shoulder. "Start at the beginning. We're listening."

I take a breath, straighten up, and tell them everything. Our early morning conversation over coffee last year. That first night at the bookstore. Our cohabitating and skills-swap plan. The promise we made each other to be brave, to explore what we could share, when we realized how much we wanted each other, how differently we saw wanting. Working together, at the store, on her book. Walking the dogs, cuddling the cats. Coaching soccer. Living life. Falling for each other.

So I hoped.

When I'm finally done, I peer up to find every one of their gazes on me, full of concern and compassion. Ren dabs his eyes. Oliver sniffs, wiping his nose with the back of his hand.

"And that, my brothers, is my sob story. I fell in love with someone who doesn't even believe in it, who said she'd try to be . . . open to it, who made me feel . . ." I shut my eyes, tears spilling again. "So fucking much. Last night, we . . ." I shake my head. "It meant so much to me, and I think I fucked it up. Then I woke up to her gone."

"So go find her," Ryder says.

Oliver massages the bridge of his nose. "Still not helping."

"No." Ryder stands. "I'm right. Listen, I know I wasn't very sensitive when we came down here, saying I hadn't had a Bergman Brothers Summit, but that's not because I couldn't have used one. I kept my pain to myself, shielded the family from what I was going through with Willa, how badly I loved her and how hard I was struggling, with her fear of my love and of her love for me."

Ryder's eyes meet mine. He drops on the storage bin beside me. It creaks ominously under our combined weight. "I wish I'd told you all. I wish I'd asked for help." He sets a hand on my back. "And I'm proud of you for opening up to us, even if it is a little late in the game. I'm sorry you've been carrying this all by yourself. I know how hard that is."

I bury my face in my hands again. "I was proud and scared and stubborn. I told myself I could wait while she figured it out; told myself I had stuff to figure out, too."

"So you kept it in," Axel says quietly. "I know something about that. How isolated it makes you feel, thinking you're alone in how you're hurting."

"But you aren't alone." Seb sets an arm on my shoulder, squeezing hard. "We're here for you. And I believe Tallulah is, too."

I wipe my nose as I meet his eyes. "You do?"

He nods, smiling softly. "I recognize a fellow thoroughly besotted scaredy-cat when I see one. She adores you, Viggo. She said it with every glance at you last night, every time you said her name, every not-so-subtle touch you snuck in. Trust her. There's a reason she's been gone this morning."

"I think he's right." Ren nods encouragingly. "Give her a chance. Don't give up on her or on what you want to share with her."

"Come on." Aiden grips me by the arm, tugging me upright. He reaches for my hair, trying to fix it.

I duck reflexively. "What are you doing?"

"Making you look presentable." He frowns. "Or trying to."

"Now." Ryder slaps a hand on my back, pointing to the stairs. "Go find Tallulah. Tell her how you feel. You deserve to be honest with your heart, Viggo. And she deserves the chance to be honest with her heart, too."

I glance around at my brothers, a glimmer of hope flickering in my heart. "Okay, I will."

They all smile. I smile back, but it falters, fear rushing through me. "But first, could I just have a—"

Gavin throws his arms around me.

"Hug," I whisper.

Axel steps up next, his hand heavy on my back. Ryder, then Ren, circle around me, then Seb and Aiden, and finally Oliver, who clasps my neck.

"Love you guys," I whisper.

"We love you," they tell me, loud and strong, and that strength, that truth, pours through me, fills me up, gives me the courage to pull back and stand tall.

Oliver's eyes meet mine as he smiles. "Now, get the hell out of here."

———

Bounding up the stairs, I bang the door open. Rooney shrieks in surprise, just a few feet down the hallway, leaping aside.

"Rooney!" Axel yells from downstairs.

"I'm fine!" she calls. "Viggo just surprised me."

Axel's flying up the stairs, shoving past the brothers like a bull in a china shop who transforms into calm control, wrapping her in his arms. "You sure?" he whispers.

Rooney smiles into his shoulder, nodding. "I'm sure."

He exhales heavily. Rooney wraps her arms low around his back and squeezes as she tells us, "Axel's been a little on edge lately."

"I have good reason," he mutters into her hair.

She glances up at him, cupping his face. "I'm pregnant, Ax, not sick."

All our mouths fall open. Rooney glances our way slowly, eyes wide. "Oh boy. I said the quiet part out loud."

Axel ignores us, smiling softly down at her. "Better go find Elin and tell her. If she hears the boys knew before her, she'll never let you live it down."

Rooney nods, a nervous smile lifting her mouth. "Let's go." She clasps his hand, tugging Axel with her.

"Wait." I lift my hands, halting them. The panic subsiding, my brain's clearer, piecing together this morning. When I came downstairs, Rooney wasn't there. She must have been in the bathroom, if she's anything like Freya, dealing with plenty of morning nausea that plagued her pregnancies. "Rooney, have *you* seen Tallulah this morning?"

Rooney smiles. "Yeah! Charlie woke up stressed about not having something blue for the wedding. You know, 'something old, something new, something borrowed, something—'"

"Blue, right."

"I told her about the blue lupine field just past the house, figured she could add a few sprigs of it to the bouquet, maybe tuck it into Charlie's hair. I was going to offer to head there myself, but then I realized I was about to upchuck my breakfast, and before I could ask her if one of the rest of us could go, she took off."

"Thank you!" I rush past her, down the hall. I'm about to dash out the door when Oliver yells my name.

I spin around, exasperated. "*What*, Oliver?"

I'm hit in the face with a soft, worn plaid shirt and a pair of lightweight chinos. I blink down at them, realization dawning as I take in my appearance. White undershirt. And blue . . . boxers. I glance up, blushing. "I coulda sworn I'd put on shorts. You could have said something!" I tell everyone.

Frankie shrugs. "We've all survived your Speedo shows at the beach. Nothing fazes us now."

Laughter echoes around the room.

I tug on the pants, buttoning them, then rip off my undershirt, tugging on my plaid flannel. It'll get warm later on, but it's still cool in the mornings, and I don't mind the idea of looking half-decent when I run into Tallulah, when I tell her what I can't hold inside me one more minute.

"Thanks, Ollie," I call, yanking open the door.

"Shoes!" Mom yells.

I freeze, then glance over my shoulder at Mom, who walks toward me, smiling, my chukka boots in her hands. "You always loved to run barefoot, Viggo, I know. But I think you're going to want shoes for this."

"Thanks, Mom." I smile as she gives me a kiss on the cheek, then take them from her, dropping the boots to the floor and stepping into them, before I turn toward the door.

"One more thing."

I glance up at Dad, a grin lifting the corner of his mouth. He gestures with his finger, an upward motion. "Left the shed door open."

His code phrase has me instantly peering down at my fly. I blush as I drag up my zipper.

"*Now* you're ready," he says, patting my cheek gently. "Be brave, Viggo. We're right here behind you."

I clasp his hand and squeeze, turn toward the open door.

And then I run.

THIRTY-ONE

Viggo

Playlist: "Blinding Lights—Acoustic,"
Matt Johnson, Jae Hall

It's not a short hike to the lupine field. You have to take the trail leading to Axel and Rooney's cabin, then stay on the trail about another half mile. I know the way by heart. I love the lupine field, played in it with my siblings when we were kids, crouching among the two-foot-tall flowers that mingled in the taller grass, leaping out and startling the hell out of each other. It developed my love of a good jump scare, taught Oliver to pop up silently out of nowhere and surprise the living daylights out of people. It's the first place Ziggy tickled me so hard after I caught her off guard, I laughed until I peed myself. It's filled with memories of playing, teasing, tipping into adolescence and growing up.

It's my favorite, most nostalgic spot on the property.

And when I turn the corner around the last big tree, breaking into the field, it's cemented as my most favorite place ever.

Because she's here. Tallulah.

Bent over the flowers, wearing a sunshine-yellow shirt, one of her stylish long cardigans tied around her waist as she picks a cluster of blue lupines.

"Excuse me, ma'am!" I call. "This is private property. You can't just help yourself to the flowers."

Tallulah jerks upright, her head whipping my way. Wide amber eyes, flushed cheeks. Her surprise dims, slipping to a wide, soft smile. "That wasn't nice," she calls.

I smile back at her, starting across the field, every step steady and sure. Sunlight kisses her skin and sparkles in her eyes. The wind caresses her blue hair, whipping it back. I stare at her, my body thrumming with purpose, with peace.

My heart thuds in my chest as warmth spills through my limbs, its truth as vital to my existence as the blood swimming in my veins: I love her.

I know my heart. With every step I take closer to her deepening smile, her glittering eyes, I feel sure of it: Tallulah knows my heart, too. And I know hers just as much.

The wind dances past me, swaying the grass.

I love you.

My smile deepens as I grow closer, holding her eyes.

I love you.

Tallulah's smile falters at my next step. Her free hand clutches her cardigan as the wind whips it back.

Suddenly, she drops the flowers, then runs toward me, barreling into my chest. "I'm sorry," she whispers.

I wrap my arms around her, breathing her in. "There's nothing to be sorry for."

"Yes, there is," she whispers, blinking up at me tearily. "I was so happy to see you at first, but then I realized that meant you were awake, that you woke up to an empty bed, and after last night, that might have thrown you, which is the last thing I wanted to do, it's just that Charlie started spiraling and—"

I set a finger to her mouth, smiling down at her. "I know you'd never want to upset me. I *was* upset, but that was my thing, not yours. I panicked. Because of what last night meant to me, and I was so afraid it didn't mean the same thing to you. Because I've been staying quiet, waiting, but I don't want to wait anymore. I want to tell you and trust you to stick with me, even if you're not where I'm at yet, Tallulah. Because—"

She kisses me, hard and long, silencing me, drugging me with her tongue stroking mine, her hands diving into my hair. I wrap my arms around her waist, savoring the taste of her, the rich, soft scent that never leaves her, soothing me.

Tallulah pulls back, dropping back on her heels, and clasps my face in her hands. Her eyes hold mine, and sunlight dances in her gaze as she blinks away tears. "Me first."

I stare at her, heart pounding. "You first?"

She smiles, soft and slow. "Since I saw you last year, about to fall on your ass off that chair, you have gone first, given your smiles, your kindness, your home, your friendship . . . your heart." One hand leaves my face, drifts down over my shoulder, before it settles on my chest. "So I want to be the one who goes first now, who tells you what I've been so terrified to believe, let alone say, but it's no less true." She swallows thickly, blinking away tears. "I *love* you, Viggo. And I know I'm no love expert, not the way you are, but I know my heart, and this is true: I love you.

"I could have danced around that word for as long as I lived, but it would never have changed what you mean to me. It could never change that my world is meant to have you right at the heart of it, that my life is wider and brighter and sweeter for sharing it with you. I want to dream dreams and work hard and hold hands and face whatever comes with you.

"I don't need the word 'love,' but I have it and I'm going to use it. Loud and often." She draws in a deep breath, holding my eyes. "I love you, Viggo Bergman. I mean it with my whole heart."

I swallow roughly, clinging to her. "Dammit, Lu. Did you have to be so good with the words?"

Her smile wobbles. "Well. I might have been rehearsing it a little while picking flowers."

I shake my head, my voice catching as I blink back tears and try to speak. I clear my throat as I bring her close and press a soft, tender kiss to her forehead. Slowly, I pull back and hold her eyes. "I love you, Tallulah. My Lulaloo, I love you so much, so deeply, I can't even find the words to describe it, which, I'll admit, after reading five hundred–plus romance novels, is a bit humbling, and yet that's just it, Tallulah—I love those love stories, but they're not ours. *Our* love story is the only one I want."

Tears slip down her cheeks. Gently, I thumb them away. "I'm no love expert, but I think I just might be an expert on loving you. Because you were meant for me, Tallulah, and I was meant for you. Your heart was meant to be with mine; I believe that." Clasping her hand where it rests over my pounding heart, I tell her, "And my heart was meant to be with yours. It *is* yours. It always has been." Bending, I kiss her, gentle and reverent, forehead to forehead. "My heart has been, and always will be, only and forever *yours.*"

A soft sob leaves her as Tallulah draws me close, crushing her mouth to mine, hard and needy. "I love you," she whispers. "I love you, I love you, I love you."

I smile against her fierce kiss until it slips, as brutal, desperate desire courses through me. My hands shake, my body aching for her as she slows our kiss and deepens it. I tug at her long sweater bunched around her waist, shoving it away from her body. She yanks it off, tosses it down, then she's at me again, kissing me, openmouthed and hot, moaning into my mouth.

I stumble into her, and my knees buckle. "Here," I whisper. "I need you here. Now."

She nods frantically, dropping onto her cardigan spread like a blanket beneath her.

I crawl over her, frowning in concern even as she tugs me down for a kiss. "Your sweater. It's fancy, isn't it? We'll ruin it."

"Fuck the sweater," she mutters, wrenching her pants down,

letting me help her tug them past her hips, while she yanks at my pants' button and zipper. "I'd throw my whole wardrobe beneath us right now and ruin it, if you asked me to."

I sigh into her kiss, slipping my hand beneath her panties, feeling her wet and slick. "God, Lu."

"I want you, in case that isn't clear," she whispers. "Verbal foreplay—big thing for me, apparently."

I smile against her mouth. "I got you horny with my words. My *romantic* words."

"I'm a woman reborn," she pants, tugging my pants lower down my hips.

"Lula, let me make you feel good first," I plead as she wraps her hand around me and drags it up to the tip. A gasp tears out of me as she strokes back down.

"Inside me," she begs. "Please."

A frustrated groan leaves me. "I don't have a condom. I was in a rush. I forgot."

"I'm on the pill." She cups my cheek and stares up at me. "And there's been no one since I was last tested. No STIs."

I stare down at her, heart flying, need racing through me, just at the thought of what that means she wants—just her body and mine, nothing between us. "Me neither. No STIs."

"Then come here," she says softly, drifting her hand inside my shirt. Her fingertips dance up my back, making me shiver. "I want you so badly." Her breath is hot in my ear, her voice threadbare and needy as I cup her breast, kiss the crook of her neck, then her shoulder. "I want you inside me. Now. *Please.*"

"Are you ready?" I whisper, slipping my fingers over her, satin smooth and slick, easing a finger inside, then two. A groan rolls up my throat. She's drenched.

She smiles, head thrown back in pleasure as I curl my fingers inside her. "You tell me."

"Fuck, Lu." My hand wanders the soft curve of her stomach, over to her hip, where her pod is adhered. "Your pod, will I bump it, if we do it this way? Is another way better?"

She peers up at me, our urgency momentarily dissolved into stillness, the breeze swaying the flowers that hide us, the sun warming my back, gilding her amber eyes.

I smooth away an ice-blue hair that dances across her face, waiting for her, drinking in her beauty as she searches my eyes.

She swallows. "You're sweet. But this is fine, just like this, as long as you don't grab it or rub hard against it." She smiles softly, lifting her head, kissing me. "Please, Viggo," she whispers. "Now."

I kiss her back, her lips, the tip of her nose, the beauty mark that lifts with a smile. Holding her eyes, I grip my aching cock, easing the tip inside her, just the tip. Air rushes out of my lungs. Lightning dances up my legs, deep into the base of my spine. Fierce need drags my hips forward, easing in farther, farther. "Christ, Lula, you feel incredible. How is it so incredible?"

She nods frantically, drawing me close, cupping my neck, until we're forehead to forehead as I roll my hips, seating myself inside her. I gasp as I feel her wrapped around me, the sensation unlike anything I've ever felt or dreamed of, hot and tight, gripping me as I drag my hips back, then thrust in.

Stars dance in my vision. This is not going to last long.

"Who the hell cares?" she pants.

Seems I said that out loud.

"I want to make you feel good," I groan into her neck, kissing beneath her ear.

She shivers and turns, taking my mouth in a hard, hungry kiss. "You are. Now—" She reaches beneath my loosened pants, my boxers, her fingers sinking like claws into my bare ass. She yanks me against her and bites my neck. "Fuck me like you want to."

"Shit." My hips jerk into her, hard and urgent. Once, twice, until

I'm scrambling at the edge of release, panting with the effort not to give in.

"Take me," she whispers.

I press my pelvis into hers, burying myself into her, and grind, leaning into the soft fullness of her body. She gasps. Yanking her top down, I bare her nipple to the cool air, latch my mouth over it as I cup her breast, heavy and spilling out of my hand. I swirl my tongue, drag my teeth against it. Tallulah shouts my name, fingers curling into my hair, holding me to her.

My cock swells, my balls draw tight. I scrunch my eyes against the glorious agony of scrambling at the edge of release. She rubs her hips up into mine, crying out hoarsely, "Viggo. Oh God. Yes, yes."

I tear my mouth from her nipple, crash down on her lips. She grips my ass hard and moves me in her. "W-wait, Tallulah, I can't—"

"Come," she whispers. "Trust me. Just come."

I swear into her neck, a hoarse, pained shout as I sink my teeth into her skin and pour into her, hot and hard, my hips jerking, legs shaking, burying myself as deep as I can.

Tallulah gasps as she works herself on me, holding my hair in her tight grip, tipping my face until my mouth meets hers, open and gasping. I grip her hair, too, and anchor myself to her as she arches up into me, and then I feel her, tight, rhythmic waves clenching around me, tearing another wave of release from me that makes me shout into her mouth, my brow scrunched, hips moving with hers again, rhythmic, rolling, until finally we slow, chests heaving, sweat on our skin, cheeks flushed.

Tallulah stares up at me, clumsily sweeping hair off my forehead. I brush fine blue strands off her face, too, breathing roughly as I stare down at her.

A slow, satisfied smile breaks across her beautiful face. "I love you," she whispers. "I'll never get tired of saying it."

"Good," I tell her, bending, kissing her once more, gentle and soft. "Because I'll never get tired of hearing it." Tipping my head, I drink her in, save this memory, vivid and precious, tucked away to have for always. "I love you, too."

Her smile deepens. "I know. Now," she whispers against my cheek, kissing it sweetly. "I hate to break up the moment, but I think we have a wedding we don't want to miss."

I grin down at her. "I think you're right. So long as I can get a guarantee that you'll save a dance for me afterward?"

"Silly man," she whispers. "Every dance is yours. *And* every karaoke song."

"Now we're talking." I sigh, burying my face in her neck again. "There's just one small problem."

Her fingers trail through my hair. "What's that?" she asks.

"My legs don't work."

Tallulah laughs.

"I'm serious," I tell her, exhaling heavily as I push up on my elbows. "God, this is euphoria, isn't it? I feel like those cows just let out of the barn after winter."

Tallulah blinks up at me. "What?"

"In Sweden, the cows, they're kept inside all winter, and it's a whole day, everyone gathers to see it, when they let them out in spring. Much like my rather speedy performance, those happy fuckers sprint out of the barn, leaping and bounding—as well as cows can—across the grass." I kiss her, my shoulders shaking as I start to laugh. "And that is the most romantic analogy ever."

Tallulah draws me in again, kissing me deep and sweet. When we finally break apart, and her eyes meet mine, I *moo* so loud a flock of birds shoots out of the nearby trees. She laughs, hard and long; it echoes through the field.

It's the most beautiful sound in the world.

THIRTY-TWO

Tallulah

Playlist: "Whole Wide World," Mindy Jones

"Your legs seem to be back to their old selves, Bergman." I smile up at Viggo as he sashays toward me, twinkly lights strung across the deck bathing him in a magical golden glow.

"And you," he says, wrapping an arm around me and pulling me close, the slow dance music swelling around us, "have finally stopped walking like you got railed in a flower field this morning."

I gasp. Viggo grins devilishly and wiggles his eyebrows. "I *love* scandalizing you."

"That's my job," I tell him. "Scandalizing *you*."

"I guess we'll just have to enjoy scandalizing each other." He leans down for a kiss that's slow and sweet. "I love you," he whispers.

"I love you," I whisper back. My smile is so wide, it makes my cheeks ache.

His eyes search mine. "How you doing?"

"Doing . . . pretty great. You?"

He smiles. "Pretty great." He clears his throat, his eyes darting to where his parents are making conversation with mine. "How you feeling about *that*?"

I glance over at my parents and sigh. "Feeling like . . . there's a lot we haven't dealt with, that we should." My mind travels back to the family selfie we took with Charlie's wedding photographer, a little stilted and awkward, but . . . trying. Charlie had Dad take a selfie, too, that we sent to Harry, telling him we missed and loved him, that we'd visit when he was ready for visitors. It felt raw and hard, but it also felt real. Like, maybe, our family will start with these tiny, humble steps, each of us trying to be healthier individually, figuring out how that makes us work together, as a family. "But I think this is a good beginning."

Viggo nods, cupping my face, his thumb skating softly along my cheek. He's quiet, which is so rare, but he doesn't *feel* quiet. His grip around my waist is tight and sure, his eyes locked on mine. I *feel* his love, its reality so visceral, so powerful, it's unlike anything I've known.

"I love you," I tell him.

He smiles. "I know. I love you, too, Lula."

I link my hands around Viggo's neck, our height difference diminished thanks to my high heels, and stare up at him as the music fades. Filled with love. With dreams. With so many hopes for what lies ahead.

Viggo's smile deepens. "What is it?"

"You and I," I tell him, taking his hand, drawing him toward the mic, "have some karaoke-ing to do."

For once, I am the furthest thing from quiet. Shameless moans leave me as I lie naked, stretched out wide on our bed in the empty A-frame, family long gone since this morning, leaving us to have what we needed—a place to be together, to love each other, just the two of us.

Hot sunlight pours into the room, painting Viggo's brown hair bronze. I grip it tight in my hand, biting my lip at the sight of his head between my thighs, his tongue lightly flicking my clit. A gasp tears out of me.

"Like that?" he whispers against my skin.

I grip his hair tighter. "Yes, like that."

Another flick of his tongue, then he swirls it slowly.

"Oh, *God*. Just like that."

He glances up, pale blue eyes blazing like blue flames, a sexy smile tipping his mouth. "Yeah?"

I nod frantically, cupping his jaw, savoring the scratch of his scruff. I stare at him with wonder, overwhelmed with knowing he loves me, knowing I love him, too.

"The way you're looking at me," he whispers. "If I had known you'd look at me like that, I'd have shaved the beard down sooner."

I shake my head. "You're always lovely to me. Bigfoot beard or not."

He laughs softly, rubbing his bristly chin right where my hip meets my pelvis. I arch up into him.

"I love you, Lula," he whispers, planting a tender kiss to my thigh.

I smile down at him. "I love you, Viggo."

He bends his head again, eager, sweet, working me up with his tongue, with one long finger, then another, crooked deep inside me.

My legs shake. My breathing stutters. Viggo wraps his hand around my thigh, traces the tributaries of stretch marks that lead to where his tongue strokes me, dragging me to a height I can barely fathom falling from.

But I will. I will fall, trusting him to catch me.

"Please," I beg, rocking my hips into him. "Please don't stop."

He hums against me, tongue and fingers moving faster, sending me flying, soaring. I arch up, shaking, crying out his name. I'm still shaking and gasping, when I grip his arm like a vise and drag him toward me. "Inside me," I tell him. "Now."

He salutes me, his face a portrait of solemn obedience. "Yes, ma'am."

I swat his butt, making him break into a laugh, making me laugh, too.

I'm so wet, from my body, his tongue, and he sinks inside me effortlessly, filling me to the hilt. I moan, my orgasm's echoes stretched into sweet, lasting pleasure.

"Fuck, Lu," he gasps into my neck, breath hot in my ear, his hips thrusting fast and desperate. "One of these times I'm gonna last longer."

We laugh into each other's mouths. Our kiss turns into wide twin smiles. "We've got lots of time for that."

He pulls back, eyes holding mine. He cups my face, and his fingers slip into my hair.

"I love you," I whisper, as he moves faster, hips faltering, his smile slipping into that beautiful furrowed-brow concentration, preceding the pure ecstasy that breaks across his face. He throws his head back, eyes shut, throat working as he comes, then falls into me, rocking into me still. I clasp him tight, kiss his forehead, hold him close to me, so close, heart to heart.

"I love you," he whispers. "I love you, Lula, with all my heart."

I nod, smiling, my forehead pressed to his, and tell him what I feel in this moment, right down to my bones: "I know."

It's late when we get back to LA, the sun only a sliver of tangerine on the horizon. I take the Vespa ride slow, savoring the wind on my skin, Viggo's arms tight around my waist, his strong warmth wrapped around me.

When I take the turn toward Donnie's shop instead of home, his grip tightens, revealing his surprise.

I smile as we soar down the road, then finally pull up to the shop. I drop the kickstand and kill the engine. Viggo yanks off his helmet, frowning in confusion. "Lula, what are we doing?"

I tug off my helmet, too. "That errand I skipped on the way out of town. Come on." Clasping his hand, I walk ahead of Viggo and guide him toward the shop. Donnie's there, just like he promised he would be, lingering at the entrance.

Viggo gives Donnie a hug, then stares after him, perplexed as Donnie backtracks. "I'll take good care of her for ya," he tells me.

"Thanks, Donnie." I smile at him.

Donnie smiles back, winking. "You bet."

Viggo sets his hands on his hips. "What is going on?"

"Pandora needs a tune-up."

His confused frown returns. "Who's Pandora?"

"My Vespa, sweet cheeks."

Viggo gaze narrows. "Since when did you name your Vespa..." His eyes widen. "Wait, *Pandora*?"

I shrug, smiling coyly. "She's a great heroine. Fiercely independent, vehemently against marriage, but she changes her stance after a sweet, determined man decides he's going to bend his world, meet her where she's at, and love her endlessly." I step up to Viggo, cupping that bristly jaw, my thumb sweeping along his temple. "She has a beautifully creative, agile brain like yours. I loved that about her, too."

Viggo swallows roughly. "Lula ... you read a romance?"

"A *historical* romance," I tell him, wrapping my arms around his waist as I smile up at him. "Tore through half of it the night before the wedding while you were sawing logs. Finished the rest of it on the plane today."

He shakes his head, staring down at me. "Lu, I don't know if I can handle this."

"You better figure out a way. I'm hooked. Soon as we get home, I'm heading straight for hist-rom aisle of the store, and you're going to give me a reading lineup."

Viggo bites his lip. "Seriously?"

I nod. "It was beautiful. A little messy. A lot hopeful." I wiggle my eyebrows. "*Very* sexy. Got me all horny."

A wide smile breaks across his face. "Like you need any help in that department."

I swat his shoulder. "Excuse me," I say primly. "I can't help that I have a very sexy boyfriend I can't get enough of."

"I'm your boyfriend," he croons.

"You are." I tip my head, still smiling up at him. "And now, boyfriend, I have something I want you to see."

"Oh?"

Reaching past him, I open the door to the shop.

There sits Ashbury, still the same eye-singeing orange, but now rust free. Shiny new tires, scrubbed-clean chocolate-brown interior. He looks very like his old self, but I know inside he's got a whole new lease on life.

Viggo stares at the car, breathing roughly. "Tallulah, you didn't."

"Define 'didn't.'"

He whips around, blinking away tears, and wipes one away from his cheek. "You spent so much money. You fixed him. Woman, how dare you!"

I clasp his hand and squeeze tight. "Don't be mad."

"I'm not mad! I'm *irate*!"

I smile softly. "Don't be irate, either. My book's selling incredibly. I could have fixed ten Ashburys and never even felt it. And I would have done that, a hundred times over, not because I think money can buy your feelings for me or our happiness, but because I want to give you things that bring you joy, Viggo, and sometimes, money is the best way to do that. So *please* accept this."

Viggo stares down at me, palming away another tear. "It's too much, Lula."

"A fixed-up car for a fixed-up life?" I wrap my arms around his neck, drawing him down. "I'd say I got by far the best end of that deal."

He tugs me close, forehead to forehead. "I didn't fix up your life," he whispers.

"I didn't fix up your car," I whisper back. "We both just used our gifts to help that effort."

Viggo sighs, and a soft smile breaks across his face. He leans in, kissing me sweetly. "You could have been a lawyer."

"I know. But I'm so glad I'm a writer instead. Now I get to spend my days working right beside you, dreaming up worlds and plans, sharing ideas and hopes. I couldn't ask for better."

Viggo squeezes me tight. "Thank you, Lula. Thank you so much."

I kiss his cheek and breathe him in. "You are so welcome, my love. Happy early birthday."

"How do you know when my birthday is?"

"Because Charlie told me, of course." I nuzzle his neck and press a kiss there, too. "You thought you could sneak a birthday past me?" I shake my head. "Oh, do I have plans for you tomorrow."

Viggo groans happily. "Those plans sound promising."

"They are," I whisper.

"As long as there aren't any more gifts," he says, pulling back and holding my eyes. "This is a bigger gift than I could ever deserve."

"You absolutely deserve it. You deserve this and so much more."

He sniffles and shakes his head as he stares at Ashbury again. "Goddamn, he looks good."

I stare at Viggo, drinking him in. "He really does."

Viggo does a double take, noticing my appreciative gaze, realizing my meaning. "Don't you look at me like that, Clarke. We're in a public place."

"Not that that's stopped us before."

He blushes fiercely.

"Well," I tell him, "we don't have to be in public much longer, if you'd take us home already."

He lifts his eyebrows, pointing to his chest. "Who, me?"

I step up to him, arms slinking around his waist, staring up at the man I love. "Yes, you. Pandora's going to be out of commission for a couple days. Guess you'll just have to drive us in Ashbury."

Viggo shakes his head, smiling. "Lula. What am I going to do with you?"

"Take me home. What do you say?"

He cups my face, thumbs sweeping across my cheeks. That breathtaking, adoring gaze dances over my face. "I'd say nothing would make me happier."

THIRTY-THREE

Viggo

Playlist: "Home," Drew Holcomb

"Hey, Bergman."

My head snaps up from where I've been watering my plants scattered throughout the bookstore. I glance toward the threshold of the store to the house, where Tallulah stands, backlit, freshly showered, wet, ice-blue hair and a swingy T-shirt dress. This one is pale pink, like the dress she wore opening night. Aching want tears through me. We've only been home for a couple of hours, dividing and conquering the tasks of taking care of the animals, unpacking, prepping baked goods for the store, which I'll open back up tomorrow, showering off the plane ride, making dinner, and I've missed her. I'm a lovesick mess.

I couldn't be happier.

"Hey, Clarke."

She smiles, but it's nervous. "The plants make it through okay?"

"Yeah." I set down my watering can. "They're okay."

"One day," she says, pushing off the threshold, "we're going to take trips that last longer than forty-eight hours, and you're going to have to trust *someone* with watering Lisa and Beverly and Tessa."

I scratch at the back of my neck. "I know. They're just . . . finicky. They need very specific care."

Tallulah's smile widens as she walks up to me and wraps her arms around my neck. I tug her close, my hands gliding up her back. "You know something about meeting the needs of a finicky lady, do you?"

I grin, then bend for a kiss. "I might know a thing or two."

"Hmm," she hums against my mouth. When she pulls away, she bites her lip and slips her fingers through my hair. "I have . . . something to give you."

I frown. "I told you no more birthday gifts. I'm still reeling from Ashbury."

"It's not a gift," she says carefully. "Well, it might *feel* like a gift. I hope it will. But it didn't cost anything. If anything, it was a gift to *me*."

"What do you mean?"

"Come on," she says quietly, tugging me by the hand.

I follow her through the store, across the threshold to the house, greeted by Romeo and Juliet, who are so happy we're home.

"Have a seat," she says, pointing to my rocker.

"Why?"

"Because . . ." Tallulah picks up a spiral-bound printout sitting at the edge of the coffee table. "You're going to be reading for a while."

I blink in shock as she walks toward me, smiling nervously. "I finished it. And I hope you like it. Please don't tell me if you don't. Well, actually, tell me if you don't, but tell me very gently?"

I drag her into my arms, her finished manuscript crushed between us. "Seriously? You want me to read it?"

"I do," she whispers.

I smile as I rest my cheek against her head. "Can I read it right now?"

"I wish you would. Get it over with! The suspense is killing me."

"Well, that makes two of us. You left me hanging with that jump scare." I pull away, peering down at the manuscript, *Dwelling*. By Z.S. Ruhig.

I tip my head. "Your pen name, Lula. What's it mean?"

Tallulah huffs a laugh. "It's silly. Our au pair, Gretchen, she always said about me, '*Sie ist sehr ruhig.*' It's German and means 'she is so 'quiet,' or 'calm,' depends on the context. I did a play on that."

I tip my head. "You're not so quiet or calm with me, are you?"

Tallulah grins. "No, I'm not. You, Viggo Bergman, seem to have a unique gift for firing me up."

I smile, too, bending to kiss her. "You're welcome."

She swats my butt and laughs. "Sit down and read that ending already."

───────

I'm a fast reader, but I'm flying even faster than normal, hooked and on tenterhooks. I tear through the last quarter of Tallulah's book, rocking in my chair as I read, my foot pressed on the coffee table, my heart in my throat.

Tallulah paces the house with two cats on her shoulders, and every time she hits the creaky floorboard outside the bathroom, I startle.

"Lu, stop pacing already!" I flip the page. "You're making me jump out of my skin."

"How do you think *I* feel?" she says. "You're reading my book. This was the worst idea ever—"

"Shh!" My eyes are flying down the page, my heart pounding. It's the last chapter of the book, and I can't believe what's happening, how this story has turned.

The wife . . . she's just thrown herself in front of the husband, protected him from the knife being swung his way. My head is spinning. I can't believe who the villain turned out to be, can't believe *this* is what the husband's been up to. I can't handle the fact that the wife is dying on the page as the husband wrestles the villain to the ground and knocks him out, then scrambles over to her, clutches her in his arms, watches the light leaving her eyes.

Tears fill my eyes as I read the last line of the wife's point of view, as darkness swallows her up. But then I gasp as I turn the page.

An epilogue.

From the husband's perspective. And the woman he's walking with slowly, hand in hand, careful of her healing body, up to a new house, a place of fresh beginnings . . .

It's his wife.

A loud, raw sob jumps out of me. I glance up at Tallulah, who clutches the cats to her chest, standing only a few feet away, her eyes wet and locked on mine. "You . . ." I swallow roughly. "You gave them a happy ending, Lu."

She nods as tears slip down her cheeks. "They still have lots to work on. They're far from perfect."

I search her eyes, hearing her hidden meaning. "I know."

"But they love each other. And they want to love each other well," she whispers. "So . . . they'll keep working on it. Keep choosing each other. No secrets, no holding back, just trust."

I reach for her and draw her onto my lap, setting the book on her legs. Tallulah peers down at me as the cats tumble around us, meowing happily, leaping off the book onto the floor. "I love it," I tell her.

"You didn't finish it," she says. "There's four pages left."

"I still know I love it," I tell her.

She smiles softly, then kisses me. "I'm glad."

I kiss her tenderly, slowly, wrapping my arm around her waist and tugging her close. "Now." I tap the book. "How about you do the honors?"

"You want me to read to you?"

I smile. "Will you?"

Tallulah blushes, slowly opening the manuscript. "All right."

"Excellent." I smile at her, leaning my head back on the rocker. "I'm trusting you to take care of my delicate heart here. Those two have put me through a lot. This book better finish with an 'and they lived happily ever after' or I'm going to riot."

Tallulah's smile turns coy. "This is the end of a thriller, Bergman, not a Hallmark movie. I can promise you that while this story ends well, it does not end with the phrase 'and they lived happily ever after.'"

I give her an exaggeratedly stricken look that makes her laugh. "What?!"

Tallulah leans in and kisses me, soft and sweet. "I guess you'll just have to find your HEA somewhere else. Maybe in one of those hundreds of beautiful books in your store."

"*Our* store," I whisper, drawing her close. "But there's actually somewhere else I plan on finding my happy ending."

She leans in, her mouth brushing mine. Her eyes glitter, filled with love. "And where is that?"

"Right here," I whisper against our kiss, "with you."

Tallulah

Playlist: "The Power of Love,"
Vitamin String Quartet

Three years later

Springtime in Washington State. Is there anything better? After that spring three years ago, lying in a sea of blue flowers, the man I love wrapped in my arms, I used to think not. But now I know, somehow, every part of life *does* keep getting better and better because I share it with him—

Viggo, my love, my forever.

Right this moment, I am keenly aware of that impossible possibility, better beyond best, joy even greater than I imagined swelling through me.

Sunlight spills across the field, warming my skin, lighting up his eyes. A warm late June breeze sways the blue lupines that dance around us. Legs straddling Viggo, I stare into his eyes, feel his love, in his gaze holding mine, in his hands on my hips, sinking into my softness, gripping me for dear life. "God," he groans, throwing his head back, writhing against the blanket beneath us, rocking underneath me. "Ride me hard, Lu. Harder."

A moan leaves me as I make a fist with his shirt, crashing down on him, teeth clacking, dancing tongues. Viggo sits us up, deftly pulls away, turns me, then hoists me up by my hips, careful of my pod adhered to my stomach. He runs his hands appreciatively over my ass as he eases back inside. A groan tears out of him, and I glance over my shoulder, thrilled at the sight of him, head back, sunshine gilding his hair and his eyelashes, glowing on his skin. He opens his eyes and finds mine, a sexy, knowing smile lifting his mouth.

Viggo bends over me and cages me in, kisses my shoulder, my neck, my cheek. He turns my face and takes my mouth with a hard, slow kiss. "I love you," he whispers.

"I love you, too," I whisper. My mouth falls open as he thrusts into me, in that controlled, teasing, wonderful way he has now, that keeps me right on edge, until I'm begging him to give me relief.

"I need it," I plead as his hand slides down, cups my breast, then trails over my belly, around my pod, until his fingers are where I need him, right between my thighs, circling, drawing wetness up and circling more.

"I know what you need," he says quietly, kissing my neck, biting it softly.

I gasp as I feel him swell inside me, and I push my hips back, seeking even more.

"That's it, Lu," he grunts, rubbing me faster, circling his hips while he's deep inside me. Heat, sweet and sharp, soars through me as he draws me closer, my back to his chest, and whispers, hot in my ear, "Come all over my cock, Lu. Come on. Give it up."

I cry out as I come and sigh with pleasure as he grips my jaw, holds my mouth to his as he swears and kisses me, lost, undone. I love to watch him, feel him, hear him, the pleasure breaking over his face as he pumps up into me, his gaze growing hazy, mouth open, his desperate sounds, his hot, panting breaths. He gasps my name, spills into me, and clutches me tight.

Clumsily, we sink down to the blanket, Viggo heavy over me, his breath in my neck. He plants a slow, savoring kiss to my shoulder, then gently eases out, falling to his side, drawing me with him until I turn and we face each other. We breathe roughly as we stare at each other, smiles softening our faces when we lean in for more gentle kisses.

Sighing, Viggo drops his head back on the blanket and smiles up at the sky. "Goddamn, Lu. You out in open nature. You're feral."

I give him a prim look, gesturing around us to the flowers hiding us, deep on the A-frame property. "We're secluded."

He snorts, head turning my way. "Not *that* secluded."

I laugh as we kiss, then laugh more when we scrounge around for our clothes, when he misses the button on his shirt and I put mine on backward. Once we're dressed, I stand, savoring the wind on my face, the sun kissing my skin, and then I offer him my hand. "Come on. We've got a schedule to keep."

He frowns. "We do?"

"We do."

Viggo takes my hand and stands, too, following me through the field. We walk hand in hand, quiet, arms swinging, sneaking smiles and kisses until we make it to the clearing in front of the A-frame, where Ashbury is parked, waiting for us, still reliable after three years and a handful of drives up and down the coast. "Where do we have to be?" Viggo asks.

I smile and give him a coy shrug. "You'll see. Now, hand over the keys, if you please."

He narrows his eyes but smiles as he hands me the keys, then follows me as I walk toward the car while checking my app quickly to be sure my sugar is in range, which I always do before driving. I pocket my phone as he opens the door for me and then shuts it after I settle in. Once Viggo's inside, too, both of us buckled in, I start the car and drive us carefully onto the main road, back toward town, toward what I hope is the future he wants to share with me.

I'm quiet because I'm nervous. I try to hide it, putting on strumming, happy music, setting my hand on his thigh, but Viggo can sense it. He watches me closely, his hand resting reassuringly over mine, humming along to the music, meeting me right where I am, like he always has.

When we stop in front of what was, until just a month ago, Sarah's general store, a beloved place for the Bergmans, owned by their good family friend, Viggo frowns. A heavy sigh leaves him.

Now it's my turn to clasp his hand. I know he's sad that the store is closed, that Sarah's packed up, ready for retirement. But I hope, soon, he'll be happy again.

"Come on," I tell him, opening my door.

Viggo opens his door, too, following me to the storefront. That's when I turn and face him, holding out the key.

His gaze drops to the key, then flies up to my face. "Tallulah Jane Clarke. What have you done?"

I smile. "I didn't spend a bunch of money behind your back this time. I promise. I'm just here with . . . an idea. A dream."

He tips his head. "What do you mean?"

Blowing out a slow, steadying breath, I clasp his hand and hold his eyes. "This place is ours, if we want it. Sarah . . . she wants us to have it, to open the next Bergman's Books."

His eyes widen.

"There's a house behind it, as you know. It's old and rough around the edges. Needs a good bit of love and elbow grease. I thought we'd work on this place together. I figured, when the time came to fix it up, that I'd be an excellent second pair of hands, that all your wonderfully handy family would help my husband, who'd lead the charge, so gifted with building things, reviving things, breathing life into them."

Viggo stares at me, eyes turning wet. "I'm . . . not your husband, Lu."

"No," I whisper, fighting my own tears. "But I want you to be."

He exhales roughly, face crumpling. "Lula—"

"I love you, Viggo." I clasp his hand tight, my heart pounding. "I want to believe and dream and hope and build a life with you, from what we already have to even more. I want kids and chaos and joy that always gets the last say, even when sorrow comes. I want that with you, only you. Will you marry me?"

He nods frantically, tugging me into his arms, kissing me hard and deep. "God, you have a way with words, Lula."

I smile nervously, peering up at him. "Is that a yes?"

He laughs softly, then kisses the tip of my nose. "You silly woman. Yes. It's a yes. Always has been. You're it. It's this life with you, only and forever *you*, that I want. Of course I want to marry you."

I wrap my arms around his neck and kiss him with all my heart, loving him more than I ever knew I could.

I smile against our kiss, joy filling me. Knowing that, in some miraculous way, every day that comes, I'll love him even more— my friend, my partner, my heart.

My happily ever after.

Viggo

Tallulah and I drive all around because it's a beautiful day, and it's something we love to do together—ride in Ashbury, windows down, music playing, talking about books we've read, her next story idea, plans for the new bookstore, dreaming for what's ahead.

We break up our drive with a picnic lunch Tallulah packed, enjoyed on Ashbury's hood, drinking in the breathtaking mountain views, emerald evergreens and sapphire sky, golden light and fields of gemstone wildflowers. Then we make our way back, low evening sunlight lancing through the trees, bathing the A-frame in a lacework of smoky shadows and pearly flickers of fading light. I'm floating on a cloud as we walk up the steps to the house, hand in hand, me and my fiancée.

My fiancée.

I grin like a goofball down at Tallulah. She smiles up at me and squeezes my hand tight. "Why don't you do the honors?" She nods toward the front door, handing me the keys.

I take them, smiling at her again as I unlock the door. I'm expecting it to swing open quietly, reveal the hushed house, space and silence for Tallulah and me to fill this week, making love, sleeping late, cooking together, reading on the deck, sipping our coffees.

But what greets me is the opposite.

"Surprise!" The sound is shocking, the sight even more so. Every member of my family beams my way, blowing kazoos, party hats on their heads, balloons floating overhead.

I shut the door behind me, stunned. Confetti dumps on my head, narrowly missing Tallulah, who somehow knew ahead of time to jump aside.

Oliver cackles, raising a triumphant fist.

I roll my eyes, but I'm smiling so wide, my face hurts. Tallulah laughs straight from her belly, pressing up on tiptoe to clear confetti from my face. "Happy birthday, Viggo."

I shake my head, trying and failing to hold a serious face as I narrow my eyes at her. "You devious woman."

"It's not every day you turn thirty," she says. "Plus, I know how much you love surprises. I had to."

I tug her close, smiling down at her. "It's not every day you get engaged, either. Best birthday present, ever."

She sets her hand over my heart. "I'm so glad you said yes."

"I'm so glad you asked," I tell her, smiling as I feel the ring in its case, burning a hole in my pocket. I know now when I'll give it to her. Tomorrow morning, when it's just the two of us on the back deck, coffee in hand, watching the world wake up, a brand new day, the start of the rest of our lives.

"When do you want to tell them?" she whispers as we start walking toward the family, blowing their kazoos still, swatting balloons at each other.

I drink in the laughter and joy, as vivid and beautiful as the sight and gift of everyone here for me, all my nieces, nephews, brothers, sisters, and my parents in one place.

Stopping us, I wrap her in my arms and kiss her, long and deep. "You kidding? Right now."

It's a big deal, changing things at the A-frame. The place's allure is its constancy—the beds are always where they've been, the spoons and forks in their same drawer, the same worn books on the bookshelf, the couch that I know personally *does* get moved for enthusiastic lovemaking in front of the fire, but is always put back afterward where it belongs.

Only for very special occasions do we change things up. And today is one of those days.

The long wood table that normally dominates the main room, after a lot of huffing and swearing through laughter, now stretches across the back deck, lights strung overhead, candles littering the table with their soft, cozy glow.

I glance around the table, my heart full at the sight of all my family, Tallulah's too, her parents and her brother, Harry, along with Charlie and Gigi. Sarah, whose store we're going to bring back to life, laughs, head to head with my mother. My dad smiles, deep in conversation with Linnea, who sits on his lap, telling him something that has him fully engrossed. Kids banging and coloring, babies babbling and cooing, being passed from one loving set of hands to another. All of these people who love us, who are overjoyed for us, celebrating the happy ending I was so scared I'd never find.

Tallulah clasps my hand beneath the table, and I meet her eyes. She smiles. "Happy?" she asks.

"More than I ever thought possible," I tell her.

She squeezes my hand hard. I bring hers to my lips and press a soft kiss across her knuckles.

"A toast," my dad says, standing slowly, glass in hand. Linnea bounds toward me, so tall and lanky now, a busy, bright ten-year-old who's become my childhood literature expert, always helping me find the newest and best books for the store. I open my arms to her, hug her hard, before she darts around me toward her youngest brother, Noah, and lifts him up onto her hip.

Noah leans toward me, and I take him, cuddling him onto my lap. He sets his head on my shoulder and sighs as I rub his back. I smile at Tallulah, who watches me, her own smile tipping her mouth.

Linnea wraps her arms around Tallulah from behind. "Lula Blue," Linnea whispers.

Tallulah glances back. "Yes, Linnie Loo?"

"Got any tissues?"

Tallulah frowns. "Why?"

"Uncle Viggo's going to need them."

I glance their way. "What?"

"We're here," Dad says, drawing my attention, "because this house is, more than any place, our family's home. This is where we come for the big moments—weddings, birthdays—"

Glasses are raised toward me, sweet calls of love and cheers to many more. I smile, swallowing against the lump in my throat.

"Engagements," Dad adds, smiling at us.

Tallulah sets her head on my shoulder and curls her hand around my arm.

"While I'm so glad we're all here for this," Dad says, "while I hope there are many more occasions and happy memories made here, I think it's fitting to remind us, on our Viggo's birthday, on his engagement to Tallulah, who we love with all our heart, that even if we lost this place, if we never came here again, this"—he gestures around the table—"would be just as vibrant, just as real."

Turning toward me with a smile, pride in his eyes, Dad says, "Viggo, you love to love unlike anyone I have ever known. You wrap up everyone you hold in your heart with so much love, even when they don't know what to do with it, even when that wrapping is a *little* tight."

My family laughs. I laugh roughly, blinking away tears.

"We are so thankful for the light you brought to our world, thirty years ago, for all the ways you've thrown yourself into loving us, reminding us that love isn't an idea but a living, breathing thing. We are so happy for you that you found someone who believes that, too, who *lives* love with you."

He lifts his glass. "To Viggo, and to Tallulah, to both of you, the happy couple whose hearts have found their home in each other." He glances toward Mom, who takes his hand and smiles. "Tell them, sweetheart. What you've always told me."

Mom glances my way, smiling brighter and says, "Home is not a place. Home is . . . this." She glances around the table. "Our hearts, our love, knitting us together, wherever we are. Wherever life takes you, may you know you have a home in our hearts, and may your hearts always be each other's home."

I raise my glass as Tallulah does, too, along with everyone around the table. "I love you all," I tell them, my voice wobbly with emotion. "Thank you."

Noah's snore on my chest makes me laugh reflexively, his dark waves tickling my chin, his sticky hand hot on my forearm. I smooth back his hair, press a kiss to his head, then peer over at Tallulah, who watches me with so much love, it makes my heart ache.

"How you doing, Lulaloo?"

"Couldn't be happier," she whispers, then kisses me. "How about you?"

"The happiest."

Tallulah tips up her head and kisses me again. I clasp her hand as it rests over my heart, sure and calm, so at peace, knowing that my heart has found its home, that Tallulah will always be by my side. I wrap my arm around the woman I love and rest my head on hers as we glance at the table, filled with my family, the breeze warm and sweet, swaying the lights and candle flames, whispering through the trees.

It could be magic, dancing through the air like fireflies sparkling in the darkness. But I know what it really is, woven between us, as elemental as the breeze, the tides, the sun that will rise and set tomorrow; what's sustained me, healed me, what gave me this life to share with the woman I adore, this future of ours that I can't wait to meet—

Love.

ACKNOWLEDGMENTS

As I sit here to write these acknowledgments, searching for words to express myself, I'm reminded of what Knightley says to Emma in Jane Austen's *Emma*; what Axel, in very similar words, says to Rooney, in their story—"If I loved you less, I might be able to talk about it more." I love this series, this concluding installment, my readers, the gift and work of writing, so much, and if I didn't love it so much, articulating what all of this means to me would most certainly be easier. But that's the beauty, the point, the heart of what I write and why I write it—that loving deeply, pouring yourself into who and what you love, is paradoxically both the easiest and hardest thing we do. It requires vulnerability and bravery and trust and hope, the risk of cracking ourselves open, our pasts, our fears, our hurts, which the world has taught us to guard and to hide. That vulnerability is hard and frightening . . . but it also grants us the most beautiful gift that would otherwise be impossible, when we find those who wrap their arms around *all* of us and love *all* of us; when we find safe spaces with those who see us in our full humanity and affirm that miraculous truth.

Without the risk, there is no reward.

So here I am, saying thank you to every reader who saw my vulnerability, my open heart pouring my belief into my writing that every one of us deserves a love story, and for rewarding that risk, for meeting my books with open arms and welcoming them. Thank you to every reader who's messaged, emailed, DMed, written notes, who's hugged me at events and trusted me with their words and their hearts to tell me that the Bergmans have given them a home, an affirmation, an encouragement that they deserve love *exactly as they are*, that there are people out there who are worthy of their love and who deserve the chance to know and love every rough and tender part of their past, present, and future. Thank you for using your voice to share about my stories and help me find new readers. Thank you, booksellers and librarians, for advocating for this series when it was self-published and so much more difficult to get in stores and in libraries. I'm so happy that it will be that much easier for you to stock these books now, but I'll never forget or be less grateful for how hard you fought for them when it wasn't.

Thank you to my publisher, Berkley, and the talented team there, who's amplified these stories and given them a chance to reach new readers, new hearts and minds who I hope will find a home away from home, a truly happy place, in the Bergmans.

I cannot express how grateful I am that this journey has given me a community I never dreamed was possible, turning something that began as a small private hope and need for myself, as a romance reading neurodivergent with chronic conditions who loves so many people living with similar realities, and who longed to see those realities not diminished or shamed or hidden but lovingly, authentically foregrounded in romances. Thank you for making it possible for me to tell happy, hopeful stories about people with real bodies and minds and hearts, with human struggles and vulnerabilities—for making it possible for this to be my job, my vocation.

Thank you to Becs and Sarah, who empathized and encouraged me as I struggled through burnout and those intense, irksome feelings writing insists on excavating from my emotions every time I sit down to write but especially in writing this conclusion to the

Bergmans; thank you for bolstering me with affirmation and understanding and kindness and care.

Thank you to Jen and Izzy, for your wisdom and feedback as authenticity sources for this story—your intention and dedication and thoughtfulness have made this book so much better, and I cannot thank you enough.

Thank you to Katie and Kayla, who have tirelessly shouted their love and poured their creativity into hyping the Bergmans, who squealed and shrieked and celebrated when I shared little snippets of this book in its drafting. It is rare and special to have people who love this world as much as I do, and I'm beyond grateful for the way you've made a space to share that with me.

Thank you to Sam, my agent, without whom I could not navigate this publishing path, not because I'm garbage at making sense of contracts (though I definitely am), but because there is so much effort and strategy and wisdom and work that go into making my stories morph from a dream to a deal, a hint of a hope to a beautiful book on shelves, and she is a rock star at making that possible.

Finally, thank you to my darling kids, who put up with their mom being so very busy this year while I wrapped up the Bergman world. You hung in there and stayed patient, and I hope I've shown you that sometimes you have to burn the candle at both ends for the things you fiercely want, and it's worth it, but it's so important to care for yourself in the wake of that grueling season, to sleep and read for fun and play goofy games and take aimless walks and stare up at the clouds with simple wonder for all we know about the world and all that's left to learn. Thanks for sticking with me—we finally made it to the pool and ate lots of hot dogs and probably too many Icees, and it went way too fast, but I drank up every moment, and I loved it, and I love you.

Last but not least, thank you, my Dr. B, for every strong long hug and reassurance that I could write this book; for making me laugh hard and making space for me to feel deeply. You are the perfect dose of chaos gremlin goodness, and I'm so happy to love you, even when you compare me and my wardrobe choices to Smee.

Viggo and Tallulah's story is about people reckoning with the ways they've learned to protect themselves from pain and hurt—a profoundly human, natural instinct—and unlearning those patterns, laying down those shields, and in doing so, opening themselves up to the messy, magical complexity of healing and love. Their story, like all my stories, is, at its core, about vulnerability. About how hard it is to practice and how beautiful it is to experience, when we finally find those who make us safe to do so. I hope, even if you don't have ADHD like Viggo or type 1 diabetes like Tallulah, that you've felt seen and affirmed in their journey—reminded and encouraged that it's okay to be afraid of the depth and risk of intimate relationships, to fear trusting your vulnerabilities to others; that, if you've been hurt or punished for that trust and vulnerability in the past, it was the fault of the people who failed you, not your own; that you deserve to be surrounded by friends, family, partners, a community, who know your aches and pains, fears and struggles, who care for you and consider you and welcome you and love all of you.

The Bergman Brothers series, concluding with this book, portrays a big messy family, found family, and friends—imperfect people trying exceptionally hard to love each other well. There are rough patches and plenty of struggles along the way, but ultimately, their love is accepting, affirming, and profoundly safe. Some might say this isn't very realistic. To which I say, I'd like it to be, and this is why I write. As Oscar Wilde said, "Life imitates Art far more than Art imitates Life." I believe stories affirming everyone's worthiness of love and belonging have life-changing power—to touch us, heal us, and deepen our empathy for ourselves and others. Stories have the power to reshape our hearts and minds, our relationships, and ultimately the world we live in.

I hope by now that, as it has been for me, this Bergman world is a haven for you, reader, where these intimate relationships with oneself and others, platonic, familial, romantic, and beyond, affirm the hope for all of us—that we can be curious, open-minded, and openhearted, without being judgmental; that we can welcome and embrace one another, just as we are, and become better, wiser, kinder, for having experienced all that is possible when we do.

Thank you for coming on this journey with me. I can't wait to see where it takes us next.

Keep reading for a preview of

TWO WRONGS MAKE A RIGHT

the first book in Chloe Liese's Wilmot Sisters series.

Bea

A word to the wise: don't have your fortune read unless you're prepared to be deeply disturbed.

> *Wrong is right and right is wrong.*
> *I foresee war—merry or misery, brief or long?*
> *A mountain looms built on deception.*
> *Surmount it and then learn your lesson.*

See what I mean? Disturbing.

I tried not to get anxious. But the morning after my grim fortune reading, I woke up to an ominous daily horoscope email. The cosmic warning was loud and clear. Duly noted, universe. Duly noted.

Quaking in my Doc Martens boots, I decided to beg off the party. That didn't go so well, seeing as this party is my twin sister's doing and my twin is hard to say no to. And by "hard" I mean impossible.

So even though the universe has all but warned me to *buckle up, buttercup*, and the air crackles like ozone before a storm, here I am. I reported for duty at the family home—wore a dress, donned my crab mask, made a cheese-and-cracker plate. And now, like any self-respecting scaredy-cat, I'm hiding in the butler's pantry.

That is, until my sister sweeps in and blows my cover. The swinging door flies open, and I'm caught in a beam of light like a crook cornered by the cops. I stash the peppermint schnapps behind my back and slide it onto the shelf just in time to prove my innocence.

"There you are," Jules says brightly.

I hiss, throwing my arms across my face. "The light. It hurts my eyes!"

"No vampires in this costumed animal kingdom. That crab mask you're wearing is scary enough. Come on." Taking me by the arm, she tugs me toward the foyer, into the jungle menagerie of masquerading guests. "There's someone I want you to meet."

"JuJu, please," I groan, dragging my feet. We pass an elephant whose trunk clips my shoulder, a tiger whose eyes hungrily trail my body, then a pair of hyenas whose laugh is spot-on. "I don't want to meet people."

"Of course you don't. You want to drink in the butler's pantry and eat half the cheese-and-cracker plate before anyone else can. But that's what you *want*, not what you *need*."

"It's a solid system," I grumble.

Jules rolls her eyes. "For eccentric spinsterhood."

"And long may those days last, but I'm talking about my anxiety."

"Having been your twin our entire lives," she says, "I'm familiar with your anxiety and its bandwidth for socializing, so trust me when I say this guy's worth it."

The peppermint-schnapps-and-hide trick *is* my social anxiety lifesaver. I'm neurodivergent; for my autistic brain, engaging strangers isn't easy or relaxing. But with the trick of a couple of covert swigs of schnapps—buzzed, calmer—I find the experience less overwhelming, and my company finds me not only passably sociable but minty fresh. At least, that's how it typically goes. Not tonight. Tonight I have grim cosmic warnings hanging over my head. And I have a bad feeling about whatever she's dragging me into.

"Juuuuules." I'm that kid wailing in the grocery store. All I need is a smear of chocolate chip cookie on my cheek, a rogue untied shoelace, and I am typecast.

"BeeBee," she singsongs back, glancing my way and failing to hide how disturbing she finds my papier-mâché crab mask. She tugs it up off my face and nestles it into my hair. I tug it back down. She tugs it back up.

I glare at her as I tug it back down again. "Lay off the mask."

"Aw, c'mon. Don't you think it's time to come out of your shell?"

"Nope, not even for that dad-level pun."

She sighs wearily. "At least you're wearing a hot dress—oops, hold on." We stop at the bottom of the steps before she yanks me behind the banister.

"What?" I ask. "You're letting me go?"

"You wish." Jules cocks a smooth dark eyebrow as her gaze dips to my dress. "Wardrobe malfunction."

When I peer down, I see my dress gaping along my ribs. Thank you, universe! "Pretty sure it's busted. I should go check it out in the bathroom."

"So you can hide again? I don't think so." She slides the zipper up my ribs, the sound of my fate being sealed.

"It could be on its last little zippery legs. Shouldn't chance it. A boob might pop out!"

"Uh-huh." Clasping my hand, Jules launches me forward. I'm a meteor hurtling toward catastrophe. As we approach our destination, sweat breaks out on my skin.

I recognize her boyfriend, Jean-Claude, and Christopher, our next-door neighbor, childhood friend, surrogate brother. But the third man, who stands with his back to us, a head above them, is a stranger—a tall, trim silhouette of dark blond waves and a smart charcoal suit. The man turns slightly as Jean-Claude speaks to him, revealing a quarter of his profile and the fact that he wears tortoiseshell glasses. A molten ribbon of longing unfurls inside me, curling toward my fingertips.

Distracted by that, I catch my toe on the carpet. I'm saved from a face-plant only because Jules, who's used to my body's abysmal proprioception, grips my elbow hard enough to keep me upright.

"Told you," she says smugly.

I'm staring at a work of art. No. Worse. I'm staring at someone I want to *make* a work of art. My hands crumple around the fabric of my dress. For the first time in ages, I ache for my oil paints, the cool polished wood of my favorite brush.

My artist's gaze feasts on him. Impeccably tailored clothes reveal the breadth of his shoulders, the long line of his legs. This man has a body. He's the jock of your dreams who forgot his contact lenses and had to wear his backup glasses. The ones he wears at night when he reads in bed.

Naked.

The fantasy floods my mind, red-hot, X-rated. I'm a walking erogenous zone.

"Who *is* that?" I mutter.

Jules stops us at the edge of their circle and takes advantage of my stunned state, lifting up my mask as she whispers, "Jean-Claude's roommate, West."

West.

Oh shit. Now, thanks to my recent deep dive into hot historical romance, I've got even higher expectations for the guy, with a name like *West*. I picture a duty-worn duke, thighs stretching his buckskin breeches as he walks broodingly across the windswept moors. Braced for ducal grandeur, I fight a swell of anxiety as Jules breaks into the trio, as *West* turns and faces me.

Stunning hazel eyes lock with mine and widen. But I don't linger on his eyes long. I'm too curious, too enthralled, my gaze traveling him, drinking in the details. His throat works as he swallows. His hand grips his glass, rough at the knuckles, his fingertips raw and red. Unlike nonchalant Jean-Claude, whose stance is arrogantly loose, his tie looser, there's nothing relaxed or casual about him. Ramrod-straight posture, not a wrinkle to be seen, not a hair out of place.

His eyes travel me, too, and while I'm poor at reading facial expressions, I'm excellent at noticing when they shift. I observe the record-scratch moment as his features tighten. And the heat previously flooding my veins cools to a chilly frost.

I watch him register the tattoos swirling over my body, starting with the bumblebee's dance down my neck, across my chest, beneath my dress. His gaze drifts upward to the frizz of my just-showered hair and messy bangs. Finally, it wanders over the family cat Puck's white hair stuck to my black dress. There's a rather aggressive tuft on my lap area, where Puck parked himself before I nudged him off. Mr. Prim and Proper looks like he thinks I forgot the lint roller. He's absolutely judging me.

"Beatrice," Jules says.

I blink, meeting her eyes. "What?"

After twenty-nine years of twinning coexistence, I know that her patient smile plus my full name means I zoned out, and she's repeating herself. "I said, this is Jamie Westenberg. He goes by West."

"Jamie's fine, too," he says, after an awkward beat of silence. His voice is deep yet quiet. It hits my bones like a tuning fork. I don't like it. Not a bit.

He's still scrutinizing me, this man I've decided most definitely doesn't get to ruin hist-rom *West*s and is instead getting called Jamie. Judgy Jamie suits him much better.

His eyes are back at it, traveling the tattoos along my neck, over my collarbone. His critical gaze is an X-ray. Heat flares in my cheeks. "See something you like?" I ask.

Jules groans as she steals Jean-Claude's drink and throws back half of it.

Jamie's gaze snaps up to mine as he clears his throat. "Apologies. You looked . . . familiar."

"Oh? How so?"

He clears his throat again and slides his glasses up the bridge of his nose. "All those tattoos. They reminded me of . . . I thought you were someone else for a moment."

"Just what someone who busts their ass on designing highly personal tattoos wants to hear," I tell him. "They're so unremarkable, they're easily mistaken for someone else's."

"I'd think you're accustomed to being mistaken for someone else," Jamie says, glancing toward my twin.

"Thus the *highly individual* tattoos," I say between clenched teeth. "To look like myself and no one else."

He frowns, assessing me. "Well, no one can say you lack commitment."

Christopher snorts into his drink. I rub my middle finger along the side of my nose.

"Maybe West recognizes those tattoos because you two *have* bumped into each other in the city . . . somewhere . . . at some point?" Jules says hopefully.

"Doubtful," I tell her. "You know I don't go out much, and definitely not to places that someone as stuffy—I mean, *serious*—as him would like."

Jamie narrows his eyes. "Considering that club Jean-Claude

dragged me to last year was a den of chaos, complete with an inappropriately handsy woman who projectile vomited on my shoes, I'm reassessing. Perhaps it was you."

Jean-Claude rubs the bridge of his nose and mutters something in French.

I smile at Jamie, but it's more like baring my teeth. "Chaos dens aren't my speed, but whoever the poor soul was that bumped into you, then upchucked, I imagine puking was an involuntary response to the misfortune of making your acquaintance."

Jules elbows me. "What's gotten into you?" she hisses.

"I remember that night and it definitely wasn't her," Jean-Claude tells Jamie, before he directs himself to me. "West is determined to die a miserable old bachelor and has grown crotchety in his solitude. You'll forgive his rusty manners."

Jamie's cheeks darken to a splotchy raspberry red as he stares into his half-empty lowball glass.

A determined bachelor? That means I'm not the only one who's been avoiding romance. Dammit. I don't want camaraderie with Mr. Bespectacled Stick Up His Ass.

"Bea, too," Jules adds, like the nosy mind-reading twin she is. "She hissed at me when I found her hiding tonight. The determined spinster's turned feral." Smiling up at Jean-Claude, she tells us, "But I'm just as determined to see her put away those claws and be as happy as I am."

The two of them share a lovey-dovey look, then a long, slow kiss that makes the cheese and crackers I ate crawl up my throat. As their kiss becomes kiss*es*, Christopher adjusts his watch. Jamie studies his lowball glass. I pick Puck fur off my dress.

Glancing up from his watch, Christopher gives me a meaningful lift of his eyebrows. I shrug my shoulders. *What?*

He sighs before turning toward Jamie. "So, West, you and Jean-Claude go way back, right?"

"Our mothers are friends," Jamie tells him. "I've known him my whole life."

"That's right," Christopher says. "You went to the same boarding school?"

"Our mothers did, in Paris, which is where they're from. Jean-Claude's family didn't move stateside until we were teens, and then we didn't cross paths academically until we went to the same university."

I roll my eyes. Of course Jamie's one of those people whose *French* mother went to *boarding school*. I bet Jamie did, too. He's got prep school written all over him.

As Christopher asks him another question, Jamie drains the rest of his cocktail. It smells like bourbon and oranges, and when he swallows, my gaze dips from his lips to his throat.

I stare at him as they talk, telling myself I don't have to like *him* for my artist's eye to love observing how the soft lighting of my family home knifes down the long line of his nose and caresses the angles of his face, revealing sharp cheekbones, a sharper jawline, a tight slash of a mouth that might be secretly soft when he's not pinning it between his teeth. A stuffy stick-in-the-mud shouldn't be allowed to be this beautiful.

"Well, Miss Crabby," Christopher says, nudging my crab mask and rudely dragging me back into the conversation. "Did you make this yourself?"

"But of course," I tell him, feeling Jamie's eyes on me and hating how that makes me blush. "I'm not even going to ask you, Christopher. This brown bear disguise is clearly store-bought."

"Sorry to disappoint. Some of us are too busy working to make our own masks for Jean-Claude's masquerade birthday party."

"Well, at least you're color coordinated." Christopher's dark hair and amber eyes are the same shades as his bear mask. I sink my fingers into his neatly styled locks and purposefully mess them up.

He flicks my ear. "Ever heard of personal space? Back up. You reek of peppermint schnapps."

I dodge the next flick. "Better than having bourbon breath."

Jamie watches us in silence, a notch in his brow, like he's never seen two people good-naturedly tease each other.

Before I can make some jab about that, the lovebirds break apart on a loud lip smack, leaving my sister breathless and pink-cheeked.

"The things Juliet comes up with," Jean-Claude says on a sigh as he stares down at my sister. "A masquerade party, full of people I have to share you with." Tucking her tighter against his side, he adjusts the neckline of her wrap dress so her cleavage is covered. "When all I need is *you*."

Jules smiles and bites her lip. "I wanted to make it special. You always have me to yourself."

"Not enough," he growls.

Something about Jean-Claude's intensity with my sister makes my skin crawl. They've been together for a bit over three months now, and rather than mellow out after the first frenzy of infatuation, like the people Jules has dated before, Jean-Claude just seems to be ramping up. It's to the point that I can't even walk around the apartment in a bathrobe because he's *always* there, on the sofa, in our kitchen, in her room. My gut says it's too much.

But Jean-Claude works at Christopher's hedge fund, and he's recently been promoted, meaning Christopher trusts him, which says a lot. More than that, Jean-Claude seems to make Jules genuinely happy. I don't understand it, but I can't deny it. That's why, so far, I've kept my concerns to myself.

"Well." Jules smiles. "Seeing as we're hosts, we should mingle, Jean-Claude." Next, she elbows Christopher, raising her eyebrows. "Mind making sure there's enough ice at the bar?"

Christopher frowns at her before his expression clears. "Oh. right. Bar duty. Gotta run."

Leaving Jamie and me. Standing together. Alone.

The air drips with tension.

If I were feeling mature, I'd make myself scarce. Be helpful. Serve drinks. Refill appetizers. But I'm not. I'm feeling my competitive streak overriding logic. I'm feeling perversely invested in proving to Jamie that he's wrong about me. I'm not someone to be mistaken for a chaos demon with unmemorable tattoos who puked on his shoes in a dingy bar months ago.

Well, I'm a bit of a chaos demon, but it's hardly my fault that I'm a little clumsy. Everything else, he's got me pegged all wrong, and I'm going to out-civilize him just to prove it. Only problem is, that requires something I'm very, very terrible at: small talk.

"What . . . are . . . you . . . drinking?" I ask. Because, you know. Small talk.

Jamie glances up and gives me a guarded look, like he's not sure what I'm up to. That makes two of us.

"Old-fashioned," he finally says, his words as neat and tidy as his looks. Then he peers at my empty hands. "Not partaking?"

"Oh, I am. I just hit the schnapps pretty hard in the kitchen. You know, a little social lubricant."

His eyes widen. I die inside.

Lubricant. I had to say *lubricant.* So much for out-civilizing him.

"I see." He adjusts the lion mask that rests on top of his impeccable dark blond hair.

My *lubricant* bomb threw the conversational waters into sky-high swells. We're seconds from drowning, but Jamie just threw me a little rescue floaty in those two words. So I grab on and throw him one, too. "Nice mask," I tell him.

"Thank you." He examines mine. "Yours is . . ."

"Gruesome?" I stroke a pincer of the papier-mâché crab mask. "Thank you. I made it myself."

He blinks at me like he's trying very hard to think of something nice to say about it. "That's . . . impressive. It seems . . ." He clears his throat. "Complicated?"

"Ah, it wasn't too bad. Besides, I'm an artist, so I like hands-on creativity." And then, because I'm feeling extra juvenile, I add, "Like my tattoos."

He swallows and blushes spectacularly as his gaze darts down my neck to my breasts, following the bumblebee's trail. Not sure what he has to blush about, since there's hardly anything to see. My black dress runs low, but unlike Jules, I was not blessed in the chestal department. The curse of fraternal twinship: similar face, different boobs.

Jamie is silent in the face of my latest move. It's gloriously rewarding. Now I'm the one smiling politely, and he's the one letting our conversation die a slow, awkward death. I'm about to declare victory when Margo pops her head in.

Smiling up at me from her diminutive height in a burnt orange jumpsuit and a fox mask that pins back her tight black curls, Margo says, "Need a cocktail, sweet cheeks?"

"God, yes." I take the glass from her, appreciating its deep red complexion and enticing aroma. Margo is a mixologist who makes the best drinks. I'll take anything she gives me. Like nearly everyone else at this party, she's also one of Jules's friends, because my twin is the nucleus of our social cell, unlike me, who's happy existing on the edge of the semipermeable social membrane.

I have friends but only through Jules, which is enough for me. Jules is how I know Margo, who's married to Sula. And because I met Sula, whom I now work for, I once again have a job as an artist that pays a living wage. My sister's social strategizing can be exhausting, but it's also made my life better. Without Jules tugging me inside her sphere, nudging me to make connections, I'd be lonelier and a lot less gainfully employed, especially since things took a nosedive nearly two years ago.

In keeping with my prove-non-chaos-demon-status campaign, I'm polite and make introductions as Margo offers Jamie her hand. "Jamie," I say, "this is Margo."

"Actually," he says, taking her hand, then releasing it, "most people call me—"

"West!" a voice yells from behind us, startling me so badly, I jump half a foot and send my bright red cocktail straight into his chest.

Jamie's jaw tics as he steps back and shakes off the liquid dripping down his hand. "Excuse me," he says, eyebrow arched in censure. *See*, that eyebrow says, *you* are *a chaos demon.* Then he turns and disappears into the jungle of guests.

I beg the ground to swallow me up.

But the universe is silent, so here I remain. The meteor that's just made impact, hissing in its crater.